FROM THE ASHES *of* 391

FROM THE ASHES of 391

TO MULES, MAD DOGS, AND MORSE CODE

ALLEN BRADY

FROM THE ASHES OF 391
TO MULES, MAD DOGS, AND MORSE CODE

iUniverse books may be ordered through booksellers or by contacting:

iUniverse
1663 Liberty Drive
Bloomington, IN 47403
www.iuniverse.com
1-800-Authors (1-800-288-4677)

ISBN: 978-1-5320-7676-3 (sc)
ISBN: 978-1-5320-7677-0 (e)

Library of Congress Control Number: 2019909144

Print information available on the last page.

iUniverse rev. date: 07/26/2019

Contents

To the memories of Lewis and Thelma Brady, my parents, and to Toshi and Zensho Chinen, my wife's parents, all of whom struggled under difficult conditions to provide safe and loving homes for their children.

I further dedicate this book to those who have served in the armed forces and to anyone who finds something in this work to which they can relate.

Acknowledgments

My thanks to all those who have long encouraged me to follow my dream of leaving something behind of my memories of a mule, a wagon, and a little farm.

To my brother in spirit and fellow Vietnam veteran, George Baird, who finally made me understand that I needed to open up a bit about that period of my life.

To Lonnie Long and Gary Blackburn, whose book, *Unlikely Warriors: The Army Security Agency's Secret War in Vietnam*, inspired me to include in this book a part of my life that I had excluded.

Thanks to my sister Dianne, who has been so helpful in many ways.

A special thanks to my daughter, Melissa (Mechi) Davis, without whose assistance this dream of mine would never have been realized.

To my wife, Yoko, for her patience and willingness to share life with me. I am eternally grateful.

Introduction

I can still smell the ashes after all these years. Our house had burned late on an autumn afternoon, and where it had stood earlier was a blackened pile of tin that had once been its roof. That jumbled tin now served only to partially obscure the ashes underneath. The ash bed was full of globules of melted glass and bits of metal that had been parts of the furniture and household goods. Rain had come since the fire, settling the ash bed a bit each time it visited and laying bare hundreds of now-rusty nails. Some nails were still straight enough to reuse, but most of them were bent. Curiously disfigured items begged to be identified, though the dish fragments scattered about were easy to recognize, even in tiny bits.

It was fascinating to dig through the debris. My little hands dug, and I investigated everything they uncovered. My life started in that pile. I had been born in it four years earlier. Only now, its form was far different from the house it had been when I made my entry into this world. In a crazy way, it seemed that the formation of that bed of ash became the real birthing event for me. The events surrounding the creation of that pile of destruction also supplied many of my earliest and most vivid memories. It was as if I was four years old when I was born.

Looking back, I see how my life started there at four. All that had occurred before only kept me in hold until the fire in 1954. Time has moved on, and an awful lot of years separate today from the day of the fire. That's the way time works, and it works all too well. Now, I find myself looking back over the years and reflecting on what time and circumstance have sent my way. More than sixty years have passed since what has become, to me, the beginning of my childhood.

This is a collection of memories, observations, and my view of changes that have occurred about me since our house burned in 1954, an event that my mind has declared "the ashes of 391." As life unfolded for me in the years that followed, it took unexpected turns. The coincidence at another 391 in a place far away and the ashes surrounding it had the effect of creating still another beginning for me.

It is as if life began for me twice, once as a four-year-old child and the second as an adult on an island that I had never heard of until shortly before my arrival there. Both times at addresses that included 391 and both times as a result of tragic events. Events that played such big parts in determining the course of my life. Would I change either of these occurrences if I could? I've asked myself that question more than once. Even though those times were painful for so many people, I must view them through my eyes and how they ultimately affected me. Selfishly, I must answer, "No! This is my life. Meddling with it is not allowed." Difficulties and even tragedies included, I accept things as they played out. I just want to remember life as it was, move on to the rest of it, and hope that it will provide me with many more of the happy moments.

On this cold, bleak December day, I find myself having just returned from one of my mental journeys in which I revisited the days of the fire and retraced events back to the present. Along the way, I visited certain people and relived moments of time. I returned to places that I thought I had left long ago, not having fully realized until now that perhaps I never really left them behind at all. An image from my childhood of beggar lice and cockleburs comes easily to mind. Anyone familiar with them knows it is next to impossible to walk through places where they are without finding them stuck to your hair and clothing. They stay with you and go along for the ride wherever you go. How often I remember sitting down and pulling away cockleburs and beggar lice from my clothing, studying them, and pitching them aside. Good riddance! But memories? Some we might wish to treat like cockleburs, but we can never leave them by the wayside. Even those that we would have liked to have pitched aside, we cannot. Like beggar lice and cockleburs, they still manage to hold on and come along with us. Whether pleasant or sad, invited or otherwise, we accumulate so many memories as we move through life. Now, I find myself in the present with a pile of them. A pile to be sorted through, reflected upon, and, perhaps, tucked away again.

Part 1

ALABAMA

1

MEMENTOS AND
SELECTED MEMORIES

THE BLEAK rawness of this December day is confined to the outside. My little room is cozy. The golden yellow of its walls and the red brown of the floor and furniture soften it and make it inviting. There is no sharpness here, just a feeling of warmth and security. The small electric fireplace hums softly and flickers its invitation to move my feet a little closer. Responding, I shift my chair and lean back with a feeling of contentment. In my comfort, I turn my attention to the items displayed on the walls about me, and I pause briefly to reflect on each. The items would convey no special meaning to the casual observer, but my glances are not casual. Everything displayed about me is important to me, each for its own reason. Each comes with its own set of memories and a bit to tell about something in my life. All of them together tell a story—or at least begin to tell it. They remind me of where I am today and invite me to examine the events of my life, all of which, happily, have worked together to bring me to where I am today. They, along with my early memories, remind me of the sweetness of life and even a bit of its bitterness. Both play their parts in making my life unique to me.

"Would you like to hear a story?" the walls softly invite. "I know the story," my mind responds, "but I'll listen to it again. Remind me of all those things that played their important parts in my life, even the difficult ones, for those times help me appreciate the sweet things all the more. Go ahead and tell it. I'll listen and remember!"

I call this room my private study, but that is misleading. I don't study anything here. Calling it a study just makes it sound official and off-limits. This is a place of reflection and remembering. My wife knows it makes me happy thinking that it is private. She allows me to think that and only pokes her head in occasionally with a comment or request. My private study is really my special place.

Hanging on the wall of my special place and just above my desk is a tri-folded American flag. It speaks volumes and clearly too. It proclaims me an American in spirit as I am also by birth. To its right is a portrait of myself in uniform, bearing witness that I have served my country. To the left of the flag is a letter of commendation given to me at Field Station Sobe, an intelligence-gathering station on Okinawa. It references "highly congratulatory correspondence" received from the National Security Agency concerning certain contributions I made. This letter says everything that I need to hear concerning my service. No military award or decoration means as much to me. I always read it with a sense of pride. It says that I made a real difference, and that leaves me knowing my work was noted by others and appreciated. That's all anyone can ask for.

The flag, the portrait, and the letter tell the short story of my military experience spanning nine years and nine months. The full version has long ago been boxed up and stored away in some dusty corner of my mind. I am content to have it so, for stored with it is a certain amount of the disagreeable and unpleasantness that was. From this short version of my military experience comes the introduction to some of the most wonderful experiences of my life. Those experiences are ongoing and continue to unfold. The things around me provide a window and highlight that part of my life starting in 1974. Somehow it seems that my adult life began in that year on the island of Okinawa, even though I had been in military service for four and a half years.

There is the portrait of Okasan (Mother) in her kimono taken several years after I married in Okinawa, Japan, on January 30, 1974. She calls me her son, and it makes me proud that she does so. A letter, displayed in three frames, is from my wife's sister, Misae. She extends family sentiments and thanks me for the "treasures" of my heart. Beside it, another frame holds an approximation of a heart with the inscription "arigato kokoro kara" (thanks from the heart). A sake set sits on the shelf along with several cultural figurines and the piece of coral that allows me to reach out and touch part of Okinawa whenever I wish. Four expired Japanese passports showing younger versions of my wife occupy two frames. Samples of simple but elegant Japanese art and life depictions are highlighted in others.

In a display located directly behind me, on top of a brown bookcase, is a samurai sword and its companion short sword. Above the swords and stretching toward the ceiling is the white flag of Japan with its rising sun. Against the top portion of the flag and canting downward where the flag meets the ceiling is the portrait of a young Japanese man. From his heavenly vantage point, he seems to survey the room. I never met this man, as he died young. He bears a striking resemblance to my own son and appears to be about the same age, probably around forty years old. It is good that he is there and keeping his eye on me because I married his daughter, Yoko. She is the second child

3

of seven and his second daughter. Sometimes I turn in my chair, look up at him, and in the Eastern fashion talk to him almost prayerfully. My mind supplies his responses.

"Yoko is fine," I tell him. "Your grandchildren and great-grandchildren are all healthy and doing well. You would be proud of all of them. Yes, we stay in touch with the family in Japan and communicate regularly with them. We help in caring for Okasan's needs. We hope to see her in the coming year."

When I look up at this man, Zensho Chinen, I think about the difficulties he faced in caring for a young family in the aftermath of the horrific battle of Okinawa. I cannot help but be reminded of the hardships my own father faced in raising a large family under difficult circumstances after he had lost everything. Sometimes, I shake my head as I consider the chain of events that took me from 391 Hope Hull, Alabama, to 391 Misatosan, Okinawa. Often, I have reflected on that chain of events that link the ashes of two different places. Also, how those events eventually led a young man and young woman from opposite sides of the earth in forming a new family.

My conversation with him continues. "I know," I tell him, "it was hard to care for a young family under the conditions that you went through. Yoko has told me so. I know she was born on the rubble and ashes of Okinawa just a year after the smoke had cleared following that great battle of World War II. How hard it must have been to raise a family on a tiny patch of ground and with a few carpentry tools. Since public buildings with their records were destroyed, you lost title to most of your property. I know it must have been hard to accept, especially under the harsh conditions that were the new reality. There was a lot of rebuilding to be done but little money to be had. There were 241,000 dead from the fighting. Two hundred and forty-one thousand people! More innocent men, women, and children than soldiers. Now their names are inscribed on the granite monuments at the world peace museum and park near Naha. Otosan (Father), it is a sight to see! I have been there, and I wish you could see it for yourself!

"Okasan's first husband, Shiroma Kotoku's, name is inscribed there. His daughter, Masako, became your daughter. The memory of all that occurred must have overwhelmed your senses! I have heard a lot about that and what you did as a family friend to help Okasan locate her husband or find out what had become of him. She was injured in the blast of shrapnel while carrying the baby, Masako, on her back. Your friend Shiroma Kotoku was terribly wounded in the stomach by the blast and taken away by the Americans. I know that you helped Okasan in her search for him among the aid stations and field hospitals. No one ever found out what had become of him or his body. I was told how everyone finally accepted that he was dead and that his body would not be recovered. I suppose he must have ended up in a common grave somewhere with others who were unknown and unclaimed. His parents later recommended that Okasan marry you. 'He is a good man and will take care of you,' they told her. That's what family members have told me.

"Masako then became your daughter, but her brother, Kousei, stayed with his grandparents to replace their lost son, his father, Kotoku. Now, Yoko, your second daughter, is born amid the ashes and the hard times. She does not like to open up to me about those times. 'No, I don't have a penny,' you answered Yoko when she was six years old and in the first grade. 'Why do you need it?' 'My pencil is too short, and I need a new one,' she answered. There was no penny and no pencil. American money had become the currency on the island instead of yen. Money is hard to get, and even food is precious.

"The family raises some food on the small plot of ground.

5

Some sweet potatoes are grown, but they are to sell for a precious few cents. The family will eat only the smallest. They are not suitable to sell. Tending the plot is a family affair with the children doing their part. Children can pull weeds and carry water. They can bring the fertilizer from the outhouse in buckets suspended on a yoke across their shoulders, if need be. You spare them from those tasks as much as possible. They still need to be children. After all, the liquid fertilizer stinks and is messy, but it is good for the plants and is ladled carefully around them and makes them grow. During the school week, there is bread and milk for the children. They get it at school for lunch, and the Catholics supply it. Yoko said that she ate her bread but brought the milk home for the younger children to drink. You know, Otosan, after more than sixty years, she still will not drink milk! Isn't it strange how things like that can stay with us for so long?"

My mind returns to the comfort of this small room and again becomes conscious of the humming of the electric fireplace. Glancing at the window, I observe the still overcast Alabama sky. My eyes scan the walls and my surroundings once more, and I consider how lucky I am. There were times in my life when I did not feel so lucky or secure. From the comfort of this time and place and surrounded by the mementos of a happy adult life, I enjoy reviewing those times and events that were a part of my own early life and younger years. So many of the memories that come flooding back are happy ones. There are a few of difficult times and an occasional one that is even frightening, but as I string together the events of my life, I can see clearly how they have all worked together to make mine a happy life.

I think about the house fire when I was four years old in which we lost everything except the clothes we were wearing. I think about how life was reconstructed from those ashes and how Dad and Mom had to start over in much the same way that another family on Okinawa had to start over. There was the terrifying period of separation when eleven children were split among various households in the community until my parents could effect a new beginning for the family. There was the one-mule farm with the wagon. A wagon that was to be the only wheeled vehicle Dad ever operated.

I recall vividly the sights and sounds of the small farm and of my part in tending the garden and fields that supplied most of our food. The smells of mink, beaver, and otters that Dad trapped in the wintertime are such familiar odors of my life. I remember, also, the smell of paint and sawdust from Dad's summertime occupation when he was not engaged in his farming activities.

I think about the importance of books in a family that had no television during the first few years of my life, the joys that came as a consequence of employing my imagination in finding new ways to entertain myself or in creating new adventures. Those adventures were certain to keep this redheaded child outside and in the woods most of the time!

There are plenty of memories involving the people of the community. Some of these people were friends from church or school or nearby houses and were playmates and partners in adventure. Others seemed to be like ancient permanent fixtures of the community. Their lives touched those of my family in so many ways. As I consider all these people who figure so prominently into my remembrances and experiences, I am keenly aware of the tremendous impact that the black residents had on me. They played a truly big part in my growing-up experience. Failure to acknowledge them and their place in my life would create gaping holes in my very existence! Such was their impact upon my life.

As I look back over my life to my childhood, with the desire to commit to paper some of those things that I remember, the starting place is not difficult to choose. As with my wife's story and with its beginning in the ashes, so does my story begin.

Toshi Chinen (Okasan, Mother), Okinawa, Japan. About 1983.

Zensho Chinen (Otosan, Father). About 1958.

2

SHOES AND FIRE: THE BEGINNING

"BE STILL, for crying out loud!" Mama scolded me as she fought to push my feet into the new pair of hard leather shoes. Having finally accomplished the task, she compressed the toe end of one shoe between her thumb and forefinger to assure herself there was adequate room between the end of my toes and the toe of the shoe. I don't know how she could tell since the leather was so hard, but she seemed satisfied that the shoe fit properly.

Tying the laces, she instructed me to stand up and walk around a bit. I did, and the edges of the leather pushed in around my ankles and above my heels. They felt unnatural on my feet, and I complained to Mama that they hurt. Like my sisters and brother, Larry, I was used to having my feet free of any constraints and fully exposed most of the time. Suddenly I felt a bit apprehensive about the new pair of shoes. Sure, they were pretty, and I was proud of them, but they were awfully uncomfortable! Mama assured me that they would soften up and stop hurting after I had worn them a few times. Hurting or not, with Mama's reassurance, I finally felt my apprehension beginning to fade and found myself even becoming happy about the shoes and a bit reluctant to take them off.

"Maybe I should wear them around awhile to get them softened up," I suggested to Mama.

Mama said no. It was too soon to start wearing them just yet. It would still be a while before wintertime came when it would become necessary to protect my feet against the frosty ground. Barefoot weather would continue for a few more weeks at least. The shoes would be there for me when the cold weather hit.

Satisfied that the shoes would be okay, Mama untied the laces and slipped them from my feet. Later as I lay in bed, I happily contemplated the shoes that I had placed nearby so that I could look at them. Sure, they were hard and uncomfortable and even hurt a bit as I had walked about in them, but they were mine! They were brown, shiny, brand-new, and mine!

Thinking back to this time, I have come to realize that the shoes were the first things that I remember getting that were uniquely mine. Of course, there must have been other things, but I don't remember them. Santa Claus was not a part of my life, and birthdays were not celebrated events, or I don't remember it so. Any new items or anything out of the ordinary certainly were of the necessary sort.

Pushing sleep away, I looked at the shoes that I had placed nearby. I lay in bed reassuring myself that the shoes were there. They were. Presently, my eyes grew heavy, and in fits and starts, sleep came. The dreams were pleasant ones, I'm sure. They must have been because my mind had only pleasant things with which to work.

This is one of my earliest memories. There were others, but they were different. This one stands out because of the comforting nature of it. It represents a time in my life when things were totally free from care and equally secure. It marks a point at which the security of my world was suddenly shattered. Everything changed because of the fire. Perhaps the events in my life were "too right."

Many years later, I became familiar with the writings of the ancient Jewish historian Josephus. He remarked, "Fate often intervenes to change our lives in a big way, especially when things are 'too right.'" It certainly intervened here and changed the course of my life and of all my family. I also remember reading in some psychology book that our earliest memories often involve either a pleasurable experience or a difficult one. My memory of the shoes and the memory of our house being destroyed so soon afterward were so powerful and close together that they seem to be a part of the same event. The memories involving total security and total devastation were so closely linked that they combined and became the signal event of my childhood.

There are other memories that I retain that are "prefire," but they only come to me in bits and pieces. At best, they can be described as fragmentary, disjointed, and without context. However, they still give some insight into that time before the fire. The front of the house faced east, toward the road. There was probably only thirty yards separating the house from the road. This was a narrow two-lane road that had only been black-topped a couple of decades earlier. It was designated US Highway 31 and extended from the extreme north of our country to the Gulf Coast. It has served as one of our country's main north-south arteries for many years. Even so, it always has seemed like a country road. Turning into our yard from the road, a visitor would have first passed the dog pen on the right with the house a few yards farther in on the left. The outhouse was very apparent in a line with the dog pen and sat slightly back from the house. On the far end of the house was the garage with its attached sheds and the hog lot between it and the road. The corncrib was behind the house near the end closest to the garage. These areas and structures also doubled as our playground. As children, we considered that their primary purpose.

3

PREFIRE MEMORIES

STANDING BESIDE the old floor lamp just inside the front door of the house, I watched Mama as she nursed my little sister, Dianne. Mama sat on the edge of the raised floor of the central room of the house that separated the living room from the kitchen. To the right side of this area was a bed that we younger children shared. I have no remembrance of any of the other rooms except a recollection of a portion of the kitchen nearest the kerosene stove. Outside the house and near the kitchen was our cistern, which caught the water from the housetop when it rained. That was our water supply, and it was drawn out with a bucket and rope. It was to be many more years before indoor plumbing and running water became a part of our home life.

~

The kids were all sick, or at least all of us younger ones were. We had the measles; I had heard Mama and Dad talking about it. As usual, all six of us younger kids were in the same bed. The bed smelled bad, like vomit and pee. We all alternated between crying, moaning, sleeping, and crying again. Sometimes one of us began to vomit, and Mama would be there to clean that one and comfort the rest and try to get us to sleep a bit. There was no doctor, and it seemed as if time was relied upon to take care of such illnesses in those days.

It was dark when Dad came in, and there was little that he could do to relieve our misery. He patted each of us softly, opened a small paper sack, and took out a lollipop for each of us. It was oddly shaped and had a piece of candy on each end of the stick like a dumbbell. I wondered later if I had imagined the shape of that lollipop in my fevered state. I did not imagine Dad's gentle touch and was conscious of his concern and comforting words for all of us.

We all survived, and the illness became a memory. I was told many years later that the nerve damage in my left eye was probably a result of that illness. I was also told that I had not imagined the shape of the lollipop.

Something was very wrong! My stomach was cramping, and I desperately needed to get to the outhouse. Running along the back side of the house, I knew that I was not going to make it! Stopping, I pulled down my short pants, backed up close to the side of the house, and squatted down. I felt as if my insides were going to come out, and it was a big relief when I had finished. I felt so much better and looked around, hoping that no one had seen me. I pulled up my pants and looked around again to see if anyone was looking. Even at four, some things were private, and I didn't want anyone to know what I had done. I marked the spot in my mind, knowing that I must remember not to step there. I decided not to warn anyone else to avoid the spot. They would have to look out for themselves, I thought. I would keep it secret so they couldn't blame me.

There was an apple in the outhouse. It had a green skin and was only partly eaten. Had I made it to the outhouse I might have looked to see if it was still there. I had seen it several times before. Looking down through the sitting hole, I had seen it among the waste and filth down there. I do not understand why someone only took a few bites and then threw it away. Uncle Frank had brought us a bag of apples from Birmingham a few days before. He had given each of us one, and I had eaten mine—core and all. Later, I saw that the apple in the waste of the outhouse had disappeared, and I wondered what had happened to it. The chickens found it, I concluded, and I wondered why it had taken them so long. *They will eat anything.* I found myself wishing that whoever threw it away had given it to me instead.

~

The family that I don't like came back to visit. They are loud, and they talk bad. The little boy and his older sister are mean and are always looking for things to get into. The adults went into the house, but all the children stayed outside playing. Mama always said, "Children should be seen, not heard." Whenever we had company, we had to leave the adults to themselves and not be a bother to them. As usual in such situations, we kept to ourselves and played. The girl climbed up onto the top of the house and called for my sister, Betty.

When Betty came around the corner of the house, the girl called Betty's name again. Betty stopped and looked up just as something fell onto her head. When Betty cried out, the girl began pulling her pants up, begging my older sister to be quiet. Scrambling down from the roof, she pulled her to the rain barrel at the corner of the house. As she began washing Betty's hair, she continued to beg her not to tell on her. It took a while for her to finish cleaning my sister's hair and for Betty to stop crying. I found myself disliking this girl and her family even more, and I hoped that they would not come back anymore!

~

Dad kept a couple of dogs in the dog pen. They were his possum dogs, and he liked to go possum hunting sometimes. They barked a lot, and sometimes we played in and around the pen. One day we were in the pen with the dogs and were told not to climb over the fence. Mama had to go somewhere, and the older girls were supposed to be watching us, but they put us in the dog pen instead and told us not to climb out. We were all crying to be let out, but they wouldn't let us out. The dogs did not like the crying and began jumping on us. They were not used to us being in the pen with them and crying like that. Mama would not have liked it if she knew. We threatened to tell on them for putting us in the dog pen, but our older sisters said that we better not! They finally let us out.

~

It was getting late into the afternoon, and I found myself very hungry, but it was too early for supper yet. *Maybe I can find something to eat in the kitchen*, I thought. Looking around the kitchen, I found nothing that was ready to eat. Perhaps there was a baked sweet potato left over somewhere, maybe in one of the drawers under the stove. I could not find one, and there was nothing in the drawer under the stove except something that looked like water. *It shouldn't be there*, I thought, and it *smells! I know what that smell is; it's kerosene. I've smelled it many times. Mama and Dad used it for lots of things, but why was it all puddled up under the stove like that?* I closed the drawer and left the kitchen because my older sister June wanted me out of the way so that she could start cooking supper. *I'll sure be happy when supper is ready,* I thought. *I'm hungry!*

I didn't say anything about the kerosene, and later, I was sorry that I had not. I kept the secret about what I had seen for many years. I know I should have said something about the kerosene, but I was only four, I reasoned when I got older. Still, I should have told.

June lit the stove after getting me out of the kitchen. Pretty soon, the screaming started—and the world as I knew it was gone before the sun went down!

4

THE FIRE

MY OLDER sister June set about preparing the evening meal when suddenly, the area around the stove was engulfed in flames. It was pointless to try to turn off the kerosene supply. The flames prevented anyone from getting close. It didn't matter anyway. The fire was being fed by the kerosene puddle in the areas under and around the stove and in the drawer beneath it. The screaming intensified and spread through the house so that all of us knew that something was dreadfully wrong.

I don't remember leaving the house, nor do I remember seeing the crowd of people begin to gather in our yard. I do remember being in the yard in the middle of a crowd of concerned people, all of whom were anxious to see if everyone had made it out. Some older sister or adult had her restraining hands on my shoulders as she peered over the heads of those between her and the house. Even in this forest of legs and bodies, I could see the line of cars stopped on both sides of the road with more vehicles stopping and people running to the scene to help.

There was no helping to be done except to ensure everyone was accounted for. The only water supply was the cistern with its bucket and rope located at the very corner of the blazing house. The bucket and rope had been employed only briefly before the heat made it impossible to continue. Very quickly, they were abandoned and lay on the ground, useless. There would be little hope of stopping such a fire even today with our volunteer fire department. This fire had gained a rapid start and secure purchase with its kerosene supply and had spread rapidly because of the fat pine lumber and asphalt-based siding of which the house was constructed.

Dad came home in a rush, though I don't know who brought him home from the carpentry job where he was working. The situation was hopeless as far as the house was concerned since there was no longer any access to the cistern. The heat was intense, and black smoke billowed upward from the kitchen end of the house.

The roaring and crackling noises seemed to be getting louder as the flames spread. Dad had a wooden box in his room on the far end of the house and was determined to try to get to it before it was destroyed by the fast-moving flames. Realizing his intentions of trying to get to the box, several men blocked him and successfully held him back from entering the house. It seemed that only seconds later, the hungry flames had engulfed that end of the house as well. The wooden box was gone along with the few valuables and little bit of money stored in it. As far as the house, its contents, and Dad's box, my father had just lost everything. In looking back, I realize that had Dad not been restrained by the quick-thinking men, we might have lost him because of that box. It would be impossible for me to ever imagine growing up without him as the virtual center of my life.

The corncrib was fairly close to the house and was getting dangerously scorched. Dad quickly enlisted the help of a number of the men in smothering the flames on it as they broke out. There had been a vain attempt to turn the crib over with levers to gain a little more room between it and the house. That turned out to be unnecessary as they were able to save the scorched corncrib using wet crocus sacks and water from the mule's watering trough.

The structure that we called the garage was also saved, though badly scorched. The garage contained the wagon, farm implements, livestock feed, and various tools. It served as our barn and had served some family member in years past as a garage and was never referred to as anything else. Attached to either side and to the back of this structure were sheds used for various purposes, one of them serving as the chicken house. The chickens were fine and had been shielded from the heat by the tin that overlay the rough board siding. The pigs in their pen on the other side of the garage were okay too. They were in a fenced enclosure between the garage and the road. It was referred to as the "hog lot."

Our family was unharmed, and everyone had made it out and been accounted for. Not even a pig or chicken had suffered injury. Though the life and future of those chickens and pigs would continue unaffected and unchanged, it was not so for me, my sisters, my brothers, or the parents who would have to care for us.

As the vehicles along the road slowly began to depart, and the crowd started dwindling by ones and twos, I was still unaware of the hushed conversations that had been taking place. Conversations about what could be done for Mama and Dad and for their eleven children.

I found out many of those details only late in my life. Mama would be staying with her foster mother, Mrs. Clara Marshall in Montgomery. Mama had been orphaned as a very young child, and Mrs. Marshall was one of several people who had cared for her as she grew up, eventually becoming her "mother."

Grandmama, Dad's mama, would look after his needs and those of my older brother, Buddy, who was nearly seventeen years old. Daisy Anne, the oldest at eighteen, had recently married and not at home any longer. June was fifteen and would be taken in by Mrs. Clara Venable. Mrs. Iva Henry took in Pat, my thirteen-year-old sister. The Brookses, who owned the small store south of us, agreed to care for my twelve-year-old sister, Verba Lee, while the Crosses took Betty, Sharron, and Sandra. Betty was eight, and Sharron and Sandra were five. They were twins. Our great-uncle, Claude, and his wife, Aunt Clara, took six-year-old Larry. Uncle Claude was my grandmama's brother. His property adjoined Grandmama's.

It had been worked out that Dianne, the two-year-old, and I would be going with Aunt Louise and Uncle Rufus. It was to be the first time either of us had been away from the family. When we were placed in the front seat of the truck and into the care of Aunt Louise and Uncle Rufus, we were reduced to a state of abject terror. The secure world of a few hours earlier was gone, and all I could do was cry out for it as we drove away in the old pickup truck. I did not understand at the time that I would never again see that which had been my home except as it continues to exist in memory. In a very real way, this was to be my beginning.

5

A FAMILY SEPARATED

THE TRIP to Aunt Louise and Uncle Rufus's house seemed to have gone on forever, but it was really only five miles. I knew that we were getting farther from home, and my crying increased even though I tried very hard not to cry. They didn't want me to cry and tried to comfort me as best they could, but I wanted to go home.

Dianne cried for Mama and would not be comforted. I sat between Aunt Louise and Uncle Rufus while Aunt Louise held Dianne in her lap. Being so small, I could not see through the window glass of the old pickup truck, but I could hear the crunching of the gravel under the tires and taste the dust that had drifted in through a partially opened window. The sound of the truck engine and that of gravel crunching under the tires changed, and I knew that we were slowing down.

Uncle Rufus brought the truck almost to a stop and turned the steering wheel to the right as the truck bounced slowly up the short approach to the house. The brakes squealed lightly as he brought the truck to a stop and shut off the engine.

Aunt Louise opened the door and climbed out with Dianne in her arms. Telling me to climb down, she shut the door after

I was on the ground beside her. The sun had gone down, and it was nearly dark.

As she turned toward the even darker house, Aunt Louise told me to follow her. There were no lights on, and the dark strangeness of the house made it look scary and uninviting. I had only been inside one house in my life, and that one had been reduced to the smoking pile we had left a few minutes before. Aunt Louise said to "come on," and I trailed along behind her to the house.

Uncle Rufus had missed his chores and headed to the barn with a flashlight to do the evening feeding of the livestock. We haven't had supper either, and Aunt Louise set about putting together something for all of us.

By the time the food was on the table, Uncle Rufus had finished his chores at the barn and had come inside. Though I had been so hungry earlier in the afternoon, thoughts of food were driven from my mind. I no longer wanted a leftover sweet potato or anything else. I only wanted the company of my sisters and brothers and the security of home, of Mama and Dad.

My aunt and uncle encouraged me to eat, but I refused to eat more than a few bites. Dianne did not want to eat either, and Aunt Louise only managed to get her to swallow a tiny amount. Even though they did not have the experience of raising children, this aunt and uncle realized that the situation was hopeless. We were not going to eat.

The bedroom looked big to us as our aunt opened the door and guided us inside. Going to the bed, she pulled the covers back and assisted us in crawling onto the bed. We were to sleep in our clothes as we had nothing else to put on. Pulling the covers up around us, she attempted to comfort us, telling us not to cry and to go to sleep. Lingering at the door, she watched us for a moment, turned off the light, pulled the door shut, and left us alone. I do not know how many times she might have checked on us during the night, but I'm sure she must have done so several times. Dianne had always slept in a baby bed, and I slept in a bed with several sisters and my brother Larry.

As Aunt Louise closed the door and left us alone in this strange place, Dianne and I huddled closer together, trying to find comfort in each other's presence. It was to be the first of many nights of sleeping with our arms wrapped around each other and comforting each other. The bond that existed between us and was so apparent through our childhood years formed on that night.

$\sim$

We lay awake side by side with the covers pulled up to our chins. It was morning, and we could see the window lightening as the sun came up. Looking about the room, we talked in hushed tones about the things a two-year-old and a four-year-old would talk about in such a frightening circumstance. We wanted to be with our sisters and brothers and with Mama and Dad. It is all we had ever known and all we could think about. We were not crying, but our eyes were wet, and Dianne was shaking like she was very cold. The muffled footsteps and slight noise at the door indicated that someone was coming into the room.

My aunt and another woman stepped into the room and stopped just inside the door. I knew they were looking at us, but I could no longer see them. I had shut my eyes as tightly as I could, and my body was stiff. There was the whispered observation from Aunt Louise, "They aren't really asleep. They're scared and just pretending." By that comment, I knew that Dianne was doing the same as me. The two continued to talk in low tones about the tragedy of the situation and how sad it was that such a thing had happened.

"I don't know how long we'll have them," Aunt Louise said, "but it will be until everything gets straightened out. They will stay with us 'til then." There were a few more low-voiced comments and then the sounds of the door closing and footsteps moving away.

Aunt Louise fixed us a special breakfast. We did not want to eat the food even though Aunt Louise said that she had fixed it just for us. The stuff on the plate was golden brown and cut into little square pieces with butter and something else on top. The plate was full of it, and it was sticky. It had a peculiar but interesting smell I'd never smelled before. Aunt Louise told me to take a bite, and I did. It had an odd sweet taste to it that I was not familiar with. She succeeded in getting me to eat some more of it, but not all of it. I didn't know if I was liking it or not. It smelled and tasted different from anything else I had ever eaten, and I was suspicious of each bite.

Dianne was suspicious too, and she did not eat much. Even today, I can see, taste, and smell those little sticky squares on that plate. It was when I was in the army many years later that I was reintroduced to pancakes and maple syrup. The mystery of what Aunt Louise had prepared special for us was finally solved.

I've never forgotten how we huddled together for comfort on that night, nor have I ever forgotten the special breakfast Aunt Louise prepared for us the following morning. Not only were these things not forgotten, but they have never dimmed in my memory. All else that occurred during our stay with these relatives, my mind did not consciously retain. Aunt Louise and Uncle Rufus were good people and kind to us, but that really did not matter. We wanted only to be back home.

6

A FAMILY REUNITED

FINALLY, DAYS or weeks later, the happy day came when the announcement was made that we were going back to our family. I remember the incredible joy and happy anticipation that I felt. We could hardly contain our excitement at the prospect of being with Mama and the rest of the family again. Our aunt and uncle had bought us several toys while we were with them, and we wondered if we were allowed to take them with us. When we asked if we could take the toys with us, the answer was, "Yes, me and Rufus don't need no toys." I picked up the sports car that they had bought for me and carried it to the truck along with the other toys they had given us. The little car was white. It was of durable metal construction and was about eighteen inches long. I could even sit on it and push myself along. It remained a favorite toy for many years until, like many things, it simply ceased to exist.

The trip from Aunt Louise's house back to my family was different from our trip to their house. The sound of gravel crunching beneath the truck tires no longer sounded ominous and frightful but had taken on a new meaning for me. Now the crunching beneath the tires and the haze of dust suspended in the cab of the truck were evidence of our progress along the graveled road that led home.

As our excitement grew, the small talk between the two grown-ups diminished and ceased altogether. Perhaps each was considering the conversations that they had had with each other and how they might propose the things that they had discussed privately. We were ignorant of such discussions, conscious only of the fact that we were finally going home. Eventually, the sound of the tires on the graveled road surface changed again as we first came to a stop and then turned onto the hard surface of the highway.

Moments later, the motion of the truck changed once more as Uncle Rufus guided it to the left onto the dirt road known as Pintlala Old Road. Although I could see none of this, it didn't matter. I could feel it, and I knew that I was going home. When the truck finally came to a stop and the engine shut off, Aunt Louise announced as a matter of fact, "Well, we're here."

Scrambling down from the truck after Aunt Louise had cleared the way, I found myself looking at very strange surroundings. We were parked in front of an old wooden house with a porch along the front side. The yard was broad and sandy. Two or three large oak trees spread their massive limbs over portions of the yard. Looking behind me, I could see the dirt road that we had come in on and noted that it was bordered on each side by a line of trees draped in spanish moss. The largeness of everything was intimidating, and in the bleak winter surroundings, my heart seemed to sink inside of me. I had never been to this place before, and it seemed very strange. The dismal quality of the winter day and the strangeness of this place sent doubts coursing through my mind. That was quickly forgotten when Aunt Louise announced, "Your mama is inside.

Let's go and see her." My heart and spirit soared as I raced for the house.

I don't remember going into the house or how I came into the room without Mama knowing. Entering the large room, I approached Mama who had her back to me. She was standing close to the wood-fired heater where the room was warmest. Smoke hung in the air in a layer from the cigarette she was smoking, and the odor of tobacco was strong but somehow familiar and comforting. Mama was slender and wore new blue jeans. I had never seen her dressed that way, but it was probably a consequence of her having gotten new clothes after losing everything in the fire.

Staring into space as if she were lost in thought, it took a moment for Mama to realize that she was no longer alone in the room. Turning, she broke into a happy smile and spread her arms. Dianne and I both ran to the security of her arms and received the hugs and kisses that we had cried out for on so many nights. In the warm room with its comforting smell of tobacco and wood smoke, we became happy and laughed again. Reassured that we were back with the family and that everything was okay and right once more, I gradually began drifting farther away from her and taking an interest in my new surroundings. They were different to me, like Mama with those new blue jeans.

Knowing that Mama was there, these unfamiliar surroundings began to lose their intimidating nature and assumed an interesting and mysterious quality instead. I enthusiastically investigated every room and everything inside and outside of the place that just a little while before had appeared so cold and forbidding. By the end of the day, the old Moseley house was well explored. I had been reunited with all my family members, and the world was a bright and happy place again!

Something was wrong with Aunt Louise. I had heard her crying in the other room. She and Uncle Rufus were arguing with Mama and Dad.

"But you have eleven children," my aunt wailed. "You'll still have nine!"

"No!" Mama said. "These are our children, not puppies. We are not going to give any of them away."

Aunt Louise's voice was shrill as she pleaded her case, but Mama and Dad could not be convinced to give up Dianne and me, their two youngest children. It had seemed a reasonable solution to these kindhearted people to their own situation. They were childless and could never bear their own children, and this was possibly the only chance to have children to raise. It would help ease the burden on Mama and Dad as well, as Aunt Louise pointed out. But Mama and Dad refused, and Dad's sister went away heartbroken. I was "home," and I was happy. Mama and Dad were not going to let our aunt and uncle keep us as their own.

I was relieved when Aunt Louise and Uncle Rufus were gone. Soon, my feeling of security was again restored, but for a long time, I found myself uneasy of Aunt Louise and was not sure that I liked her at all. She represented something that was painful in my life. Even though I did not actually blame her for it, I remembered the separation that had been so frightening. A day came many years later when I cried for Aunt Louise. It was after I came to understand her and became aware of the heartaches and disappointments in her life. She had loved us as if we were her own. We were the closest that she ever came to having children. I suppose for a few days, we were hers.

We stayed at the "old Mosley house" for several months. I do not remember most of the day-to-day events during that time. There are a few special things that I do remember, however.

The old house had been built nearly a century earlier though I was not conscious of that at the time. I was only aware of the largeness of the rooms and of the cold draftiness of the house during those winter days. Being new surroundings for me, I saw it as mysterious, and I never got tired of exploring all its nooks and dark corners. The dirt road in front of the house ran roughly parallel for nearly a mile alongside Highway 31, which lay a couple of hundred yards to the east. Both ends of this dirt road connected with the highway at points a mile apart. The ground fell away sharply behind the house and made it appear as if there were a small valley on that side. Pinchona Creek ran through this bottomland and separated the hardwood forest on the far side from the cattle pastures nearer the house. The house appeared to be on a ridge when looking at it from the lowland along the creek. In later years, I would spend a lot of time hunting, fishing, and trapping along the creek that ran through those woods that seemed to stretch for miles.

While we were staying at the Mosley house, I was not aware of all these landscape features that would become so familiar to me with time. The area in and closely around the house was enough to occupy me during the few months that we were there. Trickling out of the steep hillside about a hundred yards from the house was a cool, clear spring. It was to the north of the house and about halfway down the slope toward the bottomland. This was fascinating to me as I had never seen a spring before. A basin had been dug out about ten feet across to capture the water. When Mama came back from her frequent trips to pick turnip greens from the garden near our house that had burned, she washed the greens at this spring. I liked playing among the trees on this hillside while she washed the greens, though she would not let any of us stray too far away. Being wintertime, I knew her hands were about frozen by the time she got her turnip greens washed. Somehow, it did not seem to bother her.

Years later, while trapping along the creek that ran through the forested bottomland, I walked up the side of the slope to see if the spring was still there. It was! The water still flowed into the basin, cold and clear!

7

THE MAD DOG

MAMA HAD to leave the house for the day, and the older girls were supposed to be taking care of us younger children. They put us out of the house, locked the doors, and would not let us back in. They seemed to think it funny that we cried and carried on so about it.

A strange dog had come into the yard, and we were afraid. We had all been warned about "mad" dogs before and to stay away from them. This dog was surely "mad," and we began running from door to door, screaming to be let inside, but our sisters would not let us in. They seemed to be enjoying our terror and in no hurry to provide us any relief or comfort.

The dog was showing an awful lot of interest in us, and that caused us to cry all the more to be let inside the house. Our cries attracted the dog's full attention, and he sat down on the ground and watched us as if he was undecided about which of us he would attack first. Presently, he stood up, walked around, wagged his tail, and sat back down again. He had not made up his mind yet. He kept watching us, however, as if carefully considering his choices, but he never came too close. The longer that he remained in the yard, the more we ran around and cried.

The mad dog laid down with his head on his paws, flopping his tail, and brushed the ground with it. Occasionally, he lifted his head and studied us some more. Finally, he rose from the ground as if he had made a decision. After stretching and yawning, he wagged his tail once more. Turning toward the dirt road and with a parting glance at us, he headed south down the road.

Years later, I can laugh when I think of what must have been going through that dog's head that caused him to avoid getting too close to us. He must have been wondering what ailed that bunch of screaming, running children. Perhaps, they were "mad."

Well, even though we had never seen a mad dog before, we thought we would know one if we saw one, considering all the stories we had heard. Perhaps the dog was not foaming at the mouth. That really did not matter. We were not educated about the symptoms that might be exhibited as "curious" or "furious" behavior. Little note was taken that he wagged his tail and laid down as he studied the curious behavior and the furious activity of the younger Brady children. He was a strange dog that we had not seen before, and that qualified him as being a mad dog.

None of us wanted those awful shots in the stomach that we had heard about as a treatment for rabies. We had also heard that people who caught rabies got chained up, snapped at other people, foamed at the mouth, and chewed on themselves till they died. I know that we considered ourselves as very lucky when the dog disappeared down the dirt road. I could picture myself chained to one of the massive oak trees in the yard, chewing on myself, and everybody avoiding me. I didn't want those awful shots, and I didn't want to chew on myself or choke to death on my own saliva. Yes, I was relieved to see the mad dog disappear down the road!

Well, the mad dog was gone, but on another day, I wished

that he would come back and frighten away that family that I don't like. Maybe they would not come back again! They came to visit with Mama for a while, at least the woman and her mean boy did. The woman was loud and cursed a lot. Her boy was just a little older than me, and he cursed too. Even as a four-year-old, I knew he had learned his cursing from his mother. We had all heard words before that we were not supposed to use, but not like we heard from this family. She warned him to watch his mouth, but he continued to use the bad words. He was very disrespectful and talked back to her every time she said something to him. He continued to curse her, and she spanked him. He cursed louder. "If you don't shut up, I'll wash your mouth out with soap!" she shouted. He didn't stop, and she left the room and came back, presently, with a wet washcloth and a bar of soap. After catching him, she sat straddling his body, soaped up the washcloth, and forced it into his mouth. He thrashed and cried as she washed out his mouth with the soapy cloth. Finally, satisfied that his mouth was clean enough, she got back to her feet with the wet, soapy washcloth in her hand.

He jumped to his feet and ran from the room, cursing her as he went! I found myself wishing that the mad dog would come back again for a visit and get this boy and his mother too. *I've never seen other people act like this family, and I wish they would never come back anymore! Mad dogs don't ever seem to come around at a good time!*

8

A SUNDAY-MORNING JOURNEY

IT WAS a cool Sunday morning and time to go to church. Mama collected all of us into a group, and we set out on the quarter-mile walk to the Liberty Church building. Walking along the dirt road known as Pintlala Old Road was an adventure of new sights. The road was overhung with the moss-covered limbs of the trees that lined either side of it. The spanish moss hanging from the trees, whose limbs interlocked above our heads, gave the dirt track the appearance that it was closed in at places, almost like a tunnel. Old barbed wire fences ran along both sides of the road. At one point, the road cut through a small hill, and the cut bank on either side seemed as high as mountains to someone as small as myself. Later in my life, as I grew taller, the banks seemed to have shrunk considerably to a dozen feet on the left and to three or four feet on the right.

This dirt road gave way to pavement as it angled back into Highway 31 about three hundred yards from the house we had left. An old log house surrounded by huge pine trees occupied the spot to the right of the dirt road at this point. Continuing our Sunday-morning journey to the church building, we followed the highway about two hundred yards to the church, which was located on the right side of the highway. We had passed an old store that was known as Lassiter's Store just a few yards before entering the churchyard. Across from the store, a graveled road came in from the east and led to the Fleta community and Aunt Louise's house. Had we continued past the church for another quarter of a mile, we would have been at the site of our burned house. Dad was there now and preparing to build us another house on the clay hill across the road from the ashes of our old house. This hill was used as his sweet potato patch, and he would have to find another spot to plant his potatoes.

Liberty Church of Christ was an old church that had been built in the 1800s. The building was wooden and painted white, which was probably the only accepted color for a wooden structure of that time. The churchyard had several pecan trees, and cars were parked under the trees. Both the church building and the store, which was about fifty yards back in the direction we had walked from, sat on the edge of the ridgelike high ground that descended to the bottomland off to the west.

Upon entering the church, we all knew that we were supposed to act appropriately. Running, playing, and loudness had to be left at the door. This was the place where we worshipped God, and he would never put up with such nonsense. Neither would the thundercloud of a preacher or anyone else. It was a truly special place. It was God's house! It was awe-inspiring and intimidating at the same time.

The building was always full with everyone occupying their family's traditional seats. The talk among the women always seemed to involve the subject of hats and dresses. "This old thing? Just something I had in the back of the closet," was an often-heard response to a compliment about a new hat or dress. Secretly, the owner of the new hat or dress was thrilled to have the addition to her wardrobe noticed. Some of the hats had veils on the front and came down over the upper part of the face. They were for decoration only since they didn't really cover anything. They were of a fishnet-type construction popular at the time. Most of the men of the congregation wore fedora hats that were never worn inside the building. Between Sunday school and worship, a number of the men congregated under the pecan trees and smoked. Women who smoked did not do so at church.

My first memory of walking to church was on the occasion of walking to it from the house on the mossy, tree-lined dirt road. I suppose that is because it was the first time that we had walked to the church from a place other than our own house that had been recently reduced to ashes. The future would supply many more trips to the old church building from the site of our new house after Dad got it built.

9

THE NEW HOUSE

ONE EVENING, while we were still staying in the Mosley house, Dad made the announcement to Mama that he was ready to start painting the inside of the new house. He and Mama decided on using pale yellow, light green, and light blue on the interior walls and doors. Larry and I insisted that only red would do for our room. We were very excited to see the new red room, but we were in for a big disappointment. There was no red room. We also discovered that we had no room of our own but would share a room with our four youngest sisters. For now, one of those four sisters, Dianne, would be sleeping in a baby bed in Mama's room. Our room was to have two double beds, one for the girls and one for Larry and me. Sometimes we had to share our bed too. The older girls had a separate room, which also contained two double beds. Buddy, the older brother, had his bed in the room that later became the dining room after he went into the navy shortly after we took up residence in the new house.

Our new house was built of cinder blocks on a concrete slab. Dad poured the slab himself with the help of a couple of people from the community. It was mixed and poured from a wheelbarrow. The block walls were all constructed by Dad with the assistance of my older brother Buddy and some occasional assistance from one or two friends. The roof of the house was made of tin. Our local handyman wired the house for electricity. No plumbing was installed at the time as our water supply would be a cistern that stored water from the roof when it rained.

As in the old house, we would draw our water from the well (cistern) with a rope and bucket. Also, as in the old house, an outhouse would serve as a toilet facility for several years. A chamber pot was available for nighttime use. Emptying the pot was to become one of my duties as soon as I was able to carry it outside without spilling the contents. It was almost always full to the brim by morning since so many used it during the night. Dad was probably the only one who braved the dark and nighttime air and went to the outhouse during the night.

Our new house was painted the customary white and looked very pretty to us, even sitting in the middle of the red clay of our former potato patch. At least we had our own house again, and we were proud to call it home!

I don't remember the day that we made our move into the new house, but I am sure that it would have involved the mule and wagon. The new belongings acquired by donations from the community had to be moved from the house we had been staying in on the dirt road. Some of the furniture was already in place as different families had donated items to get us started. There was a stack of old quilts for the beds. Also, a wood and coal-fed heater in the bedroom that Mama and Dad would use. Another one was set up in the kitchen so that we could all be warm when we got out of bed on the cold, winter mornings. None of the other rooms were heated, but between the two heaters near the kitchen end of the house, that end of the house was quite warm. Our new house also had a brand-new electric stove. We were so proud of our new house even if it was a bit crowded with eleven children and two adults. We were used to that, and it was normal for us.

I got the first and only spanking from Dad soon after moving into the new house. He was working in the kitchen and watching over Dianne and me at the time. Nobody else was at home. He had put the electric stove outside on the clay ground while he was doing the work. My sister and I thought we would take advantage of the situation and play house. We soon had some of the pans out of the storage drawer at the base of the stove and began playing with them. Dad came out and told us to stop, and he put the pans back in the drawer. It wasn't long that we had them out again and started filling them with the soft clay. Dad came out and scolded us and emptied the pans and returned them to the stove drawer.

Next, he sat down on a bucket and turned each of us across his knee and spanked us. It wasn't a hard spanking, just enough to show that no meant no. He might as well have blistered me red because the effect would have been just about the same!

Dad had never spanked me before, nor did he ever do it again. I never have forgotten the very light spanking I received as a warning from Dad. I remember the incident clearly after more than sixty years. Spanking was not in Dad's nature, and he rarely administered such punishment. Mama had lots of practice in such things and was kept quite busy at times. I probably would not have remembered that spanking at all if it had come from her. It might have been lost over time among all the others.

～

The cold weather of winter was gone and was replaced with the warmer weather of early spring. Dad wanted to check the condition of his fields in the bottomland across from our new house. He would like to start his spring plowing before long if the ground is suitable, he said. The fields lay beyond the strip of woods past the ashes of our old house. I was to accompany him and was excited about being allowed to go along. When we got to the site of the burned house, Dad stopped and began searching through the debris for something. He dug through the ashes in the middle of the pile as if he was looking for something in particular.

Twisted tin and bricks were scattered about. The ashes were black and packed into a solid bed by the rains that had come since the house burned. Nails lay everywhere on top of the black ashes. There was also glass that had been melted into interesting shapes. Most of the melted glass was in the area where the kitchen had once been. I found jars that were melted flat and others that had melted into heavy globules. It was fun to collect them and admire their interesting shapes. A burned can that was heavily rusted caught my attention. It was puffed up some from the fire, and I could tell from its shape and size that it was a can of potted meat. Suddenly, I found myself very hungry for potted meat!

After placing the can on the solid surface of a brick, I searched around for something with which to open it. Finding a straight nail and a piece of brick to use as a hammer, I began my work of opening the can. After making a line of holes in a circular pattern on the can's top, I began to pry the can open. The oily meat had already covered the top of the can even before I finished prying the metal back with the nail. Wow, it sure looked and smelled good!

"Don't eat that," Dad warned. "Might make you sick ... give you ptomaine poison or something."

I did not know what ptomaine poison was, but it didn't

sound good. Putting the oozing can aside, I followed Dad out of the ash bed. I had dug through the ashes quite a bit and had uncovered interesting and mysterious things. I hoped that I would get to explore the ashes again soon. With a parting look at the scorched sides of the corncrib and garage to the south of us, we continued our westward journey to the fields that Dad wanted to check.

I have often wondered if that potted meat would have really made me sick. It sure smelled good! I have also wondered what Dad was digging for on that day and what thoughts were going through his mind as he searched. As for me, everything was okay again. I could content myself with the thoughts of a four-year-old and confine my thinking to interesting things like the melted glass that I was going to take home and show my sisters!

10

WITCHES ON HOG-KILLING DAY

MAMA IS working in Montgomery. She has a job as a waitress. Dad is supposed to be taking care of Dianne and me. He is also going to kill hogs today. It is very cold and windy. He will butcher the hogs down by the pond near Grandmama's house. There is a good water supply at the pond and a big tree too. Dad will hoist the pig using a block and tackle attached to a tree limb. There, he will butcher it after he first removes the hair on the ground. Dianne and I cannot go because it is too cold and windy for us to be outside for so long a time. Dad has put plenty of wood in the heater and has given us instructions to stay in bed and away from the heater. He assures us that he will be back to check on us now and then.

There is a dreadful howling and screeching noise around the house! We are terrified, but we remember that we are to stay in bed until Dad comes back. The screeching and howling grew louder and louder until we are convinced that witches are circling the house and trying to find a way to get to us.

"They may come down the chimney!" Dianne cried.

I told her to be quiet and maybe they would not hear us

and just go away. The sounds seemed to be getting louder and occasionally, small puffs of smoke came from the heater. *The witches won't leave and are coming down the chimney!*

Convinced that the witches would soon be inside, we scrambled out of bed and fled out the back door of the house to the place where Dad was doing his hog killing. We had not tied our shoes or fastened our coats. It was very cold, and the north wind was blowing the smoke from the fire parallel with the ground.

Dad was unhappy that we had left the house, but he did not spank us when we told him that witches were trying to get in the house. He took us back and explained how the wind made the howling sounds by blowing across the chimneys and under the eaves of the house. We felt a little better with the explanation, but we still did not like the sounds we were hearing. They still sounded like witches to us! They were a little less terrifying while Dad was with us because we knew he would protect us.

He put us back in bed and covered us again and went back to his hog-killing work down at Grandmama's. We huddled together under the covers and hoped that Dad would come back soon and check on us. Even under the thick quilts, we could still hear the shrieking and moaning of the witches.

For many years after that, I often dreamed of witches circling the house above the roof looking for a way in. Always, when I woke up from those dreams, the wind would be blowing and making the terrible noises that I remembered on that cold, windy, hog-killing day.

Lewis Brady (Dad) butchering pig,
possibly for July 4 barbecue.

11

KILLING MAMA'S PIG

"RECKON I'LL go kill your pig now," Dad said to Mama. He had designated one pig as hers and was going to barbecue it on July fourth as a "thank you" to people of the community who had been kind to us after the loss of our house. Dad had built a small wooden pen on the side of the corncrib for this pig and had been feeding it separately from the others. After sharpening his butcher knife on the brick well curbing, he went to the woodpile and got his ax. Then, granting me permission to go along, we crossed the highway and headed for the pen where he had been keeping the unlucky pig.

At the pen, Dad propped his ax up against the side of it and placed the knife on top of the piece of tin that sheltered the pig from the sun. He took an ear of corn from his pocket and shelled it out into the pig's trough. When the pig started eating, Dad picked up the ax and brought it crashing down on top of the pig's head. The pig began squealing horribly, and I began wishing that I had not come!

Quickly, Dad climbed into the pen and dealt the pig several more blows in the head with the ax. He then reached up and took his knife and cut the pig's throat. After climbing out of the pen, Dad took the ax and knocked three or four boards from the side of the pen and dragged the pig out. He was visibly upset as he wiped his bloody hands off and reached for his can of Prince Albert tobacco in his pocket. He rolled a cigarette and lit it. I saw his hands tremble as he smoked his cigarette and watched the pig bleed out on the ground.

Later, I heard him tell Mama of his intention to buy a single-shot .22 rifle so that he would not have to use an ax again in this manner. I was glad of that because I had witnessed the gruesome use of the ax. Dad did not use that pigpen again. He disassembled it and used the boards in the construction of a pen behind our new house.

For several years, Dad left intact the other structures that had not burned at the site of our former house. The hog lot, complete with its shed to shelter the pigs from the sun and its accompanying mud wallow, remained exactly as it was. The barnlike "garage" that had been scorched heavily on one end by the fire continued to be used as before even though we were living in our new house a hundred yards away and across the highway. Attached to the garage on the back and two sides were sheds that were used for different purposes. The shed on the opposite side of the garage from the hog lot (which was by the road) was used as a chicken house and contained roosting poles for the chickens as well as a number of nesting boxes in which they could lay eggs.

Later, Dad built a small chicken house a few yards to the west under a very large but hollow oak tree that was always referred to simply as "the hollow tree." Beside this chicken house, he also built a small pigpen of thick lumber that would hold one or two pigs to be fattened up. The corncrib remained for some time to come as well and had a shed attached to it to hold hay.

Eventually, Dad stopped keeping any pigs at the old house

site, and the time came when the old corncrib, garage, sheds, and chicken house needed to be moved to a new location across the road to where we now lived. The small chicken house was dragged to the new location with the mule. Dad nailed timbers under the chicken house after he had raised it with levers and put bricks under it to give him room to do so. The timbers had been shaped at each end to prevent them from digging into the ground. Dad nailed trace chains to the timbers and hooked the mule to the singletree that he had attached to the chains. It was fascinating for me to see the mule pull the chicken house to its new location.

When Dad crossed the highway with it, I was very worried for him. I expected the mule to stop or perhaps a chain would come loose from one of the runners that they were attached to. It would have been a big surprise to any driver coming down the road to see a mule and chicken house blocking the road! The small chicken house made it to its new location without mishap. It was used for many years in this new location and eventually had a nice chicken pen built around it. A wooden hog pen was built next to it, and Dad used it also for many years to keep one or two hogs at a time in it for our winter smoked meat.

The corncrib and garage with their attached sheds were torn down, and the wood and tin were used in the construction of a barn near the place where Dad had placed the chicken house and hog pen. This barn remains to this day, but it is in a sad state of disrepair. Much of the lumber used in the construction of the corncrib portion of the barn is heavily charred from the house fire in 1954. None of the wood came from the house itself as it was totally burned up. Rather, it came from the garage, corncrib, and other structures at the house site.

After more than sixty years, those boards look nearly the same as they did when they were removed from their original structures. However, most are eaten up on the inside by termites. Though those structures were torn down so long ago—and their materials reused to build a newer one—the memories of the older ones live on. Some of these memories will be recounted later in this story.

12

GUILTY BY ASSOCIATION

THERE WAS a period of time between moving into the new house and my starting school where Dianne and I were the only children at home during the day. A lot of this time is fuzzy in my mind as to the day-to-day activities and exactly who cared for us during most of that time. Mama had a job as a waitress in Montgomery then, but I also have a lot of memories of her with us at the house. Usually, they are memories of my getting into trouble because of something that Dianne had instigated or caused me to be guilty of by association. I suppose that I remember certain things because the punishment following any particular incident imprinted it in my mind. After all, a spanking or switching is supposed to remind a child that a particular behavior is not acceptable.

Dianne was quite good at suggesting and even setting up an activity in such a way that if it went sour, she could be perceived as blameless. She may not have understood the term "plausible deniability," but she was a master of the concept, even by the time she was three or four years old. Because we were so close in age and at heart, we were generally involved in the same misdeed. Dianne, the baby of the family, regularly escaped blame by virtue of that position. I, being a little older, was judged guilty since I was "old enough to know better."

Tom Sawyer would know what I'm talking about. He had Sid, and Sid could do no wrong. The difference between Tom and Sid and ourselves was the lack of resentment and in the closeness that Dianne and I felt for each other.

"I want to show you something," Dianne whispered. Mama was in the older girls' bedroom taking a nap. We were supposed to play quietly and behave ourselves while she did so. Taking me into Mama's bedroom, Dianne pointed out the large bag of vanilla wafers placed high enough up to be considered safe from our eyes or reach. They were on top of a stack of items resting on the top of the tall chest of drawers in the corner of the room. Mama had misjudged both our eyes and our ability to extend our reach!

Studying the situation, we were careful to discuss it in whispers. We suddenly realized our first mistake when Mama called out from the back room, "It's mighty quiet in there. What are you young 'uns up to?" We quickly learned that quietness was not the key to the cookies, but deception was.

Assuring Mama that we were not up to anything, we began carrying on two conversations at once. One for Mama's ears and the other, conducted in whispers, with which we worked out our plans for getting to the bag of cookies.

Presently, a workable plan was agreed upon and involved a chair and other items that could be easily stacked without too much noise. We continued our distracting conversations and sounds to mask our activity as we put the plan into action. Before long, I had the bag of cookies on the floor between us and had succeeded in getting the cellophane bag open. Helping ourselves to a generous supply of them, I then climbed back up and replaced the bag in its original position. A little fluffing was required as the contents of the bag appeared less. Satisfied that Mama would never know the difference, I climbed back down.

Sitting on the floor and enjoying the fruits of our labor, we made sure that we kept up the distracting noise and conversation. The picnic was over all too soon, and we began thinking that a few more cookies would not be missed. We could fluff the bag up again. In short order, we had a second helping of cookies and then a third go at the bag. The bag didn't fluff up much anymore and there was a lot of empty space showing through the cellophane. We decided that we had best call a halt at this point since most of the cookies were gone.

We were beginning to feel concerned that Mama just might notice the bag was practically empty. If we cleared away all the evidence of what we had been up to, she might not notice anything right away. Perhaps our sisters and Larry would be home before she noticed, and the issue of guilt would be less clear. That was a consoling thought that had barely entered our minds before Mama fairly flew into the room and headed straight to the place where the cookie bag was.

Snatching the bag down and discovering that it was nearly empty, she cried out, "I knew it! I knew you young 'uns were up to something! Those were for a banana pudding on Sunday!"

We enjoyed the cookies and the adventure in getting them, but we didn't enjoy what came next. At least, I didn't! Mama rightly surmised that I was the one who had managed to get the cookies down, but she did not know, as Paul Harvey was famous for saying, "the rest of the story." I got the blame for the misdeed, and Dianne, the ringleader, got off pretty lightly. I'm sure if Mama could have seen the affair through our eyes, she would have been proud of the ingenuity and resourcefulness of her two youngest children. I don't recall if we had any banana pudding on that Sunday. If we didn't, it was a pity to have missed such a treat because Mama made very good banana pudding!

I recall another incident that occurred shortly after moving to the new house. "Let's go look for money," Dianne proposed. I had been playing quietly by myself, and the idea of an adventure of this sort appealed to me. Mama was taking an afternoon nap, and our sisters and Larry were at school.

It was not an uncommon thing for her to lie down for a few minutes' rest during the afternoon before everyone came home and things got hectic again. Dianne and I knew to play quietly during those times and not to disturb her. Looking for money was a fun thing to do, even though there was none ever to be found unless it was a penny somewhere in Dad's chest of drawers. If we were ever lucky enough to find one, we always hid it a few more times so that we could continue the experience of finding something valuable. In this way, we could keep an adventure going.

My first experience of finding money was at the home of a very nice family in our community. There were a couple of older boys is the family who convinced us that they often found money in a white sandy spot in their yard. Taking us to the spot, they casually dragged the toes of their shoes through the powdery sand and uncovered a coin. Encouraging us to do the same, we dug through the sand with our hands and bare feet and found several nickels and dimes. We left that house feeling as if we had been to a magical place and always talked about going back and finding more money.

With Dianne's suggestion to "go look for money" hardly out of her mouth, I was already moving for the treasure hunt. "Let's go outside and look," she said. I was headed for the back door when she suggested, "Let's go out the front door and look." She allowed me to lead the way and cautioned me to look carefully around the front door as I went out. She certainly knew her treasure-hunting business, because there it was—a dollar bill was laying on the grass to the right of the door!

I saw it immediately and could not believe my good luck of finding a whole dollar, and so quickly too! Had I not been overcome with the excitement of my good fortune, I would have paid attention to the fleeting suspicion that darted through my mind. Until that moment, I had never seen a dollar up close and had certainly never held one. Snatching up the dollar, I did the first thing that came to my mind: I ran into the house and woke Mama.

Big mistake! Showing the dollar to Mama and telling her where I had found it, I thought she would be happy. Mama was very unhappy when she looked in her purse and found that the only dollar she owned was no longer there. I knew rather quickly why I had been so lucky in my treasure hunt and why Dianne had been able to narrow the search area down so effectively. I was judged guilty of having taken the dollar from the purse and was reminded rather forcefully about the sins of stealing and lying. Dianne hung back and kept quiet. She knew something about this business, but she wasn't telling!

13

THE FIELDS

WE ARE going to the fields with Dad today. Mama is working, and Dad has to take care of Dianne and me while he is plowing. We have to go with him quite often to the fields. No matter what part of the farmland that he is working, we simply call it all "the fields."

Today, he will be plowing in the big low-lying field that he calls "the bottom." Sometimes, we go in the wagon, and at other times, we ride the mule as Dad leads him down the wagon trail to one of the fields across the road. They are west or behind the place where our house burned. Dad plants mostly corn for the livestock and chickens, but he plants a lot of things that we eat too. He likes peanuts, and we always have a peanut patch for that. The peanut vines also make good hay for the cows and mule.

We always have lots of watermelons and cantaloupes in the summer. We can eat as many as we want, and he also gives some to the pigs. There are peas planted everywhere, even among the cornstalks. There is a big sweet potato patch every year as well as Irish potatoes. There is also a vegetable garden where lots of vegetables are raised. Dad raises most of the food that we eat.

Today, we are following Dad to the fields. He is leading the mule, and I am pulling Dianne in the red wagon. We have brought a quilt and a half-gallon jar of water.

Dad stopped the mule near the sweet gum tree where he will leave us while he does his plowing. While he hooked the mule's trace chains to the singletree of the plow, we spread the quilt out on the bare hard ground under the tree. We always use this spot, and it's like our own little home while we are in the fields.

The water jar is put to the side, but it's always kept in the shade. Even so, the water gets very warm during the day. We play house and any other game that we can think up to pass the time. There are little wormholes in the ground with grains of sand around them. We know that there is a small fuzzy worm in each hole, and we like trying to catch them. A long, fine straw can be inserted into the hole and left. When the straw starts moving about, we know that the worm is crawling on it, and we pull the straw out quickly. If we time it just right, we can snatch the worm out of the hole before he can let go. There are small black beetles that come by occasionally pushing a ball of stuff that they have collected. They are the most interesting insects around and seem to be very hard workers. Sometimes the ball gets away from one of them and starts rolling. The beetle runs and gets control of it and begins pushing it again. Often, a beetle has to push the ball over or around something, but it seems to get the job done. I've often thought that these beetles must be smart enough to figure out anything! Dragonflies, moths, and butterflies fly around now and then, and we like to catch the butterflies if we can. They are very pretty, and there are many different kinds. The yellow ones are the most plentiful, but the large monarchs are the most beautiful.

I think that I would like to go into the field where Dad is plowing and follow the fresh furrows that he is making. The freshly turned dirt is damp and cool and feels good under my bare feet. As I followed behind Dad and the plow, I noticed that his feet turn outward as he guides the plow along. I try to match his footprints and step in them. It's hard to do because they are so far apart. My legs get tired quickly from trying to take such long steps while keeping my feet turned out the way he does. The mule has lifted his tail, and I know what that means. He is about to drop something on the ground, and I need to walk in another furrow for a while. The droppings are brownish-green and shaped like big marshmallows. They have a strong, but not unpleasant smell. I smell this odor all the time and am not repelled by it. It smells like the barn or livestock. It is a farm smell. I don't want to step in it though and get it between my toes. At least, not now. It's okay when I'm with the others and do it on a dare.

Dianne is standing at the edge of the field, and I know that she wants me to come. I take long steps over the furrows and soon come to where she is waiting near the shade of the sweet gum tree. She wants to make "frog houses" in the freshly turned dirt. We found a place that was still in the shade at the edge of the field and sat down. Each of us mounded dirt up over one foot and patted it down until it was firm. Pulling the foot back out of the dirt left a small house for a toad to get in. We made lots of these frog houses and are convinced that the toads will be happy that we did so. Tomorrow, when we come back, we will look inside each one and see if any toads have moved in!

I have become thirsty and want a drink of water. Dianne is thirsty too. The half-gallon jar is heavy, but I unscrewed the lid, and we both had a drink. The water is already getting warm even though we have kept it in the shade. I put the lid back on, but it is crooked, and I can't straighten it out. That's okay. Dad can get it back off and put it on straight.

Soon, Dad stopped the plow in the field and walked across to us to get some water. He cannot get the top off, no matter how he tries. He is upset with me. Finally, he took his knife and cut a hole in the lid and drank some water. Perhaps he can get the lid off at home, he said, but I should have been more careful about what I was doing.

We have gotten hungry and want to pick some dewberries to eat. Dewberries are early blackberries. We know there are lots of them about because they are in season, and we saw plenty of them as we came to the fields.

"Dad, is it okay if we go and pick berries?" we asked.

"You are liable to step on briars with your bare feet," he answered.

"We'll be careful," we assured him, knowing that the soles of our feet were tough as leather.

"I reckon so," he said. "Watch out for snakes and don't get turned around. Listen out for me when I'm plowing, and you'll know where I am."

We knew the layout of the various fields around the wooded hills and how the wagon trail went to each field. We also knew of the sounds that were generated in the course of Dad's plowing: the "gee" and "haw" and "giddup there" and the occasional "dammittohell" that he threw in now and then when the mule was slow to respond. Occasionally, we could hear the creak of the harness or jingle of a trace chain.

We found lots of berries and ate them until we could not hold anymore. Afterward, we started picking them for fun. We had no container to put them in except our shirts. Making pouches of the shirtfronts, we filled them until juice was running everywhere. We could have a cobbler with supper tonight, and we could also eat them with milk and sugar. There seemed to be loads of berries everywhere, and we didn't want to stop picking them. We carried as many berries back with us to the quilt as our shirts would hold. The stains left by the berry juice had ruined the shirts, but that did not concern us. We had lots of berries and had plenty of fun picking them!

Dad came out of the field with the mule and plow. He unhooked the plow nearby and laid it on its side. He hooked the ends of the trace chains onto the hames portion of the harness so that they would not drag the ground. Dianne and I folded the quilt and loaded it into the wagon with the water jar and with the berries piled in one end of the wagon. We bunched the quilt up against them so they would stay together in one place. Dad led the way back up the wagon road toward home as we followed along behind with our red wagon. Dianne rode, seated on the quilt, while I pulled, but I didn't mind. The jingling of the chains hanging from the harness of the mule made a pleasant, musical sound.

We knew that we would not go straight home without making one stop. This was at a small pond that had been dug out years before to catch water for livestock. There were trees all around it, and the ground was soft, muddy, and smelly. It smelled like rotten leaves and crawfish. Crawfish mounds jutted up everywhere around the little pond, and we could see the crawfish scuttling away from the water's edge.

We knew that we would be here for a few minutes and began playing around the edge of the pond in the mud and water. Mussel shells and live mussels were scattered on the bottom in the shallow water. The mule walked out into the water to drink, and his feet made sucking sounds in the soft mud. Dad allowed the mule to stay as long as he wanted.

As he waited for the mule to cool a bit in the shade and the water, Dad took out his tobacco can and rolled a cigarette. As he stood quietly smoking, we began catching the big, soft tadpoles. We were careful about where we put our feet because of the sharp edges of the open mussel shells that were scattered about in the water.

Presently, the mule turned and pulled his feet free of the mud in which they had sunk while he had been drinking and cooling off. The sucking sounds were loud as he pulled his feet free. The tired mule staggered a bit from the effort but made his way out of the mud and onto firm ground.

"Wash your feet," Dad said. "Let's go home."

We quickly hurried to an undisturbed spot where the ground was firm, stepped into the water, and cleaned the mud from our feet. Dad watched until he was satisfied that we were done, threw the cigarette butt into the water, and led the mule up the wagon path. I followed behind with the red wagon, and Dianne walked behind me. She can walk home instead of riding. We are going slightly uphill now, and I don't want to pull the extra weight. It's been a long, warm day, and the heat is starting to make me tired. Later in the afternoon, it will cool off again. Larry and the girls will be home from school, and we can all play together. I am always happy to see them come home because it's so nice to have more people to play with.

Allen Brady (author) and youngest sister, Dianne.

Allen and sister Dianne cleaned up for church.

Six youngest Brady children on a typical summer day (left to right: Larry, Allen, Sharron, Sandra, Dianne, Betty).

14

WATERMELONS
AND PEANUTS

DAD AND I are going to the fields to see how everything is growing and to pick some peas. All of the fields have trees around them, and they are broken up by low hills covered with young pine and sweet gum trees. The wagon path follows the side of one of these low hills through the pines and sweet gums. It goes past the small pond that was dug out many years ago for livestock watering. Dad always waters his mule there when he is plowing or using the wagon.

After passing the small pond that seems to be almost enveloped by large trees around it, the wagon path branches. Straight ahead, it goes to the bottom where the biggest cornfield is. The sweet gum tree is there, to the left side of the field as the wagon path enters it. When anyone says, "The sweet gum tree," everyone knows that it is the special tree where we often spread our quilt or play house. The wagon path that branches to the right at the "watering hole," as we call it, goes to a long bottom field where Dad has more corn, but also peas, watermelons, and sweet potatoes.

Today, we will take the path to the right at the hole and

follow it as it meets the open field at an old, overgrown barbed wire fence. There is an opening called a "gap" that Dad no longer bothers to close. Passing through the gap, we entered into a watermelon patch. These watermelons are different from the ones that Dad usually plants. They are round and striped with alternating light and darker green stripes. There are lots of watermelons scattered among the vines, but they are not ready to pick yet.

"This is your little patch," Dad said. "Take care of it."

I could scarcely believe my ears and my good fortune! I'm not sure what he meant by "take care of it" because the watermelons were practically grown, and there was little to do but wait for them to be fully ripe. It made me very happy to know that I had a watermelon patch all for myself!

Leaving the watermelon patch, we walked around the edge of the field as it circled to the left and joined the field that was called "the bottom." To our left was the sweet gum tree, and just before it the other branch of the wagon path that came down along the side of the hill from the watering hole. On the side of the hill behind the sweet gum tree was a narrow terrace of a field that wrapped partially around this pine-covered hill in a crescent shape. More corn was planted there. As we walked the edge of "the bottom" field, we followed the low embankment that separated it from the narrow terraced field to the left.

Soon the strip of terraced ground came to an end in a point, and we began to circle the slope of the hillside upon which it lay. Several sweet gum trees grew here in a clump, and the ground underneath them was bare clay and smooth. It was a place that we called "the sweet gum trees," and it was another of our favorite spots. The bottom field continued on our right until it butted up against the barbed wire fence separating the field from Tabernacle Road. This roadbed was built several feet above the surrounding ground because of frequent flooding. The "bottom field" was appropriately named. Sometimes, Dad lost his corn crop in this field due to flooding.

To the left of us were two more terraced fields. The first was planted with peanuts and ladyfinger peas. The last was another cornfield that disappeared into the woods around the hill. We had come here today to look at the peanuts and the ladyfinger peas. They were growing very well, and Dad said that the peanuts should be "making" now. He pulled up a clump of peanut vines, and the roots were covered with young peanuts. *They smell good, and Dad thinks that they will "make" very good.*

Pulling his Prince Albert can from the pocket in the bib of his overalls, Dad rolled a cigarette and lit it. He does this whenever he is going to stop and relax for several minutes. He surveyed the fields about him, and I think that he is satisfied with what he sees. Everything has been "laid by," and there is no more work to be done in the fields until each crop is ready to gather. I know that we will soon be backtracking along the path at the edges of the fields when Dad finishes his cigarette. I am still excited about the watermelons, and I will get to see them again. We are going to pick some peas on the way back, and they are in the cornfield next to the watermelon patch.

Finally, he was through and stamped out the cigarette butt in the dirt under his shoe. With a last look at the peanut patch, he turned and began walking quickly in the direction from which we came. I hurried to keep up as my bare feet brushed through the occasional bits of fine straw and tickleweed that grew along the dusty path at the edge of the bottom.

Suddenly, I realized that something was moving up my leg inside my pants! I stopped and grabbed my pant leg, but I could not feel anything there. Hitting the pants leg several times to dislodge any creature, I hurried to catch up. There it was again, but it had moved up higher inside the leg of my pants! Grabbing the cloth of my pant leg to keep the creature from moving any farther up, I called out to Dad, "Something's in my pants! Something's in my pants!"

Stopping, he told me to pull up my pant leg and see what it was, but I could not relax my hands from the hold that I had on my leg. If I did, whatever it was might go farther up into my pants and maybe bite me!

"It's a spider," I cried out. "It feels like a big spider, and he's going to bite me!"

Dad came back and told me to sit down. Pushing my britches leg up several inches, he reached in with his fingers and pulled out the thin, spidery tickleweed.

"That's all it was," he said. "Just a tickleweed."

As I followed him along the path, I kept wondering how such a delicate thing as a tickleweed could feel so creepy inside my pants. It was to be the first of many encounters with tickleweed. I never got used to the feel of them and could not seem to get rid of them quickly enough. They always felt like spiders crawling up my leg!

The crescent-shaped terraced field is now on our right, and we have come to the sweet gum tree. A few yards farther, there is an old corner post of an ancient barbed wire fence that once protected the field. This is the point where the wagon path enters the bottom. It also marks the inside corner where the two big bottom cornfields come together.

Dad has purple-hulled peas and other peas planted among the cornstalks between here and the watermelon patch. Wading into the corn, Dad began to pull the peas from the vines growing up the cornstalks. He has brought along a croker sack to put the peas in. He shows me which peas to pick. The ones that are filled out and have pink to very purple hulls are ready.

"Don't pick the ones that feel hard and dry," he said. "Check the black-looking ones close because they might be dry. Leave them alone."

Each time I filled my hands up, I went over and put them in the croker sack that he was holding in one hand. While Dad went down the middle between the rows and picked peas on both sides of him, I ran here and there and picked where they grew the thickest.

Cockleburs grew everywhere, but they were still green and not a problem. Later, as they matured, they would grab hold of anything that moved through them. The mule's tail, croker sacks, and clothing would quickly become matted with them, and it would be a difficult job to remove them.

The sack has a lot of peas in it, and Dad thinks that we have enough. We will be going home now and will pass the watermelon patch and take the wagon path that comes into the field there. As we passed the watermelons, I hung back a little for another look before hurrying to catch up. I can't wait to get home and tell the others that I have a watermelon patch of my own—and they don't!

In the days that followed, I made many trips to the watermelon patch to check on my watermelons. As they matured, some started getting a lighter color on top because of the sun. I was concerned that they might get sunbaked. I had seen Dad pull weeds and lay them on top of certain watermelons to protect them, so I did the same to several of the largest. One in particular lay at the back-left corner of the patch and was the biggest of all. Each time that I came to the patch, I hurried to uncover it and make sure that it was still okay.

One day, I went to check on my watermelons and knew something was wrong as soon as I entered the patch. The straw and weeds that had been protecting my biggest watermelon had been pushed aside, and there was only a nest-like depression where the watermelon had been. At supper that night, I tearfully recounted to Dad about my discovery of the theft of my biggest watermelon.

"It must have been Frank," he said. "I told him to stop by over there and get him one. I didn't think he would get the biggest one though."

There was little more that he could say about the matter. I know that it bothered him. Frank was "Cousin Frank," and he lived on the wooded hill south of our pasture fence. He was an old man, and he lived alone. His wife had died years before, and his son lived in Montgomery. The land that we described as "the fields" was actually his, but Dad had always farmed them since Cousin Frank didn't use the land for anything. Dad gave him a couple of wagonloads of corn each year in return. I could not understand why he had to have the biggest watermelon too, and I have never forgotten it!

The peanuts are ready now. Fall is not far away, and Dad has been pulling up his peanuts. Today, I am going to go with him and help him stack them. He has his pitchfork with him. At the field, there is something that was not there before. There are several tall poles set into the ground at different spots around the patch. They have timbers nailed to them about a foot off the ground and stick out in different directions from the poles. Dad has built these several platforms so that he can stack the peanut vines clear of the ground while the vines and peanuts finish drying.

Using his pitchfork, he gathered the peanuts on the vines and built a stack at each pole. I ate the green peanuts and watched him. The smell of the peanuts was very strong and pleasant. I found myself wishing that I could smell them all the time. The stacking is finished now, and Dad is shaping the stacks so that they will be steady and neat. The field looks different with the several tall stacks scattered around and is very pretty. Dad said that he would leave them to finish drying for a few days before he brought the wagon back to start moving them to the old corncrib by the house that had burned. To put them in the crib now would cause them to ruin and get moldy, he explained. He would also have to move them before any wet weather moved in, but that wasn't likely to happen this time of year.

~

Dad has been pulling corn. He has enough of it pulled so that he can take the wagon to the fields and start bringing the corn to the corncrib. It is not good to have too much of it on the ground at once. I am going to go with him. I like to ride in the wagon with him.

He backed the mule up between the shafts of the wagon and hooked the trace chains to the singletree of the wagon. Straps on the harness hold the shafts of the wagon up close to the mule's sides. Dad used two ropes that fed through rings on the harness and were fastened to either side of the bit in the mule's mouth. The ropes were called plow lines even if the mule was pulling the wagon. Dad controlled the mule with these lines as well as various voice commands.

After putting his cotton basket and a jar of water in the wagon, he indicated that he was ready to go. Today, I was going to take my red wagon too and fill it with corn. As Dad stood in the wagon holding the lines in his hands, he shook them slightly once and gave the command, "Come up!" He guided the mule and wagon into the wagon path. I was sitting on the back with my feet hanging off. My wagon, which I was holding by the handle, followed behind.

Entering the big field that we called "the bottom," Dad swung the wagon so that it would follow a straight line down the corn rows. Through the corn and cockleburs, I could see the occasional piles into which Dad had tossed the corn after he pulled the ears from the stalks. Climbing down from the wagon, he loosely tied the lines to a metal ring fastened to a corner of the wagon body. Taking the cotton basket to a pile, he tossed the ears into the basket and emptied them into the wagon. When he finished with the first pile, he gave the command, "Come up!"

As the wagon came along to the next pile, he gave the command, "Whoa!" He did not have to guide the mule until we came to the end of the long field and needed to turn and go back the other way. After untying the lines and turning the wagon, Dad retied the lines and continued to gather in the corn from the piles to the wagon. Sometimes, Dad did not have to command the mule to move forward. It seemed as if they had developed a rhythm.

What had started out to be a comfortable day was quickly becoming uncomfortable. The sun had heated up everything considerably, and the dust raised as Dad dumped the contents of the large round basket made things seem hotter and dryer somehow. The mule's ears flopped around in different directions to keep the flies confused, and he switched his tail against his body, first one way and then another. I knew that he was trying to keep the flies away, but I also felt that he was trying to stir up a little fresh air. It was getting more difficult for him to use his tail because of the solid mat of cockleburs in the hair of his tail. Dad kept an eye on the mule with each trip with the basket and occasionally approached the mule with his hat in his hand and talking in soothing tones. Suddenly, he would strike the mule with the hat and kill another horsefly that had been a misery for the mule. The mule knew what was going on, and I know that he appreciated the help. Horseflies hurt bad when they bite and are no joy to have around.

The wagon was eventually full, and it was time to take it to the corncrib for unloading. My little wagon had nothing in it as I was unsuccessful in keeping it upright as I pulled it behind the big wagon in the cornfield. I left it behind at the edge of the field as we started out the wagon path. I could get it later. Now, I was perched on top of the load of corn and trying not to slide around too much. It seemed a long way to the ground from atop the load of corn. Dad had increased the depth of the wagon bed so that he could haul more corn than the wagon would normally hold. He had nailed wooden brackets onto the sides of four wide boards that were cut to the right length and slipped them onto the wooden wagon body.

As we headed up the wagon path to the crib, Dad walked alongside the wagon with the lines in his hands. Approaching the watering hole, he stopped the wagon in the middle of the path, unhooked the mule, and led him into the water. There, Dad waited and rolled a cigarette as the mule drank his fill. Bringing the mule back from the water, he backed him between the shafts and hooked him up again. We continued our journey up the path to the corncrib.

At the corncrib, Dad backed the wagon up to the door and removed the board and the end gate from the back of the wagon and stood behind the wagon shoveling the corn into the crib with a corn fork. A lot of it had fallen to the ground as he removed the back boards, but he shoveled them up and tossed them into the open door of the crib. He was going to stop for a while to eat and let the mule cool as well before we went for the next load. After that, we would stop for the day as he had other things to do. Then he would start pulling more corn and piling it up for hauling. Gathering the corn was very hard and dusty work, even though my part was just keeping Dad company.

In the days that followed, the corn was finally gathered in, as well as the peanuts. The peanuts still on the vines were brought to the crib and its attached shed and piled inside. Dad wanted to return to the fields and pick some of the peas that had been left to dry on the vines. They could be kept for winter use as well as for seed in the spring. I did not like pushing my way through the cockleburs that were taller than me and clinging to every part of my clothing. We picked the dry peas for a long time, and I was very happy when Dad said that we had picked enough for today. He had several sacks nearly full of the peas.

A cool dry breeze had sprung up from the west, and Dad commented about how good it felt. He took his hat off and used the brim of it to rake the sweat from his brow and stood with the hat in his hand enjoying the breeze. It felt very good against my sweaty skin, soft and gentle. I hoped that it would not stop, but it soon faded away, and the air was still again. Replacing his hat, Dad asked me if I could carry the smaller of the bags. When I lifted it, I realized that the bag of dried peas had very little weight, and I indicated that I could carry it okay. Picking up the two larger sacks, Dad slung one across his left shoulder and the other across his right and headed up the wagon path toward home.

Once home, he tied the mouths of the sacks closed and hung them in the smokehouse until he could "beat them out." I found out what that entailed a few days later when he produced a fairly heavy stick about three feet long and showed me and my sisters how to beat the peas out of the hulls. Placing one of the sacks of peas on the ground, he gave it a number of strong blows with the stick and then rotated the sack and repeated the process. The demonstration completed, he then turned the operation over to us. It was not an unpleasant task to perform, and between us, we soon had all the sacks of peas pulverized quite well. However, separating the peas from the crushed hulls turned out to be more work than we cared to be involved in. It seemed that removing the chaff was a task that would never be completed. Though we all enjoyed beating the sacks with the stick, we all secretly hoped that he would not pick any more of the peas.

~

The weather has turned cooler as late fall comes on, and today is a cold and windy day. I am with my four youngest sisters and Larry at the corncrib. We are helping pick the peanuts from the vines. Annie, an older colored woman, is in charge and is watching over us today. There is a younger woman and a young girl with Annie. The young girl, Rosetta, is Annie's granddaughter. She is about the same age as I am, or maybe a year older, and she often plays "dolls" with my sisters. She is a playmate of ours whenever Annie is watching us.

I have my coat on but can't seem to get warm. Sometimes we run around outside the crib and play and warm up. Afterward, we pick more peanuts for a while, but I do not feel good and have begun to throw up. I begin shaking and can no longer get warm—even in the crib out of the wind. Annie is concerned and says that I have a fever. She does not want me to go outside in the cold wind again and tries to keep me warm in the peanut hay. The peanut hay smells good, but I cannot enjoy it. I want the day to be over so that I can be in the warm house and in bed. Occasionally, I run outside in the cold air and throw up again. Returning to my nest in the peanut hay, I try to sleep. I'll be so glad when Dad or Mama gets home, but I also know it will be a while. For now, I'll stay here in my little nest and try to keep warm.

15

THE BEGINNING OF MY CHRISTMASES

I WAS so very happy when I learned about Christmas! When I discovered Christmas, I found out that it was the best day of the year! Since that time, I came to realize that there was nothing else that could compare to it. It seemed that the entire year revolved around that particular day for the Brady children. Christmases, for me, began when I was five years old. I have no memory of those that came and went before that date. We were in the new house at this time and had spent a good portion of the year getting used to our new surroundings.

The day came when Dad came into the yard dragging a cedar tree that he had cut from one of the hillsides on Uncle Frank Anderson's place across the road. Uncle Frank was also a doctor.

Dad dragged the tree to the well and left it on the ground there and placed his handsaw on top of the boards that formed the well top. From the smokehouse, he brought his hammer, nails, and a couple of one-by-four boards. After cutting the butt of the tree off square, he cut the two boards into equal lengths and nailed them in a cross pattern to the bottom of the tree.

He had first nailed two short blocks of the same boards to the ends of one of the boards so that the tree would sit level when he stood it up.

Satisfied that it would stand straight, he took it into the house and placed it in the corner of the living room. We were very excited about the tree and knew that a very special time of the year had come! Mama had gotten some thin, glass ornaments of different colors and allowed us to put them on the tree along with the red and silver garland rope. Next, she strung the strands of multicolored lights and plugged the cord into the wall. It was very pretty when the lights came on. She draped tinsel on the branches and put a white sheet on the floor to cover the wooden base that Dad had made. The sheet looked like snow under the tree. We could not wait for Christmas, but we also wished that when it got here, it could last forever!

Sharron and Sandra are the twins and are thirteen months older than me. They wanted to show me something, but first, I had to promise not to tell. I promised them that I wouldn't say anything about the secret that they were going to share with me.

"There is something in the garage for you and Dianne," they said, "but you are not supposed to see it."

Unlatching and swinging one of the garage doors open enough to send the pigeons into flight and out through the various openings around the eaves, we stopped and peered inside.

"Look!" The two of them said, almost simultaneously, as both of them pointed to the back, left corner of the dim garage. There, beyond several pigeons that had not been quite convinced that they should leave, hung something that we had not seen before. High up in the corner were two small chairs. They were very small versions of the wicker-bottomed straight-backed chairs that we were familiar with. They were painted white and hung, suspended, from two nails. Below the chairs, in the near darkness of the corner was a little, square table, also painted white. It was the perfect size for two little children such as Dianne and me.

"Dad built that," they said, indicating the table. "And Mama bought the chairs. They are going to give them to you for Christmas. We heard them talking about it."

I thought that the chairs and table were a beautiful sight to behold and could not wait for Christmas to come. Several times, I eased the door of the garage open when no one seemed to be around and checked to see if the table and chairs were still there. Whenever I eased the door open and the sudden burst of activity from the pigeons diminished, I could see that they were!

As Christmas grew nearer, the white sheet under the tree began to disappear. Slowly, a pile of wrapped presents was accumulating under the branches of the tree. Mama came home from work in Montgomery on the Greyhound bus at six o'clock each evening and always seemed to have one or two shopping bags as she climbed down from the bus. From the privacy of her room, after we had gone to bed, came more wrapped gifts to add to those under the tree.

Finally, it happened. Christmas morning had actually arrived! Everything was different. The smell of wood smoke from the two heaters was the same, but there was a new odor that was always to be associated only with Christmas morning. That was the smell of apples and oranges that Mama had brought home the evening before and laid out for us to eat as we wished. With the cry, "It's morning!" from one of the children, we all rushed from the cold, back rooms to the kitchen and living room where it was warm and Christmas waited!

There they were: our table and chairs! In the middle of the living room and with bows attached were the two chairs and table that had hung in the garage for so many days! These were to be the first of many gifts that I was destined to receive from my parents at Christmas from that day forward. Of all the good things that I would receive over the years, nothing would ever equal the very practical gift that I received on the first Christmas in my memory. It took only a few minutes for Dianne and me to move the table and chairs into the kitchen and set them up near the wall, close to the heater. It was here, at our own table, that we ate our meals for some time to come.

There were other things that we became familiar with on that Christmas morning and were to become a staple around our house at this time of year from that day forward. There were raisins, lots of them. Mama bought a big box of those, and we could eat all we wanted. The smell of coconut became familiar as well. Mama made a coconut cake every Christmas after that, and opening the coconut with a hammer became a regular Christmas activity. Mama bought big bags of the special hard candy that came in so many different colors and flavors. We never referred to it as anything but "Christmas candy."

The memory of my first Christmas experience—and of the special nature of the gift that I received on that day—has never been surpassed by any that came after it. I can truthfully say, every Christmas was something that we anticipated with unbridled joy, hope, and anticipation. I can also say that we were sorry when the day had passed, and we had to wait another year before it came around again. I believe that the calendar should mark Christmas on every day of the year. Then, Christmas would never be over!

16

MAMA'S UNREASONABLE REQUIREMENTS

MAMA COULD be very unreasonable at times. I don't recall a time when I was a child that I was constipated. Our farm diet included lots of vegetables, which probably ensured that our systems stayed regular. Mama took no chances, however, and dosed us up regularly with a laxative. When I say regularly, I don't mean that she was really consistent over the long term. The dosing might be for two or three weeks and then stop for a number of weeks before occurring again. I think that her own periods of irregularity might spark her to start dosing us again. These dosing sessions were always done on a Friday evening when we had no school the next day. Also, we would not be going to church, either. That left us the whole day of Saturday to compete for the use of the outhouse while we got "worked out."

On Friday evenings, Mama lined all of us younger children up and administered a dose of liquid laxative to each one. Perhaps the laxative did not actually taste bad, but since it was medicine, she met with resistance and had to be a bit forceful in jamming the spoon in our mouths. I suppose that part of our balking at the medicine was the knowledge of what was going to happen the following morning and over the course of a good part of the day. On Saturday morning, there was a mad dash for the outhouse. It was almost a sure thing that while one person was in the outhouse, there were one or two more outside complaining that the one inside was taking too much time. Our outhouse was often a very busy place on Saturday mornings! It might have been noisy too—both from what was going on inside it and the desperate arguing going on outside the door!

While Mama was dosing us on Friday evenings, she also took advantage of that time to make sure our ears were cleaned out. That was far worse for all of us than taking the laxative. As a matter of fact, it was a frightening thing to endure and was an act of pure torture. Dropping to my knees, I laid my head in Mama's lap so she could look into my ear and assess the wax buildup. Next, she inserted a bobby pin and dug the wax out while holding my head down with the other hand. It felt as if she was gouging my eardrum out!

In later years, I told her that I thought she might have been getting the wax out of one ear by going through the opposing ear. It is a wonder that we made it through our childhood with our eardrums intact, but somehow, we did.

Having received a good "working out" and surviving the torture with the bobby pin on Friday night, Mama insisted that we have an allover bath on Saturday night whether we needed it or not. She wanted to make sure that we would be clean for church on Sunday morning. During the week, a pan and washcloth was sufficient. Saturday-night baths, however, involved the washtub.

In summer months, the washtub could be filled from the well and left outside for the afternoon sun to heat the water. It would then be carried inside at bath time. The winter months were different, and the water was heated on the two wood heaters in large pans and poured into the tub. One heater was in the kitchen and the other in Mama and Dad's room where we set the tub in the middle of the floor. Baths were not pleasant during the winter months. The area near the heater was warm, but the room was too cool just three or four feet farther away. I didn't like wintertime baths!

~

Like it or not, it is Saturday night and Mama insists that we all take a bath. The weather is very cold, and the two wood heaters don't seem to warm the house up as much as we would have liked at bath time. The washtub is in place and full of water that was heated on the tops of the two heaters. Mama bathed Dianne on the kitchen table near the wood heater there. Her bathtub doubles as the dishpan when the dishes are washed after meals.

Betty, Sharron, and Sandra take their baths in the tub in the bedroom while Mama washes Dianne. The girls are always allowed to go first while the water is cleanest. It is assumed that Larry and I are the dirtiest, and we always go last. There is probably a lot of truth in that assumption as our sisters are better at maintaining a state of cleanliness during the week. Were it summertime, the dirt behind the boys' ears and the black beads around the neck would be pretty evident by Saturday evening. On those occasions, the water in the tub might begin to look a little thick by the time Larry and I were through bathing!

On this winter night, it was particularly cold, and we were not too anxious to get undressed and get into the tub of water.

"It's too cold!" Larry complained after he had removed his clothes. Going to the corner where the wood was stacked, he picked up several pieces of wood and brought them back to the front of the heater. Opening the upper door, he dropped the wood into the heater and closed it again. Next, he opened the lower door to allow a larger draft of air to enter the burning chamber. Quickly, the metal began to expand as indicated by the slight popping noises.

Larry hurriedly got into the tub of warm water and settled into it as deeply as he could. I settled in a little deeper as I was a bit smaller. I was warm below the suds line, but cold above it on the side away from the heat. A red glow started at the middle of the heater and began to spread downward and upward until the entire heater body and flue pipe was red. I had never seen the heater so red before or felt it put out so much heat! My body closest to the heater felt as if were roasting while I could still feel the cold air on the side away from it. Kind of like how the planet Mercury might feel in its orbit around the sun.

We stood it as long as we could when Larry jumped from the tub and closed the door of the heater to stop the draft of air and allow the heater to cool down somewhat. It quickly began to lose the red glow, first at the pipe going into the chimney and gradually down the body of the heater. Larry decided that he had enough bathing for one session even though little cleaning had been accomplished on any region above the suds line.

Grabbing a towel as the red glow disappeared, he began to towel off, not realizing that he had begun backing closer to the hot metal. When he bent over to dry his lower legs, he put his butt against the searing hot heater, or at least, one cheek. There was a slight sizzling noise from the wet flesh followed by loud screaming. Perhaps I imagined the sizzling sound, but I didn't imagine anything else! Prompted by the loud screaming and the furious activity, my bath also came to a quick end. I was completely shaken by what I had witnessed. Mama rushed into the room to see what had happened. Feeling sick and terrified, I backed away from Mama and Larry. I wanted to be someplace else! I found myself in the kitchen never remembering afterward ever drying off and getting dressed.

~

All the children are in the kitchen and have become very quiet. Larry is still in Mama's room and crying in a way I've never heard before. We are frightened by what has occurred, but we are trying to get into a better position to see across the living room and into the bedroom through the open door. Mama seems very frightened too, but she is trying to comfort Larry and quieten his cries. I have never known such quietness in our house before from us children. That quietness made Larry's cries all the more frightful to us.

~

Mama put Larry in the baby bed. The bed was in the corner of her room, and Dianne usually sleeps there. Mama laid Larry on his stomach and began fanning his bottom with a folded newspaper. The skin has been pulled away for at least two inches and is stuck to the side of the heater. Mama mixed a paste of cornmeal and water and applied it to the burn. She said that it would help to cool the area. She continued to fan him and tried to comfort him. When I went to bed that night, Mama was still fanning Larry, and he had not stopped crying. She kept him in her room for several more nights in the baby bed so she could care for him.

The spot on the heater where Larry's butt had contacted it was evident for a long time after that night. The area showed up as a grease spot and was darker than the deep gray of the surrounding metal. It seems to have remained there for a couple of years before it completely disappeared. Whenever I saw it, I remembered, vividly, what had occurred that had brought my Saturday-night bath to such a sudden end.

I suppose that if Mama had not been so unreasonable in her requirements, this incident might not have happened. We probably didn't need a bath every Saturday night and would probably have been fine having missed taking one on such a cold night as that one had been! After all, we certainly hadn't been sweaty under those cold conditions, but she was Mama. As unreasonable as the rule was, "A bath every Saturday whether you need it or not" was still her rule!

17

THE GOOD OLD DAYS? MAY THEY NEVER COME AGAIN

"THOSE WERE the good old days ... may they never come again!"

This was an expression that my older brother Buddy often repeated. Buddy was referring to the hard times that are so often forgotten when we get nostalgic and revisit, in our conversations, the "good old days." Those days that we are so fond of remembering, generally concern our childhood and simpler times. A time that was less complicated for us, more secure, and there was less required of us. Worries and cares of life had not yet become a part of our existence.

Buddy was referring to the harsher things that we may have forgotten in our desire to relive a simpler and, seemingly, less cluttered life.

"We forget," he tells us "about the cold, smelly outhouse in winter. We forget about no running water and not enough heat. We forget about the farm chores, no car, no doctor, and no television. We forget about a lot of things that were unpleasant, and we don't care to remember. You can have the good old days, and I'll stay right here!"

My brother had this way of emphasizing the positive changes that he had seen and in so doing, he reminded me that some changes are for the best. He would be quick to agree with me that some of the older ways were better. There were fun and enjoyable times. There was a simplicity in so many facets of our lives that we all remember and yearn for from time to time.

People visited and socialized more back then on a face-to-face basis. In so doing, there seemed to be more good times with their accompanying close physical relationships. We created ways to entertain ourselves back then. Most of this entertainment included other people. When we think back to earlier times, we generally consider these pleasant memories. Often, we bury or at least push aside those memories that are unpleasant. Though I am fond of remembering those good times and cherish the happy memories, I agree fully with him that a lot of the good old days were not so good.

I further agree that a lot of change that has occurred since my childhood has been for the better. If some of the newer ways are better than the old, why then should we ever even desire the older ways? These conversations between Buddy and me tended to include societal changes that he had seen and viewed as good. Changes that both of us agreed had made a positive impact on all of us. These changes have helped my family and society as a whole evolve to a better state. In this better state, my desire to remember can become more focused when considering the pleasant things and the simpler lifestyle of years gone by. I can remember the good of the "good old days" while having the pleasure of experiencing the better of the present days. Somehow, this attitude makes life more complete and without a sense of loss. For I have lost nothing—I have only gained.

Alabama is a unique state. I am becoming more convinced of it as time passes, and I see the very face and character of it changing before my eyes. The suddenness of the change has been remarkable, and most of it is for the better. In many ways, it bears little resemblance to the state that existed when I was a child. Some of these changes came about because of a shift in the perspective from which I was viewing the world around me.

Children grow up, and the view of their surroundings changes with them. Those times that once seemed so simple to me gradually gave way to the reality that they were more complex and complicated than my young mind had comprehended.

Many of the changes that I have witnessed in growing up in Alabama have been very real and not just a matter of changing perspective. The most obvious has been in the area of its shifting demographics and the changes in attitudes concerning race and the interaction of people from different racial backgrounds. The strict rules and customs regarding interaction along racial lines are gone and have been replaced by a new sense of what is appropriate. Faces in the crowds at shopping centers and in malls no longer reflect the demographics of old Alabama.

Those faces were white and black. They represented two societies that interacted but did not mix. The catchphrase then was "separate but equal." However, anyone with sense knows that no two such distinct groups can coexist separately and be on an equal footing. This was the lie of the old South and my home state of Alabama. The forced integration of these two societies was a painful process, not unlike that of a mother who has suffered a hard labor ordeal, but after the labor, a new generation was given birth to. It, in turn, gave birth to another. Each generation has brought to us a new idea of what is normal until we have come to a generational acceptance that society should never again be divided by color or class.

Now, a new society exists in my native state that is no longer divided into separate racial entities that are forbidden to mix.

The faces of this generation have also changed. There are many biracial persons to be seen, and some are even multiracial. The once white and black faces in public areas now include large numbers of Hispanic, Indian, Korean, and other Asian groups.

On a much larger scale, it reflects what has happened within my own family. Outsiders? There are no outsiders in my family. Show up at a family gathering, and you are accepted as one of us. While this attitude has not gained total acceptance among my state's populace, it has made very significant progress. Enough, though, that the Alabama of today can be characterized as a totally different place than it was just a few years ago. This is a positive and heartwarming aspect of Alabama's new normal. It is because of the particular history of this state and the progress that it has made that I can characterize it as unique.

"When I was a child, I thought as a child, I spoke as a child, I understood as a child."

Most of us recognize these words from the scriptures as written by the apostle Paul. We do not have any trouble accepting the obvious truth of such words. Therefore, I can honestly say that I feel it unreasonable for anyone to judge me too harshly as I attempt to describe some of the interactions with the black community in my earlier years. My description of the attitudes, relationships, and interactions between those of the "white" side of society and the "colored" side may cause offense to some. My intent is to be honest and straightforward, not hurtful. My view of the matters recounted and of certain people are described as I saw them from my point of view as a child. Others were described from my adult point of view and looking back on those times.

It may appear to the reader that I am saying all people in a particular grouping might hold to the same view or mind-set that I have stated. However, these are really generalizations and speak to the predominant attitude of people concerning a certain point. The interactions I will recount later in this section involve real events and situations from earlier times in my life. Some occurred in my adult years. There are a couple of stories that were told to me by other members of my family. All things stated are true and are recorded as reminders of how things were and of various and real people who played parts in making my life richer. Some things are not about specific people, but as I stated, they concern attitudes and conditions at a particular time in my life.

It would be truly difficult for anyone to grasp, fully, what I recount without a rough understanding of the dictates of society, law, and custom of the time. The existence of the two separate societies came about by historical events as old as our nation. By the time that it was decreed that all men should be free, certain customs were fully entrenched. Custom and tradition had already separated the people of my state by race. It was then just a matter of passing enough laws to ensure that the separation would continue. No doubt, the rationale was that continued separation would be good. Our society would be more orderly, and there would be fewer causes of friction as well.

"Yes, we will keep our societies separate," it was decided. Generations followed and grew up on each side of this dividing line and adapted to it. By the time I came along, there was a general acceptance that "this is just the way things are."

"The way things are." That is the mind-set that locks people into a system and then perpetuates it. Things were "that way" because of law—and because of custom and tradition that ended in this mind-set that seemed impossible to overcome. As children, we knew only part of how things really were and not the "why" of it. We knew nothing of any laws restricting anyone's rights or preventing them from achieving a better level of existence. We wondered at certain customs and practices at the time and occasionally asked questions. The uncomfortable response might be: "That's just the way things are. Don't ask why."

Mama and Dad never taught us to look down on anyone or to mistreat anyone. They would not have stood for that. I don't recall them disparaging the black folks we all knew. We were taught to be respectful and not to "sass" or talk back to them. We understood that a certain level of behavior was expected regardless of who we were around, and race was not an exception. It seemed that most of what we learned early on in our lives concerning what was appropriate in racial interaction was through something akin to osmosis.

Children are wonderful observers. Much of what they absorb is through their powers of observation. In our day-to-day lives, we could see how the older white and black folks interacted. We were not blind to the fact that the black folks were deferential to the whites. Nor did it escape us that they never entered or left by the front door or even ate with us. By the time we were three or four years old, I'm sure it was beginning to imprint on us that there was a difference even though it had never been taught in any overt manner. As we got older, we also realized that everyone on both sides of the issue was aware of certain unwritten rules that governed our relationships. Only on rare occasions were we ever actually told that something was not allowed.

It was only after I had started school that I began to develop a fuller comprehension of our society's rules. There were white schools and black schools, and there were laws dictating such. The laws demanded a separation. They further demanded separation in other aspects of our lives, and we all learned. In time, I was to find out that it included toilets, water fountains, waiting rooms, eating establishments, and any other such places. Violations were not tolerated. Mama and Dad were bound by these same laws and could not answer the "why" questions. They were uncomfortable with them and knew that I would have my answers by and by. For now, "that's the way things are" must do.

It would be very difficult for anyone not having grown up in such a system to actually fathom how firm its control was over everyone. It might be equally difficult for such a person to understand how such a system could actually operate for so long and do so rather smoothly. The relative smoothness of its operation was due to the details having been worked out so completely over a long period of time. A time in which everyone within the system had a thorough understanding of how to get along under its often unwritten dictates.

As I got older, I began hearing about occasional incidents that had occurred somewhere in the state directed toward the black community. Some of these incidents may have been in the way of punishment for breaking some rule or to serve as a general warning not to do so. They served as constant reminders that everyone should know their place and remember what was expected of them. We only became aware of incidents like these as we got older. As young children, we were blissfully ignorant of such matters.

Warm, personal relationships between black and white people not only existed, but they were commonplace. Many of the families I knew enjoyed such relationships. My own family was fortunate in that we enjoyed a number of them. These were not casual acquaintances, but they were with people we really cared about and were always happy to see. Some seemed to be such a part of our very existence and day-to-day lives that to remove them from my remembrance would leave gaping holes in the history of my life. I can truthfully say that I cannot think of one unhappy memory or unpleasant experience that I can associate with any of our black residents as I grew up in Alabama. I enjoy the memory of my interactions with them just as I enjoy those with my own extended family. It is as if they added a dimension that I can neither describe nor imagine existing without.

We did not refer to anyone as "black" in my childhood. That terminology came along years later after I had reached adulthood. The term "Negro" was official usage and was not generally used by the average person. However, corruptions of this word as expressed by "Nigra" or "Negra" were. They meant the same thing, just pronounced differently in a very southern way. The mother of all forbidden words was what we now call the "N-word." It was used to demean and was generally used to be derogatory. I say "generally" because the "N-word" was so common in its usage by some people that it was no longer intended to be derogatory, but was used exactly as the term "black" is used today. In other words, it was a habitual term for some.

The common, polite term in referring to a black person was "colored." There was no demeaning connotation attached to the word at all nor was there a word that could have been substituted that would have been considered as equally acceptable at the time. I suppose that the NAACP was cognizant of that fact when they included the word in the title of that organization. The terminology "colored" is not generally used now and is frowned upon by some. As I record some of my memories on the following pages, I use this word in its polite sense as I was taught as a child. I would not want to be impolite to anyone who I remember on these pages or demean the memory of a single special person in my life. If I alternate between the usage of the terms "black" and "colored," I am alternating between two polite terms: one learned as a child and the other learned when I became an adult. However, I will use the term "black" as much as possible and hope that the reader will understand the use of the older term "colored" and not be offended.

18

GENERAL REMEMBRANCES OF HOW THINGS WERE

AS YOUNG children, we were always close to home. We did not own a car, and Mama and Dad never learned to drive. Usually, wherever we went, we walked. As a young child, I don't remember going anywhere at all, except to church. Worship at our church was an all-white affair. From the time I started school, and continuing into high school, it was white kids only.

A "Mexican" boy attended school for one year when I was in the seventh or eighth grade. Though olive skinned, he was not considered "colored" by those who ran the school system in our state. He was the first Hispanic person most of us had ever met, and we were in awe of him. His daddy was an air force officer who had been stationed at Maxwell AFB. His family rented a house in our community during that time. As the school systems within the state were not really set up to accommodate anyone but white or colored, anyone not black would have to be treated as if they were Caucasian. Most of us had never actually seen a person who was not white or black. We lived in a white and black world. Integration of the schools and of these two separate parts of our world began about the same time that I started high school.

Early on in my school years, the idea of race never really came up at all. After all, why should it? We were totally separated, and our part of the world was white. In those early years, my contact with members of the colored community was with those who came by the house for some purpose or lived around us or close by. All of these were people with whom we had a special relationship and often had warm feelings for.

We were never taught in any overt manner as to how we were to interact with them. As I stated earlier, we learned by observation. Colored folks always said, "Yes, ma'am" or "No, sir," just like we children were taught to answer older people. In fact, white adults were also careful to use this polite speech in talking to each other. However, it was not extended to a colored person by white adults. We soon learned to answer using only a "yes" or "no" to a member of the colored community. No white adult used "Mr." or "Mrs." when addressing or referring to a colored person that I was ever aware of. As a result of this, we learned to address every colored person by their first and last names only. No honorifics were ever attached to their names. Almost all that we learned from our parents concerning relationships between the "white" and "colored" folks was learned in this manner.

As the school bus began picking up each of us when we were old enough to start school, our world—and our perceptions of it—began to change. It was slow at first, but as several years passed, we all had absorbed information from classmates and from things we had observed. By then, I had become aware of the "white" and "colored" signs on the restroom doors of a nearby store. I had come to understand that all restrooms open to the public were so designated. On a trip into Montgomery on the Greyhound bus with Mama, my knowledge was expanded even more.

The trip was occasioned by my need to see a doctor. The white folks sat in the front of the bus, and the colored folks sat in the back. "That's the way it is," Mama said. At the bus station, when we were waiting to board the bus to return home, I learned even more details about how things were. There were separate waiting rooms in which passengers rested and waited for the buses to begin boarding. When it came time for us to board our bus, which was to take us the twenty miles back home, I became further educated as to the dictates of the system. The white passengers boarded first. When it was certain that all the white passengers were aboard, the colored passengers were then allowed to board and claim their seats in the rear of the bus. Later, I was to wonder about the separate lunch counters at the bus station that I had become aware of on that trip. Also, about the water fountains that were designated "white" and "colored." I learned later that no colored person was allowed to eat at an establishment that served white people. They were also forbidden rooms at hotels where white guests stayed.

My first experience in actually witnessing this system in action was occasioned by a weekend visit to a friend's house. We were allowed to ride the school bus to a house other than our own if we had a note of permission from a parent. It must also have been approved by our school principal. I had such a note, which had the effect of granting me the rare privilege of riding the bus to the home of a friend who lived about twenty miles to the south of us. His daddy had acquired a little gas station on the outskirts of the small town of Fort Deposit. I had heard a lot from my friend and his brothers about the good and adventurous times that we would have that weekend. I was pretty excited and felt that I was going to heaven itself! I was not disappointed either. There was actually a television set, and we were allowed to watch it when we were indoors. My family had no television—so this was a real treat! While outdoors, I learned that there were prickly pear spines and sandspurs to avoid. These things and bare feet do not get along. At lunchtime, I learned two more new things. I learned that hamburgers are wonderful, especially those made in that day and time. They were much tastier than those of today. The fat content of the meat then was much higher, and the meat was actually fried. Hamburgers were a new experience for me, and I loved them!

While enjoying my hamburger, I learned something else. I looked around and studied the small room with the three or four tables. This room was an extension of the small gas station. Short-order meals were served to the public at lunchtime, and patrons were allowed to sit at one of the tables if they desired. I was curious about the very small window on one side of the room. It was obviously designed to open and close by sliding. In response to my question about what the window was for, my good friend informed me that if was for the colored folks to use when ordering food.

"Why don't they just come inside like everybody else?" I asked.

He abruptly stopped eating and looked at me with an incredulous expression. "You know that colored folks can't eat in here or come in here with white folks! It's the law!" he exclaimed.

I looked at the window from time to time as we continued to eat. Presently, a colored man came by and was served at that window. It was true: I had never seen white and colored people eat together, but I had also never witnessed, outright, this manner of enforcement of the system that demanded total separation.

On that later trip to Montgomery with Mama, I learned much more about the requirements that ensured the separation of our society by color. I was learning "that is how things are." I was also learning that it had always been that way—and that was how things were *supposed* to be—but things went along surprisingly smoothly because everyone knew exactly what was expected. Children of the time learned of society's dictates along with their walking, talking, and social manners.

There came a time when I was old enough to accompany my father on one of his trips to the Brooks' store. It was several hundred yards to the south of our house and was situated where the graveled Tabernacle Road intersected the highway on the right side. Dad walked up to this store quite often on Friday evenings to purchase some small items and to socialize. I knew that if I was lucky enough to go with him, I could also watch television.

On Friday nights, there were televised boxing and wrestling matches. At one end of the small and narrow building was the television set, which always seemed to be on. It was mounted just high enough to allow good viewing over the heads of people like me who were seated on the various sacks of feed stacked near the television. By the time the matches began, several young black men of the area would have made their entry into the store and congregated near the set to spend the evening enjoying the events.

I was usually the lucky one, having found a hundred-pound sack of feed nearest the last cold drink box. This allowed me to lean back against the box and be very comfortable. Dad was always seated toward the other end of the small room with Mr. and Mrs. Brooks and one or two others. I was normally somewhere in the middle of the group of young black men. They always kept their voices respectfully low so as not to disturb the white folks a few feet away in their little group. Their speech was often decorated with just enough profanity to make it interesting, but I was the only one close enough to be aware of it. Occasionally, one or another would go to the drink box and get a cold drink and hold it up so that Mrs. Brooks could see it and make a note of it. Nehi seemed to be the drink of choice, with strawberry being the favorite.

When the matches were over and everyone knew that it was time to go home, the young men settled their accounts and departed to their respective homes. They were always polite and courteous in their manner. They knew that it was a privilege for them to watch television on those evenings and did not want to jeopardize being allowed to do so. They also knew that such courtesy was required and had learned, just like me, to practice it. I never witnessed any breach of courtesy on those occasions. That was just the way it was.

19

PAUL

MY DADDY was a farmer. No matter what else he did to support the family, he always described himself as a farmer. He was also a housepainter and carpenter. In the wintertime, he trapped fur-bearing animals during the three-month-long trapping season. When the season ended, the traps were put away, and he and the mule went back to plowing the fields. He had farmed ever since he was old enough to use a hoe or hook up the mule, and he liked watching the crops grow and produce. Before I was born, he hired himself out on a farm for a number of years. He was the only white employee and as such was a sort of headman. All the other workers were colored.

His job was to plow and hoe just like everyone else, but he had the added responsibility of seeing that everyone else did what they were being paid to do. The adult colored workers received fifty cents a day in wages, and Dad received sixty because of his additional duties. The workday started well before the sun came up. Plowmen were already in place with their mules hooked to the plows. Anyone not willing to do so was considered lazy and not dependable. Such people quickly lost their positions to someone who "wanted" to work. Those who hired themselves out in this fashion usually had their own small subsistence plots as well. Dad was no exception as he had a small farm of his own and had to balance his time between the two.

My older brother Buddy remembers these times since he was a number of years older than me. Even though he was very small during the time of many of the experiences that he liked telling me about, he had no problem recalling them. He shared them freely with me, and I enjoyed reliving them along with him. Some of these experiences involved a young colored teenage boy named Paul.

Paul was often given the responsibility of keeping an eye on Buddy and making sure nothing happened to him while Dad gave his attention to his work. Paul had other things to attend to at the same time, which meant Buddy was mainly following Paul around. There were often a number of colored children around either participating in the work or hanging about because their mama or daddy was working. Paul was a bit older and bigger than the other colored children and seemed to enjoy reminding the others of the fact. When Paul carried things too far or when things got a bit out of hand, Dad would have to step in and restore order. While general tattling by children was always frowned on, occasionally, something serious would come up that might be a breach of order or safety.

"Mr. Lewis, Paul done busted me in the mouth with his water jug!" The little boy with the bloody nose and mouth cried from the pain as he presented his damaged features as evidence.

"All right," Dad said. "I'll take care of it at dinnertime." At the noon break, or dinnertime, several other children showed up with a complaint: "Paul won't let us in the water to cool off. He's trying to drown us when we get in!" They were referring to their routine at noontime of taking a dip in the pond to cool off. Dad, now in the process of unhitching the mule for the noon break, took loose one of the ropes that served as a plow line and began doubling it a number of times until it was about two feet long.

Walking down to the water with the folded rope in his hand, he called out, "Paul, get out of the water and come up here!" Walking over to a stump and sitting down, he waited for Paul to come. Paul was already crying when he got to where Dad was sitting. "Lay across my knees," he was commanded. Paul did so, all the while repenting and promising to behave better. Nevertheless, the plow line was applied to his wet back side as punishment for the bloody mouth and not allowing the other children the luxury of cooling off. The misbehaving stopped, and order had been restored. However, it is a likely probability that Paul got his revenge somewhere between the fields and home after the workday was over.

～

Paul is driving the mule and wagon down the wagon trail on the back side of the Venable property, and a very young Buddy is sitting in the wagon as it bounces down the trail. Paul is in charge of Buddy's care while carrying out some errand for Dad. It happened to be at the time of day when the colored children were walking home from school along that same wagon trail. This trail that alternated through wooded areas and farmland was the shortest route between their school and their homes.

On this particular occasion, Paul decided to take the opportunity to impress the teenage girls in the group of children. Stopping the wagon, he began his posturing and challenging of any male who might think himself a better man than he. Eventually, one teenaged boy responded to the challenge, at which time, Paul climbed down to establish that he was the man of the group.

After tying off the mule, he took out his pocketknife, cut down a small sapling, and trimmed it into a long, slender club. Meanwhile, the other "man" had taken out his knife and done the same. Finding a broad area that suited their purpose, they began circling each other with the knife in one hand and club in the other. All the while feinting and dodging, they jabbed and swung their sticks at each other. Now and then, there would be a swipe with a knife, but not close enough to make contact. The knives were more for show and effect, and cutting really wasn't necessary. A few gashes cut through the air was sufficient as long as they were close enough.

It was a bit too much for little Buddy who climbed down from the wagon unnoticed and disappeared into the brush. Presently, one of the girls turned and discovered that the little white child was no longer in the wagon and shouted the alarm: "Paul, Buddy done gone!"

The "knife fight" came to an abrupt end as everyone began to look about with increasing alarm. Everyone fanned out and began searching through the brush and honeysuckle vines and calling Buddy's name. Buddy did not respond though he could clearly hear the searchers all around him. Presently, the vines were pulled aside, and Buddy was staring into the face of a young girl who loudly announced, "Here he, here he!" She pulled him out with a relieved smile and carried him back to the wagon.

All thoughts of hostilities were over, and the entertained group of children resumed its journey down the wagon trail to their respective homes. Paul and Buddy continued on in the bouncing wagon with Paul reminding Buddy of how well he had established himself as the "man." That fact having been established, he then returned to the never-ending task of educating Buddy in the use of new words and names to call people. On one occasion, after finally being worn down by promises by Paul of not telling, Buddy repeated what Paul had taught him.

"Mr. Lewis," Paul called out when he saw Dad, "Buddy done called me a -----------------!"

"Yeah? If he does it again, I'll beat hell out of him too!" Dad responded.

I wish that I could record the other things Paul enjoyed teaching Buddy, but I cannot. Though Buddy and I laughed a lot about those things, I cannot repeat them.

Paul, in later years, became a very special person to me as well when I came along, even though he was a grown man by then. He always enjoyed a close, personal relationship with Dad. It was Paul who helped Dad when he was building our house, and Dad sometimes needed the extra pair of hands and strong back that Paul could supply. I was told that Paul volunteered his help with the house. On more than one occasion, in years following, I saw Dad hand Paul two or three dollars. I knew that Paul was in a "tight" and needed a little help to see him through. This was at a time when two or three dollars was considered a day's pay for a farmworker, so it was no small thing to do.

On a late spring day, I happened to walk over to a place in the fields where Paul was plowing for Dad. I had heard Dad tell Mama that he was going to have Paul do some plowing for him while he worked on a carpentry job somewhere. I decided that I would go and find him and visit with him a bit. It turned out that he was plowing the crescent-shaped terraced field above the sweet gum tree.

When I got there, he had plowed half of it with the turn plow, and I began following behind him as he plowed. Noticing that I was there and thankful for the company, he stopped plowing so that we could talk awhile. We talked while he made a cigarette and smoked. Later, he put his hand in his pocket and discovered that he had a hole in it and had lost thirty-five cents. It was all the money he owned. We started backtracking through the furrows and eventually found the quarter and dime very close together and on top of the dirt. I could not believe how lucky we were to actually find the two coins in that field of big dirt clods. Paul was a happy person, and I was very happy for him because I knew how much that money meant to him. When it represents your life's savings, thirty-five cents is important!

I remember Paul as a man who seemed to be physically capable of anything. He was incredibly strong and seemed indestructible. It was difficult for me to digest the information, later, that he had died of an injury. From what I was told, he died after contracting blood poisoning from an injury he had received while using a crowbar. Apparently, he did not have the means to seek proper medical attention, and it had been left untreated. It may be difficult for a person now to understand that in times as recent as those days, so many people did not have access to a doctor because of money and transportation, but that was the reality of things at the time, and it proved fatal for Paul.

I am glad that I knew Paul, and I'm thankful for the blessing of his memory. I wish that he could have lived a longer life and experienced the change in our society that I was privileged to witness. I would have enjoyed talking over some of the old times with him. Perhaps he could have educated me in some of the things that he taught my brother Buddy. I guess I'll just have to enjoy them in the way Buddy passed them on to me! Remembering Paul is to remember pleasant things of the "good old days." Paul's death at an early adult age from poor economic conditions and lack of medical care highlights the bad of those times.

20

ANNIE AUSBORNE: A FOLK DOCTOR

THERE WERE a lot of Osbornes and Ausbornes around our community when I was a child, and there continues to be a number of people around with these surnames today, mainly Osborne. One of the most well-known people to us and a person we liked and respected was Annie Ausborne. Annie lived in a house on the same side of the road as our house that burned in 1954. When we moved into the new house across the highway, she was still only about two hundred yards away from us. She lived in a small two-room tenant house surrounded by brush and wooded areas. It also included a covered wooden porch or "stoop." On the back of the house was attached a small added room that served as a kitchen. The front room of the house was used as a bedroom and living room and had the house's only fireplace. The fireplace or hearth was very important to the house. It was not only a heat source; it was also used in the summer to heat the flat irons for ironing clothes as well as for cooking, if need be. I liked Annie's house and felt very comfortable there. A number of times as I got older, her house appeared in my dreams, and I never really understood the reason for that happening. I suppose it represented a place both comforting and secure.

Annie played a very important part in the beginning of my life and also the lives of my sisters and brothers. Annie was a midwife and folk doctor in the "colored" community and either delivered some of us children or assisted in those deliveries. Some of my sisters remember seeing her tying Dianne's umbilical cord with a string.

Annie had a granddaughter named Rosetta who lived with her. They seemed to be together just about all the time. When Annie came to our house to watch over us while Mama was working, Rosetta came with her. She played house with Sharron, Sandra, and Dianne. They played with their dolls and dressed them up. I remember they argued with Rosetta about whether or not she really had a "colored" doll at home. They refused to believe there was such a thing since they had only seen white baby dolls before. Rosetta brought her doll with her the next day to prove it was so!

One day almost ended in tragedy at our house. Annie was watching over us, and Rosetta was there with us. Later in the day, Annie decided she should go to the mailbox to retrieve the mail and newspaper. The mailbox was across the highway. She took all of us children to the mailbox with her to check the mail and to pick up the newspaper. The trip across the road went very well, but the trip back did not go quite as well. The traffic in the northbound lane suddenly got pretty heavy, and Annie kept all of us close around her to keep us safe. The heavy traffic was probably due to people going home after their trip to the beaches in Florida. The time was likely around one of the holidays, possibly Memorial Day or one of the other holidays when so many people from northern areas spent vacation time on the coast.

Annie was waiting for a break in the traffic when it would be safe enough for us to cross. As she kept us close around her, she said, "Don't go 'til I say go!"

Unfortunately, Rosetta only heard the word "go" and darted out into the traffic.

The next thing I heard was the sound of a "thump" and then the skidding of tires. A black car pulled over to the side of the road and a young man and woman came running back to where Rosetta was still in the road. There was a break in the traffic as Annie picked up Rosetta and took her to the side of the road with all of us still around her. The young man and woman were still dressed in their beachwear and were horrified at what had happened.

Annie examined Rosetta and determined that other than being shook up and scared, she had escaped with only a badly scraped knee. As it turned out, she had run into the side of the car rather than being run over by it.

After talking with Annie a bit, the young man returned to the car, opened a cooler, and took out a Coca-Cola, which he opened and brought back to Rosetta. He gave the drink to her, and then he and the young woman went back to the car and drove away to the north. We all knew Rosetta was a very lucky person to have escaped with only bruises and a skinned knee. She was also lucky enough to get a Coca-Cola out of the deal! Unfortunately, that's where her luck ran out. Annie did not want Rosetta to appear selfish by not sharing the drink with the rest of us children. She dutifully passed the small bottle of Coke around the crowd of Brady children, and when she got it back, poor Rosetta got only a swallow or two!

Annie had a custom of making herself a jar of sugar water whenever she came to our house to spend a few hours or the day with us. She filled a quart jar nearly full of water from the water bucket and then added several spoons of sugar. After making sure the sugar was dissolved, she put the top on the jar and placed it in the refrigerator. From time to time during the day, she took it out and drank from it. At the end of the day, she washed the jar and put it away. I have often wondered if she drank the sugar water to give her energy or whether she just liked the taste of the sugar water.

Annie also dipped snuff, which was not an uncommon thing for people to do at the time. I knew a number of people who did, both white and black, women and men. It sure did look good too! She seemed to enjoy it so much. At some point, I was able to try a little, though I'm not sure of the source of the snuff. When I finally got it cleaned out of my mouth and my stomach had settled down, I determined that I would not be a snuff dipper. I would probably smoke instead since Mama and Dad did, and it smelled so good, but I did like to watch Annie spit because she did it so well. She generally had a can near the ironing board she spat into and seemed never to miss even though the stream of juice appeared to go several feet through the air. Perhaps it just seemed to travel a big distance due to my small size. Whatever the distance, she never missed! When I watched her ironing at her house, she spat the several feet into the fireplace and the juice sizzled as it hit the coals. I thought it was a pleasant sound.

Annie used old-style flat irons to do her ironing at home. At our house, she used the electric iron. At home, she had two or three of the flat irons sitting on the edge of the hearth and close to the fire to heat up. They were solid iron and heavy. When she picked one up to use, she used a rag as a type of pot holder to keep from burning her hand. She wrapped the rag around the handle of the iron. She used one iron until it began to get too cool to use, and then she replaced it on the hearth and picked up a fresh, hot iron and continued ironing. On one occasion, I watched Annie as she combed Rosetta's hair with a hot comb. The comb was metal and was heated by the fire and was also held with a rag to keep from burning Annie's hand. I thought it was an interesting thing to see as she fixed her granddaughter's hair with the comb.

As a folk doctor, Annie's services were in demand among the colored people of the community and also in our family when Mama was having her annual baby. I am happy to say she was there and available to me when an occasion came up in which I needed some help. One day while playing ball with David Massey, a friend of mine, I ran under a low-hanging tree to retrieve a ball. When I raised up, my head struck a tree limb pretty hard. I almost passed out from the pain and from the force of the blow. It seemed quite a while before my head had cleared enough for me to be steady on my feet. The following day, my head was still throbbing, and I had a small knot in the "cowlick" part of my head. There also seemed to be something hard in the middle of it, though I could not see it. I happened to be at Annie's house a day or two later and told her about it. She wanted to see it, and after examining the injury, she said there appeared to be something stuck in my head. After cleaning around it, she took a large sewing needle and began trying to remove it, but it was too deeply embedded. Next, she bored a hole through what she had determined was a large thorn and tried to extract it, but she could not. After applying an ointment she called "drawing salve," she told me to go home and come back the following day.

When I came back, she reinserted the needle through the hole she had bored through the thorn and began to turn the thorn like a screw as she pulled it out. The thorn turned out to be rather thick and at least three-quarters of an inch long. She said it probably had completely penetrated the skull. It was quite a relief for me to have it out, and I got over it without any complications. I never told my Mama or Dad about the incident, and I'm not aware of Annie saying anything about it either. If the thorn had indeed completely penetrated my skull, and if she had not extracted it, the situation could have gotten out of hand and led to some bad consequences for me. Her long experience in taking care of so many people really paid off for me. She had never gotten excited, but she had approached the situation in the cool and methodical manner she was known for. I will always remember her fondly and with a thankful heart! Annie moved to Montgomery while I was in my middle teen years, and I visited her there a couple of times in the area known as Washington Park. After that, it was a dozen or more years before I saw her again, and that was the final time.

I don't know how old Annie was when I last saw her. She had always looked ancient to me, and I had never known a time when she wasn't around. She was one of those persons who seemed like a fixture in the community and had always been there. I do know how old I was when I last saw her. The last time I saw her face was on July 18, 1979. It was my twenty-ninth birthday, and I remember remarking that I knew what she had been doing on that day, twenty-nine years before. She had brought me into the world. Sadly, I'm not sure she knew me, one of the Brady children she had delivered. Thank you again, Annie!

Annie Ausborne: A "fixture in the community," late 1970s.

Rosetta Ausborne Thomas, Annie's granddaughter, 2017.

21

PRESTON AUSBORNE DIES IN THE BLOWOUT

THE "BLOWOUT" is a peculiar name for a peculiar body of water near my house. Everyone who grew up in my community in my day was very familiar with this body of water and may have played around it or fished in it. I did both, and I was fascinated by it.

About three hundred yards south of my house was a graveled road (now paved) that comes up the hill from the west and intersects with Highway 31 at a spot where Brooks' Store once stood. Turning down this graveled road at Brooks' Store and traveling about half a mile would bring a person to Pinchona Creek, which has a wooden bridge spanning it. At this point, that person would have passed, a couple hundred yards back, the old "bottom" field my dad planted in corn. That field abuts the road on the right or east side as one travels in the direction of the bridge. The bridge that spans the creek first crosses a large hole of water that would probably cover an acre. The origin of this hole is a mystery as it has always been there, right beside the creek, for as long as anyone can remember. Since the creek comes down through some extensive bottomland that floods frequently, it is likely that swirling floodwaters gradually created the Blowout over many years. It also happens that the creek makes a turn there to a more northwesterly direction. The Blowout is separated from the creek by a strip of land about twenty or thirty yards wide. The bridge that spans this body of water and then the creek is a wooden affair that bends in somewhat of a crescent shape and is bounded on either side by wooden guardrails. Travelers using this road knew to be careful during rainy periods as the surface contained a lot of clay and was slick, especially on the bridge itself.

The Blowout has had its share of stories told about it, and it does have an eerie quality, especially when a person surveys it from underneath the bridge and looks up at the heavy creosoted timbers. The smell of the creosote lends an even greater air of mystery to the deep, murky waters. I had always wondered at the secrets those waters were keeping and what stories they could tell. One of the saddest that could be told is of Preston Ausborne, who died there when I was a boy.

We all knew Preston Ausborne, and each of us could identify him as he passed our house each day in his old pickup truck, but I don't remember what he looked like. The truck, however, was a light greenish color. During one of those dismal rainy spells that lasted two or three days, Dad announced Preston had been killed in an accident when his truck went through the flimsy, wooden guardrail of the bridge. The road surface was slippery, and because of the immediate bend the road takes upon entering the bridge, he lost control. Breaking through the wooden guardrails, he plunged into the water below. Some said his neck was broken when the truck hit the water, while others maintained he had drowned.

On the day after the accident, I was standing in our front yard when the wrecker came down the road from the direction of Brooks' store, towing the truck I knew immediately was Preston Ausborne's. One of the panels along the bed of the truck was missing. I was in a bit of a somber mood for quite some time afterward. It seemed my mood fit perfectly with the drizzly weather conditions and the circumstances.

Strangely, this story picks up again after the passing of a few years. I had gotten my driver's license and my first car. On a particular day, I happened to turn on to Tabernacle Road at Brooks' store and started down it. A black woman was walking in the same direction as I was going (toward the Blowout), and I stopped to see if she needed a ride. She gratefully accepted the offer and got into the passenger seat. As I continued toward the bridge, she explained she had just gotten off the Greyhound Bus from Montgomery. We engaged in small talk as we approached the Blowout. Glancing in her direction, I was surprised to see she had slid down in the seat and was almost in the floorboard of the car. I quickly hit the brake to stop the car on the bridge when she cried out, "Don't stop! Don't stop!" I continued across the bridge, and she knew when we had reached the other side by the sound the car made as moved from the bridge's surface to the roadbed. I slowed down almost to a stop as she sat up erect in the seat once more.

"My husband died back there," she said. "I've seen him on the bridge before, so now I close my eyes whenever I go across it!"

I felt some tingles on the back of my neck when she said that. It obviously was very real to her that the ghost of her dead husband was still there. In my mind, it only added to the eerie feeling the Blowout has always caused me to experience. Looking back in my mind to the time I saw the wrecker hauling away Preston Ausborne's truck, I still have a sense of what I was feeling at the time. As a child, I was unfamiliar with the death of another person until that moment. The death of Preston Ausborne put a face on the experience and made it something very real. Though I did not know him in a close and personal way, I have never forgotten the incident or forgotten his name.

22

ALEXANDER

ALEXANDER WAS a black man who had been a part of our community for as long as I can remember. As a child, I knew him, and he continued to touch my life even after I had left the military service in 1979. He had a habit of showing up unannounced, and I eventually accepted that as just a normal trait of his. Even my children have recollections of his appearing from the woods at the corner of the pasture and following the fence and tree line up to the highway. Sometimes, he cut across the pasture to the house to sit and chat a spell. After uttering barely intelligible greetings, he would usually ask, "Got a cigarette?" That was a way to ensure his own meager supply lasted a bit longer. I always accommodated him and enjoyed the time we spent together during those little visits.

I don't believe Alexander, or Alec, as we called him most of the time, ever had what might be called a permanent home. As a child, he spent a lot of time with a white family whom I knew very well. One of those family members was a schoolmate and friend of mine, and I spent a weekend with him every now and then. His father was about the same age as Alec, and they had been boyhood friends. That family had, in a sense, taken Alec in and looked out for him for quite some time. Later, he would move about a good bit and lived in several households in the black community. It is possible he might have been married at some point and may have even been a father, but I'm not sure about that.

Alexander was very dark and had a pronounced lower lip that protruded and showed the red color of the inside most of the time. It was very difficult to understand Alec when he talked because of his lip, and I never got to the point where it got easier for me to understand him. One old man I knew had even given up on trying to understand him. He relied on someone else to interpret for him. When Alec said something, the old man would simply turn his head to someone else and ask, "What'd that damn fool say?" I guess being old and hard of hearing, he figured it was a waste of his time and energy to even try to understand him. Usually, I would have to ask Alec to repeat something a couple of times. After the general course of a conversation was set, understanding became a little easier as the context proved helpful.

Alec never held a job in the traditional sense or at least what could be reasonably termed as such, as far as I know. Somehow, he got by, though. He generally managed to have a bit of tobacco or a cigarette or two. Alexander always seemed to wear overalls with rubber boots or the traditional high-topped work shoes and carried a big stick. The stick was used as a staff and could also be used for protection should he encounter a snake along the many paths he often traveled through the woods. His was not a fast-paced or high-pressure existence. He took the days as they came and whatever life and circumstance sent his way. Somehow, he got by and seemed content. Various people did extend to him opportunities to pick up a few dollars here and there for assisting in some small project or another. I remember

Dad doing so on a number of occasions, and they proved pretty exasperating most of the time.

On one occasion, Dad had Alec stand on a ladder and brace the bottom of another ladder he had laid on a roof. That ladder was placed there for Dad to put his feet against on the steep tin roof to keep him from sliding off the roof. It was a very easy job and didn't require much effort to brace the other ladder. The problem was, it was so easy that Alec would doze off now and then and allow the ladder to slip a bit. This always prompted a yelp from Dad followed by a bit of cursing to encourage Alec to stay awake.

One day, Alec was helping to replace tin on a small building that had been storm damaged. Dad was putting the first piece on while Alec was to cut the next piece. He never got beyond the preliminaries required before cutting the tin. Dad would climb down, cut the tin, and tell Alec to cut the next sheet. He never got it measured, much less cut. Dad would climb down and cut it and climb back up on the roof and nail it. So continued the entire operation. It turned out Alec was ashamed to say he could not read the folding rule. Dad finally got the tin on the roof with less help than he had counted on. At least Alec was able to push the cut sheets up to Dad each time he climbed back up.

The fence did not go much better. It was not that Alec did not know or understand what to do. He had built or repaired fences before. I have seen some of his fence work. I have also seen the little wooden footbridges he had built across ditches he crossed regularly. They even had handrails. The difference was he knew what he wanted to accomplish and did it in his own time and way. When he was doing something for someone else, he had to have very complete instructions. When Dad, who was working on one end of a quarter-mile fence, sent Alec to help me at the other end, Alec did a lot of walking. He showed up at my end with his hammer but had left his bucket of staples at the other end. When he went back and got the staples, he had left his hammer at the far end. By the time Alec got everything together in the right place, I had most of the work done. In retrospect, I feel we had not really hired him to do work—but to keep us company and to make him feel he had contributed. I don't really regret that at all and am happy for the pleasant memories.

When I returned to Alabama after nearly ten years in the military, I returned with a wife and three children. It was often difficult for us to make ends meet, but we always managed to pay our bills on time, and we always had something to eat. However, there was rarely more than a few dollars in my wallet at any given time. We really had to watch every penny closely. Early on a Saturday morning, I walked around my house to the front yard and found Alexander sitting on my front steps. It turned out he needed a little money and was offering his services for the morning. I protested I had nothing for him to do and was practically broke besides, but he persisted.

Eventually, I gave in and told him he could dig up the four small hedge bushes that had sprouted along my chain-link yard fence. They were not very big, and I thought he would have them out in a few minutes, and I could be rid of him. I went to the shed and got several tools for him to do the job. As I deposited the tools by the fence, he announced "I ain't et yet!"

Well, I had not had breakfast either, so I went to the house and asked Yoko to fix breakfast for the two of us. She fixed a very generous breakfast, and Alec was content to allow the work to hold off until breakfast was over. Afterward, he set to work on one of the hedge bushes, and I went off on some other Saturday-morning project. After about three hours, I came back fully expecting he would have been long through with the job. What I found was he had only removed one bush, but he had dug a large hole in the soft ground beside the bush. The hole was dug so he could sit on the ground with his feet in the hole while he whittled the bush away from the fence with his pocketknife. That wasn't exactly the approach I had expected or would have used myself! He began filling in the hole at that point and informed me he was through for the day.

After collecting my few tools, I reached into my wallet and took out twenty of the very few dollars I had in the world. *My God*, I thought. *I can't believe this!* I gave the money to Alec and said, "I appreciate your helping me, but I can finish this myself another time."

Alec indicated he would appreciate a ride down to Cassidy's Store, which was about three miles to the south of my house. I told him I would be glad to take him there, and so I did. I was happy to drop him off, but I couldn't stop mourning the loss of the precious twenty dollars. Anyway, I was rid of him.

The following Saturday morning, Alec was on my porch steps again. Again, he was ready to go to work. I could not believe this was actually happening again. When I delivered the tools, he reminded me he had not "et yet." My wife dutifully prepared us another Saturday-morning breakfast, after which Alec set to work on the second small bush.

Coming back a couple of hours later, I found he had removed the second bush and filled the hole and was through for the day. Wondering how I might convince him the project was over, I picked up the mattock, and with a couple of strokes under the roots of the two remaining bushes, I pulled them from the ground. It took only about a minute to remove both bushes from the fence. Again, I gave up a generous amount of the precious few dollars I had. This time, I told him I had no more work for him to do. After taking him down to the store and dropping him off, I thanked him and prayed as I drove away he would not show up again the following week. I truly did not want to hurt his feelings. He did not show up the next Saturday or any thereafter, so I'm not sure where he might have been getting breakfast.

For a number of years, I continued to see Alec from time to time. Now and then, he would come through the fence at the highway on the far side of the pasture. He would then follow the fence and tree line to the back corner, which was nearly a quarter of a mile, and then disappear through the back fence and into the woods beyond. At other times, I would see him take the same course, but in reverse. Sometimes, he would cut across the pasture and come up to the house and sit awhile, as always, dressed in overalls and with staff in hand.

On fairly frequent occasions, I would observe Alec standing beside the road in the shade of the trees that generally line the highway's right-of-way. The place he would be standing would usually mark the spot from which he had exited the woods and might indicate the end of a trail through the woods known only to him. Some of those trails were the remnants of old wagon roads or cow paths he had negotiated all his life and would be virtually invisible to anyone else. No doubt, he had kept these paths clear enough for walking by his own frequent use.

From his shady spot along the road, Alec would observe the passing vehicles and raise his arm occasionally to those he recognized. He also knew who would stop and give him a ride to wherever he might be going. If Alec raised his arm once as I passed, I would wave back at him and continue on my journey. If he raised his hand more than once or held it up, I knew it was a signal to stop. In most cases, he was always headed to Cassidy's store for cigarettes or tobacco. Sometimes he would ask me to wait until he got his cigarettes so I could drop him off several miles in the opposite direction at someone's house. Most of the time, he simply wanted a ride back to a certain spot along the road where one of his paths came out of the woods. Whenever I let him out, he would raise his arm over his head as he walked away in a parting gesture of thanks. While I might have known where he was staying at any particular time, I did not always know for sure. The path he used indicated which house he might be headed toward on the far side of the woods, at least.

I eventually stopped seeing Alexander, and I knew he had died. I heard he had developed serious problems that often affect older males. I don't remember a distinct time when he disappeared from my life. As with many people, I began seeing him less and less until he wasn't there anymore. He was an interesting part of my life, and I'm happy that, in my mind, I can still hear that hard-to-understand speech of his and see him waving backward to me as he walks away.

23

MANDY NORMAN

OF ALL the people who I developed affection for and have fond memories of, Mandy is very high on my list. Because I knew her for so long and saw her so frequently, I was never conscious of any physical change in her appearance as she grew older, at least, not until I had been away from her for the period of time when I was in the military. She had fairly short, gray hair that she kept twisted into a number of small tight braids. She wore a perpetual broad smile on her nut-brown face as if she were genuinely happy with life and pleased with my company. Even during the summer months, she dressed in layers of clothing and heavy stockings. As a child, whenever I went to see her, she pulled me into an embrace that threatened to smother me in the folds of clothing she wore.

Mandy lived to the east of our property across an expanse of wooded land broken up by several very large grassy "hammocks" that served as pastureland and was owned by Mrs. Ethel Todd, a neighbor and one of my schoolteachers. Our back fence separated this portion of Mrs. Todd's property from ours. In the edge of the woods, across the fence from us, two or three deep ditches of water meandered through the woods and emptied into a much larger stream called Ball Branch. One of these ditches actually had its beginning at the far end of our property near the highway about a thousand feet across the pasture. It ran under our back fence where, with the other two ditches helped to drain the low-lying areas in the woods on Mrs. Todd's side. The courses of those other ditches extended for great distances and also drained the low areas belonging to others to the southeast and south of us. They served as the headwaters of Ball Branch, which fed into Pintlala Creek almost a mile to the north.

After climbing over or crawling under the back fence, I was in position to begin one of my frequent treks to Mandy's house about half a mile away. First, I had to get across two of the ditches of water that were pretty wide and deep in most places. I knew the spots where they narrowed to a point I could jump across or cross on the roots of the trees exposed on either side and above the waterline. Keeping a careful eye out for snakes, I crossed these ditches and headed through the Cherokee roses and sparse trees that made up this narrow and bottlenecked area of the woods.

After a couple of hundred yards, the land ascended to higher ground and a very extensive grassy hammock stretched away to the east and to Mandy's back fence. To my left, or north, were several more of these grassy hammocks ringed with hardwood-forested areas that sometimes intruded in lines partly across these pretty pastures. Also, to my left and tucked away in the tree lines on two opposing sides of one hammock, were two old cemeteries. They were not visible unless a person actually entered into the tree lines. Though I explored them on occasion, they were of some distance from the route I usually took when I went to visit Mandy.

Mandy's back fence also protected her cornfield where she also had peas planted among the cornstalks. To the left of the cornfield, she often had a patch of cotton and a few watermelon vines scattered throughout it. Mandy's second fence separated this cultivated area from the pond and the few acres of pasture where she kept her mule and a few poor-looking cows. On the far side of the pond was another area fenced in various ways containing the barn, pigpen, fruit trees, and the house with its yard and chicken coops. Before I entered this area, I took time to figure out how I wanted to approach the house. She always had a dog chained that was already announcing my arrival. I wanted to make sure he was securely chained and would not break free before I made it to the house. He invariably seemed very anxious to get to me, and I was fearful he might someday have the opportunity. Mandy always quieted him down while I worked my way through the various gates and fence openings to her house. I made sure to stay as far away from the dog as I possibly could. Having finally made it all the way to her backyard and house steps, I felt safe from the dog and would get my smothering embrace from Mandy.

Mandy's place seemed like a throwback to a much earlier time. I felt I had entered a world that might have existed fifty or a hundred years before. It seemed totally isolated in this area of woods and fields with no other house close around. There was quite an array of pens and outbuildings around the house and barn. The yard was fenced with various forms of wire, pickets, and tin to separate and protect it from the livestock and wild animals. Mandy's yard was bare dirt and swept with a brush broom with a roof-covered well in one corner. Beside the well was a log that had been hollowed out like a dugout canoe that served as a water trough for the animals that had access to it. Mandy had chickens everywhere; some ranged free in the yard, while others were in several coops scattered about under the fruit trees. These usually contained mother hens with their chicks or a brood of chicks that were not yet grown. Some had "setting" hens hatching clutches of eggs.

Mandy liked taking me around, showing all of them to me, and catching me up on everything going on with the chickens. She showed me the fruit trees and expressed her thoughts that the apples were coming along good and the plums seemed to be relatively free from worms. She put wood ashes around the base of the trees and said it helped in controlling the worms. The brood sow had a nice litter of pigs, and they were growing just fine, and she had not lost any. I could see them with the big sow over in the hog lot by the big pine tree that separated the lot from the pond. The pigs had a nice hog wallow with plenty of mud to cool themselves off during the hot sunny days. The quiet isolation of Mandy's house seemed so peaceful and secure to me, and I often dreamed of living in that kind of environment, especially as I got older, and life became more complicated.

Will was there too in those earlier years. He seemed to be as old as the world and walked with his back stooped over. When he walked, he eased about slowly as if the effort was painful for him. I know he did his part in the fields of corn and peas and did a lot in the tending of the pigs and chickens. Will was bald on top of his head and had a ring of gray hair on the sides and back of his head. He had the appearance of someone who had been pulled out of an old movie. During the warmest part of the day, he seemed to enjoy a comfortable spot in the shade and worked on some sort of simple, but soothing project.

On one visit, I watched him smoothing a new hoe handle with a piece of broken glass. He did not get in a hurry, but he worked patiently at it until it was perfectly smooth. During another visit, he was working on a ring he was fashioning from a piece of bone. He had taken the circular piece of bone and slid it onto a strong length of wood the diameter of his finger. Using a piece of glass, he was shaping it into a ring. He explained it would take a long time to finish, but it would be pretty when he got through. He was going to work on it from time to time, he said.

Now and then, he would make a new basket if one was required. They were made of strips of white oak because that type of wood split very well into strips when it was green and was very tough and pliable. He once showed me a large "cotton" basket he had started on. My dad was fond of those baskets and used one frequently for gathering corn in the fields and loading it in to the wagon. He used the basket for all kinds of things. Every few years, he would replace the old one when it became worn and ragged. I suppose Will had determined it was time to replace his basket with a new one.

It was a very pleasurable time for me to sit and talk with Will while he worked on some project in the shade or to follow Mandy as she showed me about. On one visit, I was aware Will was not there. I did not ask Mandy about his absence, and she did not volunteer any information. I suppose his age had caught up with him, and he had passed on from this life. I felt Mandy's place had lost something very special, but it was still a favorite place for me to visit. As I got into my teen years, I continued to visit her regularly. She told me I could fish in her pond as I wished, and I did so. Whatever fish I caught, I took to her, and she seemed to appreciate having the fresh fish.

When Dad bought a large freezer to keep meat and vegetables in, he told Mandy she could store her peas in it as well. During the summer months, she sometimes showed up with several bags of peas for the freezer, and by fall, she had stored a good supply of them. During the winter months, she sometimes came to the house at night to pick up a few bags of the peas. Her son, Hamp, who worked at one of the old hotels in Montgomery, would come down from Montgomery and bring her over. We all liked Hamp as he was a very pleasant person. He had an air of quiet confidence and a pleasing, courteous demeanor. No doubt, all his years of service at that hotel had perfected his skills in dealing with people. He had a smile that seemed to cover his whole face and made the world brighter. I suppose Mandy had her family at her house on Christmas because she and Hamp always showed up before Christmas Eve for some of her peas. For several years, Hamp brought Dad a bottle of wine for Christmas when he came with his mother, Mandy. He said it was one of the perks he enjoyed by virtue of his position. The guests often presented him with wine they had ordered but had not opened. Dad gratefully accepted the gift and put it on the shelf with his homemade wine in the smokehouse.

In my later teen years, I started a tradition of sorts in which I visited Mandy around the time of her birthday and carried with me a box of Whitman's chocolates. As I entered the military, I could only go infrequently as the visits were dictated by the timing of the few opportunities I had to come home to Alabama on leave, a number of those years having been spent in Japan, Korea, and Vietnam. Whenever I was home, I always made it a point to go see her and take her a box of chocolates.

Sometime during the winter of 1975, or in one of the winters shortly thereafter, I determined to take my bride, Yoko, to meet Mandy. I had set some animal traps along Ball Branch and the ditches in the woods behind my house. Some of this trapline followed along the edge of Mandy's property about three hundred yards from her house. My wife dressed warmly and set out with me on the trapline. We were at that portion of the line closest to Mandy's house by the time the sun was fully up and showing over the treetops to the east. I kept an eye on her house for signs she was up and stirring about on the very cold winter morning.

Presently, I saw smoke coming from her fireplace chimney and knew she was awake and had built the fire up. Giving her a few extra minutes, I then started in the direction of the house with my bride in tow. Calling her name several times before I got to the house, I was pleased to find Mandy standing in the doorway with a big smile on her face. I'm sure it was not what she had expected when she had gotten out of bed a few minutes earlier. She had just lit a fire in the wood cookstove in the kitchen and was starting to warm up the kitchen. She smothered both of us with her hugs as we came inside and took seats at the kitchen table near the warming stove. She filled the coffeepot with water and placed it on the stove to heat while she chatted with me and studied my wife intently. She had never seen an Oriental before and seemed to be fascinated by her. Not only was she different-looking from anyone she had ever seen but was also so tiny. I talked to her about the faraway place called Okinawa, Japan, and told her I had married there and brought Yoko back to Alabama to live.

I could not help noticing there were some obvious changes that had occurred involving Mandy in the years I had not seen her as often. She moved with great difficulty and told me how her knees were swollen and troubling her so. She said some days were a pure misery, and she had a hard time getting about. As I looked about the kitchen, I could see the inside of her house was no longer as neat as it once was. The table was covered with yesterday's dishes, and an old pan of dishwater sat on one corner of the table. True, it was early morning, but it was still an indicator something was not as it once was.

As the coffee water heated, she poured a handful of coffee grounds into the pot and set it on the back of the stove to finish making. She took two coffee cups from the table, dipped them into the old dishwater, and dried them with a well-used dish towel. I knew my wife was watching the proceedings with foreboding and a growing sense of panic. I also knew what her background was and of the Japanese mentality concerning germs and sanitation. Making eye contact with her, I tried to reassure her everything would be okay.

Mandy continued our visit by telling us a son of hers had been to Mississippi and had come by the day before for a visit. That, no doubt, explained the dishes on the table that morning. He had brought with him some wonderful smoked pork sausage, and she indicated it was on top of a tall cabinet on the opposite side of the kitchen. It was not refrigerated, but at least the weather was cold. However, it was lying with its paper wrapping spread apart, and I wondered if anything had gotten a taste of it during the night. She insisted we try the sausage and was convinced we would enjoy it as much as she had last night.

Taking an iron skillet from one side of the stove, she dipped it in yesterday's dishwater and washed it. Drying it with the same towel as the cups, she put the skillet on the stove and began heating it. Hobbling across the room, she broke off two big pieces of sausage and came back and dropped them into the skillet. Washing two plates in the same manner as the cups and skillet, she then dried them and put them on the table. After putting two slices of bread onto each plate, she tended the sausage as it swelled, split apart, and began to turn a beautiful brown. She poured two cups of coffee as I shot warning glances to my wife that she better not run or get sick. The sausage being ready, she took the pieces from the skillet, put them on the plates with the bread, and pushed the plates toward us. One thing I knew for sure at that moment: my wife was not going to touch that food!

Knowing in advance she would not, I explained to Mandy my wife was not feeling well that morning and couldn't eat or drink anything. I ate both sandwiches and drank two cups of coffee and enjoyed the fact that I got my wife's portion because I was very hungry! Mandy was right too! The sausage was every bit as good as she had said. She watched me with a happy smile as I finished the sandwiches and coffee and expressed my agreement about the quality of the sausage from Mississippi.

Our visit in Mandy's warm kitchen soon came to an end, and we had to go back into the frosty air and continue checking the trapline and setting additional traps. We were barely clear of the yard before Yoko started expressing her concern for my health in a horror-filled voice. "You gonna get sick. You gonna get sick! How you eat that? You know you gonna get sick!"

"Honey," I said, "when I was in Okinawa, I ate a lot of things I wasn't too sure about, and I didn't get sick! I did not like raw fish, but I ate it too, and I was fine afterward. I did not want to offend your family by refusing what they offered. Mandy means all the world to me, and I would never dream of offending her in any way." After all, I had truly enjoyed the breakfast and was somewhat amused at my wife's reaction. I saw no need to inform my wife of the conditions in which I had been brought up. Conditions that might have, on occasion, been very similar to what we had just experienced. I went on and explained Mandy had been so neat and tidy in all her ways until her health had obviously caused her to be unable to keep up those same standards. I asked her to be understanding.

She said she would, but from time to time during the day, she would ask, "How you feel ... you feel okay?" Anyone reading this must understand the hypersensitivity the Japanese have when it comes to germs and sanitation. Yoko was also suspicious of my mother's dishes and kitchen as well and was not convinced they were clean enough. She had always been quick to volunteer to wash the dishes and clean the kitchen for Mama.

On the several subsequent trips to see Mandy, I made sure she received her box of Whitman's chocolates. I enjoyed the visits and the few minutes I could sit down and listen to her recount how the chickens were doing and about the latest fox sighting. Once or twice, she wanted my opinion of the plum wine she had made that year. Bringing the gallon jug out, she would set it down, take the inverted glass off the top of the jug, and pour me a couple of ounces into the glass. After trying it, I would testify that it was very good, which pleased her greatly. Taking the glass, she would invert it onto the top of the jug and put it away.

Our talk would then go to the issue of chicken snakes, chicken hawks, and foxes. Those were the biggest things she had to worry about with her chickens, both old and young. Now and then, she had a problem with a possum or coon—but not so much as with the hawks and foxes.

"I was settin' here 'bout three weeks ago," she might start. "It wasn't long after the sun come over them trees when I seed a fox come out of the woods 'bout where dat big pine is down there in the corner." She rose and pointed toward the tree as she craned her neck and peered intently in its direction. She continued the account of the fox sighting as if she were seeing him come out of the woods at that very moment. She continued to describe his every action and movement in detail, where he went, in which brush pile he nosed around, how long he stayed in each location, and finally the point where she lost sight of him. She may have sighted him a few days later and included that as an encore of the first appearance.

I enjoyed hearing her tell about these happenings, and it seemed more pleasant than reading a story or watching a fictional drama unfold on television. As I sit here now recording these memories of those moments, I find myself wishing I could walk with her again across her well-swept yard and sit down and listen to her tell me again about her chickens and about the foxes. I would give anything to sit in her kitchen again on a frosty morning next to the warm cookstove and enjoy another sausage sandwich and cup of coffee!

She finally came to the end of her days during a time when my life had become increasingly dedicated to working and raising my family, but I made sure I had a chicken pen in my yard so I could continue to enjoy gathering eggs and tending the chickens with their chicks. I also learned about the chicken snakes, hawks, and possums that posed an ever-present threat to them. I waged a constant battle against snakes that were swallowing eggs and chicks, as well as the hawks that swooped in regularly on the chickens. Though, like Mandy, I had to be ever vigilant, the memories of those experiences are precious to me. It pained me greatly that I had to make a decision about whether to continue to keep some chickens or get rid of them. I took the chicken pen down, finally, and I have often wondered at what point Mandy had done the same.

24

FRANK MATHEWS (GO-ME)

ONE PERSON all of us children were very familiar with was a black man who we knew as Go-me. He was of medium-dark complexion and of medium height. He, like so many at that time, kept himself fit with his hardworking lifestyle. Though we only knew him as Go-me, I found out later that was not his real name. It was a number of years before I knew his real name was Frank Mathews. He was a man we all liked and respected. He was also a man Dad depended on for his feed and fertilizer. Dad did not own a motorized vehicle and had no way to get his feed and fertilizer from Montgomery. It happened that Go-me worked at a feed store in Montgomery named Sylvest. He had a pickup truck and was willing to bring Dad the feed and supplies he needed.

Go-me lived about a mile from us down Pettus Road in the direction Aunt Louise and Uncle Rufus lived. When Dad needed certain feed or other items, he would get word to Go-me in some manner that is still a mystery to me since we did not have a telephone. Oftentimes, Dad would tell me to be on the lookout for him on a certain day, just in case he was doing something at the time that Go-me showed up. He almost always came late in the day, just before dusk-dark to deliver what he had brought to Dad. As Dad instructed, I was on the lookout for him and had the wheelbarrow ready for unloading the truck.

After notifying Dad he had come, I would go and meet Go-me and try to unload the truck myself. He would caution me that the hundred-pound sacks were too big for me, but I wanted to prove I could do it. The fifty-pound bags of scratch feed and chick starter were easy to unload as were the bags of fertilizer. Sometimes I was able to handle the heavier bags by myself as well. Those bags weighed much more than I did, but it made me feel good to be able to unload one now and then. I felt as if I were proving myself somehow. Go-me knew what was going on in my head and seemed amused by it. He also seemed to know it was something that, as a boy, I had to do.

Go-me went over the bill with Dad and gave him the final figure, and then Dad pulled his purse from his pocket and began counting out the money. I know he had a pretty good idea of the final figure before it was announced and had prepared the amount in his pocket purse. Once the business was concluded, the two of them conversed for a few minutes before Go-me had to leave and head home to take care of his evening farm business there.

This man was very helpful to Dad in so many ways, and I don't know how my father could have managed getting certain things around the place done without him. He brought his bull over when the cows were "in season," and it was breeding time. This was before Dad had his own bull. At times, when Dad planted a couple of acres of oats for the cows, it was Go-me who came and cut it down and baled it for us. He was an intelligent and accomplished man, and it showed in so many ways. He owned a mule, a tractor, and other farm equipment. This was unusual for a black resident of the community at the time and serves as an indicator of his exceptional abilities. It was not easy for a black man to "get ahead" or distinguish himself as he did in rural Alabama during that period of our history. To say he was a good man and respected is an understatement.

It was a pitiful sight I beheld one evening when he showed up with the feed with a rather large bandage covering part of his mouth. He had had an unfortunate experience of having been kicked in the mouth by his mule. Looking at the bandage and imagining the pain he must have suffered made me shudder. To think he had worked all that day and previous days with such an injury was difficult to imagine. Lesser men would have been out of work for quite a while. You really cannot help but respect a person like this man with his determination, honesty, and hardworking spirit. I am very happy my family had the privilege of knowing Frank Mathews and appreciate all the ways he was so helpful to Dad. I also appreciate the example of character that he left behind for others to look to. If I was to hear again the expression "They don't make men like they used to," I would have to answer, "Amen!"

25

LAURA

LAURA WAS an unusual woman. She dressed like a man. She also worked like a man when it came to any kind of farmwork. As a matter of fact, she probably could outwork most men. In the years I knew Laura, she did not own a mule, though she probably had in previous years. Dad would loan his mule to Laura to do her plowing with an admonition: "Don't go working him to death. Let him rest now and then!"

When she brought the mule back each time, Dad would vow he would not allow her to borrow it again. The mule would be staggering and barely holding his head up as she led him home. Dad would not allow the mule to be used for a couple of days after Laura had plowed her field with him. It took that long, in Dad's estimation, for the mule to recover from the ordeal. Laura expected the mule to work just as hard as she did. I think Dad always gave in to Laura's requests to use the mule, even though he swore each time would be the last. Dad had a certain tenderness toward his farm animals and did not want to see any animal abused. However, I feel he also had sympathy to Laura's plight and admired her hardworking spirit.

As I grew older and Laura visibly aged and began to grow

feeble, I began seeing certain other changes coming over her as well. I rarely saw her in men's clothing anymore, but she was usually wearing dresses. It occurred to me she had preferred the men's attire because it better suited the way she worked. In her later years, she often stopped by the house and inquired if I or anyone known to me might have any old batteries she could have. She apparently got a couple of dollars apiece for them when she sold them for salvage. There were certain other items she would accept as well.

Whenever Laura showed up at my house, she drove a fairly nice pickup truck. She had evidently gotten ahead economically since those days of walking the mile to our house to borrow the mule. She was always grateful for an old battery or for anything she could get a dollar or two for as salvage. Because I admired her hardworking spirit, I often slipped her five dollars or so as a gift. A relative of mine said he too admired her and did the same. She was appreciative and full of praise and thanksgiving to God. A kiss and a hug became a part of our parting ritual. She was one of a kind, and I'm happy our mule survived it. Had I owned a mule as my dad had, I might have been apprehensive rather than happy when Laura showed up!

26

AUNT LOUISE AND
UNCLE RUFUS

WHEN OUR house burned in 1954, it was Aunt Louise and Uncle Rufus who took Dianne and me in and cared for us until our family was able to reunite. As I previously stated, Dianne was two years old at the time, and I was four. This aunt and uncle of ours would have liked to have made the situation of their caring for us a permanent arrangement, as they had no children of their own. However, that was not to be as Mama and Dad would not agree to such a permanent arrangement.

Aunt Louise was one of Dad's sisters and lived her life in the very simple fashion farm living usually dictates. There was no fanciness or frivolity in her life. Aunt Louise was a plain woman. The plainness of her features reflected the plainness of her life. Hers was a life of chores and the day-to-day activities required in the operation of a small subsistence farm. Uncle Rufus could be described as a subsistence farmer, much like my dad and many other such people in the rural environment in which we lived. He and Aunt Louise raised a lot of their own food just like our family did. They also had a number of cows on the forty acres they owned. Like my dad, Uncle Rufus also worked outside his farming activities to bring in the extra money needed to make ends meet. Uncle Rufus brought in this extra money by working in the community as a housepainter.

There is very little I can actually remember about Uncle Rufus when I was very young, but I remember certain things about him as I got a little older. The name "Gomer" comes to mind for some reason I can't really explain. Perhaps, in physical appearance, he may remind me of the Gomer on television who most of us are familiar with. Uncle Rufus drove an old pickup truck, dressed plainly, and rolled his own cigarettes from Prince Albert tobacco just as my dad did. He also had a speech impediment that caused him to talk in the funny manner of the cartoon character Elmer Fudd. It gave his manner of speaking a very interesting quality. When he tried to make a "G" sound, it came out sounding like a "D." His "R" always came out sounding like a "W." When he tried to make a "C" sound, it came out as a "T." He had difficulty pronouncing other letters as well.

When I became an adult and began working alongside my dad from time to time, Dad would recount incidents and stories he found amusing. One of these stories involved Uncle Rufus's speech impediment and the television he had recently purchased. Uncle Rufus had become very fond of a television western that aired in the afternoon at three thirty. The show was called *Cheyenne* and starred Clint Walker. Uncle Rufus's work schedule was tailored in such a fashion as to allow him to be at home when his favorite show came on.

Dad recounted to me that he and Uncle Rufus had been hired to paint the Liberty Church of Christ building. It was an old clapboard building built in the 1800s and was where my whole family had always attended church. On a particular day, Uncle Rufus did not pay as close attention to the time as he usually did. Stopping his painting to check the time on his pocket watch, he exclaimed loudly, "Oh my doodness, Tchi anne tums on in fifteen minutes!" Scampering down from the ladder, he set his bucket down and called out, "Cwose my paint, Dewis … I'll wash my bwush when I dit home!" (Dewis is Lewis, my father.)

Throwing his brush into the back of his truck, he jumped in and headed out of the churchyard as quick as he could get the engine started. He lived about five miles away down Pettus Road which intersects Highway 31 almost across from the church building. According to Dad, Uncle Rufus made it on time but also paid closer attention to his watch during the rest of the afternoons they were working together. Dad also affirmed he did indeed "cwose the paint can" for Uncle Rufus and put away his ladder and drop cloths.

Aunt Louise was a woman I found myself uncomfortable around and disliking somewhat when I was a young child. As I got older, and I began to understand her, I found I had begun to like and appreciate her. It's pretty amazing what a little understanding can do as far as effecting attitude shifts. I thought her to be a bit stingy and miserly and maybe even somewhat hard-hearted. She had always appeared to be a little brusque in her manner, and sometimes her voice became a bit shrill as if she was angry or frustrated. There may well have been reason for some anger and frustration to affect her state of mind and voice control. At least, that is what I eventually came to understand. She had no children, and that had been a major disappointment for her. She had gone through some frustrating times in other areas as well and often struggled to make ends meet. She was a closed-mouth person about private matters, and she kept certain things to herself. It was only when we had developed a close relationship in the years following my uncle's death that I learned of the difficulties she had kept silent about.

Uncle Rufus had a tendency to drink some now and then. On numerous occasions, he also gambled away the money he had earned. When that happened, Aunt Louise was forced to surrender the meager savings she had accumulated and squirreled away in a drawer. When I became aware of this, I understood why she had pinched every penny and looked for ways to make a few extra nickels and dimes. I was reminded of the time when I had seen her retrieve an old purse Mama had tossed into the trash pile. I also remember her wonderment that Mama would throw away something someone might pay her twenty-five cents for! The shame I felt for her at that moment changed to admiration as I got older and more understanding. It was from her "butter and egg" money and other little ways like salvaging the purse from the trash that she was able to put those few dollars in a drawer, dollars that allowed her to get through some difficult times. She had grown up in the Depression and knew to be prudent in all things. In time, Aunt Louise was revealed to me as kind, tenderhearted, and generous, but she was never wasteful, for life had taught her not to be.

In the early 1980s, after having spent a number of years away in military service, I found myself making a living as a housepainter as Uncle Rufus and Dad had done. Aunt Louise needed her house painted and asked me if I would do it for her. Uncle Rufus had died several years before. I happily accepted the job and the opportunity to do something for her. To have done the job for nothing would have hurt her pride, so I charged her a small amount. While painting the back of the house, I heard a loud commotion from inside. Aunt Louise was crying out and seemed to be shouting at someone. I thought that, possibly, an intruder had come in through the front door and was assaulting her.

Jumping off the ladder and dropping my brush in the dirt, I

ran to the back door. Expecting the worst as I pushed the door open and ran inside, I was confronted with a spectacle that both surprised and relieved me. Aunt Louise was standing in front of the television and shouting warnings to the soap opera actress in the television drama.

"Watch out," she shouted. "He's right behind you! He's gonna get you ... watch out!"

I stopped abruptly and waited for her to turn around, but she was so intent on the program she never knew that I was there behind her. I backed out the way I had come in and then closed the door. I could not help shaking my head and smiling at what I had seen. She apparently got very involved in the shows when she watched television. I picked up my paintbrush from the dirt, cleaned it, and resumed my painting. Later, I was reminded of how Uncle Rufus had reacted when he thought he would be late in getting home to watch his afternoon show, *Cheyenne*. I wonder how it must have been when my aunt and uncle watched an exciting show together.

After completing the painting of the house, I was introduced to Aunt Louise's pickles, preserves, and other canned items she was proud of. She insisted I have some of each to take home with me. She also showed me a large crock she was using to ferment corncobs for wine. I had never heard of corncob wine before, but she assured me anything that could ferment could be made into wine. She had processed a good amount of fresh corn and had begun making wine of the cobs from which she had sliced the corn away. Smelling the contents of the crock, I could quickly detect the odor of sour corn. She showed me some bottles of a previous batch she had made and asked me to sample a bit and give my opinion. The wine had a distinct sour corncob taste, but it also possessed the soothing warmth and goodness of homemade wine. She added a bottle of the wine to my collection of pickles and preserves.

After a moment's reflection, she asked, "Your daddy drinks, don't he?"

"No ma'am," I said. "Dad doesn't drink."

Responding in surprise, she continued, "He don't? All painters drink. They have to ... Rufus said so. He said they needed the alcohol to cut the fumes out of the blood."

I could not help smiling when she said that, and I could picture Uncle Rufus assuring her he was really taking medicine and not just drinking because he enjoyed it.

"Well, Aunt Louise," I replied, "if a person wants to take a drink, that's about as good a reason as I ever heard." I did take Dad a small bottle of the wine home so he could taste it. Though he had never been given to drinking, I remembered he had enjoyed a taste of homemade wine now and then when I was a child.

Aunt Louise had always depended on Uncle Rufus and his truck for transportation throughout their married life. When he died, she had no way to get around except through the generosity of family members or friends. This continued for a number of years until she finally got her driver's license and, later, a car. It was a liberating experience for her, and she was finally able to get away from her house and socialize. This added a whole new dimension to her life and made her a much happier person.

One day, several years after her husband had died, Aunt Louise tearfully recounted an incident to me that had distressed her greatly when it occurred and continued to bother her years afterward. She told me she had gotten a visit from the preacher one afternoon. She had missed church services for two or three weeks, and the preacher came to see her. Uncle Rufus was suffering from lung cancer and had gotten to the point that he was confined to the house and bed. When she explained that she did not wish to leave her husband unattended during this stage of his illness, she was shocked by the reaction of the preacher.

"He will be fine while you are gone," the man said. "Your place on Sunday morning is in worship service." As she recounted to me, he then went on and chastised her for "forsaking the assembly."

"Did I do wrong, Allen? I couldn't just leave Rufus," she said. "He needed me!"

I was flabbergasted by what she had told me and could not believe the lack of understanding the preacher had shown. "Aunt Louise," I said, "Part of what we do in church is learn about duties and responsibilities. By being at Uncle Rufus's side, you put religion into practice. That is doing God's work. Don't doubt for a minute that you were doing the right thing."

Aunt Louise was the possessor of a simple, pure, and honest heart. That someone might suggest that her devotion to Uncle Rufus indicated a lack of devotion to God and to his service still causes me to get angry.

Aunt Louise eventually came down with cancer and was confined to bed herself in her final weeks. On one occasion, several of us family members went to visit her. We could all tell she was in a lot of pain and suffering mental anguish over her condition. As our visit grew to a close, and the family members began to leave the room, she called out to me to wait.

She obviously had something she wanted to say, so I remained behind.

When the last of the others had left, she looked at me and began crying. Through her tears, she acknowledged, "Allen, I'm afraid to die … I'm so afraid to die!"

My experience in such situations was very limited at that time, and I was at a loss as to how to respond and comfort her. "Everything is going to be okay, Aunt Louise. Everything is going to be okay." These were the only words I could think of to say to this dear, frightened woman. Since that time, I've thought of a dozen things I would have liked to have said. She had experienced a lifetime of hard teaching about the severity of God and his judgment. She knew her time was growing short, and she would soon be facing God and his judgment. I know Aunt Louise had a good heart, and she had always tried to do the right thing. It was painful for me to see her in her physical and mental misery. I wish I could have thought of the right words to say to her, but I did not possess them. The memory of that moment is still with me, though I'm confident that soon afterward she got the comfort she needed from someone far greater than me.

27

THE HANDSOMEST
MAN IN ALL OF INDIA

CHARLES EDWARD Brady was my uncle and my dad's youngest brother. As the baby of the family, he had been pampered somewhat by my grandmother. At least, that is what I was told. Uncle Charles served in the army during World War II and retired from service around 1962 or '63. In a lengthy newspaper article his wife, Aunt Bea, had saved, he was described as the "handsomest man in all of India." The article was written by a female correspondent who had spent a day with him in India where he was serving at the time. The photograph Aunt Bea had stored with the article attested to the fact that he was, indeed, a very handsome man.

Charles Edward Brady (Uncle Charles): "the
handsomest man in all of India."

When Uncle Charles retired from the service, he was still
a young man in a relative sense as he was barely in his forties.
However, I was only twelve years old, and forty seemed like
forever. Dad and Uncle Charles came to terms on the small plot
of ground where our burned house had stood.

Shortly afterward, Dad built a small wood-frame house on
the spot for Uncle Charles and Aunt Bea. I was Dad's helper
during the building of the house and learned a lot about
carpentry from the building of it. Dad often commented I could
handle a hammer and saw better than most grown men. It made
me proud to hear such compliments from Dad—and sometimes
Uncle Charles. Even though I only received five dollars in pay
for the whole job, I enjoyed it and got to know Uncle Charles a

bit. Uncle Charles did not particularly like children, and I was still on the brink of that distinction, so we really did not forge a close relationship for some time to come. He never had children of his own and was happy with that fact.

Uncle Charles had an amazing regularity in everything he did. I suppose that was chiefly because of the discipline instilled during his twenty years of military service. His appearance was always neat, and his shoes were softly shined. He would call it "squared away." He never threw a cigarette butt on the ground, and he always disposed of them in a proper container or by "field stripping" them and putting the paper and filter in his pocket to be discarded later. For several years after retiring, he wore his green fatigue cap and always removed it when entering a building. This cap was not the softer baseball-type cap; it was the round, rigid kind favored by Fidel Castro. I never knew the proper name for this style of cap. I have often referred to it as a "Patton cap," but I don't have any idea where that thought came from. Eventually, he stopped wearing a cap at all unless conditions called for one. He would not be in the hot sun without one or out in wet or foul weather with his head uncovered.

I don't recall very many instances in which Uncle Charles did work that required a lot of physical exertion. Occasionally, I might see him putting away some tool or another or rearranging them, but he seldom actually used them. He preferred to do the supervising while someone else actually employed the tools to some task. Often, the person using the tools would be me. He had a bad back due to a motorcycle accident when he was in the service and was quick to remind me the back still bothered him and prevented his doing anything too physically demanding. Dad scoffed at the reality of the bad back and was quick to point out to me that it likely went back to his pampered childhood.

Uncle Charles became a barber after attending Patterson

Trade School in the early sixties. He was actually attending the school while we built his house. Dad built him a small barbershop beside his house after finishing the house. Uncle Charles operated it for many years until he became ill and started hurting all over his body. It was one of the very few barbershops around that existed outside of the city limits to the south of Montgomery. Even so, business got off to a pretty slow start, but he eventually attracted the locals as loyal customers.

Saturday was his busy day. People who were not farmers had jobs that required them to be in Montgomery on weekdays. The slow pace of the weekdays suited him just fine as it left him with some flexibility to do other things as he wished. He was able to get by pretty well on the money earned cutting hair and his military pension. Dad had always cut my hair with an old pair of hand clippers that pulled as much hair as they cut. At some point, Uncle Charles gave him an electric clipper set.

My dad had one style of cutting ... whitewalls on the side with a little thatch on top. By the time I reached fifteen and was in Junior ROTC in high school, I was getting ribbed a bit about my hair by the other boys. Uncle Charles became my barber and promised to give me military-style haircuts at no cost. I'm not sure if my dad's feelings were hurt or not, but it relieved him of the burden of having to keep my hair cut. I was more comfortable with the professional haircuts and did not have to put up with the kidding anymore. The haircuts by my uncle became partial payment for little things I did for him.

There were some people my uncle refused to accommodate in his barbershop. Long hair was coming into style, and he associated long hair with dirty hair. He had no desire to put his clippers or other equipment in danger of possible contamination by cutting the hair of some "hippie." The one or two who he consented to do, he intentionally humiliated so they would be discouraged from coming back. That seemed to do the trick, and he was satisfied without their business. The low opinion of males with long hair was widespread at the time. Uncle Charles also did not like to cut the hair of children. Certain ones were tolerated, but not very many. It was good he was not dependent on his barbershop for his livelihood, for he served a narrow clientele. Sometimes, I feel it was more of a hobby for him and gave him a way to use some free time and visit with people.

Uncle Charles liked to stand in front of his barbershop to do his smoking. He rarely smoked inside, though he did it occasionally and also permitted his customers to smoke inside if they wished. When I came home on the school bus in the afternoon, I would often observe him standing outside and watching for the bus. When I saw him, I knew he would likely call me over for some task or project. If he didn't need me, he might just throw up a hand and wave. Sometimes, my heart would drop inside me when I heard him call out "Hey, hey," and motion for me to come. I knew my fishing or hunting plans had just gotten dashed to pieces! However, if I had no such plans, I enjoyed going to see him and spending time with him on one task or another.

Uncle Charles liked his yard to be orderly and well "policed." I learned the proper way to police an area was to walk back and forth across it in such a way as to miss no spots while picking up anything that didn't belong on the ground. Even small sticks had to be removed along with any rocks a lawn mower blade might strike. After the yard was cleaned of anything that might dull a mower blade, it was time to get the mower out. The oil and gas were checked even though it had been done as a part of putting the mower away. After starting, the mower was warmed up a prescribed amount of time and its throttle set at a very definite speed he felt did not overwork the mower. Then the mowing began under the watchful eye of my vigilant uncle whose ears could detect the sound of the blade striking anything that was not grass. I would almost cringe at the sound of the blade hitting a twig or acorn and glance across in time to see him stiffen and look in my direction.

If the sound was loud enough, he might motion for me to stop the mower. That meant I had to police the area again before I could continue. With the mowing completed, I had to clean the equipment and put it away. This involved wiping or washing the mower down, cleaning the air filter, checking the oil, changing the blade, and filling the gas tank. After the lawn mower had fully cooled, it was put away. My uncle made sure there were no missed steps. He sure could supervise! His military training ensured his equipment was always ready for use and never failed him.

When there seemed to be nothing else to do, Uncle Charles liked to clean out his garage and organize it. This meant I took everything out, cleaned the floor, and put everything back in its proper place. Water had to be sprinkled on the floor before I swept it to minimize the risk of the dust getting airborne. When the floor was completely dry, I could start putting the items back into place. I did not mind doing these projects for Uncle Charles as long as I got to do my fishing too. He never expected me to do the work for nothing, and he was always generous with me. If he did not have anything to give me at the moment he might say, "Come see me later," or "I'll settle up with you later." He was true to his word, and I never felt unappreciated or taken advantage of.

Fishing was quite an experience with Uncle Charles. Several times, he and I went fishing in the little pond where Dad watered his cows. I got to dig the worms or capture some catalpa worms from the uppermost branches of an infected catalpa tree. With the bait and a couple of long cane poles, we were ready to go. Of course, a camp stool was a necessary item for him, as well. Fishing together meant I fished, and he supervised.

"Bait this hook," he might say. "Drop it in the water over there ... ho ... a little farther toward that stump. Watch your cork ... you're getting a bite! Pull it in!" If the pole was set down while waiting for a fish to bite, my uncle might pick it up and pull the fish in for me to take the hook from his mouth. That is generally how we fished together.

On one excursion to the creek for night fishing, Uncle Charles accompanied Dad and me. A neighbor, Dan Fuller, who was about Uncle Charles's age went along too. I seemed to be Uncle Charles's baggage handler, camp custodian, and cook. We parked the car (Mr. Fuller's) along the dirt road at its closest point to the creek, which was about three hundred yards down a wooded hillside to the creek. Dad and Dan Fuller carried their own items while I made a couple of trips to the car for Uncle Charles's after I had gotten mine to the spot we had selected to make a camp. There was plenty of deadfall wood for a fire as well as a nice log on the ground for a back log for the fire.

Having set up the camp and setting out the poles along the creek at promising spots, we got the fire going. By that time, it had gotten fully dark, and the air began to chill quickly as it was still early spring. Uncle Charles and our neighbor had begun this fishing expedition in a pretty high state and had also brought some whiskey along to ensure they remained in that state. The whiskey was of the illegal variety and was brought along in a jug that had originally contained Wesson cooking oil. In the darkness, Uncle Charles enquired as to the whereabouts of the whiskey and was told where to find it. Pulling the Wesson bottle out, he took a big swallow and began cursing.

After some spitting and sputtering and a good deal more

cursing, he complained to his companion, "My God, Dan, that's the nastiest stuff I've ever tasted! It tastes like cooking oil!"

"Give me that bottle, Charles," Dan said. Taking it to the light of the fire for a closer inspection, he announced, "I reckon so, Charles, you're drinking the cooking oil! There is another bottle there just like this one," he said. Finding the other bottle, Uncle Charles spent a little time washing his mouth out with the whiskey.

Once we began taking a few eels and catfish from the lines, I began to clean them and cook them in the pot we had brought along for that purpose. Fortunately, we still had most of the contents of the bottle of cooking oil in which to fry our fish.

I set up the folding army cot near the fire for my uncle and spread the several wool blankets on it that Uncle Charles had insisted I bring along for him. He enjoyed a pleasant night's sleep near the fire while the rest of us slept poorly on the ground with our blankets and kept the fire going. Somehow, I made it through the cold and smoke-filled night and found enough energy to get mine and Uncle Charles's stuff back to the car the next morning. I'm certainly glad he did not make it a habit of accompanying us on other outings like this. It seemed he did not mind roughing it a bit as long as he did it in comfort and style. Having a personal aide seemed to be a must for him as well.

As a teenager, I was invited to go on a deep-sea fishing trip with Uncle Charles and this same neighbor. As before, they made the trip in "high spirits." Dan drove to Destin, Florida, while my uncle sat in the navigator's seat. I occupied the back seat and was designated the bartender. It was my first experience at such a thing, and I was complimented on how quickly I learned to accommodate the tastes of my traveling companions in the front seat. My sole purpose on the trip down was to keep the drinks coming. I don't think Mom, Dad, or my Sunday school teacher would have approved.

We arrived at the pier in Destin while it was still dark as we had made the trip late at night. The two adults of our small group had consumed a good bit of alcohol on the trip down and were not too steady on their feet as we boarded the boat that would take us out for a day of deep-sea fishing. I was pretty excited at the prospect of catching some huge ocean fish I had heard so much about. This would be my first experience in fishing in salt water.

The boat left the pier before the sun came up and began making the long trip out to the proposed fishing grounds. The crew of the boat prepared breakfast for the couple of dozen fishermen aboard, but Uncle Charles and our neighbor decided they were not hungry. I noticed they had also grown very quiet in the hour or so since we had left the dock. First, one, and then the other announced they were "tired" and would lie down and rest a bit. When we got to the fishing grounds, they continued to rest while everyone else fished. Uncle Charles's rest was interrupted quite often by trips to the rail to throw up and moan a bit.

Presently, Dan began fishing, but he was quieter than usual, and I knew he was not feeling well. However, as the day wore on, and we went from one fishing spot to another, he started becoming his old self again and began giving me pointers to improve my fishing. Uncle Charles's condition never improved enough to allow him to do any fishing. He continued to lay down most of the time and only got up for brief intervals during the day at sea. When we got back to the dock in the afternoon, my uncle was the happiest person on the boat and one of the first off. This had been his first experience at deep-sea fishing, and he never had any desire to go again.

The trip back to Alabama during that evening and night was

far different from the trip of the preceding night. I was tired from the trip of the evening before and from the day's fishing. I sat in the back seat and dozed a lot and even managed to get a little sleep. There was no need of my bartending services on the return trip as the stomachs of the two patrons of this rolling bar had not recovered sufficiently to tolerate any alcohol. Only short bits of conversation interrupted the occasional sounds of road traffic going in the opposite direction as we made our way back home. It was a tired and very relieved uncle of mine who wasted no time in heading for his own bed within minutes after our return trip. It was as if he were a magician performing a disappearing act!

Another of Dad's favorite stories that he shared with me on occasion while we were working together involved Uncle Charles. The incident Dad recounted to me occurred when they were still teenage boys. They, along with their older brother, Frank, and a couple of other boys had decided to spend the night on the creek, fishing. It was decided that they needed a few items from home, and Uncle Charles, the youngest of the group, was selected to be the one to go home and pick up what they needed. He was not allowed to take the one lantern they had and would have to make the trip in the dark.

On his return trip to the campsite, he began to call out to be guided in by his companions. They answered his calls, and he began following their replies back to the camp. They knew between the campsite and Uncle Charles's position was a deep depression that had once been a section of the creek but was now dry and bordered by a high bank on the side from which he was approaching. This area was also full of cypress "knees" that ranged from a few inches to several feet high, like a thick forest of thin rounded stumps. They continued to call their companion in and guided him to the brink of the old creek bank.

Seeing the fire ahead of him, he headed directly to it and plunged down among the cypress knees after having stepped off the high bank. He was bruised up pretty badly from the fall, but he was able to finally work his way out of the cypress knees after someone brought the lantern. Everyone had a fine time over the affair except for this youngest member of the group. It was surely a young people's way of having fun at someone else's expense. It was also a way of equaling things out since he was the pampered one at home. Left to their own devices, young people have a way of doing that. I'm sure Grandma had some questions about the bruising later, but Dad never told me about that, and I never thought to ask.

While growing up, Dad was the one who kept the place going for Grandma, even though Uncle Frank was older. There were times he had to take his younger brother, Charles, to task over one thing or another. I'm sure my uncle did not care to be bossed by his brother and that resentment became evident from time to time. On one occasion, Dad had instructed his younger brother to hitch up the mule for some plowing he was to do. Likely, he was passing on the instructions from Grandma, but Dad's brother let his temper get the best of him. Uncle Charles took out his anger on the mule and began abusing him. That was a mistake. Nobody did that around Dad!

Dad quickly got fed up with the whole affair and doubled up a plow line several times and whipped his brother soundly with it. He could never tolerate the abuse of an animal nor could he tolerate someone acting out in this way. I don't think my uncle cared much for mules or farming, but that was part of his existence for the time being, and he was expected to do his part. When he became old enough to get out on his own, then he would be free to choose his way of life. Until then, he was to follow Grandma's and his brother's instructions and pull his weight without abusing the livestock. He was probably relieved when December 7, 1941, arrived and with it, the knowledge that the Japanese had bombed Pearl Harbor. Suddenly, my uncle Charles had his purpose, and it did not include farming.

He left the farm, joined the army, and soon found himself in India. It was there that the female reporter came across him and described him to people back home as the "handsomest man in all of India." As a youngster, I saw him one evening in the late 1950s at Grandma's house when he had come home on leave. It was the first time I had seen anyone in a military uniform, and it was an awe-inspiring experience for me. Several years later, my relationship as nephew to uncle began when he retired and hung up his uniform for good. I was twelve years old at the time.

After having spent almost ten years in the army myself, I went to see Uncle Charles one day. I was still just shy of my twenty-ninth birthday. With me was a small boy who was not yet three years old. His name was Charles Lewis Brady, and he was my youngest child and only son.

"Uncle Charles," I said, "I want you to meet your namesake. He is named for you, and I brought him to spend the afternoon with you. Do you want to nursemaid him for a few hours?" I pushed little Charlie over to his great-uncle who grinned down at him. After a few uncomfortable seconds, he reached into his wallet and took out a dollar. Handing the dollar down to Charlie, he gently pushed him back to me.

"I don't think so," he said.

Several years later, Uncle Charles started hurting all over and took to bed. After three or four weeks of not getting any better, he asked me if I could take him to the veteran's hospital in Montgomery. It was a weekend, and he was chastised by the staff for not coming in during regular sick call hours. However, after being checked out by a staff doctor, he was admitted for a week. During that time, the cause of his weakness and pain was not diagnosed, but he regained some of his strength and energy, and he began to feel more normal, though he was still in pain. When he left the hospital, he resumed his normal activities and began to cut hair on a limited basis. However, in a few days, he had again taken to his bed with no energy and pain in his extremities.

Larry, my brother, and I took him to Maxwell AFB Hospital in Montgomery to have him checked out. He was initially told everything checked out, and he was "as healthy as a horse." We insisted something was very wrong and recounted what had been going on the past few weeks. Several people checked him out to see if something had been missed. The third doctor who looked at the chest x-rays became suspicious and studied them at length and checked my uncle's breathing several times. After consulting with the other medical staff, he came forward with the news that Uncle Charles needed to be admitted. He voiced his concern that lung cancer was a possibility, but further testing was called for. The following day, we were informed he had lung cancer in both lungs as well as bone cancer throughout his body.

The diagnosis came as a blow to all of us, especially to my uncle. Treatment was not an option. He remained at this hospital for a few days until it was agreed that he should be transferred to the military hospital in Biloxi, Mississippi, which had a terminal ward. The purpose of this ward was to provide terminal patients the greatest degree of comfort possible in their final days. It was a good decision as he was now in terrible pain and discomfort. The treatment protocol at Maxwell Hospital limited the amount of morphine and possibly other drugs they were allowed to administer. The terminal ward of the military hospital in Biloxi was not limited in that regard. The staff promised us his stay there during his final days would be as pain free as they could make it.

In the three weeks he was there, Larry and I also spent most of our time there. Whenever I came home to sleep and clean up, there would be a telephone message from the hospital to come back if it were any way possible. The trip each way took several hours, but we made the trip a number of times. Uncle Charles did not want to die alone.

After a number of trips back and forth to Alabama, we realized the end would be coming soon. We were determined on our final trip to remain with our uncle until the end. During the last night and day, we did not leave his bedside except for brief moments to eat or drink something. At those times, we assured him we were not leaving except for a few minutes. We made our absences from his bedside as brief as possible. Uncle Charles told us that he loved us, and I know that he meant it. He wanted to die quickly and expressed a number of times, "I hope the good Lord takes me soon!" His breathing was very labored during the last few hours, and he fought hard for each breath he pulled in. Presently, he was no longer conscious, and his breathing began to slow. Larry and I agreed it was time to summon the medical staff. The nurse and doctor came in as our uncle, once described as the "handsomest man in all of India," drew his last breath.

The young doctor sat on the side of Uncle Charles's bed with her hand on his arm and began to cry softy. This was the first person she had seen die, she said. She looked like a young girl, not a doctor in training. After a few moments, she asked us to accompany her to her small office where she talked with us a while. She seemed shocked when she saw my smile. I explained Uncle Charles's prayer had just been answered, and I was happy he was not suffering anymore. I was touched by the tears on her face and the genuine emotion she displayed.

The staff of that terminal ward could not have been better chosen. Each person serving in it treated their dying patients as if they were their own family members. Later, I chose a nice card to send to that staff on behalf of my family. In it, I expressed those very thoughts. I never realized how much I would miss Uncle Charles until after he was gone. It was good his suffering had come to a quick end, though. As time went on, I began thinking of the questions I should have asked. It would have been good to talk about his military experience. Neither of us had ever spoken about our military experiences. I don't know why we didn't. I suppose we must have felt there was no need to do so.

Aunt Bea died a little over a year after Uncle Charles. She had tripped and fallen while coming out the small building that had been the barbershop. A young black man stopped at our house across the road and told me there was a woman lying in the yard across the road. He did not just drive away as if it were not his business. He was also concerned about stopping and checking on her without someone with him. He didn't have to tell me why. This was still Alabama, and he was obviously concerned his good intentions might be misunderstood should someone show up and see him bending over her. He was obviously still conscious of certain things he had been taught. I wish I knew who he was. I never got the opportunity to thank him properly.

As it turned out, Aunt Bea's hip was broken. She was transported to a hospital in Montgomery where she later died of a stroke. Uncle Charles and Aunt Bea are buried side by side in our family cemetery next to Mama and Dad. The cemetery is practically in my front yard, and I spend a lot of time there cleaning, visiting, and remembering.

28

UNCLE FRANK

MY DAD'S oldest brother was Frank Brady. Frank is a name that appears quite often in my family tree. Before I was born, Uncle Frank lived in a small tenant house near the spot where our burned house had stood. Where our house had been became the site of Uncle Charles's house. The little house nearby that Uncle Frank inhabited later became the home of a black woman named Annie Ausborne. It was the type of small cabin that might be associated as a sharecropper's shack or maybe quarters attached to an old plantation. There were many of these types of small dwellings about when I was a child. Most have since disappeared, but there are some still around. Sometime around the time I was born, or just before, Uncle Frank moved to Birmingham. He lived and worked there until the end of his life.

Uncle Frank was a big man. His facial features always reminded me of King Henry VIII, the biggest differences being the nature of their births and the clothes they wore. I guess I should throw in their social status and jobs too. Uncle Frank generally dressed in long-sleeved, "blue-collar" work clothes, though they were actually green work uniforms. His working career was with the Dupont Company in Birmingham. We did not see him very often. I remember him coming at least twice a year, but he may have come more often in the years before I knew him. In the wintertime, he came to visit for two or three days and do some squirrel hunting. When summer came around, he came for two or three more days and caught up on his fishing. I began to look forward to his visits and enjoyed the times we spent together.

The first order of business for my uncle when he came down to visit was to pick up a gallon of whiskey to enjoy while vacationing. He knew the backwoods location where there was sure to be some ready for him. I don't think he was ever disappointed. On one occasion when I was about twelve years old, he had me hide his jug for him until he called for it the next morning. It was dusk-dark when he pulled up in the driveway and honked to get my attention. Making sure that Dad or Mom could not see us, he took the jug out of the car and handed it to me.

With a grin, he said, "Hide my water somewhere for me, lad. I'll be back in the morning to pick it up." This was a gallon he was planning to take back to Birmingham with him the next morning. I did hide it for him—but not before pouring out a bit of it in a pint jar and refilling the jug an equal amount of water. I just wanted to taste it and see what the big attraction was. When I sampled it later, I found it was not something I wanted! The following day, my uncle came by and picked up his jug and headed back north again. Some people pick up trinkets or T-shirts as souvenirs of their vacations, but not my uncle Frank. He was a practical-minded person!

The first time I remember seeing Uncle Frank was when I was four years old, even though I obviously knew him and was excited about his visit. He showed up at our old house with a bag of green-colored apples and that made us all the more excited about his coming. He gave each of us children an apple from the bag. I have already described how one of my sisters had thrown away the biggest part of her apple into the waste hole of the outhouse. I was very sorrowful over the waste of the apple, which was in evidence on several subsequent visits to the outhouse. However, one of the chickens eventually found it and enjoyed a special treat!

Uncle Frank had a very distinct odor about him that I could have easily identified in the dark. He smoked a pipe, and his clothes and belongings were infused with the smell of pipe tobacco. His car was permeated with the same smell. The aroma of burned pipe tobacco was coupled with that of the whiskey he kept on hand. Though he obviously took a few drinks from a bottle during certain times of the day, he was reasonably moderate and discreet about it. I never saw him intoxicated. On one occasion, I happened upon him and Uncle Charles fishing at a nearby pond. As I stood talking to him, he nodded to a thick cord tied to a jug bobbing in the water. The cord was fastened to a small willow at the edge of the pond.

"Pull in my water, lad," he said. "I need a drink."

I dutifully pulled in the gallon jug from the water and handed it to him.

He unscrewed the lid, took a big swallow, and handed it to his brother, Uncle Charles, who took a swallow or two. It was a warm day, and I was a bit thirsty and indicated my need for a bit of water too. This drew a laugh from both of my uncles.

"This ain't that kind of water, lad," Uncle Frank informed me. "This is firewater!" They both chuckled a bit over that. The jug's cap was screwed back on, and the jug was tossed into the water where it began bobbing around as before. I tied the cord back to the base of the small willow from which I had untied it. They were still chuckling about the "firewater" jest as I walked away. I went away thirsty and had to stay that way until I got back home.

My older brother Buddy recounted how he had gone fishing with Uncle Frank when he was a youngster. Buddy knew of the quart jar in the back seat of the car and decided to help himself to a drink when his uncle was not looking. He had seen Uncle Frank drink from it and knew it was moonshine whiskey. What was the big attraction—and why did Uncle Frank seem to enjoy it so much? My brother decided he would find out for himself. Going to the car while Uncle Frank's attention was fully on his fishing, Buddy sneaked a drink from the jar.

"It was awful," he told me in later years, "and burned like fire!" After a while, he decided he might want a second opinion and went back to the car and sneaked another drink. It was still awful and still burned—but not quite as bad as the first time. He began to feel a bit "different" after the second swallow from the jar. On the third trip to the car, he decided to stay right there in the back seat, but he kept an eye out for his uncle. After all, there was more in the jar, and Uncle Frank probably would not miss a little bit more. He decided to have another drink. At some point, my brother gave in to the effects of the whiskey and lost consciousness. He awoke later in a very sad condition with Uncle Frank standing over him.

"How do you feel? Do you feel that you're going to die?"

All Buddy could do was moan and puke. He wished he could go ahead and die!

"Well, I hope you do die, you little b——! You didn't even save me a drink!" Uncle Frank was in no mood to extend any sympathy to Buddy under the circumstances and punctuated his thoughts with a solid cursing of the "dying" Buddy. He probably didn't mind Buddy trying the whiskey, but the fact that he was so insensitive as to drink it all was unpardonable!

Uncle Frank rarely wore a jacket or coat, even in the coldest of weather. Most of the time, his long shirtsleeves were turned up one or two times at the cuff. He seemed to be immune to the effects of cold weather. Perhaps it was because he was fairly large even though he could not be said to be fat. When we squirrel hunted, he wore a hunting jacket for the purpose of carrying extra shotgun shells and the squirrels he would shoot.

On one occasion, he went with Buddy, Dad, and me as we were going to check traps we had set on Pintlala Creek about three miles from our house. The temperature was in the twenties, and a heavy frost was on everything. The traps were on the opposite side of the creek, and we needed to cross on a foot log to get to that side. Dad told his brother not to cross the log but wait for us as we went to the other side and checked the traps we had along a ditch there. The log was very slippery with frost and was quite long. It crossed a deep hole of water in the creek. I was the last to cross, and I heard a loud whoop and a splash. I turned to find my uncle thrashing his way back to the creek bank. He pulled himself out of the water at the creek bank with the aid of small tree growing there. Cursing and swearing, he stamped his feet and swung his arms about to try to shake off some of the water and warm back up. I could see the steam rising from his clothing in the cold air. He finally pulled the bottle from his hip pocket and took a drink to warm himself a bit more. Though he had no coat and was wet all over, he stayed with us until we finished with our traps and headed back home. He may have been miserable, but he never complained about his situation at all. I suppose the whiskey bottle in his hip pocket helped keep him warm and comfortable enough. He probably wished he had stayed off that foot log, though!

Whenever Uncle Frank visited with us, he never slept in any other way than sitting in a chair in the living room, that I was aware of. It is probable that he laid down and slept sometimes, but I just didn't notice. He simply sat there with his head tilted forward and snored through the night. I got the impression it did not take much in the way of creature comforts for this uncle of mine. He was a big and tough man. He did not want to be a bother to anyone or have anyone making a fuss over him. He was an unusual person, and I enjoyed being with him. I know Dad did too because they saw so little of each other. We always hated to see him leave and head back home to Birmingham.

29

COUSIN FRANK ANDERSON

COUSIN FRANK was a first cousin of my grandmother. He was about the same age as she was. He lived on the wooded hill just south of our pasture fence. His son, David, lived in Montgomery and came down occasionally to visit with him. His wife, Betty, was dead, and he lived alone in a house that had never been finished on the inside. It was built of wood and overlaid on the sides with asphalt siding in a brick pattern. The roof was tin, and the floor was concrete. The two-by-four studs of the walls were still exposed inside the house. Many of the areas between the studs were plastered with newspaper or cardboard to help insulate it against the wind. The ceilings had been closed in with large pieces of cardboard. I suppose he never finished it because after his wife died, he had no one to push him to complete the structure. He spent most of his time while inside sitting beside the kitchen table with a radio to keep him company. Before him was an old cast-iron wood-and-coal-fired heater to push the chill away and comfort him on winter days. Many items of daily use were scattered within reach across the old brown table. Always, there was the cake of corn bread on a plate on the table or on top of the heater during the summer months. His water supply was a cistern outside where he drew the water up with a bucket and rope.

A few yards to the east stood the corncrib and a shed or two for stored items and to give shelter to his few chickens. He had no other livestock about during the years I knew him as he had no further need of pigs or milk cows. He no longer planted any of his fifty or so acres of land and had no need of a mule. The land that had once been cultivated was overgrown to a large extent, and much of it had begun to revert to forestland. The exception was the acres Dad farmed in return for a portion of the corn crop he made. The yard around the house was kept relatively free of weeds and brush with the use of a hoe and a swing blade. A very ancient oak tree with massive limbs stood at the front corner of his yard. An aggressive red rooster prowled the yard and kept better watch over the place than most watchdogs could have done. It was the aggressiveness of this rooster that did him in when he chased Larry home one day. Larry was afraid of that rooster, but, as it turned out, the rooster should have been afraid of Larry. I'll get to that later, however.

Cousin Frank was advanced in years, and I cannot account for all the ways he might have used his time. I visited him a lot and listened for hours as he reminisced over old times and told many interesting tales. Many involved pranks he had heard about or been involved in during his youth. There were times when he caught the Greyhound bus and headed to Montgomery for the day. His favorite cigar was a King Edward, which cost five cents each at the small country stores scattered about. He complained mightily when they went to six cents. He usually did not smoke a whole cigar at once; he preferred to economize by making one last through two smoking sessions.

Often, he walked the hundred and fifty yards to Brooks' store, which was the closest neighboring structure to his house.

This somewhat small country store occupied a spot beside Highway 31 at the point where the graveled Tabernacle Road intersected it from the west. Cousin Frank's house was on a hill on the east side of the highway and about three hundred yards from our house to the north.

When Cousin Frank made one of his frequent trips to Brooks' store, he usually purchased only two or three cigars at a time. By not having an overabundance on hand, it probably forced him to smoke a little less and stretch his meager resources. It also allowed him to make more trips to the store for human contact. Often, he walked the nearly half mile to the north past our house to Lassiter's store for cigars or social interaction. Lassiter's store had become Tom Ganey's store by that time.

There were times when I observed Cousin Frank emerge from the woods behind our house and walk up the fence line of our pasture before crossing the barbed wire fence and going back up the wooded hill to his house. On these occasions, he was likely to have a hoe across his shoulder and a few small fish wrapped in a brown paper sack in his hand. He told me he used the hoe to muddy the water of some small hole in a ditch or in Ball Branch. When the water was well muddied, he was often able to scoop out a few small fish that came to the top. He said he cleaned them and ate them whole after frying them. I thought it would have been much better to use a fishing pole and hook to catch larger fish, but I suppose he did that too. I asked about the terrible scars he had on one of his hands, which made it look as if that hand had been split apart in several places. It had indeed been badly injured when a shotgun exploded in his hand as he fired it. Apparently, he had used a shell not designed for that particular gun.

I have often heard the older people referred to this older cousin of mine as "Laughing Frank," obviously, because he liked a practical joke and enjoyed a good laugh following one. At least, if it was at someone else's expense. On one particular day, I sat with him for hours by his kitchen table and in front of the old wood heater as I listened to the retelling of many old stories. On that day, there was a bar of segmented chocolate on a silver foil wrapper next to the usual plate of corn bread on the table. It was obviously displayed by design and presently caught my attention.

"Do you like chocolate?" The twinkle in his eye should have told me something, but I paid it no mind as I bobbed my head that I did like chocolate. He broke off two squares and handed them to me. I ate the chocolate slowly as he continued his stories. After a period of time, he broke off a bit more, handed it to me, and continued the tale he was on. As the day wore on into afternoon, he had fed me several more pieces of the chocolate, and I began to feel uncomfortable. Realizing I might need to go home and visit the outhouse, I began to make my way to the door. He accompanied me to the door, but he managed to stay between the door and me to prevent my leaving too quickly.

Judging my body language correctly, he knew it was time to step aside, and when he did so, I left the house like a rocket! I made it to the shelter of a large bush partly down the hill toward home when my bowels fairly exploded. Eventually, I felt relieved enough to believe I could safely continue my trip down the wooded hill to our pasture fence and home on the hill at the far side of the pasture. I didn't make it! Fortunately, there was another large bush handy, and I took advantage of that fact. I was also fortunate in that the red rooster of Cousin Frank's had not followed me. Either I had left too quickly or he was occupied somewhere else and did not see me run out the door and dash down the hillside. I believe Cousin Frank would have enjoyed the addition of the rooster in his practical joke.

Leaving the refuge of the second bush, I fairly sailed across the barbed wire fence at the base of the hill and ran across the pasture as fast as I could go without losing control of myself again. Having gained the safety of the outhouse, I visited it quickly and many times afterward during the rest of the day. Though I was not positive about the reason for my sudden distress, I became increasingly suspicious during the following few days. I recalled Mama had some chocolate she ate a bit of now and then, and it looked mighty similar to what I had been eating in the hours before the onset of my condition.

After a few days, I went to visit Cousin Frank again, and he invited me in to visit for a spell. He seemed to be in a pretty happy mood as if he were laughing on the inside. Giving me my usual seat between the heater and the table and facing him, he smiled as he unwrapped and punctured his cigar with the wire he kept for the purpose. He watched me all the while as he lit it and knew I was also studying the chocolate still sitting on the open wrapper on the table.

"Want some chocolate?" he asked with a laugh as he nodded in the direction of the table.

By then, I had confirmed my suspicions and had seen the Ex-Lax markings on the wrapper. "No, sir, I don't guess so," I answered.

Laughing Frank? Yeah, it's easy to laugh, I suppose, at someone else's expense.

Being barefoot most of the time when I was young, I learned early to watch where I stepped. Even though the bottom of my feet were as tough as leather, thorns and such still hurt when they managed to penetrate the thick skin. It so happened that I came upon Cousin Frank in his front yard standing on the far side of a large area of gray ashes with a hoe in his hand. The bed of gray ash was ten or twelve feet across. Thinking the ashes might still be hot, I stopped before I got to them.

"It's okay," he said. "They're cold."

Taking him at his word, I continued toward him until the coals under the ash began to burn my feet. A particularly hot coal lodged between my big toe and second toe, and I skipped around a lot before getting out of the ash bed and dislodging the red coal from between my toes.

Laughing Frank laughed again and thought it great fun to see me jumping around like that.

I failed to see the humor in it, and so did my toes. As it turned out, he had cleared the weeds and brush from his yard and piled them up and burned them. It was something he did every year in an attempt to keep as much bare dirt as possible in the yard around his house.

Several years before these events, when the outbuildings of our old house were still in place across the road from our new house, I had a rather frightening experience involving Cousin Frank. Convict labor was used to maintain many of the roadways and rights-of-way along them. It was a common sight to see a gang of men dressed in white prison garb, attended by armed guards, working at one project or another along the roadway. Usually it had to do with grass cutting and brush control. On this day, I had been exploring in the woods around the fields Dad was farming.

As I came back up the wagon path to the garage of the old house site, I saw the gang of convicts working along the road between me and my house on the other side of the road. Darting to a safe location at the corner of the garage, I sneaked peeks around the corner at them. I knew for sure they were all bloodthirsty killers and would very likely kill me too if they happened to see me. I determined to stay hidden and safe until they had moved on down the road. I stayed where I was, hidden by the garage, and kept a close eye on them. Suddenly, I felt a rough hand over my mouth and an arm around me as I was being dragged backward by the person who was about to kill me! The fact that I had been in the process of peeking around the corner at that very moment added to my surprise and terror. Obviously, one of them had sneaked up on me, and I was about to be dead! When the hands let go, I spun around in terror to see Cousin Frank's laughing face. I was added to his list of pranks that day and became another of his funny stories. I accompanied him across the road and made it back home without being murdered and considered myself lucky to still be living.

Cousin Frank did not laugh on the day his rooster died. Nor did he ever laugh, when afterward, he remembered what had happened to his vicious pet rooster that was such a good watchman for his house and property. My brother Larry killed him. The rooster had ventured down the hill through the woods one day and saw Larry across the pasture at our house. He came running across the pasture as if he were bent on destruction but wound up sparring with one of our roosters near the barn. Larry ran inside and got his 410-gauge shotgun Dad had bought for him for Christmas. Expressing the intention to "run him off," Larry miscalculated his shot, hit the rooster in the head, and killed it. He looked in horror at what he had done and lamented, "I only meant to scare him!"

The rooster had begun running back in the direction of his home when Larry fired. The intention was to shoot close enough to the rooster to send him on his way, but Larry rolled the rooster up on the dead run. He had shot in front of the rooster instead of behind it, and the rooster ran directly into the shot.

Larry was pretty badly frightened by what he had done and

decided to hide the rooster. Grabbing it by the feet, he hurled it up onto the top of the barn where the roof began to flatten out. It could be seen perfectly from the direction of Cousin Frank's house, and after a few hours, he discovered it there. However, by the time the dead rooster was found, and the sun having heated the tin up so, it was too late to eat it as the flesh was spoiled.

Confronting Larry later, Cousin Frank bemoaned the loss of his rooster and the fact that Larry had not at least brought it to him to eat. He did not allow Larry to forget the deed for a long time to come. This was no laughing matter! No, Laughing Frank was not laughing. Cousin Frank Anderson never stopped mourning the loss of his vicious pet rooster! He was the only one who mourned though. It was our time to laugh, and we did so whenever the incident came up in our conversations!

30

GRANDMA (MAMA DOWN YONDER)

MY DAD'S mother, Grandma, lived in an old house toward the lower side of our property. This was near the woods through which Ball Branch flowed. That property belonged to Mrs. Ethel Mae Todd and was across the back barbed wire fence about 150 yards behind Grandma's house. Because Grandma's house sat at a slightly lower elevation at the lower end of the pasture, we referred to that location as "down yonder." Dad called her "Mama," and that is how we called her when speaking to her. We also called our mother Mama. To distinguish the two and to keep confusion down when referring to either of them, we often included (as a clarification when we talked) the phrases "Mama down yonder" and "Mama up here." That may seem an odd or quaint way of distinguishing between the two, but it worked for us. Once it was determined which "Mama" we were talking about, the descriptive phrase was dropped as unnecessary in further conversation. So, we always referred to Grandma as "Mama" or "Mama Down Yonder."

Mama's house had been built in the 1800s in a style that had been popular at the time. The basic structure of the house had originally been two rooms with a breezeway separating the two and open to the elements on both ends. This was often referred to as a "dog trot-style" house, and the open hallway between the two rooms was referred to as a breezeway or dog trot. The house was heated by a fireplace in each of the two main rooms. The kitchen had originally been separate from the house. I suppose that was partly for safety reasons and partly to keep the house cooler in the summer. However, later, a sloped ceiling addition had been made to the backside of the house to accommodate a small kitchen and an additional bedroom. This also had the effect of extending the breezeway for eight more feet and provided a small dining area. A small screened porch was added to accommodate the various potted plants Mama liked to have. The addition on the back of the house had also closed off the breezeway on that side of the house. The opening on the front was also closed in at that time, and a large covered wooden porch was added to the front side and ran the forty-foot length of the house. This porch contained several rocking chairs and was shaded by two very large oak trees.

The house was hedged about by various bushes and fencing to keep the cows out of the yard. Pastureland surrounded the house on the front and two sides with a large vegetable garden behind it. The whole affair presented both a cottage-like and an "old-timey" appearance. Behind the house stood the brick curbing of the covered well that supplied the house with water. This was a true well and was fed from cool, underground water. A bucket and rope hung there, ready to bring up the water. The water was particularly good compared to the brackish water of our cistern. Also, on the back side of the house, stood the smokehouse and a shed for the chickens and stored items. Between the acre-sized vegetable garden and the small backyard were several fruit trees. There were plum, apple, fig, and pear trees. A large scuppernong arbor was just inside the garden with an outhouse between the garden and the back of the house.

Mama's outhouse had gotten pretty dilapidated. Dad was devoted to his mother and thought it was time to build her an outhouse she could be proud of. The old one just would not do for his mother any longer. Securing the necessary bricks and mortar, he laid the foundation of the new outhouse near the old one by the scuppernong vine. Using new lumber left over from the building of Uncle Charles's house, he constructed an outhouse anyone would have been proud to own. Rather than a door, an opening was left on the front side with a baffle-type partition to provide privacy and shielded the entry from the cold north wind in winter. Dad painted it a brilliant white on the inside as well as the exterior. The seat platform was elegantly made and finished out with a store-bought commode seat. A toilet paper holder was mounted on the wall to the left, and a bottle of turpentine was placed on a shelf in the eventuality a wasp might catch her unawares and sting her. The floor was smooth concrete. Being so well ventilated, the outhouse promised to be a low-odor affair as well as being cool in the summer.

I don't suppose anyone else in our community ever had such a nice outhouse as Mama, but it was not complete until Dad and I had poured a two-foot-wide sidewalk from the steps coming from Mama's screened back porch and extending the full forty feet to the outhouse. She did not have to worry about getting her feet wet from the dew or rain. Though I was young, I had done my part in helping Dad mix the cement in the wheelbarrow and pour the walkway. When I heard the story behind the building of the Taj Mahal and the love that inspired that structure, it was not hard for me to grasp the reason why Dad had built something so nice for his mother. For me, it therefore became the "Taj Mahal." It was with regret that I removed it many years later when I had inherited the site and renovated the house that had fallen into disrepair. I have always regretted my having removed what my dad had so lovingly built for his mother.

Mama's name was Daisy Brady. She had been born an Anderson. Her mother was Anne McPherson. These surnames have been fixtures in this area from the time the land was acquired from the Indians. The McPhersons were somewhat well-to-do and accomplished in years gone by. The name is most commonly associated with black residents now, which might serve as an indicator of the history of the McPherson family. Mama never knew that her family line through the Andersons included an ancestor who came over on the *Mayflower* and settled in the New World. His name was Edward Doty. Mama's husband, who I never knew as a grandpa, was Shilton Uriah Brady of a large clan of landholding Bradys in the hilly Mt. Carmel community several miles to the southeast. I never knew any of these things about her family history when I was young. It didn't matter anyway. She was just "Mama Down Yonder," Dad's mama, and she lived down yonder, alone, toward the lower end of the pasture. That's all I knew about her at the time.

She lived alone because her children were grown and gone to other places. They were now scattered over the state, country, and world. Only Lewis, my dad, lived on the place now with his large brood of children, livestock, and chickens. He watched over his mama and kept her place going as a dutiful son. I knew her as one who did no unnecessary talking and commanded respect. She dressed plainly, in layers, and always protected herself from the effects of the sun. On several occasions, she scolded me gently for being in the sun without protecting my head. She would quickly make a hat of newspaper and put it on my head. If she did not have newspaper, she substituted a brown paper bag. I only wore those hats until I was out of sight and could safely abandon them.

My oldest sister, Daisy Anne, married a member of the air force and was sent to Turkey with her husband who had been transferred there. They owned a television set and decided to leave it with Mama while they were overseas. This turned out to be a treat for us as well because we did not have a television. It quickly became a weekly part of our routine to walk down to her house on Friday evenings for several hours of excitement. The six youngest of us showed up at her house around six-thirty and were allowed to watch television until ten o'clock at night. We filed into the room very quietly and sat in a semicircle in front of the television. We were always still and quiet and never let our excitement get the best of us. Mama would not have tolerated it. We did not want to lose the privilege of coming down for these special gatherings. I think she enjoyed the company too since she was always alone. It was an excited and satisfied group of children who made the journey home in the dark when ten o'clock came around. Sometimes it would be a pell-mell dash back to the house for the pleasure of hearing the stragglers crying out not to be left behind in the dark with God knows what creature or ghost. Mama had not shown us any affection during our visit as it was not her way to display it. Later, I realized she showed it through her allowing us to remain there so late into the night each week. It was her way of extending to us a very special kindness and demonstrating feelings she would not give voice to.

Once, Betty sassed Mama, and that was a mistake! Being disrespectful or talking back was next to a mortal sin in that time. She was well reminded of it before the day was over. Several of us had perched ourselves on the top strand of the barbed wire pasture fence about forty yards from Mama's house and were causing the already sagging wire to be in danger of pulling loose from the old posts. Mama appeared on the front porch and called out for us to get off the fence.

Betty, the oldest, muttered an inappropriate response she supposed Mama could not hear. She supposed wrong.

"What's that you said, Betty?" she called out. "I'll be speaking with your daddy about this when he comes home."

Betty may have assumed Mama was forgetful and deaf, but she came to regret those assumptions before the sun went down that day. In the late afternoon, Dad and I came out of the garden behind Mama's house, only to be stopped as we rounded the front side of the house during our trip home.

Mama was waiting on the front porch and called out, "Lewis, I want to speak with you." After he had stopped under the shade of one of the large oak trees, he began to hear the account of what had transpired.

Asking the question, "What did she say, Mama?" he reached up and pulled down a small branch from the tree. Listening to her response, he began to cut the branch with his pocketknife. While they continued their conversation, he fashioned a finger-thick, three-foot-long implement of punishment.

"I'll take care of it, Mama," he said as he bid her goodbye and turned for home. I followed at his heels, feeling very relieved she had not implicated anyone other than Betty in the crime. The sitting on the fence had become an unimportant issue and was not a punishable offense anyway. Sassing and talking back to Mama was likely to get Betty killed! Walking up the slight rise into the backyard, I could hear the playing and laughter of the other children in the house.

Concealing the trimmed limb behind him, Dad called out, "Betty! Betty! Come out here. I have something for you!"

My sister ran out the door toward Dad as the word "What?" was exploding from her lips.

"This," Dad announced loudly as he grabbed her arm and brought the heavy switch out from behind his back and began to apply it forcefully.

Betty screamed and jumped about as our very angry father continued the whipping for quite some time. All the while, Dad was reminding her of the severity of what she had done. It was not accidental the punishment had taken place at that particular spot in the backyard. That Dad had carried out his duty to Mama and to Betty could be clearly seen and heard at Mama's house. The deterrent value of the punishment was not lost on the rest of us, and we were quite subdued for some time to come. The rod of correction had certainly done its work in driving any urge out of our minds to sass a grown-up. Especially, Mama Down Yonder!

When I got old enough to do so, I began going down to Mama's house on Thursday afternoons and drawing her well water for her. She had begun filling various crocks with water inside her kitchen to supply indoor needs for several days. She had gotten to the point where she could not draw the water herself, and I had started helping draw a supply for her each week. I was very happy to be able to do it for her, and she always had a homemade cookie or some treat to give me in return. She often commented, "You look like your daddy did at your age," or "You are just like your daddy." I knew she was thinking back in time and meant the comments as affectionate compliments. It made me feel good she should compare me with him. On Saturday mornings, I took her short list of needs to Brooks' store and spent a couple of hours watching television as I waited for the bread truck to arrive with fresh bread. She wanted her bread right off the truck while it was practically still warm. It made me feel special she trusted me to do those things.

Mama's house always felt cool inside on summer days. I suppose the big oaks protecting it from the sun were the reason. It had a soft, sweet smell of vanilla and also of the cold cream she used on her face. The breezeway of the house had been closed in and formed a narrow room in the middle of the house and was decorated with interesting keepsakes. There was a table with dishes containing bird eggs of different sizes and colors. Several odd chicken eggs that were abnormally small or large were included in the display. The small handmade settee fashioned by a former slave as a gift to her was placed in an inviting spot just inside the door. It was of split white oak and fastened together in the manner of homemade furniture with small nails, pegs, and thin wrapping strands of oak. The settee had been painted yellow and black, and its seat and back were covered with delicate cushions. This was one of her prized possessions and had been given to her as a young girl by the former slave remembered only by his last name, Palmer.

A very large shellacked gourd occupied a visible spot so the unusual quality of it could be seen by anyone who visited. It was shaped like an eighteen-inch fig and was given to her by her son Frank who had prepared it for her as a container for her knitting or sewing. The polished bony head of a garfish with its long, spiny, beak-like mouth sat on a shelf along with a Civil War cannonball someone had brought home so many years before. There were oval, bubble-glassed frames that contained the portraits of her mother, Anne McPherson, and of Mama's brothers who had already departed this world. They represented, to me, some of the ghosts of the house. Only Mama's brother Dr. Benjamin Franklin Anderson was still alive at the time. Mama's mother, Anne, had died in this house as had my great-grandpapa, Frank Goff Anderson. I don't know who else, but I'm sure there were others.

Grandma had a woolen buggy blanket and a story to tell about it. More than a hundred years old at present, it is now in the possession of my son who is three generations further removed from Mama's time. The blanket helped keep her children warm on the winter day when she drove her buggy from Mt. Carmel to come back home to continue her life in residence with her parents. She never went back to the hills at Mt. Carmel or to her husband, but she raised her children in this house.

I am sitting in a small room of that old house now, though I have changed the house somewhat since it became mine nearly forty years ago. It had become water damaged, termite eaten, and near collapse after so many generations, but I have repaired it and restored it to a livable condition. The basic structure of the original house remains as a part of the present structure. A few of the original furnishings still occupy their places in the house to keep company with the abundance of memories contained within its walls. The added-on, sloped ceiling extension that served as a kitchen and small bedroom was removed and built back in a larger form. A large kitchen and dining area as well as a bathroom are now included in that extension. Also, the small study that serves as my private place and was described early in this narrative is there. Three steps lead down from this extension of the house to a large added sunporch. The well and a portion of the walkway to the outhouse were removed to accommodate it. As the Taj Mahal, Mama's outhouse, had gotten so dilapidated, I felt compelled to remove it along with the rest of the two-foot wide walkway that no longer served a purpose. On the south end of the original house, I have added a large bedroom and a second bath as well. Three steps also lead down into this addition.

Mama would be surprised if she saw her house now. Somehow, I don't think she would feel any disappointment though. The toilet facilities are inside now, and there is running water, both hot and cold. There is no need any more to fill all those crocks every week or break the skim of ice on top of them in the wintertime. There is electric and gas heat as well as a gas stove. I, too, miss the house as it was, but I think Mama Down Yonder would be pleased with the changes. The original structure, unchanged, still exists in my mind along with its accompanying memories. In that sense, it will always be here as long as I exist.

Sunday afternoon with friends. Daisy
Anderson (Grandmama), far right.

Daisy Anderson Brady ("Mama Down Yonder"), about 1970.

31

THE MAN IN THE LOFT

THE MAN in the Loft was not a member of our family, but he lived with us. He seemed to have firmly ensconced himself as a part of the house if not the household. He secretly moved in with us one day and took up residence in our attic. There, he was to remain for many years, never seen, but often heard. It was Betty, the sixth from the bottom in order of age, who first realized the presence of this uninvited and unwelcome guest. We had been living in the new house on the site of the old potato patch for three or four years before his presence was discovered.

The six younger children had gone for a day of play and adventure around the pine hills and bottomland where Dad planted his crops. There were no adults at home on this day, and it was Betty's duty as the oldest to look after the younger children. As always, we were full of energy as we played in the pine thickets and weed-infested bottoms that made up a large part of our known world. The summers being hot in Alabama, it was only natural we would become thirsty after a few hours of nonstop activity. As the sun moved overhead and the temperature climbed, we became keenly aware of our mistake in failing to bring along a jug of water.

Someone said, "I'm thirsty," and another said, "Me too." The condition was duly noted and quickly ratified by all. The need for water having been clearly established by unanimous complaint, the assignment fell to Betty to return home and bring a gallon of water back from the well. As she left, we encouraged her to hurry since we were getting awfully thirsty.

Passing through the scattered broom straw and weeds at the edge of the bottom, she moved up the wagon path through the pines and sweet gums toward home. We drifted ever deeper into the shade of our favorite sweet gum tree to continue our play until she had returned. There, on the flat clay ground under the sweet gum tree's low-hanging branches and surrounded by a fringe of weeds and low brush, we continued our activities and waited for the water. Very soon, we were disappointed in our expectation of water by the speedy return of a breathless sister. However, our thirst was completely forgotten when Betty delivered the report that both excited and terrified us.

There was someone in the house! No, she had not seen the person, she said, but she had heard him when she went inside for the jar for the water. It didn't matter at that point that she came back without the water. We had forgotten all about that anyway. We fearfully inquired of each other, "What are we going to do?" He might have followed Betty and at that very moment be closing in on us!

Amid the ducking and shushing that followed, we studied Betty's back trail. We took heart in the absence of any strange presence or noise of anyone approaching from that direction. Perhaps, realizing his discovery, he had already fled the house and disappeared. We began to find a degree of comfort in that thought. How were we to know for sure unless someone was to investigate? There was no grown-up about to give us a hand in the matter. We certainly could not stay here all day with nothing to eat or drink!

Our best solution was to confront the invader ourselves, through our strength of numbers. After all, there were six of us, even though a somewhat small six. The trick would be to stick close together and protect each other as we entered the house and made our search. Should we confront the stranger, that strength of numbers should be enough to frighten him into leaving the house. It would be even better if we could convince the intruder we were the police. Everyone agreed that was the thing to do, and we began to practice our police commands until we were sure that anyone would be fooled. Our plan having been formulated, we completed our cautious trip up the wagon trail toward home.

Tentatively approaching the house, we began marshaling the courage it would take for us to push open the back door and make our entry. No one wanted to be first, so we all entered in a knot armed with brooms and anything else that was handy and available as weapons. We knew we would be safer if we stayed together, so we shuffled through the house in what appeared a close approximation of a rugby scrum. Holding, pushing, and jostling for a secure position, it was only the combined strength of our legs that propelled us forward. In the deepest, high-pitched voices we could generate, we put on our best exhibition of a force to be reckoned with.

"We are the police!" we announced. "Give yourself up. You are outnumbered, and the house is surrounded!"

Perhaps our announcement startled someone for there was a slight noise somewhere in the depths of the shadows before us. With shrieks and shouts of alarm, our scrum came apart and reversed course to the door. The knot reformed at the door as we all tried to exit at once. The policemen were in full retreat!

Brooms and other weapons were left behind. Murder was surely about to occur, and none of us wanted to be the first victim. Somehow, we made it out and withdrew to a secure location until afternoon. We would have to wait a while, but it would be a lot safer to enter the house when Dad got home.

With the increased courage the presence of adults can inspire, we made a thorough search of the closets and inspected the dark recesses under the beds. The cedar robe was opened and inspected. We knew all the hiding places well, as we had used them ourselves, and we were careful not to overlook any one of them. He was gone, yet we felt in the back of our minds he really was not gone and was aware of our every move.

From time to time, we inspected the hiding places in the days to come, but we never succeeded in our searches to locate his hiding place. We continued to speculate among ourselves as to where this intruder may have secreted himself. Eventually, we came to a conclusion, in common, that he had withdrawn into the recesses of our dark attic. We never called it an attic, of course, and only knew it as "the loft." It made perfect sense to us as the only explanation as to why we had not discovered him.

The loft was accessed through a removable panel in the hallway ceiling near the center of the house. It would have been so easy for him to have reached up, pushed the panel back, and then hoisted himself up through the opening and replaced the panel. Perhaps he had been there all along, and we had never suspected. Maybe he had been in the house for a long time before Betty had made the discovery. He could have been there for months or years! That could explain the frequent noises we had heard in times past that sounded like mice running across the uninsulated ceiling that formed the floor of the loft. It was the logical explanation for items that were not in their usual places or had turned up missing. We had been in the loft many times exploring the dark recesses and areas around the chimneys in our play, and we knew that he must now have concealed himself there. There were piles of old clothes he could have buried himself under.

I began making repeated, tentative trips into the loft in fruitless searches to locate him, but I knew he could easily have slipped from one dim hiding place to another. After all, I could not see everywhere at once.

He was a large man with cadaverous features and a slouch hat. That is how I saw him in my mind countless times as months and even years went by. He was crafty and stealthy and was able to survive for those years without any of us actually seeing him, but he was there. He was as real as any member of the family who could be seen or touched. Only the slight sounds gave his presence away. He was most active when one of us would be in the house alone or during the night when everyone was in bed. Oftentimes, I heard him in my sleep and woke with a start and lay there listening and afraid this would be the time he would appear before my eyes and that would be the end of me!

I never passed the access hatch to the loft in the darkened central hall of the house without looking up to confirm it was in place. Sometimes I thought I saw it move slightly as if someone had been watching the goings on down below. Occasionally, the hatch was left open from a recent exploration. My skin crawled as I passed under it! Such passing required keeping my eyes firmly fixed on it so I would not be taken unawares. Nighttime trips to relieve myself or getting to bed after everyone else had retired were especially bad. He was always nearby, watching, and I could feel his presence. He had the remarkable ability to always remain on the side of me in the dark where I was not looking. Someday I would be able to turn fast enough to see him though. That thought brought me no comfort, only terror.

The six youngest of our family had these similar experiences, and we shared our fears with each other. After we got older, those fears and experiences began to lessen. One by one, we grew up, married, and moved out. The day came when there were no more children left at home. The Man in the Loft was left alone and without purpose in the Brady household. He needed to move on too, move on to some other dark haunt and to some renewed purpose. His special talent of producing the whispering movements and slight bumps in the darkness of night would have been wasted had he remained. The adults left there would likely have misinterpreted the sounds as scurrying mice or structural shifting of the house. It was time to move on and make his presence known to other children. He had done his job well in the Brady house and would never be forgotten. Thanks for the scary nights, the heart-stopping moments, and the memories, Man in the Loft, but please don't come back anymore!

32

DAVID: THE
CONFIDENT ONE

DAVID MASSEY became one of my closest friends. He moved into our community from Montgomery at an early age. His daddy was a general contractor, and his mother was a housewife. His sister, Judy, was a year or so older than me while his older brother, George, was a number of years older than me. My first introduction to David was not face-to-face, but rather, from hearing his voice in a thicket of young pines from which I had fled a minute or two earlier. The sound of the strange voices of unknown people approaching us had frightened Larry, Phillip, and me into abandoning our log cabin idea.

Our log cabin idea came about from a mutual desire to visit the frontier days we had recently become interested in. Frontier times and log cabins sounded really adventurous. Phillip, a friend from church and school, said he knew how to do it. Build a log cabin, that is. His daddy had built a small garage out of skinned pine logs, and he had seen him do it. All we needed was an ax, a hatchet, and a saw, he said, and a thicket of smaller pine trees. We had all of that available to us, so we set about to build us a real frontier log cabin. The thick stand of young pines stood right behind the old garage and corncrib where our house had been before the fire. We chose a spot in the middle of the stand of young pines and began cutting them down with the ax. We had not gotten very far into the operation when we heard the voices of people approaching the spot where we were. We did not know who the voices belonged to as they were strange to us. They were coming from the direction of the house on the other side of the pine thicket that had been vacant for some time now. Hearing the voices took us by surprise, and the prospect of being discovered by strangers was frightening to us. The tree cutting came to a quick end, and we fled from the pine thicket.

Our tools and red wagon were left behind in our panic to get away. We may have begun our adventure imagining ourselves as brave frontiersmen, but at that moment, we could not have been described as such. The voices we heard might as well have belonged to wild Indians because we took to our heels and ran! We ran and hid in the nearest place we could think of. That place was in the hay piled inside the shed next to the old corncrib. Larry and Philip were bigger and faster than me and got to the shed first. They crawled up the pile of hay to the back of the shed and looked out the cracks between the boards at the strange people gathered at our building site about thirty yards away. I couldn't see since I was behind the two bigger boys in the hay, but I could hear the voices clearly. From the safety of the hay shed, I listened in alarm at the exchange between the small boy I could not see and his father.

"Can I keep the wagon?" he asked.

I was relieved when his Daddy said no. We had not gotten far along in our cabin building. As a matter of fact, we had only cleared a small circle of young pines and began trimming their limbs off when we had been frightened away. We listened as the man and woman who I could not see talked about the situation and how they had obviously frightened some children away. I could hear the voices of a young boy and girl. I heard laughter from the man and then the sound of the voices receding as they were disappearing in the direction of the house on the other side of the pines. We stayed in the hay until all was quiet again and scrambled down and retreated to our house on the other side of the road. We came back later in the afternoon for our wagon and tools and scrapped the idea of building the little log cabin.

Nearly sixty years after this event, I think back to the time when I first heard the voice of the boy who would later become one of my closest friends and almost constant companion. This closeness continued until I was in my upper teen years and the circumstances of life dictated that we would go separate ways. I saw him again when I was nineteen and had come home on leave after military training. He had been spending a lot of time in Louisiana where he later moved, married, and raised his family.

The Masseys were rich people—or so we thought at the time. Mr. Massey had taken the modest concrete block house just down the road from us and transformed it into a brick, ranch-style house. He added a second floor above a large portion of the house, complete with an added two-car garage as a part of the lower floor. He then installed a swimming pool behind the house. The rambling brick house and accompanying pool were impressive and unique in our rural community. As I got older, I often swam in the pool with David's family and occasionally stayed the night with them. Most of our time, however, was spent in playing at our house or off in the woods and countryside.

We first became acquainted on the school bus. Each morning, we could see David and Judy waiting at the end of their driveway for the bus. Our driveway was a hundred yards away from theirs, and we waved at one another and often shouted back and forth until the bus came. We were not used to new people in our rural community, and it took a little time to forge the close relationship that developed. Most of the families and children we knew had firm ancestral ties to our area. Many of these families were distantly related to us, even though we were not aware of it at the time. The Masseys were town folk and outsiders but soon established themselves in our community and in our hearts.

David was of fair complexion and sandy-haired. He was slightly shorter than me but carried himself with an air of confidence. I don't think I ever saw David in a bashful moment, nor was he loud or cocky. He just seemed to be self-assured and willing to take advantage of the moment and whatever life sent his way. His sister, Judy, was dark-haired and of a light olive complexion. George, the older brother, was in his teen years when this family came to be our neighbors. He was an interesting person we seldom interacted with since he was older than we were and had other interests.

George spent at least some of his time helping his daddy in his business interests. From time to time, we were all entertained as George roared past the house on his motorcycle. It was a Harley-Davidson 165 and had the deep, rumbling sound older motorcycles were known for. Sometimes, he wore a pair of goggles of a type that people had worn in an earlier time. They gave him a very comical appearance when he really put on the full show. This show consisted of his laying prone on the motorcycle with his head between the handlebars and his legs stretched out behind. As he roared past the house, there was no way to miss the big grin on his face. Continuing up the road, he assumed a seated position and threw up his hand in a parting wave. Dad would often chuckle and comment, "He looks like a big owl coming straight at you with those goggles on!"

As the relationship between David and I began to grow, we began spending a lot of time together. There were the usual childhood games with my brother and sisters which sometimes involved Judy as well. We played cowboys and Indians and also became explorers or frontiersmen. We included chickens, cats, cows, and other creatures in our play, which made their lives a bit miserable at times.

As we got older, swimming in the various ponds and in the creek was a favorite pastime. We scavenged for old inner tubes that could be patched and used in our swimming in the local ponds. Two or three tubes lashed together and covered with wood made good rafts or pirate ships to do battle from. We were pretty imaginative in our play, and it often proved to be learning experiences for us.

One day, I had a notion to dive into the water with a hunting knife clenched between my teeth. It was something pirates and seamen did all the time. I knew because I had seen it myself in book illustrations and in the movies. My intention was to come up under David's raft and cut the burlap bindings holding the inner tubes together. I could push the raft apart and put him in the water! The operations never got beyond the diving phase.

As I dove into the water, the tip of the knife blade stuck me in the left bicep. My teeth grated on the metal of the blade, and the corners of my mouth felt as if they were being torn apart. As I crawled out of the water onto the pond bank, I examined my injured arm. The knife lay on the ground where I had thrown it after surfacing from my dive. I did not like the feel of the metal grating between my teeth and was determined not to suffer that tooth-crumbling sensation again. The corners of my mouth were awfully sore for some time. The bleeding from my arm soon stopped, and I could see the puncture was not as deep as I had feared. How did the pirates do it, and how was it done in the movies without these kinds of things happening? They did it just fine and smooth as silk and didn't get hurt in the process.

I pondered this question a number of times afterward and eventually came to the conclusion I had been hoodwinked. Diving into the water with a big knife blade clenched between the teeth was one of those make-believe things from books and movies that does not translate well into reality. To be sure, while I had been defeated in my aims to disable David's raft, I still came out a winner of sorts. I had learned a lesson that has never been forgotten and cataloged it along with other facts I had stored. Through day-to-day existence, by simply surviving adventures, I seemed to be getting a bit smarter as I accumulated facts. Facts accumulated from events that I and others had somehow survived: People really can't fly, no matter how much will and imagination they have. Umbrellas do not make good parachutes. Fire walking is not really a good idea, even if the feet are tough. You can wrap rope around a sister as many times as you want before snatching it really hard, but you can't make a sister spin like a top. You just produce a howling and bruised sister. I'm not sure how many more things like these David and I tested together, but I know there were a lot.

Hot Rod Hill was a place well known to us and one of our favorite places to play. It was a steep hillside just across from our south pasture fence and was on Cousin Frank Anderson's property. The hill was forested with old hardwood trees all the way down to our pasture fence. It was the perfect place for us to lay out trails on which we could coast our "hot rods" down the hillside. The three trails began as one but diverged partway down the hill and followed different routes to the pasture fence. Two of the trails crossed each other about halfway down, and we took advantage of this fact in our "knockout contests." The trails were cleaned of leaves or debris that would slow us down, and we raced each other down the hillside or attempted to knock each other off the course or into one of the trees around which the trails were laid out. It was good that no adult ever witnessed what we were doing or one of our favorite pastimes would have been outlawed. We were always on the lookout for new wheels from which to construct our hot rods, and no trash pile in the community was overlooked in our search. We always had two or three hot rods constructed at any given time. One day, a search turned up a treasure that almost proved a disaster for David and me.

Among the trash in a refuse pile in the woods belonging to the Venables, we found the remains of a motorcycle. The rubber of the tires was dried and cracked, but we decided to see if we could resurrect them and create the ultimate downhill hot rod. We came back later with the tools needed to remove them and soon had possession of the wheels. We took the wheels to Brooks' store, which was close by and "aired" the tires. To our delight, they both held air, and we began designing our new hot rod. Two small bicycle wheels were found, which would serve as our front wheels, and we could use the large, heavy motorcycle wheels for the back. Suitable rods were found or were removed from our other contraptions that could be used as axles.

Soon, we had a real beauty constructed! It was nearly eight feet long due to the long timber that connected the two sets of wheels together. Far back and between the large back wheels was the passenger seat, and just in front of it was the driver's seat. Both seats were boards nailed to the timber connecting the front and back wheels. Footrests were installed for both riders, and a rope was attached to a board between the front wheels for steering on a downhill run or for pulling it uphill. When we had finished, we looked at it with justifiable pride. It was a masterpiece! This vehicle certainly demanded a much better course to run than Hot Rod Hill. This one needed a hill on an open road due to its size and obvious speed potential. We knew the perfect place: Tabernacle Road.

Tabernacle Road intersects the highway at Brooks' store and travels west behind the store and crosses the Blowout about half a mile away. At the store, where the road begins, it has a dramatic descent for about a hundred yards and a more gradual incline for another hundred or more yards before leveling off in its journey northwesterly. It was maintained well by the county, and its graveled surface was as hard and nearly as smooth as concrete on the downhill portion. Being only lightly traveled, it would be the perfect place to put our new racer through its paces.

A couple of trips down the steep roadway were an unparalleled success. It was great! We had never coasted so fast before. It seemed we could make it halfway to the Blowout before coming to a stop. As we were preparing to make another run down the hill, a school bus carrying black students home from school turned off from the highway onto Tabernacle Road. This was the perfect time for us to show off a bit, and we were not inclined to waste it. As the bus passed us, we maneuvered ourselves into position behind it and began trailing it down the hill. I was in the front position with David seated on the seat behind me between the motorcycle tires. He was wearing his Penn State-style football helmet and had a firm grip on both of my shoulders. The black kids seemed impressed as they gathered at the back glass to witness this unusual event. More and more faces appeared at the back window of the bus with everyone waving and grinning. At the moment, we were the two proudest white kids on the planet, and we grinned back and continued to trail the bus. Nobody had such a fine contraption as this, and we were overjoyed to have a whole busload of witnesses!

Suddenly, I noticed the faces gathered at the bus's back windows were getting closer at an alarming rate. We were gaining on the bus, and it appeared the driver was slowing the bus to see what all the excitement was about. We were going too fast, I realized. If I didn't turn, we would soon go under the back end of the bus! If I turned at that speed, we would probably flip. I didn't relish the idea of sliding down a hard, graveled surface and having the hide ripped off me. If I turned, but didn't flip, we likely would be shredded by the tight barbed wire fence that bordered the road. I determined to hold steady and hope that we would begin losing speed before going under the bus. This didn't seem to be going as well as I had hoped, and I was beginning to wish I didn't have so many witnesses. Some of the faces began to turn away from the window glass as their owners appeared to begin shouting to the driver about our predicament.

Suddenly, the bus picked up speed, and it began to pull away just as the front wheels of our racer began to go under its back bumper. We finally coasted to a stop, and the bus disappeared across the Blowout bridge. The event proved more exciting than we could have anticipated and one we never wanted to repeat. It was something else we had survived and learned from. This proved to be a good example of what I've often heard. *Anything that doesn't kill you, you can learn from.* David and I were continually advancing our education and, somehow, surviving. I've often wondered how the kids on the bus told the story!

We began building tree houses together, and there were a number of them scattered about. One of them was pretty big and was constructed on the limbs of the most massive oak tree around. One of the supporting limbs also served as a sort of sidewalk for us. It stretched for quite a distance out from the tree trunk before it dipped to about eight feet from the ground. We put our ladder against it at this point. The thicker portion of this limb was probably close to three feet in diameter. After we got used to the height, we were able to walk and even run along it as comfortably as on a sidewalk. It was good to have such a nice place to go to and be alone or be with others, whatever the time and situation dictated. We could lay in a good supply of watermelons or cantaloupes from the garden, which we did. We raided the garden and stole a pile of them! We weren't really stealing them, but it fit in with our play to call these "raids." Dad actually planted them so we could enjoy them, but it was more exciting to "steal" them.

Being a couple of hundred yards from any of the surrounding houses, our tree house was the perfect location to smoke the tobacco we kept on hand. We had learned to make pipes out of bamboo and roll cigarettes as well. Later, we learned how to make "Indian cigars" out of the sixteen-inch catalpa beans that grew on the catalpa trees. They were cut into desired lengths and laid out to turn brown as the sun dried them a couple of days. We then smoked them if we had no tobacco, but tobacco was much better than catalpa bean cigars.

From time to time, David was not around, and I might find myself alone for a day or two. I really did not have a big problem with that since I had a pretty active imagination and a willingness to use it. I built a tree house in a large pine tree behind the house and close to the barn and pigpen. This was a personal space and gave me a place to be alone and read a book or imagine other adventures. One day, on a search of the barn for building materials or any other interesting things, I came across the remains of an umbrella. I recognized the potential of it and began construction of a parachute. With a little bit of time and a good amount of hay string, I produced a parachute I was sure I could use.

Looking up into my pine tree, I saw a limb very high up

that had no real obstructing limbs between it and the ground. I climbed up to it with my newly constructed apparatus with the intention of trying it out. All I would have to do was to grasp the ends of the strings in both hands and jump. It would be a matter of just floating to the ground. I could see myself floating down and was anxious to give it a try. The ground, though, looked a long way down, and I began to wonder if the chute would work as well in reality as it did in my mind. *It wouldn't hurt to test it first,* I thought. *As a matter of fact, that would be the wise thing to do.* Later, I was relieved that my mind had taken a more scientific approach to the affair. Leaving the chute high up in the tree, I climbed down for a brick to take my place as a test subject.

Climbing back up to the jumping-off limb, I fastened the brick onto the strings of my parachute. Holding the chute out by its upper point and letting the brick dangle, I let go. The brick dropped fast with the parachute streaming behind like a kite's tail and hit the ground with a thud. I don't know what I did wrong, but I know it should have worked. I was suddenly relieved it was a brick down there on the ground and not me. On that day, my own imagination had laid another trap for me, but I had somehow avoided it. It may well be so that we each have a guardian angel watching over us and intervening at such times. If this is true, mine was a busy angel!

We dug tunnels a lot. David was there, along with my sisters Betty, Sharron, Sandra, and Dianne, and our brother Larry. We dug a large hole first, and then we dug a tunnel into the wall on one side of the hole. Afterward, we constructed another tunnel on a different side of the hole. Soon we had tunnels in different directions, each with chambers large enough to sit up in. The soil was damp and cool, and the interior of our chambers was much cooler than the outside air. We began congregating at this place from time to time at night and building a fire. Now and then, we would have some weenies or marshmallows to roast.

The tunnels eventually began collapsing from the weight of the cows walking above them, and we had to finish collapsing them and fill them in. Dad worried a cow might break a leg there at some point. Today, two large pine trees grow near this spot. As an adult, I enclosed this area as a part of our family cemetery. Any holes that may be dug there now will have a much more somber purpose than in our childhood. The grave markers in the cemetery are creeping ever closer to the spot we once knew as "the tunnels" and where we held our weenie roasts and frightened each other with scary stories.

Across the pasture fence on the north side is the property that once belonged to my great-uncle Claude Anderson, Grandma's brother. On a low-lying, but prominent hill near the fence, there was an ancient cemetery. By the time I came along, the old wooden markers had long since disappeared. Dad had even planted okra and other vegetables on this hill for a time while it was still a possession of our family. When the Todd family bought the property from Aunt Clara Anderson, the old cemetery site became another of our playgrounds and an excavation ground as well. David and I, along with the Todd boys, began digging there.

First, we dug for bones, but we had no luck in finding any. Next, we expanded our diggings into very large foxholes complete with burlap sandbags. We fought wars between these fortified positions and staged frequent assaults up the hill and "took" these fortifications from each other. Sometimes, we were Rough Riders charging San Juan Hill, and at other times, we were Germans dying on the hillside until we had to swap sides and become soon-to-be-dying Germans.

It was David who was able to produce the firecrackers, bottle rockets, and cherry bombs that made things more realistic. Wet clay was molded around firecrackers and cherry bombs and the sun dried them for a couple of days to make grenades. Bottle rockets were set up along the sandbags in a row and fired as the enemy advanced up the hill. The grenades were fearsome and were effective in stopping an advance. The hard clay fragments of the grenades really hurt when they hit someone. Somehow, we all managed to grow up still having both eyes intact, which was a testament to our good luck or to the hard work of our guardian angels.

We often divided our forces at night and set up different encampments. We made tents or other shelters and built our fires and sat down to plan raids on each other's camps. We continued until late in the night when exhaustion or someone's parents declared it was time to stop. For several years, David and I were almost always together. Whatever games we played and conflicts we fought, we were on the same side.

One day, Danny, a neighborhood friend, was crying, and Dad was laughing. Danny had fresh horse manure in his mouth. He was in the kitchen washing out his mouth at the sink when I came through the back door.

Dad sat in his chair in the living room with his newspaper in his lap still laughing at what he had heard.

"Mr. Brady," Danny had cried out as he ran into the house, "David and Allen threw fresh horse manure into my mouth!"

"Go wash it out," Dad told him, recognizing the humor in the situation. He was not one to intervene unless the goings-on jeopardized life or limb. Tattling was not really approved of either. Children were expected to work out or settle their own disagreements.

We had been having another of our little wars we often had. In this one, the ammunition consisted of fresh horse manure.

We were in the barn and engaged in all-out combat with the inexhaustible supply available to us. Danny was advancing on David with a handful of manure and laughing with his mouth wide open when David hit him square in the mouth with a wet "muffin" of his own. The duel was over quickly as Danny ran crying for the house. It was a shot in a million! I don't remember a corncob fight or a rotten egg fight that ever ended in such a beautiful fashion. There was no harm actually done. Danny eventually got his mouth cleaned out and was none the worse for the experience. He learned to keep his mouth shut in a horse manure fight too.

The smell of chlorine was something new to me. It was an odor I came to associate with the Masseys' swimming pool. Water I was used to had been the brackish water from our cistern or the water in ponds, branches, or creeks. That water was often discolored and usually had sour or fishy odors. Ponds were often cooling-off places for livestock and contained a fair amount of their waste. The edges of these bodies of water were normally covered in algae and aquatic plants. Most of our swimming was done in the ponds around. We swam in the branch that coursed through the woods behind Grandma's house. The water there was very acidic and sour-smelling due to the decomposition of all those leaves and woody material in the water. It was also a very snaky place, and we were careful and watchful for them. We knew our best defense against snakes was to make our presence well known to them. Plenty of noise and water disturbance was the best prescription for getting the snakes to loan us the swimming hole for a while.

Swimming at David's house was very different though. The water was sparkling and looked beautifully blue and inviting. There were no snakes or "moss" and no fallen tree limbs lurking beneath the surface. It smelled clean too. The strong, clean smell of chlorine. There was no mud or leaves around it, just clean concrete. So, when David sometimes suggested, "Let's go swimming in the pool," I was always happy to go along with the idea. Each time seemed like a new experience for me, and the smell of chlorine today sometimes reminds me of the specialness of those occasions, of David, and of the times we enjoyed together.

Occasionally, the Massey family had others over to enjoy their pool with them. One was a rather heavyset woman who lived about a mile away. The way Annie Ausborne told the story gave the grown-ups of the community something to laugh about anytime the story was repeated. Annie lived about fifty yards from the Masseys' pool. Her old, tiny house was beyond a sagging barbed wire fence and separated from the pool by an area of weeds and scattered brush. The pool was perfectly visible to her as she sat on her front porch cooling in the summer heat. The big woman in the pool decided to test her diving skills and positioned herself at the end of the diving board. Bobbing up and down a time or two, she launched herself from the end of the board. The shock of the impact sent much of the pool's water skyward like a broad, enormous geyser. A tidal wave surged outward in all directions. When the water made its return trip to earth and rolled backward to the place of impact, there was less of it in the pool. The surroundings were drenched for many yards out from the pool.

Annie described the scene and the reverberating boom of impact like this: "It wuz like boom! Ah-whoosh-ah-moom-moom! Water went way up in de air and ever-where!" She laughed. Each time the story was told, the boom got louder, the water went higher, and less of it returned to the pool.

Dad never got tired of repeating the story and getting

another good laugh out of it. I've grinned about it a lot myself in the fifty-five or so years since the event.

One day, David and I decided to barbecue a chicken. I would supply the cooking expertise, and David agreed to supply the chicken. There was nobody home at his house, and it would not be hard to catch a chicken without anyone knowing. Since I had seen Dad barbecue pigs before on the Fourth of July, that was enough to qualify me as an expert so I would have no problem cooking the chicken. We would not use hot coals and would build a small fire instead. David's selection of a victim turned out to be an old white-gold bantam rooster he did not like. The rooster did not like David either. It would be the perfect opportunity to settle old scores by eating the enemy, but this rooster was, in fact, very old and turned out to be a poor choice.

I was also the expert in killing and plucking a chicken. After all, I had seen Dad kill plenty of them, and I had plucked a lot of them after he had dipped them in hot water and handed them to me. How hard could it be to do the whole process? We caught the bantam using a bit of feed, and that turned out to be the easiest part of the affair. I would wring its neck, I decided. Grasping the chicken by the neck, I swung it furiously in circles a few times and let it go. The rooster began running when I dropped it to the ground. It was not hurt at all. Obviously, I wasn't very good at wringing chicken necks. We would have to find an ax and a chopping block. We cornered the old bantam rooster and soon had it back in custody. Locating a dull ax, we eventually accomplished the deed and succeeded in getting the feathers off as well. The rest of the operation was an equally ragged affair, but we eventually got it done.

Our barbecue pit was constructed of several bricks with an old oven rack laid across them. The day was cloudy, slightly breezy, and misty. We gathered a small pile of the driest fuel we could find. A small smoky fire of grass and twigs was built under the rack, and the "cooking" began. We had chosen a nice spot for our barbecue. It was under the spreading limbs of the massive oak tree in our pasture. Our big tree house was nearby and practically overhead. We would enjoy our meal there, we had agreed. We had a bit of trouble keeping the fire going and had to stop now and then to gather more grass and twigs and whatever else that looked like it would burn. A lot of smoke but very little heat was generated, but we persisted.

David had a bottle of barbecue sauce from Mrs. Massey's refrigerator, and we slathered a thick coating of it on the chicken. The cooking process was not going as well as we had hoped. The chicken did not seem to be heating up much. After thirty minutes or so, the red barbecue sauce finally began to darken from the soot of the pitiful fire of smoldering grass and twigs, and we were satisfied it must be about done. In turn, both of us tried to take a bite of the old rooster, but we were only successful in getting a taste of very smoky barbecue sauce. An examination of the layer under the sauce revealed the tough skin of an uncooked rooster. Our barbecue came to an unsuccessful conclusion and left us with nothing to show for half a day's work except a dead rooster and an empty barbecue sauce bottle. We would have to find something else to eat. We were beginning to get pretty hungry. The old bantam rooster, lately owned by Mr. Massey, was tossed aside for the wild animals to enjoy. We went off to see if we could come up with something else to eat.

Well behind the Massey house and at the fringe of tall, but still young pines, stood a wooden structure. On this piney hill, David's brother, George, had built a square, wooden building about sixteen feet square. It was built entirely of rough-cut one-by-twelve lumber. The floor, walls, and flat roof were built of the same material. He had constructed it as a tack room for the bridles and saddles on hand for the several ponies they purchased. David decided it was a perfect place to build a fire and roast some weenies from his mother's refrigerator. I agreed it was a fine place, but I had some reservations about building the fire directly on the wooden floor. Nevertheless, we had a small fire going and set about roasting the weenies. By the time we had finished roasting and eating them, we realized the small coals from the fire were beginning to drop through the cracks between the boards of the floor.

In a panic, we managed to smother the fire and ran to the horse-watering tank near the house for some water. Pouring the water on the remains of our cooking fire and in the cracks between the floorboards, we watched in alarm as smoke continued to drift upward through the cracks between the boards. If the little building burned, it was likely the straw on the hillside would burn—and the fire might spread into the pines. After that, the woods all around might catch fire and burn! Our solution was obvious. Get away from there! If bad turned to worse, we could always do what anyone would do. Lie!

David said we could blame George. His daddy might believe that.

At that point, I was not going to argue against such an obviously good alibi, so I did what David did. I ran! Fortunately, my overworked guardian angel must have intervened in the affair. When we later returned to the scene, we found the smoke gone, the ashes cold, and the structure intact. We didn't have to sacrifice George, after all. It was a big relief for us, and both of us had learned another important lesson. Today, our lessons were on some of the dos and don'ts about fires and cooking.

It was with David and his family that I attended my first rodeo. The rodeo was at the Garrett Coliseum in Montgomery and was an annual event. I was fascinated by the bull riders, bucking horses, bull-dogging, and calf-roping. I touched hands with Hugh O' Brien, who starred as Wyatt Earp on the television series of the time. It was a time when western movies, television westerns, and cowboys were all the rage. The only thing that could have made it better were some Indians. They were part of every child's play at the time. I wanted more than anything else to be an Indian. If I couldn't be an Indian, I would have gladly accepted cowboy as my second choice. Still, my temperament was best suited to being a wild Indian. Even Mama said that more times than I probably could count.

My first experience in seeing a live football contest was with David and his family. It occurred on a Saturday morning in Montgomery with Catholic High School playing someone who I don't recall. Standing along the sidelines near the goal line, I witnessed a long run directly toward me and a ground-shaking tackle almost at my feet. I was conscious of the sound of the approaching players as they got closer to me. The equipment seemed to rattle as they came down together amid huffing and grunting sounds. It seemed I felt the impact travel through my feet and radiate over my whole body. Their helmets and shoulder pads made them appear taller and bigger than anyone I had ever seen. It was an awe-inspiring experience for me.

Later, there were two trips to Florida with David, Judy, and Mrs. Massey. David's mom wanted to visit a relative for a few hours. Seeing palm trees and white sand was exciting. David and I rambled about on those occasions.

Still later, we experienced Panama City and its beaches during spring break, though we were somewhat younger than the high school and college kids there. Still, it had a bit of the excitement and feel of the Annette and Frankie beach movies that had come out. I wish I had been old enough to have been part the fun. Those who were did not want us hanging around and let us know it too. They sure were having a good time and didn't need any kids around as a distraction.

Drive-in movie theaters were common during my early teen years. David and I went whenever we had an opportunity to go. This meant finding someone older than us who was willing to take us along. At times, a carload of people could get in for one dollar. On those occasions, the car would usually be crowded. On regular-admission nights, there were fewer people in the passenger compartment and two or three in the trunk. It would be a safe bet David and I were the ones in the trunk.

On one occasion, my brother Larry was driving his large copper-colored 1961 Chevrolet Bel Air with Phillip Murrell in the passenger seat. Pulling to the side of the street about three hundred yards from the drive in, Larry opened the trunk so David and I could get in. We expected to be in the trunk for less than five minutes, but we were surprised at being taken all over Montgomery while Larry and Phillip pretended to be chased by the police. The speeds were horrifying to us, and occasionally the tires squealed as they made sharp turns. We were being thrown about a good bit and getting battered by items in the trunk. The outside temperature was hot, and the car's trunk was sweltering. Our cries to stop only encouraged Larry to continue. I found it difficult to breathe and searched for some point where I might find a bit of air coming in from the outside.

After half an hour or so, Larry and Philip finally decided it was time to head back toward the theater, and the speed and motion of the car became normal. We could hear Larry and Phillip laughing and rehashing the fine time they had with the "police chase" through Montgomery.

David decided it was time to have a cigarette, and I begged him not to light one. We were barely teenagers, but we still smoked as often as we could. Now was not the time. I was already having trouble breathing and did not need the addition of smoke in the hot, suffocating trunk. I was sure I smelled gasoline and sounded the alarm. He lit the cigarette anyway and began smoking while I prayed to God the explosion would get me and not the fire. I may have also sworn off this method of getting into a drive-in movie as well. If so, it was an oath I forgot later.

About half the attempts to sneak into the drive-in were failures. Now and then, a driver would be asked to open his trunk. Perhaps the attendant at the entrance thought he could see guilt in the driver's eyes, or perhaps he was just spot-checking. Occasionally, when climbing out of the trunk, a flashlight would come on followed by the command, "Now, let's hold it right there, boys!" It appears the folks who worked in those places knew the tricks and were prepared for them. It was time to pay up at that point and was usually handled in a good-natured way. After all, it was somewhat like a game. Our part was to try to sneak in, and their part was to try to catch us at it.

On one occasion, an attendant holding the flashlight on David said, "I bet your little heart is going pitter pat, pitter pat."

David responded, "No, sir, it's going pitter pat boom, boom! Pitter pat boom, boom!" We each handed the attendant a dollar for admission, and he went away chuckling over the affair. I'm not sure where we may have gotten the money because we rarely had any. Perhaps I had earned it from Uncle Charles. He was always generous with me when I did little jobs for him.

I had an old car when I was sixteen and my driver's license. I was attending Sidney Lanier High School in Montgomery and was also a cadet in the Army Junior ROTC program. During football season, I often volunteered to hand out game programs at the stadium. This allowed me to see the games for free. After handing out the programs, I was free to do as I pleased. By kickoff, I was already in my seat alongside my buddy, David. On one particular game night, he had a girl sitting beside him to whom he introduced me. She was obviously a new girlfriend I had not met. Presently, another girl began walking our way, saw David, and flashed him a smile.

David leaned over to the girl beside him and said, "Here comes someone I want you to meet. Play along with me."

When the new girl stopped, I could see the questioning look in her eyes about who the person was my friend was sitting with. David introduced the two and identified the girl sitting beside him as his cousin. I made room for the newcomer, and she sat down beside David. Before the girls had a chance to find out anything about each other, a third girl approached.

David, seeing her coming, said quickly to the two girls beside him, "Don't ask questions. Just play along with me." When this latest girl stopped and greeted David, she gave each of the two girls beside him looks that showed her displeasure. David introduced the girls as his cousins. Maybe the girls were only fourteen or fifteen years old, but they figured out the situation really fast. They stormed away together, and David found himself with no girlfriend to enjoy the game with. He was stuck with me for the rest of the evening.

"What are the odds of that happening?" he asked. "All three showing up at the same place and at the same time!" He didn't seem to let it bother him, though. As I stated earlier, David was confident and self-assured, taking life as it came to him and making the most of the moment. Knowing him as I did, I knew he would have a new girlfriend or two before long and maybe have made up with these girls as well. This boyhood friend of mine was no social introvert and was the most confident person I have ever known!

Several years ago, I saw David Massey after not having seen

him for forty years. He cried as he hugged my neck, and I had tears in my own eyes as well.

"You were not just my best friend," he said. "You were my brother!"

A few months later, my confident childhood friend was dead of liver cancer.

33

JIMMY AND PAT

JIMMY KNOWLES is a friend of mine. My first remembrance of him was when I was seven years old. His stepfather was a lifelong friend of my father. Jimmy's stepfather's name was Pascal Owens. He was one of those people we children called by his first name. Instances of dropping the honorific of "mister" when speaking to an adult were rare when I was a child. Pascal Owens was one of those rare ones who many people simply referred to by his first name. My father and Pascal were friends throughout their childhood and teen years, and their closeness continued to the end of their lives. The close friendship they enjoyed also created the environment in which Jimmy and I forged our own friendship.

"Lewis, I've got me a girl," Pascal informed my father one day. "Oh, she's so pretty! She's as pretty as a speckled puppy!" Along with other humorous moments Dad shared with me about his friend, Pascal, this was one of his favorites. I was to hear those "speckled puppy" sentiments expressed many times as an adult when my father and I worked together following my ten years of military service. We rarely spoke as we worked because we were almost extensions of each other and anticipated each other's movements and needs as we worked. When Dad broke the silence, it was frequently to remind me of something from the past he thought was funny. It made me aware that, like me, he also spent some of his time mentally reflecting and remembering moments of time long past, moments that concerned his childhood, friends, family, and experiences. He shared them freely with me as they occurred to him even though I heard many of them over and over.

"Dad, do you have a nickel Lewis and I can have to buy a sack of Bull Durham? We are out of tobacco," Pascal asked his father in the story recounted by my own father. Dad laughed every time he told this story about the two of them being out of tobacco as teenaged boys.

"Yeah, I've got a nickel and sense too, but you're not getting either," was the reply.

As many times as I heard this story, followed by chuckles from Dad, he never indicated whether they got the nickel or not, but I know the conclusion of the "pretty as a speckled puppy" story. Pascal married this young woman, Jimmy's mother, Louise. The friendship between Jimmy and myself, which still endures, began forming shortly after that marriage.

I was going to get to go with Dad to Jimmy's house. Pascal had come over and spent some time with us and wanted Dad to go back to his house with him for a while and look at something. My brother Larry and I were going to go too, but my sister Betty was not allowed to go. She was not happy about that and was crying. I felt sorry for her—but not enough I would have changed places with her and stayed behind. Going anywhere away from home was a rare event for me unless it was to church or school. I was going to a new place with a friend and with Dad. This was just about as exciting as life, for me, could ever get! Betty was still crying, but I was happy. I can still see her begging and crying after the sixty years that have passed since Pascal began backing his car out onto the road for the trip to his house.

Before we began our trip, Pascal took a water bucket out of his car, and we filled it with water we had drawn up from the well with the bucket and rope. I can say "we" because I was there, and I watched. He said he had a leaky radiator on his car, and it needed filling with water. With the radiator filled, the bucket was put back into the car with water in it. He said we would add that water into the radiator along the way. When that water was gone, the bucket could be refilled at one of the streams we would pass on our trip to his house. It was a very leaky radiator.

We only stayed on the main road for a mile and a half before turning on to the graveled, old "Federal Road" that ran west past Pintlala School, where we attended—and my father had before us. The road went west for about two miles before it ended at the fence of a farm. There, my dad got out and opened the "gap" in the barbed wire fence, and Pascal drove the car through the opening. Dad closed the gap and got back into the car. We continued on a rough, rutted track across the farm until we got to another gap and graveled road on the opposite side. This road was bordered closely on each side by mostly mock orange trees and brush, but there were many more assorted large trees along the way. It was a little spooky for someone as small as me, but I was still happy I was allowed to go.

We stopped once or twice to put water in the radiator. Once we stopped at a small stream of water and refilled our bucket after putting water in the radiator again. Somehow, we made the trip with water dripping and trickling from the radiator and a little steam coming from under the hood of the car. Later, we made the trip back home in the same manner.

I do not remember what all of us kids did on that day while

at Pascal's house, but I'm sure I explored the place a bit with Jimmy, Larry, and Jimmy's younger sisters, Sue and Cathy. At that young age and in that time, visiting another house was an event. Especially on a small farm with a barn, corncrib, various animal pens, and all, there was so much to investigate. In the coming years, we visited back and forth at each other's homes for days at a time during summer months. They were always interesting times of fun and adventure with a good many farm chores thrown in. The chores didn't really seem so much like work since we enjoyed each other's company and made every activity fun.

Jimmy had come to our house for a few days, and on one of those days, we were supposed to pick butter beans. Along with the bean picking, we also sampled some of the vegetables growing on the rows around us. Occasionally, we opened a pod and ate the beans from it. We ate the fresh tomatoes as if we were eating apples, and they tasted very good. We scratched sweet potatoes from the ground under the vines. After rubbing off the dirt and nibbling the skin from mine, I spit out the skin and then ate the raw sweet potato. Bell peppers were good eaten fresh from the plant as were the cucumbers too. The skin of the cucumber was a little bitter, so I spit that part out as I had the potato skin. Jimmy decided to try the hot pepper. I didn't think he would do it, but he said he would try it anyway. He took a small bite from the little end of the pepper and chewed it. I thought he would spit it out pretty quickly, but he didn't. He told me, rather proudly, he knew the trick of eating it without it burning him.

"Take a bite from the small end and breathe through your nose as you chew, and it won't burn you," he said. He decided to show me again and took a bigger bite and began breathing through his nose. It didn't work! His mouth was on fire! Out came the pepper as he began hollering that he had to wash out his mouth. I indicated the well in Grandma's backyard about fifty yards away, and he ran for Grandma's house. Beating on the back door of her screened porch, he succeeded in getting her attention and a water glass. In all the excitement, he upset her dog, Shep, who bit Jimmy as a warning. He was the only person Shep ever bit. Shep was a gentle dog!

Jimmy got his water though. The dog bite was less of a concern at the moment than the fire in his mouth. He presently came back to the garden, still suffering even though he said he had drunk eight glasses of water. I wondered about that, because he didn't look big enough to hold eight glasses of water, but he said he did and that his mouth still burned. Now he had a dog bite as well. We spent the next few minutes trying to figure out what had gone wrong with his theory about the proper way to eat a hot pepper without setting the mouth afire. We don't know what happened. Maybe he had accidentally breathed through his mouth. Anyway, I decided not to try the hot pepper or Jimmy's theory about eating peppers, and confine my grazing to the other vegetables around me. Jimmy didn't eat any more peppers either. We finally got the butter beans picked. Picking them had never been my favorite job, but it went much better with a friend helping because then it didn't feel like work. Still, I would rather pick peas than butter beans because the bushel hamper filled up so much faster with the peas.

When I was small and Pascal came to our house, we were always very excited because we knew we would get a special treat. He came in his old pickup truck with a lot of bread in the back he had purchased from the bread store as too old to sell for human consumption. He purchased a truckload of it at very little cost and fed it to his pigs and dogs. He left a lot of it at our house, and we also fed it to our pigs in addition to the pig feed and slop.

He had plenty of cakes, cinnamon rolls, and other sweets as well. We didn't share these with the pigs, as we did the bread. We ate cinnamon rolls, chocolate cupcakes, and other sweets until we couldn't hold any more. Because these opportunities were so infrequent and irregular, we took full advantage of them when they arose. We didn't know when Pascal would visit again with another load from the bread store, so we ate 'til we couldn't eat any more.

Pascal was a man who made his living in various ways. While he had a subsistence farm like we had, he farmed with a tractor and not with a mule as my dad did. This cut down on the time and labor substantially and left him with more time to follow some of his other pursuits. He owned and grazed a number of cows and sold their offspring as he needed money. He owned a pulpwood truck and chainsaws and spent some of his time in the woods cutting pulpwood. He cut and baled hay for himself and for others on a limited basis. He also owned and operated a small country store in front of his house. In the wintertime, he trapped fur-bearing animals as my own father did. He was not lazy, but he was willing to make a living for his family with the means available to him. Even so, life was sometimes a struggle for him as it was for so many others trying to make ends meet.

I looked forward to going to Pascal's house and spending a few days with my friend, Jimmy, even though I was afraid of Pascal. He had a different temperament from my dad who was gentle and soft-spoken, though tough and hard physically. Dad rarely shouted. He didn't need to. We were obedient and respectful toward him and his instructions. He also gave us plenty of room to be children and to act accordingly, within bounds. Pascal was different. His manner in dealing with the children was not what I was used to. That was why I was afraid of him. He was louder, more demanding, and, seemingly, less patient. He seemed quick to whip Jimmy, and the usual suddenness of those punishments frightened me. Jimmy knew that I was affected so, and one day made me an offer I was not quick to refuse.

We were helping his father, Pascal, pick squash one day. Pascal had showed us the size of squash he wanted picked. Any below the size of the one he showed to us would be too small.

Jimmy picked a squash and asked, "How about this one?"

"That's too little" was the response. "I already showed you how big. Don't ask me again."

On picking the next squash, Jimmy asked again. Big mistake! He was immediately howling and jumping around as his father whipped him with the weedy plant he had ripped from the ground.

"Don't ask me again!" his father ordered.

Jimmy went back to his interrupted squash picking as if nothing had happened. He had his usual pleasant smile on his face as if the interruption had never occurred at all! It seemed as soon as the whipping had stopped, the howling did too, and the smile had come back.

Reading my face and thoughts accurately, my friend said to me, "Don't worry about getting a whipping from Pat, Allen. If he wants to whip you, I'll take your whipping for you. They don't bother me none." Jimmy often referred to his stepfather, Pascal, as Pat. I reminded him of this unselfish offer many years later and the fact that it demonstrated remarkable friendship. After all, how many people would take someone else's punishment?

With his characteristic good humor and smile, Jimmy responded, "Yeah, I remember, and I lied. Those whippings hurt like hell, but you were my friend, and I knew you were scared. I would never have let Pat whip you." Jimmy has never backed off that friendship nor has he ever lost his smile, quick wit, and willingness not to let things get him down for long.

Jimmy had also learned something about his father that I did not learn until well into my adult years. At least a part of what went on between him and Pascal was a game. Jimmy needled his father, trying to get a reaction until Pat reacted like an angry bear. Much of that reaction was pure bluster.

Years later, I learned Jimmy really loved Pascal, and Pascal loved Jimmy. When I came to that conclusion, I was able to look back at incidents that had occurred and see little things I had missed at the time. I remember also the times when Pascal took time away from his work to take Jimmy and me, as well as Cathy and Sue, swimming in the creek. A railroad track crossed a part of his land and also over a trestle that bridged the creek on the backside of his property. The bottom of the creek was hard at this point, and one side was bordered by a sugar-white sandbar. Pascal allowed us to swim for an hour or more on these occasions. Almost always, trains would pass over the trestle bridging the creek while we played in the waters below.

Walking behind Pascal on a cow path one day, Jimmy and I began mimicking the sounds we were hearing from Pascal's stomach. It was a sloshing sound like water sloshing in a barrel or from inside a washing machine. Pascal was short and very big around the middle. His measurement around his stomach seemed far greater than his height. He had just drunk a lot of water before setting off down the cow path checking fences and cows. The sloshing sounds from his stomach were so loud we could not let the moment pass without having fun with it. Pascal growled out his threats toward us a time or two before turning and lunging at us. He missed. We stayed far enough back to be safe. We knew even though he was short and big around, he was incredibly quick and strong.

Presently, we let our guard down and Pascal turned unexpectedly and grabbed Jimmy. He pulled Jimmy's head under his arm and rubbed it real hard with his knuckles. I jumped back out of reach. When the payback was over, we continued following Pascal along the path, still having a good time over the unusual sloshing noises coming from the stomach ahead of us. Pascal was still growling and breathing out threats, but I think he enjoyed the moment as much as we did.

"We are going to Sylvest Seed Company tomorrow," Jimmy informed me while we were lying in bed. "I always like to go there. Pat goes every Saturday. You like peanuts?"

I affirmed I did like peanuts. I couldn't imagine anyone not liking peanuts. I could eat them every day. Dad planted a peanut patch each year because he liked them too. I liked the smell of them and of the peanut hay we stored in the shed beside the corncrib for the cows. Sometimes I had lain awhile in that hay just so I could smell it. Yes, I did like peanuts.

"Do you have pants with deep pockets?" he asked.

I did, and I told him so. As a matter of fact, my other pants had the deepest pockets of any I had ever owned, but I didn't know why he would want to know about the depth of my pants pockets.

"Make sure you wear them tomorrow," he said. "Mr. Sylvest will tell us to fill our pockets up with peanuts while we are there. He always does, so I wear my pants with the deepest pockets."

I was already looking forward to tomorrow, and I knew which pants I would be wearing. It would be my other pair, the ones with the pockets that seemed to reach my knees.

The following day was an exciting one for me. We were going to town. It was just Pascal, Jimmy, and me. Town was Montgomery, and I had never been there on an occasion such as this. We would be traveling on Wasden Road, a graveled road that ran east into US 31 and went into Montgomery. There were old wooden bridges along the way that appeared rickety, and I wondered if we would make it safely across. Some of the boards were a little loose and moved around a bit as we crossed the bridges. The one spanning Pintlala Creek was a long and ancient covered bridge. Everybody always talked about how scary it was to go through it. We would be crossing it going to town and coming back. That was very exciting even though it was so scary and ghostly. I felt like I was in a haunted house whenever I crossed that bridge.

Montgomery was far different from the way it is now. As with most towns then, all the businesses seemed to be concentrated in the downtown area. Going downtown was practically a new experience for me. It seemed everyone was in town, and the streets and sidewalks were crowded. I knew this was going to be an exciting day. It wasn't crowded around the feed-and-seed store, but there were still a number of people there.

Mr. Sylvest and Pascal greeted each other when we went inside the store.

Looking at us, Mr. Sylvest smiled and said, "Hello, boys! Y'all go over to that sack there and fill your pockets with those peanuts."

We went over to the large crocus sack that looked like it had a hundred pounds of peanuts in it. He had told us to help ourselves, so we did. I bet he would have really been surprised at our big pockets. I'm glad Pascal was talking to him—or he might have noticed how big our pockets were and stopped us. Both of us really liked peanuts. I found I liked Mr. Sylvest, and I wanted to come back every Saturday.

Jimmy told me we had to go and gather the eggs for the day. They had a lot of chickens roaming around just like we did at home. Some were around the house, while others were around his grandma's house about a hundred yards away in the direction of the barn. There were a lot of chickens around the barn too.

Jimmy knew where to go and get the eggs and went straight to the nests he knew about. With all that hay in the barn and weed patches about, I knew he must have been overlooking a lot of secret nests. I liked hunting eggs and enjoyed finding undiscovered nests at home. To me, finding a new nest was like finding buried treasure. Gathering eggs was not a chore for me. It was an adventure. I was not about to pass up a chance to find those undiscovered nests that had to be in that hay barn and in the weed patches around it.

Jimmy finished gathering the eggs from the usual places, but I was ready to search for ones I knew he must have been overlooking each day. We found eggs everywhere. There were several nests in the hay with lots of eggs in them. In the weeds, we found two or three nests with twenty or thirty eggs in each. We found more eggs than I could have hoped to find.

Jimmy was a little quiet, as if something was on his mind. I did not fully realize what his concern was until later that night. We had to get extra buckets to carry all the eggs back to the house, and I was very happy to have helped him locate the secret nests. Later, I wished we had not found them.

Pascal was not happy that night when he found we had brought in such a big haul of eggs, especially since there were fresh eggs mixed in with old ones. Some were very old and obviously rotten. I was wishing I could have been somewhere else when the sorting process started. The obviously rotten ones were easy to pick out and discard. Then came the process of getting rid of the probably rotten ones and then the highly suspicious ones. I didn't know at which point Jimmy's father was going to stop and beat us both. He threatened it continually through the whole process. Once the obviously rotten to the highly suspicious eggs were culled, the rest had to be checked by a series of tests. They were shaken, floated on water, held to the light, and put through any other test that might determine if the egg was too old. They were then judged to be possibly bad, probably good, and unknown.

The probably good were put into cartons while the possibly bad and unknown were broken into a saucer. Of those, the ones that were obviously good were then poured into a large bowl. Those that showed signs of blood were discarded. Most of the eggs broken open were good and went into the large bowl for eating. There were a lot of eggs to be eaten by someone. All in all, the process for culling the bad eggs from the good seemed to have gone very well, even though it was an unpleasant experience for all of us, especially for Jimmy and me. Strangely enough, Pascal did not punish Jimmy as I had feared. Jimmy had never put him in a situation like this before I showed up, so it wasn't hard to figure out it wasn't all Jimmy's fault.

Pascal had an egg route where he delivered eggs to certain houses each week. He had now been placed in a difficult situation because of my love for egg hunting. He could deliver eggs this week and keep his mouth shut and run the risk someone might get a surprise when they cracked an egg. He chose to be honest. Jimmy and I were in the car with him as he made his stops at the homes of his customers along his egg route. We watched from the back seat of the car as he told each customer of his concern about the possibility an old egg might have been inadvertently put into their egg carton.

"Crack them into a saucer," he told each customer, "just to be sure." At most stops, he came back to his car with his eggs. Later, he received notice from others that he need not deliver them any more eggs. Apparently, people do not like having to check their eggs in this manner and would rather assume all their eggs were fresh. I think that was the end of Pascal's delivering eggs on an egg route. It seems his customers found another source for their eggs.

Years later, I admitted to Jimmy of my sorrow at bringing about the demise of his father's egg business. He got very serious and almost emotional when he told me of how Pascal had suffered when his customers lost confidence in him and stopped buying his eggs.

"He really depended on that egg route," he told me.

I never could have imagined that my love for hunting eggs and knack for finding them would have caused such a thing as the loss of someone's egg business.

Jimmy and I spent a lot of time visiting back and forth and spending time at each other's homes over the next several years. Both of us have so many memories of the times we shared. Some things we can talk about, and maybe some things we can't, but that's life. When you're together and work doesn't seem to be work, you know that you enjoy each other's company. Time continued to pass until I wasn't seeing him much at all anymore. I still saw his father, Pascal, a lot and developed a close relationship with him.

After nearly ten years in the military, we continued that close relationship. Jimmy and I picked up again in our relationship from the new standpoint of being married with families of our own. The difference being, from our new perspective, we could appreciate the present, anticipate the future, and have a fond remembrance of the past. Looking at it like that, our time together and friendship seemed to be more full and complete.

By the time I had gotten to my midteens and began moving toward my upper teens was the period in which I did not see Jimmy as much. Pascal had moved his residence from the small tin-roofed house that was a few hundred yards behind his little store. He moved into the house right across the road from his store. My older brother Buddy moved into Pascal's vacated house with the promise that he would help out with farm-related activities in exchange for this place to stay.

I visited with my brother a lot during the next couple of years and often stayed with him for extended periods of time. It was quite an experience too. We helped with the farm-related activities, including the hot, dusty hayfield. I cut several hundred saplings from the woods for beanpoles and put them in the ground in the bean patch behind Pascal's store. That was so the running green beans would have something to support their vines. We had done the same thing at home, but usually only about three dozen or so each year. Several hundred poles were a lot and represented a number of days' work.

Every morning, I got up early and fed the pigs, chickens, and then the hunting dogs in the pen next to the house where I was staying with my brother Buddy. Afterward, I drove the old Jeep to the catch pen in Pascal's pasture and doctored the sick calves there. When all these things were taken care of, we could go to the hayfield if there was any haying going on. Otherwise, we might go fishing on the creek or spend the day doing something else.

We went rabbit hunting once during the fall with the hunting dogs Pascal kept. They were beagles, and he had three or four of them—and also one cat who lived with the beagles and ate and slept with them. Pascal had dozens of cats, but this one stayed with the dogs. She did not associate with the other cats. When we went hunting, the cat went too. When we got to the first ditch of water, my brother told me to help the cat across, so I did. When we got to the creek, I thought it would be best to let the cat stay there and pick her up on the way back, but she cried most pitifully when I got to the other side of the creek. I had to go back and get her. I was afraid she would get lost in the woods while looking for us if we left her there. On the trip back, we might not be able to find her. I carried the cat across the creek, and she stayed with us while we hunted. She never strayed and refused to be left behind. She was the only cat I had ever seen that insisted on spending her life with the dogs and going rabbit hunting with them as well. Her cries on the creek bank reminded me of how my sister Betty cried so hard when she got left behind on my first trip to visit with Jimmy and Pascal so many years before.

Buddy learned to make butter and buttermilk, and I often sat on the old porch in the evenings talking with him while we alternated using the churn. We began to drink lots of buttermilk and soon ran out of places to keep the fresh buttermilk and butter. Pascal and everyone else were well supplied until we finally had our fill of making and drinking buttermilk. You can only drink so much buttermilk. Too much of a good thing is not so good. Butter had begun to pile up too. It seemed most people, myself included, preferred margarine. We decided to quit our evening churning on the front porch.

Buddy trapped with Pascal in the wintertime on halves. Actually, Buddy did most of the trapping, and Pascal did a lot of the skinning as he minded his store. While most of the skinning was done under a shed near the store, some of it was done inside between the table where the locals played dominoes and the wood-and-coal-fired heater that warmed the store. Obviously, this was somewhat of a laid-back and informal place, but it was also warm with a pleasant atmosphere. A domino game was going on almost every night and often during the daytime as well. Nobody seemed to think it odd that Pascal often sat near the heater skinning a mink and chitchatting while the domino players played, smoked, and enjoyed a beer or something a little harder. Occasionally, Pascal would put the knife down, wipe his hands, and wait on a customer. This was business as usual at this little country store. It was the favorite—and, as a matter of fact, *only*—hangout for the locals to gather and sit awhile.

Pascal was not squeamish in his dietary habits. He was, without question, the most unsqueamish person I ever met when it came to eating. He admitted to me he would try anything once. By the end of his life, he had probably tried most things that lived in the woods or elsewhere in Alabama. Were he alive today, he could probably have his own reality television show along those lines. He did not view his "trying things" as something to be ashamed of. The one failure he admitted to me was his inability to stomach a bo mink. It had been "too strong," he said. At least he tried it.

After I had begun driving, I took a trip to Florida for a couple of days with my brother Buddy and a good friend, Danny B. While there, we became aware of a creature that was new to us: the armadillo. The roadways seemed to be fairly littered with these strange animals. They had not yet made it as far north as central Alabama. When we got back home and told Pascal about them, the one question he asked was "Can you eat 'em?" Well, the answer to that is yes, but we didn't know that at the time.

Having gone through our butter-and-buttermilk-making period and having put that aside, we started experimenting with different things to eat. We had eaten small beavers on occasion when we were growing up. Dad boiled a small one now and then and put the meat in a roasting pan. He then covered it with his own barbecue sauce concoction. It consisted of vinegar, onions, salt, pepper, and a small bottle of ketchup. It was actually pretty good and was the only way I had ever eaten beaver. Pascal had eaten it cooked in a similar fashion and had eaten beaver tail fried in his younger years.

Buddy and Pascal both liked liver and wanted to try some beaver liver. Buddy was a good cook, so it fell to him to cook some up for everyone. It was a smashing success and ushered in our beaver-liver-eating period. It was surprisingly mild flavored, and it appeared just about everyone wanted to try it. It seemed to have set off a beaver-liver-eating craze around the community for several weeks before everyone began to get a little burned out on liver. Older beavers are a bit strong flavored, but someone came up with the idea that we might be able to run one through a meat grinder and make some hamburger meat out of it. We could fry some up in patties and make beaver burgers. Again, Pascal and Buddy thought the idea deserved a try, so we ground up a beaver and made patties. The patties had a dark red, soft, and pulpy texture, but they fried up quite well even though they smelled very strong while frying. The liver was suddenly put aside and temporarily forgotten about as various ones in the community began trying the new beaver burgers. Some actually enjoyed them, it was reported, but I believe they were lying!

About that same time period, someone handed me a sandwich consisting of two slices of bread with the hindquarter of a young coon between them. I had never eaten a coon sandwich before and wasn't really hungry for one. However, I took a bite or two, but I managed to discard it in the weeds when no one was looking. Some people may not have been squeamish about their food, but I was not one of those. I was very particular about the varmints I wanted to eat. Guess I was a bit spoiled because I kind of preferred chicken, beef, and pork.

A few years later, I was talking with a friend of mine who was there during our period of experimentation with beaver liver and burgers. We got a few chuckles out of those remembrances. What he said next was a real shocker though.

"Did you know that later we made otter burgers?" he asked.

I didn't and expressed my surprise they had actually done that. He went on to tell me he had tasted one and that it was pretty strong tasting with a hint of fishiness about it. I guess I had left at about the right time to miss the otter-burger-eating period in that community.

I suppose our tastes in foods are often dictated by the times and circumstances as well as the environments in which we are raised. These factors obviously contribute heavily to whether we will even try to eat certain things. Also, after having eaten those things, whether we might appreciate having done so. I am reminded of the first meal I remember eating with my friend Jimmy and his family. It was a supper meal, and Jimmy's mama had cooked squirrel and gravy. That was in no way an odd or strange meal for me or for anyone else at the time. We ate it all the time at home and often had rabbit and gravy. Jimmy's younger sister, Cathy, was given the head to eat. It was her favorite part. I watched her chew the meat from the head. I was fascinated by that because we didn't cook that part at home. It was always discarded.

When she finished chewing the meat off the skull, she asked her daddy, "Pat, can you crack the skull for me?" He took it as she handed it over, cracked it with a big spoon, pulled the skull apart, and handed it back. She pulled out the brain and ate it as if she were eating a little plum.

Jimmy said, "He always cracks the skull for her because she can't do it. She looks forward to that every time we eat squirrel!"

So, I guess it's not always a matter of whether we consider something edible or appetizing, but what we are used to eating or whether we are willing to try something different. I really didn't want to pull out a squirrel's brain and eat it or chew on its head. I wasn't used to that. One of my older sisters informed me later if I had been around when they were young, I would have seen this same practice at our dinner table. My brother Larry seconded that and affirmed that the brain tasted good.

Dad told me the story of a classmate of his at Pintlala School during his childhood days who had a very special Sunday dinner the day before. During that period, many families did not have the means to acquire meat except on rare occasions. Even some of the forests were depleted of game due to people having hunted out just about anything that could be eaten. Squirrels, rabbits, coons, and everything else had become scarce. Dad's young friend told him of how his mama had cooked the "best Sunday dinner ever!" He went on to say his daddy had shot a hawk, and his Mama had cooked a hawk pie.

"Oh, Lewis, it was so good!" he said. It was another of Dad's favorite stories from the past, which he told a number of times while he and I worked side by side. I could very easily have imagined Pascal eating and enjoying that hawk pie too. He had grown up in the same era.

I mentioned the first meal I remembered eating at Pascal's house and of watching Cathy chew on the squirrel's head. I also remember the last meal. This was the chitlin supper. Several of us had assisted Pascal in butchering a hog or two that morning and were invited to eat chitlins and tenderloin with him that night. I love fresh tenderloin, but I had not developed a taste for chitlins yet. Years later, I developed an appreciation for fried chitlins.

Earlier that morning, while the hog killing had been underway, a very pregnant young woman showed up and offered to help. She had been raised on a farm and loved being involved in any farm-related activity. Pascal happily accepted the extra help and disregarded the warnings of a couple of the men there not to let the woman come around. They warned him of the old tradition that a pregnant woman's involvement in hog killing would cause the meat to spoil. Pascal, happy for the extra help, disregarded the warnings from these two men. A couple of months later, he was mourning over the fact that his meat in the smokehouse had "tainted." It was the first meat he had ever had ruin in this fashion. I remember him cursing the fact that he had not listened to the warnings of his friends. It is good he had enjoyed that nice tenderloin and chitlin supper with his friends the night following the hog killing because that's about all he got out of his hog killing that year—besides a lesson about pregnant women that might serve him well in the future.

Having returned from military service in 1979 after nearly ten years, I renewed the close relationship that had developed with Pascal in the years I had been around him while growing up. Whenever I had come home on furlough during my service period, I had often visited with him as I did with others I felt close to. During the winter months, I began trapping with my father as did my older brother Buddy who was living with Dad and Mom and helping make things easier for them. Buddy had a good job in Montgomery with a large book-publishing company. He had recently lost his wife and unborn daughter to a sudden illness. He found himself unable to remain in the house he and his wife, Virginia, had shared, and he moved back in with our parents. That move proved very beneficial for everyone. For a number of years, Buddy took his annual leave from work during the late fall and early winter. This allowed him to have several uninterrupted weeks in which to trap each year. With Buddy, Dad, and me trapping—and also Pascal—it gave us a lot to talk about and a good-natured rivalry developed.

During the decades of the seventies and eighties, fur prices surged to their highest level because of the worldwide demand. Fur-bearing animals that had previously been practically worthless were in demand at unbelievable prices. It seemed only wild mink had lost some value in favor of the ranch mink that had become popular. Still, they had some value, but not that which they once had. Because of that, we devoted our energy to going after the more plentiful coons, foxes, bobcats, and otters. We trapped beaver on occasion for nuisance control as they were so plentiful and created problems for landowners. While beavers created new habitat beneficial for other wildlife, they often did it at the expense of exasperated farmers, pond owners, and landholders. Anyone willing to help control them through trapping was usually granted permission to trap the other more desirable fur-bearing animals as well. With the trapping boom that developed because of the demand for furs, it was important to hold on to traditional trapping areas and find new territory as well. We used beaver control as a tool in holding and securing trapping rights, as did others.

A new tradition was started that involved Pascal and Dad by the time I had come back home in 1979. They called each other by phone every night during trapping season, which ran from November 20 to February 20 each year. They compared their catch total for the day and often ribbed each other a bit. It was a friendly competition that involved us all, and we would never have dreamed of not making that call. Those calls were interrupted for a lengthy period in 1985 when my father died unexpectedly. I had lost my best friend, and I felt as if my very soul had been sucked right out of my body. For a while, I had no interest at all in trapping, day-to-day activities, or even living. One of the greatest things in life is the sharing of one's life with others, and the one I shared so much of mine with was gone. I did not know what to do with the tremendous void it created.

As I began to refocus a bit, I found myself becoming even closer to my father's lifelong friend, Pascal Owens. In a sense, it was like having a part of my father with me still. Pascal and I resumed the daily calls to one another after a while, and we continued those calls as long as his health allowed it. In that, I could again share my life as before and bring back some of the meaning that had been lost with the death of my father. Pascal became more than just Dad's friend or my friend. I began to accept him as more fatherly from that point on.

We continued our friendly rivalry when comparing our daily catches even though we both knew I had the advantage. I was younger and more physically capable. He was far older and heavier, and he got about with extreme difficulty. He had to depend on a helper to help him maintain his traplines. He could no longer struggle up and down creek banks or do the walking trapping required. He drove his helper along his lines to check and reset traps, while he remained with the Jeep. He loved trapping. It was in his blood as it had been with my own father, and he continued it until almost the very end of his life.

We continued the tradition we had begun several years earlier of going to sell furs together for as long as he was able to do so. Long ago, he had stopped sending his furs away by mail to buyers as my father had as well. With the great demand for furs had also come a lot of buyers who established scheduled routes so they could operate effectively in the very competitive market. We took advantage of this method of selling our furs. Every two weeks or so, we loaded up the furs that were ready for sale and journeyed to the advertised location of our buyer. That was a very special day full of anticipation and optimism about fur prices. We dedicated the whole day to it because it was the culmination of so much work over the past couple of weeks. While it might have been a lot of work, it was also exciting to the point that it did not seem like work. It was a part of us. The selling of the furs was like celebrating Christmas. Christmas that came around about every two weeks or so.

It was difficult going to the hospital to see Pascal, knowing his death was imminent. His kidneys had failed completely. A lot of his family members were there. His room appeared to be the most popular place around and reminded me so much of how people had sat around in his little country store and socialized. It seemed people had just moved their socializing from there to his hospital room. I watched him as he looked from one to another of the people who had gathered in his room. People were carrying on various conversations around him. It wasn't that they didn't care. They did. Their presence around him spoke of the feelings they had for him. They just wanted to be there and spend a little more time with him, just like I did. We all wanted to avoid talking about the obvious.

As I sat there among the other visitors, I continued to watch him looking at those about him. Even then, I knew I would miss him terribly when he was gone. Everyone would. He died peacefully on January 14, 1987, two years and one month after Lewis Brady, my dad. He had been one of my father's closest friends and mine as well.

Trapping lost its appeal to me after Pascal died. Dad was already gone, and Buddy had lost his passion for trapping after our father's death. I struggled to maintain my interest in it for another year or two after Pascal's, but I finally admitted I no longer had my heart in it. The traps began rusting away. A beautiful desert island may be a fine place to be as long as it can be shared and enjoyed with others, but by yourself? No, it would probably become just a lonely place without joy. Trapping, for me, had become terribly lonesome when Pascal died. I no longer had anyone to share it with.

Just before writing the above couple of paragraphs, I stopped writing, picked up my truck keys, and took a little ride. I drove to the little cemetery at the edge of the woods behind an old, white-clapboard Methodist Church. A weathered wrought iron fence encloses the cemetery. I opened the gate, went inside, and stood beside the grave of Pascal Owens for a while. It turned out to be an emotional few minutes, but I am so happy I gave in to the impulse to go visit him once again. Perhaps, in a few days, I will make another visit there. Maybe when his son Jimmy gets back from his business trip to Canada. I'm going to suggest a couple of folding chairs so we can sit there and visit for a while. Pascal would like that—and so would the two of us.

34

THE GRIEVING TIME

LEWIS BRADY, my dad, was the hardest-working man I ever knew. I do not say that lightly; I am firmly convinced of the fact. I never knew him to play or waste time. There was too much he wanted and needed to do. His day started well before daylight and continued until the evening. He rarely varied from this type of schedule, except on Sunday. That was a special day. He got his farm chores and feeding done in time to dress for church. Later, after the usual Sunday dinner, he spent much of the afternoon relaxing with the family. Though he was such a hard and tough man, physically, he had a soft and tender heart for his family and enjoyed the few special hours with them each Sunday. Evening chores rounded out this very special day, and he went to bed early and was ready to begin another busy week on Monday morning.

A short time before the end of his life, he expressed to me the two regrets of his life.

"Allen," he said, "if I had it to do over again, I would stop and play some. I wish I had just played some."

I took that admission as an apology that he hadn't done any fun things with me and the rest of the family, an apology none of us would have considered necessary. He was Dad, a hardworking man we respected and loved with all our hearts. Just living life with him was a pleasure, and I wish he had known just how deeply we all felt that. I also took his words as an admonition to remember that life is not all work. "Enjoy the time with your children and do things together," he seemed to be telling me.

"I wish that I had never picked up my first cigarette," he said, stating his second regret. "But I was young and wanted to keep up with the older chaps and do what they did."

At this latter stage of his life, he did not have the breath to exert himself or walk more than a few steps. A lifetime of smoking had taken its toll on him. No matter how much exercise he got from constant walking and physical exertion, those activities could not stave off the effects of the smoking. He also had become badly stricken with gout in his shoulders and had difficulty in getting dressed. Because of these two conditions, in the last year or so of his life, he found he was unable to do the two things he enjoyed most: gardening and trapping.

A very respected physician, Dr. B. F. Dorough, confided to me that Dad's white blood count was high and that he suspected leukemia. "I don't want to put him through any testing or pursue it," he said. "Something else will probably get him first."

Shortly afterward, Dad told me he was passing blood regularly and could not tolerate food. It seemed everything he ate caused him to have considerable amounts of gas and intestinal distress. He began living on Rice Krispies. They seemed to cause him the least distress. Quickly, the pain was becoming unbearable, but he did not want to see the doctor. I believe he knew what was going on inside his body.

On a Friday afternoon, he sent one of my children to tell me to come. He was sitting on the edge of his bed when I arrived, holding both hands against his abdomen and rocking back and forth in pain.

"I hurt so bad that I don't know what to do!" he groaned, with his voice shaking. "Do you have anything that I can take?" I told him I would bring something, and I asked him about going to the doctor.

"It won't do any good," he told me. "Just bring me something for my stomach."

I went home and returned with some stomach medication, but I knew we were just going through the motions.

I called my children together that night and told them their granddaddy was very sick and probably would not last through the winter. "He has told me many times you are some of the best children he has ever known. Make sure you go in and see him whenever you come home from school," I told them. "It means so much to him."

"We always do," they all answered together.

"I just don't want you to forget," I reminded them. I did not know how things would unfold over the next couple of days at the time I had this talk with my children. Dad, obviously, spent some time between then and Monday morning writing a final letter to all of us. He expressed his love for us and left final instructions concerning the handling of his affairs.

"The pain," he expressed in the letter, "was unbearable." Placing the letter on the pillow of the bed he had obviously not slept in, he went into an adjoining room on Monday morning and sat down. The muzzle of the .22 rifle he had bought many years before for a more humane death for his pigs was placed to his forehead. He pulled the trigger and stopped the pain.

The days and weeks that followed can only be described as a horrible and mind-numbing period for me. I felt I was locked into a persistent nightmare I could not awaken from. *This cannot be real!* It seemed I was alternating between the feeling that I was going out of my mind and the feeling that I would just keel over and die at any moment. I truly felt I could not survive that time and wondered if I really wanted to. Thoughts of my wife and children and their dependence on me helped dispel certain ideas that had come into my mind. *How can I continue to exist without Dad?* I could not wrap my mind around such a thought. He was my best friend, not just my father, and he was suddenly gone.

Danny Bradford Yell showed up at the right time. It was a couple of days after Dad's funeral when he dropped in unexpectedly. He did not know of Dad's death, and I had not seen him for a number of years. "Danny B," as we always called him, just dropped in. Danny B was like a brother to me, and in years gone by, he had lived with us for weeks at a time over a period of several years. Even Dad felt a closeness to Danny B, almost as if he were his fourth son. Danny B told me that he had come because he felt a strong impulse to come.

"It was like I knew something was wrong and that you needed me," he said.

Whatever it was that caused him to make the decision to come proved a blessing to me. He stayed all day, and he came back the next day. He continued to make the thirty-mile drive to my house for many days thereafter. We spent those days together walking, talking, and hunting. At least, *he* hunted. I just appreciated his company and the distraction his company afforded me in my grief. I think God knew who I needed at that moment in my life, and he sent Danny B. I've wondered how I could have possibly made it through that time had he not shown up.

I am not unique in having to suffer grief, and I recognize that. All normal people will suffer it at some point in their lives, but the level of grief I experienced over the death of my father, for me, was unique. Never has the death of another human being affected me so. It was a deep, profound, and mind-numbing grief. I had left the military after nearly ten years so I could be with him. He begged me to do so. He was so lonesome after having raised eleven children and having seen them scatter all over the world. I gave in to his pleas and came home to be with him again. We worked together doing painting and carpentry. We spent the winters trapping together. He became my best friend. I could not imagine a world without him. He had always been there, and I could not imagine it being otherwise.

Things did get better though. It was a slow process, and I dreamed a lot about him. One night, he called my name, and I sat bolt upright in bed. It was called in the same manner as I had heard him call countless times in my life. I sat there awhile, hoping I would hear it again, but there was only silence.

For the next couple of years, while working on some house or another, I would think of something funny or have a question in my mind about something. *I'll stop and mention that to Dad when I get home. He'll get a kick out of that,* I would think. Just as quickly, I would remember he was not there.

Eventually, the grief began to subside, and I found it being replaced with happy memories of my father. There were so many of them too—so many that I found my mind had little room for unhappy ones when I remembered the pleasure of living life with Dad. Some of those memories I have already recorded on the pages about my youngest years. I would like to shift this narrative back to the time of those precious memories.

Dad on Sunday morning.

Allen and Yoko on the day of Dad's
funeral. It's a nightmare day.

Allen, Larry, and Buddy on the day of Dad's funeral.

35

LOOKING BACK ON
LIFE WITH DAD

DAD WAS a farmer first. He was not a farmer of the commercial type; he was a subsistence farmer. He grew food for the family and livestock. Some things, he still had to buy, but most of it, he raised on the dozen or so acres he cultivated with his mule and plow. In the wintertime, he trapped for three months to bring in money for the family. For an income in the warmer months, he took on local carpentry and painting jobs.

There were a number of odors I associated with Dad from my childhood 'til now. In the winter, there was the ever-present scent of beaver, otters, and mink. In the summer, there was the smell of sawdust, paint thinner, and sweat. When evening came, and he had "cleaned up," he smelled pleasantly of medicated heat powder and soap. From childhood, he had taken a pan bath every night and meticulously continued that habit throughout his life. Dad liked peppermint, and he kept a supply with him at all times and put a piece in his mouth at frequent intervals throughout the day. The smell of his peppermint mingled with the aroma of the tobacco he smoked. For many years, it was Prince Albert tobacco. In the later years of his life, he smoked regular cigarettes. When the weather was cold, he used Vick's Salve and Soltice Cream on his chest at bedtime. He was a firm believer those products helped him breathe better and stay healthier during the cold and flu season. I do not believe Dad could ever have slipped up on me in the dark. Any one of these odors would have telegraphed his presence.

Dad raised a lot of different things on his small farm. He raised a pretty good bit of corn because of the needs of the cows, mule, pigs, and chickens. We certainly ate our share of the corn too when it was in the "roasting ear" stage. We also had cornmeal made from the mature, dry corn. Dad raised a large patch of sweet potatoes and constructed "potato banks" to preserve them safely through the winter. It was good we all liked sweet potatoes because we ate them almost every day during the winter months. Every year, there were lots of field peas, butter beans, and okra. Also, pumpkins, watermelons, and cantaloupes. For many years, there was a peanut patch because Dad liked parched peanuts. The livestock was fond of the peanut hay. In the garden patch, there were various types of greens, tomatoes, peppers, beets, Irish potatoes, and onions. There were cucumbers, squash, and more watermelons. There had to be a good supply of watermelons.

Dad always owned a mule. A mule was a necessity for plowing, cultivating, and pulling the wagon. He also had seven or eight cows and calves on the place most of the time. They provided us with milk, and sometimes Dad slaughtered a yearling for meat. This was after he had bought a large freezer from Sears. It was only in the last several years of my father's life that he did not have a pig. Until then, he had kept at least one—and often two or three—for a supply of fresh and smoked meat. Sometimes there were a lot of pigs around because a sow had a litter of little ones. What Dad really had a lot of were chickens. There seemed to be chickens roaming everywhere. Let me tell you a little bit about Dad's chickens and chickens in general—perhaps more than you ever wanted to know about chickens!

There probably isn't any creature as cute as a baby chick. As they grow, they go through the awkward stage as their mature feathers are forming. They are not cute then, but they make it through that stage and eventually get pretty as they begin to get full-grown. Each year, they go through a molting state in which they are somewhat unattractive, but they quickly grow their new feathers.

It's an eye-opening experience to live with chickens that are free to roam. There is nothing they will not eat, and I mean nothing. They like their corn and other grain, but they like bugs and grasshoppers too. Being relatives to buzzards, anything dead, no matter how decayed, is on their menu. If they can get under the outhouse ... well, you can figure that one out for yourself. Take a good look down there before you sit down—or, better yet, don't sit!

With all the chickens Dad had on the place, we had to be careful about where we stepped, especially when we were barefoot, which was most of the time in our younger years. They left their droppings everywhere, and we were all educated in keeping our feet clear of them. No matter how careful we were, it was impossible to never make a mistake. Though I never understood exactly why it was so, I learned chicken "stuff" came in two distinct types. One was a well-formed, fairly firm, white and black or white and gray dropping. The other was brown and resembled a bit of melted chocolate on the ground. We learned it was in our best interest to avoid the brown. The white and black didn't smell too bad and could be cleaned away with a stick or corncob. The brown was purely awful! Stepping in it resulting in a hurried foot washing accompanied by a shuddering queasiness and maybe things said that I best not write. The brown did not clean away too easily. At least, not the smell. It had to be scrubbed away. It was not difficult to tell from a distance what kind of stuff someone had stepped on. A simple "Ew" indicated the not-so-bad black and white. A gut-wrenching "Kiiiiii-yahhhh" confirmed the brown. Nobody wanted a second experience with the brown!

With all those chickens, Dad had to construct a lot of chicken "nests" so they would have plenty of places to lay their eggs. He built some in the chicken house and others on the exterior walls around the chicken house. There were nesting boxes nailed in various places throughout the barn. Old coal scuttles and foot tubs would be recycled as places for the hens to lay eggs. With all of these ready-made nests, it would seem that the chickens would be satisfied, and most probably were. There were some who insisted on following nature's dictate and laid their eggs in secret places. Finding old and very large clutches of eggs was common among the hay bales in the barn. We made occasional searches in patches of weeds from time to time for undiscovered nests. We could usually find a big batch of eggs in the dim recess under the outhouse. Whenever we found some previously unknown treasure trove of eggs, we all hoped, secretly, that they were rotten. The outward appearance usually suggested that they were, and a shake or two of a couple of them would confirm it. A joyful call to arms went out from that spot, and there was a mad scramble for the ammunition. While corncob fights were fun, especially if I could bean a sister with a particularly heavy corncob, they could not compare to a rotten egg fight. We divided up the rotten eggs and allowed everyone to disperse and prepare for battle.

Once we started, it was every person for himself or herself. Rotten eggs, like chicken "stuff" came in two forms, depending on the age of the egg. The rotten ones with less age tended to be heavier and sloshed like the shell was half full of water. These heavier eggs could be thrown farther and usually a bit more accurately. The oldest eggs were much lighter and did not slosh when shaken. The rotten contents of the egg had been reduced to a paste-like consistency. They could not be thrown as far, and it was a bit more difficult to be accurate with them, but, boy, were they bad! Those eggs exploded and spread a smell worse than the brown stuff that someone might step on. You didn't want to get this stuff on you either! The trick was to get it on someone else.

After a good fight with the rotten eggs, just like any other battlefield, the evidence was everywhere. It was plastered to tree trunks. There was lots of it on the corners of the house and outbuildings where different ones had darted behind to find cover and even around the door of the house, which indicated a pursued withdrawal. I don't recall Dad ever getting really mad about it or making us clean up the mess unless it was around a door of the house. Since the doors stayed open to help cool the house, it was best not to have rotten eggs spattered all around them. Dad allowed us to have our fun as long as we weren't hurting each other or "tearing the place down." I don't know how he could be so patient with us. He was an understanding man and allowed us to experience the joys of being children—even if he had to put up with the disagreeable odor and aftermath of our rotten egg fights.

We ate chicken fairly regularly. Most of the time we had chicken, it would be on a holiday like Christmas or Thanksgiving. We also ate it frequently on Sundays. Chicken was almost always cooked in gravy. However, we did have periods when we had fried chicken because Dad would have us help him process a number of young "fryers" for the freezer. Simmering chickens in gravy was probably the best way since most of the chickens we ate would have been far too tough to fry. If the chicken was not cooked in gravy, it might have been cooked with rice, dumplings, or dressing. We never had the experience of having turkey and dressing. I suppose that is why I still prefer chicken and dressing at my holiday meals.

When I was very young, and we had fried chicken, Mama fried just about everything that could be fried from the chicken. I think the feathers and guts were about the only thing that didn't go into the skillet. I remember seeing the feet being fried and knowing Dianne and I would have those on our plates. As the two youngest, those were reserved for us. Believe me when I say there is no meat on the chicken feet. We gnawed the crust of batter off and thought we had just eaten something special. I thought about this in later years and wondered if Mama couldn't have battered and fried a couple of sticks for us. Except for the toes, we probably would not have known the difference. Eventually, we moved up to necks and gizzards. It was probably about the time that Dad had all his teeth pulled. He had always favored the neck and gizzard as his part of the chicken. Unfortunately, teeth are just about a must for these two parts. Fortunately, for Dianne and myself, we had teeth and were willing to put them to use. As we got older, the fried chicken all but disappeared from our table. It was easier for Dad to eat the chicken that had been simmered in gravy.

One chicken became a pet of ours. When she was just a baby chick, we took over her care. She was the only chick hatched by the mother hen, and the hen refused to care for her. We children began feeding the chick a mush made of cornmeal and water. We kept her in a box and pampered her. Taking her out of her box frequently to play with her, she became the center of attention. After all, how can anyone resist coddling a baby chick? Naturally, she bonded with us and not with the other chickens. She stayed in the house with us and was left out of the box to roam for long periods of time.

As she got older and messier, we were discouraged from keeping her in the house and were told to put her outside with the rest of the chickens. "Peep," as we had named her, never gave up on trying to reclaim her place as part of our household. She often hung around the door, waiting for someone to open it so she could get inside. She succeeded quite often, and we had to take her outside again.

When nighttime came, Peep would see us through one window or another and peck on it in an attempt to get inside. As pitiful as is was, we had to ignore her. She usually roosted on the ledge of the window through which she had last seen us. Sometimes, at night, when I had to get up and relieve myself, I would be startled at the appearance of a white "face" at the window. It would be the white feathers of our pet hen, Peep. If there is such a thing as happiness for chickens, Peep was happy. Being awakened by the light, she seemed excited to see me and moved around and pecked on the window. I had to ignore her.

One day, Peep disappeared. It was on a Sunday. We had chicken and gravy that day, and I didn't eat any. Even before I asked Dad, I knew it was Peep. He confirmed that it was, and I didn't say any more about it. Peep had gotten into the house too many times and had roosted on the window ledges too many times. She had pecked on the windows too often. She had grown too pleasingly plump and had attracted too much of Dad's attention. Her need for attention did her in. We were to learn that on a small farm such as ours, there was no line drawn between pets and food.

When Dad bought his large freezer so we could keep frozen vegetables and meat, he started a new tradition of sorts for us. This was the annual chicken killing that all the children dreaded. Each year, he would announce to all of us at evening time, "We are going to kill chickens tomorrow." We knew each of us had to help and could not go anywhere. Dad would already have isolated about thirty or so unlucky birds in the chicken pen. The ax was sharpened and standing by at the log round that served as the chopping block.

On the following day, Dad heated several gallons of water and filled the foot tub with it for scalding the chickens. Selecting six or seven victims at a time, which we held for him, he began chopping their heads off with the ax as we handed them to him. As he tossed each chicken aside, the chicken began to flop and jump around the yard. I fully understand the expression "running around like a chicken with its head cut off." Blood was sprinkled everywhere, and it was an unpleasant experience for us and the chickens too.

When the chickens were still, Dad dipped each in the hot water and handed one to each of us. We were expected to pick them clean enough to pass Dad's inspection. When the first batch was cleaned to his satisfaction, Dad repeated the process with several more victims. We were very happy children when our part was done and Dad finished processing the chickens and put them in the freezer. The smell of hot, wet feathers is one that is hard to forget. The sight of headless and bloody chickens bouncing around the yard is equally unforgettable. But that was life with my dad. He did it all. He spared us from these things when he could, but sometimes he just couldn't do it all alone.

Buddy, my oldest brother, was many years older than me. He figured out how to get a chicken dinner when the craving for one hit him. On more than one occasion, he sprinkled a line of corn from the yard to the middle of the road where he spread a handful of the corn. Hiding in the weeds, he waited for a car to come by. Sometimes, he got lucky and a chicken got unlucky. Announcing the unfortunate event to Mama and presenting her with the chicken, he happily anticipated the evening meal. He used this method of getting chicken on the table a couple of times before a disappointing incident occurred. Waiting in the weeds one day for the car to come by and do its work, he was rehearsing the sad tidings he would deliver to Mama. A car did come by, presently, and the sad deed was done, but this car stopped! The driver of the car backed up to the spot where the chicken was lying in the road. A door opened, and a dark hand reached down and retrieved the chicken. When the car sped away, Buddy was left very disappointed. There may have been joy around someone's table that evening, but not the one that Buddy sat at!

Chickens are great entertainers—at least they are if you have a good imagination. We had good imaginations. Swing one around a bit and let it go, and you have one sick, crazy-acting chicken! They make good targets for arrows, blunt ones, of course. When there are lots of chickens, there are lots of targets to pursue. Trapping them with a box and a rope was fun and also killed a little time on a hot summer day. With the box propped up at one end with a stick with a rope attached, and a line of corn leading to it, it became a matter of time before capturing a chicken. Chickens may be stupid, but even they learn, quickly, that they are being set up. Soon, they refused to approach the box, and I would have figure out another method of entertainment. I was doing a service to the chickens, apparently, by sharpening their survival skills. Theirs was a humdrum life of scratching and pecking. I felt duty bound to liven up their existence a bit, but it seemed the chickens just didn't appreciate it. It did liven up my existence, and I never stopped trying to figure out some new way to have fun at the chickens' expense.

Dad did not seem to mind it as long as I didn't "devil" them too much or harm them.

My sister Betty and brother Larry forgot the "do not harm" part one day. This was just before Dad had torn the outbuildings down at the old house site. The roof of the "garage" was made of tin and was quite steep. Somehow, they developed the idea it would be fun to watch a chicken slide down that roof. Who knows, the chicken might enjoy the experience too. They decided to give it a try. Grabbing an older hen that couldn't escape them, they tossed her as far up on the roof as they could manage. Boy, did she slide! She also flopped around and squawked a lot while coming down. It was such a fun thing to see that they had already decided to do it again by the time she hit the ground. Heaving her up onto the roof a second time, they enjoyed the spectacle of her descent as she repeated her terrified performance. Several encores were in order. It was too much for the old hen, and she died on stage. Her heart just gave out.

When the old hen "became dead," it was an unexpected turn of events for Larry and Betty. They knew they could not explain the dead chicken, so the best thing to do was to hide the body. They were not as imaginative in this as they had been in the entertainment phase. They picked the first spot their eyes fell on. In the front yard, there was a patch of weeds several feet across that had grown up around an old stump. That would be the place. They concealed the old chicken there. When Dad came home, he saw the dead chicken almost at once. He also judged, rather quickly, that something had occurred other than natural death. Somehow, his children were involved in this. Dad had seen his share of chickens that had been killed in various ways and those that had sickened and died. This one was stuffed into the weeds, head down and feet up. That ruled out foxes, dogs, and nature. It was proof that children were involved since chickens claimed by nature are not hidden away in a weed clump.

Hiding of a body means someone is trying to escape guilt. Dad was very good at adding two and two and getting the right answer. Since tattling was frowned on by everyone in that day, he knew none of us would tell who did it. He got very angry but didn't pursue the issue. Unlike Mama, Dad would not punish all the children to ensure that the guilty had been punished. I'm sure Larry and Betty lived in dread for a while afterward, and that was, in a sense, punishment. They were the older of the youngest group of children in our family, and they knew that Dad suspected them. Suspicion was not proof, however. Dad never whipped a child unless guilt was clearly established and the offense really called for such measures. Happily, that was rare. Dad loved his children and could put up with a lot.

I do not know how many pigs Dad raised in his life so that the family could have a good meat supply. We always seemed to have meat hanging in the smokehouse during most of the year. Dad raised and butchered quite a few pigs during the time that I remember from early childhood until several years before his death. Often, he butchered one around the Fourth of July and invited many from the community to a barbecue. At the first real cold weather of winter, he would butcher one or two pigs and salt the meat for later smoking. Sometimes he would do this again in late winter as well. This would guarantee we would have smoked meat through most of the year. I don't remember a time when we did not have young pigs and grown ones around. Quite often, before a pig ever got to the butchering stage, we had already created a few memories involving that animal. We were always on the lookout for some new way to entertain ourselves. We had good imaginations too.

My first memories of Dad's pigs were at the old house site

where we lived before our house burned. His hog lot was a large pie slice-shaped wire enclosure between the garage and highway. There was a tin shed to protect the pigs from the cold winter weather and from the sun in the summer. The pigs had created a huge mud wallow that they enjoyed during the summer months to help them stay cooler. This hog lot remained in place for several years after the house had burned. During those years we were living on the other side of the highway, Dad constructed a couple of smaller wooden pens close by to keep certain pigs in for fattening. Eventually, he stopped keeping any pigs on that side of the road and moved them all to the other side where the new house stood.

As I said, we always looked for new ways to have fun, and we tried it with the pigs, as we did with everything else. Though we had never been to a rodeo before, we had heard about them and came up with a version of rodeo on our own. We wanted to ride the pigs. That sounded like fun when it was proposed, but how were we to get them to cooperate? The idea turned out to be rather simple. Shelling the kernels from an ear of corn, we dropped them inside the fence of the pigpen. Catching one of the pigs parallel to the fence, we would lay an opened magazine or newspaper sheet on its muddy back. Quickly dropping onto its back, we tried to hold on as it bolted away from the fence. Usually it headed for the wallow or shed, squealing as it went. No matter how hard we tried to stay on, we couldn't manage more than a few feet or a couple of seconds. I tried this on a number of occasions and never really succeeded in much more than getting my clothes pretty muddy. Every time I picked myself up from the ground, I had to run for the fence. We did not really understand the danger of what we were doing and that we could have gotten a nasty bite if the pig was so inclined. Maybe this thought was in the back of my mind somewhere because I always ran pretty hard back to the fence. We never let Dad know we had done these things. He probably would not have liked it. Mama didn't know either, but she likely wondered why her magazines sometimes disappeared.

Often, through the years, my father would have a dozen or more young pigs to care for because of the brood sows he sometimes kept. Most of these pigs would be sold for about five dollars each when they were old enough to be away from their mothers. Often, I saw someone come by the house and then leave with a crocus sack with a squealing pig inside. They were usually sold to various black families who did not have a brood sow of their own. The pigs would be raised and butchered in the early winter when they were fully grown. There were years when my father also had to purchase his pigs from someone else. In those years that Dad had a lot of young pigs, there was a certain thing he had to do that was unpleasant for the pigs and for everyone else. That was castration.

When I was very young, Dad told me to take Dianne in the house while he and one of the local black men took care of the business. There was no way to block out the squealing of the pigs while this task was underway. It was nerve-racking for Dad and no picnic for the pigs. If I had been born a pig, I would rather not have been born a male. As I got a couple of years older, I stayed with Dad while he performed this disagreeable task. After all, I could hold the can of petroleum-based grease he slathered onto the wound of each pig. This was to keep flies and infection out of the open wound. It always amazed me at how quickly each pig returned to normal activity—just a minute or two.

As I got a little older, I became Dad's helper on these occasions. I developed my own technique for holding the pig so Dad could fully concentrate on what he was doing. I simply grabbed a hind leg in each hand, placed my foot underneath the pig's tail, and lay backward onto the ground. The pig could not move anything but the forward part of its body and front feet. That didn't matter anyway since I had it belly up. The technique worked great with calves too.

When I was about eleven or twelve years old, Dad gave me instructions to move several pigs from a shed down in the pasture to a wooden pen near the house. He had sold them and was going to hold them away from the mother sow. The shed in the pasture was enclosed by a nice hog lot constructed of fencing wire. It was fairly new and had been built under the shade of the oldest and largest oak tree I have ever seen. At a place where Dad proposed to put a gate, he nailed a board across the top of two fence posts he had installed about four feet apart. Later, he could cut this section of wire out and put the gate in between the two posts. The board on top would prevent the posts from spreading and cause the wire to sag, but that was still in the future.

Climbing over the fence at this point, I cautiously approached the shed where the pigs were. Carrying my croker sack, I climbed over the low tin wall that enclosed the shed. Things went well until I got inside. The situation deteriorated once the pigs started squealing as I caught one and then another and got them into the sack. The mama in the hog lot had gotten pretty agitated and responded to the squeals of her little ones. I was safe in the shed though. The problem was, I had to get out of the shed and then out of the hog lot with the sack containing two pretty heavy pigs. Watching the sow as she ran to and fro in her distress, I timed my exit from the shed. Catching the sow as she was running away from the shed, I vaulted over the side wall, dragged the sack over, and ran for the fence. I didn't make it—at least not with the two pigs.

The sow was right behind me, and the open mouth with all those teeth sent cold chills over my body. Dropping the sack, I darted to the fence and dove through the narrow opening between the board across the two posts and the wire underneath. It was the narrowest of openings, probably no more than fourteen inches or so. I did not touch the wire or the board at all and have never understood how I accomplished such a neat trick. Had I tried it ten more times, I probably would have brained myself on that board or hung up on the wire every time. I knew I had been very fortunate to have escaped being chewed up by a very mad hog. There was no way I would venture back into the lot for the sack containing the two pigs. I had only one choice: go home and tell Dad.

Dad had assigned me this job because he had so many other things he needed to do. I knew he was disappointed I hadn't carried out the assignment, but he wasn't hard on me about it. He stopped what he was doing and headed for the hog lot. All the way there, I was wondering how he was going to retrieve the sack without getting eaten alive. As it turned out, he kept the sow at bay while I got the sack out of the pen. We deposited these two pigs in the wooden pen at the house and returned for a couple more. Dad kept the sow away while I sacked up two more pigs and got out of the lot.

On the final trip, the sow was so enraged my father had his hands full trying to keep her away. She was so determined to get to him and me that Dad became desperate to stop her. On the ground was a waterlogged board that he grabbed and hit the sow with. He brought it down on her with such force I was sure he must have killed her. It did knock her over and stunned her. Both of us got over the fence with the sack containing the last two pigs. Dad was cussing a blue streak the whole time. We did not leave right away but waited to see if the sow was going to be okay. She was. Dad used the time to roll and smoke a cigarette and settle down a bit.

As we walked back to the house with the sack containing the two pigs, I somehow felt vindicated. Dad, too, had experienced a little of what I had felt. I'm sure he was relieved nothing had happened to me. He had defended me pretty vigorously just as the sow had defended her young ones.

When Dad butchered his pigs, or rather hogs, in the wintertime, it was quite an event. When I was very young, it really wasn't bad for me since little was required of me. I liked being near the fire even though the smoke was terrible. The north wind always seemed to be blowing very hard and pushing smoke around. The weather at hog-killing time was cold. Dad watched the weather closely for the right time to butcher the hogs. He wanted to be sure the temperature remained very cold for several days from the time he started to be sure that the meat did not spoil. He usually did this when a cold system was coming through, which accounted for the windy conditions.

I have already described the scene where my father killed Mama's pig with the ax. It was a gruesome thing to see, and it affected Dad too. It was then that he decided to buy a single-shot .22 rifle to dispatch the pigs with. All the pigs he butchered after that were dispatched with one clean shot to the brain. This was far less stressful for Dad and more humane for the animal.

At hog-killing time, Dad enlisted the help of one or two of our black neighbors. Usually, they were from the Osborne family. It was always good to have help. Hog killing was not only messy but a labor-intensive affair, especially if more than one hog was butchered. My dad had his own way of scalding the pig to start the hair removal process. He dug a depression in the ground and put a fifty-five-gallon drum in it. The mouth of the drum had its lower edge even with the ground, while the base was in the hole. The barrel lay at an angle, and the pig was slid into this barrel of hot water and rotated to wet all parts of it.

Afterward, it was pulled out onto a couple of pieces of tin for the hair removal. Working quickly and occasionally pouring more hot water on the pig, the hair was scraped away with butcher knives.

I helped by staying out of the way and fetching one thing or another that was called for. Otherwise, I was just hanging around. For some reason, I always had the urge to roast a sweet potato in the coals of the fire at hog-killing time. They did not get soft throughout like an oven-roasted potato, but the outer part softened a little. The skin of the potato was burned black. I peeled the outer layer of the potato away with my teeth and spit it into the fire. It was always very hot, and I had to be careful not to burn my lips and hands. The potato was only slightly softened by the fire and had a smoky, caramelized taste. By the time I put my potato in the fire, one of those helping Dad would be laying strips of the liver or heart in the coals to cook. The meat smelled good and sizzled as it cooked, but I never ate any of it. Liver had never appealed to me, and the idea of eating a heart did not either. Those who did eat it as it came out of the coals seemed to enjoy it. It must have been good by the way they carried on about it.

All the inner parts of the pig were saved in a large washtub and cleaned later. Some were cleaned and cooked as chitlins, which my father was crazy about. Much, if not all, of the small intestine was cleaned and used as the casing for the stuffed sausage. I watched Annie Ausborne clean the chitlins on several occasions. She pushed the contents of an intestine out by pulling it through one hand. Afterward, she continued doing this as she poured water into one end of it. She continued the process until she had them fairly clean. However, it was necessary to clean them again before cooking them.

When the cleaning of the pig was complete, Dad cut it up

into hams, shoulders, jowls, and "middlins," or bacon. These sections of meat were laid on top of the smokehouse late in the evening to chill in the cold night air. The following morning, they were taken down and salted away in the big wooden box Dad had in the smokehouse for that purpose. After a prescribed number of days, they would be taken out, rinsed of excess salt, and hung in the smokehouse for smoking. By then, the sausage had already been stuffed, hung, and smoked. Dad smoked his meat with green hickory chips for several days, and the color of the meat turned a beautiful golden brown and smelled very good.

The extra fat that had been trimmed away was cut up and rendered into lard and cracklings. The cracklings were salted and eaten as snacks, and they were also added to corn bread to make crackling bread. I preferred eating them as a snack. The lard was poured into five-gallon lard cans and put in the smokehouse where we dipped out a supply for cooking each day.

For supper on hog-killing day, we ate lots of tenderloin. This was the best part of the pig, and we could eat as much as we wanted. It was always best to cook it while fresh. When frozen, it loses the really good flavor that fresh tenderloin has. The following day, Dad always cooked a concoction of what he called liver hash or liver and light stew. The "lights" are the lungs and have a spongy texture when cooked. We left all of this special concoction for Dad. I didn't even like the smell of it and didn't like liver anyway. The head, feet, and ears were boiled. The feet, ears, and the meat from the head were coarsely ground after all the bones had been removed. Onion was added to the meat while it was being ground. After seasoning the meat with vinegar, salt, pepper, and sage, it was pressed into a bowl and chilled as souse meat. It had a very good flavor and could be sliced and eaten as a snack.

Within a couple of days of hog killing, Dad cooked his chitlins. If you have never smelled chitlins boiling, especially those that have recently been a part of your freshly killed, farm-raised pig, you don't want to be around. The smell of them boiling is a heavy, clinging stink that is difficult to purge from your nostrils. To hard-core chitlin lovers, it probably would make their mouths water as they anticipated this special treat. To everyone else, the smell might make the eyes water. It was truly a nauseating odor that would make the average person wish they were somewhere else.

On a couple of occasions, while Dad was boiling chitlins, visitors dropped in. I watched one man and his wife fidget a bit and try to make small talk with Dad. All the time, both had distracted and funny looks on their faces. Several minutes into their visit, they excused themselves, saying they had some pretty important business to attend to. As I recall, the visitors on the other occasion also remembered some forgotten engagement that they were already late for. Dad did not have to share this special treat of his with anyone at suppertime. We left them all to him, whether just boiled or boiled and then battered and fried.

Perhaps we did not have some of the things the neighbor kids or our schoolmates had, but we also had things they were deprived of. Not only did we have the experience of the mule and wagon and possibly a simpler life and farming style, we also enjoyed the produce of the farm that so many did not have the pleasure of. Meat from the smokehouse was one of those pleasures. It was so much better than the grocery-store versions I've had to content myself with since then. It is very difficult to describe how good the smoked sausage actually was. There was no stinginess with the sausage or any of the other smoked meat at meals. Ham was cut in thick slices and always had a lot of fat around the edge of it. We were allowed to eat as much as we wanted. Often it was cooked at suppertime, and the smell was terrific! There were times I could smell it frying while I was a hundred or more yards from the house and ran home for supper.

If I want to record my most special memories about Dad's pigs, it would have to be the memory of ham frying at evening time. It is a warm, pleasant memory that makes me hungry even now. I know there were times when Dad had no money, but we were never hungry. He loved his family and made sure there was plenty of food for us. In later years, I came to appreciate the fact that we enjoyed so many good things that others did not have the pleasure of experiencing. When my father expressed one of his life's regrets shortly before his death about not having "played" some, I wish he could have known how precious the memories were that he had left us. None were created by his playing games with us. All were a result of his hard and unselfish work and his desire to take care of us. If playing is about excitement, joy, and pleasure, we enjoyed a lot of that with him.

36

THE NECESSITY OF CATS

DAD WAS a firm believer in the necessity of keeping some cats about. On a farm with all the corn and other feed grains, and with all those pigs and chickens, there are going to be rats. Not just rats, but plenty of mice as well. Anyone can accept the wisdom of having cats about to help keep the rat and mouse population from getting completely out of hand. Even so, it seemed it was a losing battle, at times. The cats severely were outnumbered, and not all of them had the temperament required to go forth and do battle.

On a Sunday morning, Dad was standing at the table while eating his breakfast. He often ate standing when he had a lot to do. Sitting might encourage him to stay longer than he wanted to and make him feel as if he had wasted time. He had a lot to do on Sunday mornings before getting dressed for church.

As I entered the kitchen, he told me, "There is a rat in the feed barrel in the smokehouse. Take that cat there, drop it in, and let him take care of it."

Picking up the half-grown cat that he indicated, I headed to the smokehouse expecting a little excitement. Little did I know how that excitement was about to involve me. Opening the door and approaching the barrel just inside, I looked in and saw the rat in the bottom looking back at me.

Holding the cat over the barrel until it saw the rat, I dropped it in. What happened next was totally unexpected. I thought the cat would land in the bottom and then quickly pounce on the rat. Or perhaps it would hem the rat up on one side of the barrel and then seize it. I would have used either of these approaches if I were a cat, but I am not a cat, especially a cowardly one as this cat was. It happened so fast I'm still confused about what actually happened. Did the cat actually reverse course in midair and latch onto my arms or did it hit the bottom of the barrel before bouncing upward and latching onto my arms? All I know, for sure, is that I had a frantic cat trying to use my still extended hands and arms as an escape ladder. The claws not embedded in my arms were sliding down my arms trying to gain purchase. I don't think a meat grinder could have been more painful! The cat was out the door in a flash, and I was left with two somewhat shredded arms.

As I headed out the door too, I happened to see an older cat nearby. I quickly picked her up, took her to the feed barrel, and allowed her to look down. She stiffened and growled softly as if interested, so I dropped her in, but made sure I did it in a bit of a pitching motion to keep my arms clear. When she landed in the bottom, she acted like a true cat with hunting experience and not the young 'fraidy cat that had put me in misery a minute earlier. Staying just long enough to watch her capture the rat, I headed for the house to doctor my wounds.

Dad seemed a little amused when I related what had happened. He was careful to advise me to wash my arms and put plenty of rubbing alcohol on them. That was not fun! It was like a meat grinder all over again. My clawed-up arms and shoulder were on fire. At some point, the burning subsided, and I began to appreciate the humorous side of the affair.

Dad was going to show me how it was to be properly done. Catch a cat, that is. Apparently, I had done it all wrong and had been bitten by the cat I was trying to capture. We already had one half-grown cat in the bag and were trying to catch the second one too. It was the same one that had clawed me up pretty good at the feed barrel.

Mandy Norman had a rat problem at her house and needed a couple of cats. We were about to provide her with two of them that would have to earn their keep at her house or starve. It would be a good time to get rid of the cowardly cat and its littermate while doing a good deed for someone we cared about. It would also afford a perfect opportunity for these two cats to lead productive lives.

We had hemmed the second cat up in the living room, and I had closed the doors to keep it from getting out. My index finger was hurting and throbbing where the cat had bitten me. I had not grabbed it correctly, according to Dad, or it would not have happened. He was about to show me how it was supposed to be done. The cat was on top of the drapery rod, having clawed its way up Mama's drapes a few seconds earlier.

"You have to grab the cat behind the neck and hold tight," he said. "That way, he can't bite you." As he reached up for the cat, he instructed me to have the bag open and ready.

The cat turned and tried to advance to the other end of the rod when Dad seized him by the neck from behind. With his other hand, he grabbed it by its rear legs. His intention became apparent as he pulled the cat down from the rod. He would keep the cat stretched out enough that it would be more difficult for it to scratch him. Dad apparently paid more attention to avoiding the claws than he should. His grip on the cat's neck loosened enough for the cat to twist his head and latch on to Dad's thumb.

"Good God Almighty!" Dad bellowed. The air turned fairly blue with the words that came as he vainly tried to get his thumb out of the cat's mouth. Nothing seemed to work, and I could see the cat's jaw muscles working as if he were chewing deeper.

In desperation, Dad finally yelled, "Get him off. Good God—get him off!" I did not know how to proceed without maybe winding up with my hand in that cat's mouth, but Dad managed to quit hollering and cussing enough to advise me.

"Push in hard on each side of his mouth and push his jaws apart," he instructed.

I did so, and he was able to pull his chewed-up thumb back far enough from the cat's jaws to get a good hold of the cat's neck. I opened the bag that was now on the floor, and the cat was quickly thrown into it before he could grab Dad again. After tying the sack closed, Dad went to get his bottle of rubbing alcohol. I knew better than to critique my father's lesson on how to catch a cat because he was in a pretty foul humor, so I kept my thoughts to myself. One thing I did learn for sure from the whole episode. If you grab a scared and frantic cat, things will not go well with you!

Dad finished doctoring himself with the alcohol, and we stopped to take care of a couple of things before heading off to Mandy's house. Arriving at the fence on the back side of the pasture, we began our trek through the woods to deliver the cats to Mandy. Dad carried the sack with the two cats. I followed along behind, excited about going to a place I loved to visit. He had returned to his normal self, it appeared, but I was sure his thumb was probably throbbing worse than my finger. After all, in his demonstration about how it was supposed to be done, he had taken a far worse chewing than I had. Walking fast behind him so I didn't fall behind, I was in a perfect position to watch his every movement. Occasionally, I saw him flex the fingers and thumb of the injured hand, shake it, lift it up, and take a close look at the thumb. I knew it was hurting him and that he was probably embarrassed too. I kept seeing the cat's jaw muscles bunched up as he worked his teeth deeper into Dad's thumb. As I was seeing it, he must have been feeling it because he kept shaking that hand and flexing it from time to time throughout our journey to Mandy Norman's house.

Standing on the bare dirt of Mandy's well-swept yard, Dad engaged her in conversation about the goings-on around her place while he untied the sack. The cats, finding themselves suddenly free when Dad dumped them out, took off for the barn. They apparently did well, for in subsequent visits, I found they were still there. They had not starved and looked healthy and content. They had, obviously, perfected their cat skills and got along quite well with the business of being cats.

Cats just seemed to be part of the place when I was growing up. We investigated everything about our place for its entertainment value. Cats were not exempt. With a little imagination, you can actually have fun with a cat. Sure, it is basically a one-sided fun-filled event, but sometimes cats will even tolerate efforts by children to include them in these things. The girls had more success in getting the cooperation of the cats because their approach was somewhat different from that of the boys. Their approach to the cats was more nurturing as if the cats were babies or just needed some loving care. Cats respond to this kind of attention and will hang around until such time that they feel it's time to get away for a little while. When this time comes, they simply get up and walk away.

My youngest sisters adored the kittens. They diapered them, put ribbons and bows on them, and supplied items that would pass as kitten blankets. Bassinets were made of baskets and small boxes so that they would have little beds to put the kittens in. Yes, I suppose most people are unable to resist the temptation to smile at and even pick up a kitten, but my sisters took it to a sickening extreme! Those kittens loved it and thrived on the attention my sisters freely gave. My sister Dianne told me that her one failure with the kittens was at bath time. Kittens don't like baths unless they are being licked clean. Baptisms are not for them. Her one effort to bathe a kitten did not go well, and she did not repeat the mistake. She had to content herself with supplying saucers of milk and with the dressing up and the putting to bed of the little ones. The mama cat would have to attend to the licking.

While the girls were entertaining themselves with the kittens, the boys made sure that the slightly older ones were not left out. This was where the real fun was, and it was completely one-sided.

Locating a cat that didn't seem to be doing anything in particular at the time and didn't know enough to be wary of us, the fun would start. These were usually the younger cats that didn't have experience enough to have developed highly suspicious natures. They were about to get educated! Older ones had a tendency to keep at least one eye trained on us when they detected that we were moving in their direction. If we continued our course toward them, prudence and experience dictated that they get up and move away. Oftentimes, the older ones just didn't trust the boys enough to stay put.

Picking up the cat with both hands and extending my arms, I began spinning around. I could always feel the cat stiffen and then begin to twist a bit it my hands as I continued to spin. Sometimes, it made little noises of surprise as it viewed the scenery rushing by, but these were not "oohs and ahs." They were more like light squealing sounds.

When I felt I could not continue to spin without falling over myself, I stopped and set the cat down. It immediately fell over, regained its feet, and fell over again. Soon, it was on his feet again and off and running. The destination would be a tree or outbuilding that promised a degree of safety. It is a funny thing to watch a cat run sideways and falling a lot as it runs. The cat often missed the tree it was heading for, or ran headfirst, or side first, into it.

Sometimes, the cat ran for the safety of the house and its screen door. Screen doors at our house almost always had large holes torn in them by our play or by cats trying to get inside. Getting to the screen door meant safety for the cat was almost assured. It is apparently difficult to zero in on a hole in the screen door while running sideways with your head still spinning. This fact was confirmed many times over by cats that missed their marks and ran into the brick pillar to the right of the door. Never the left side, always the right.

Looking around for another cat that might be handy, the process was repeated. Sometimes, an observer cat would excuse himself, not wishing to be a part of the fun. I searched the place, high and low, for cats that hadn't had a turn yet and continued until I could not find another victim. I could not repeat this performance until some amount of time had passed and the memory of the experience had dimmed in the minds of the cats. New generations were always coming along too, and they deserved a chance of having the experience. To those who would be angry with me, be assured that I never did permanent damage to any cat. At least, not in my pursuit of fun. I might add that, like with the chickens, I was sharpening the survival skills of our cats.

Cats are not entirely innocent. They enjoyed a little fun now and then too. Some people might chalk up what I describe here as a cat honing his predator skills, but I saw what I saw. What this cat did was for pure entertainment purposes and could be seconded by the other witness: another cat. This other witness would have been a willing participant in the fun had the first cat allowed it.

Coming into the kitchen one morning and backing up to the gas heater to warm up, I glanced down to see a cat engrossed in some sort of activity. She was lying on the floor with her front paws stretched in front of her while studying the small mouse between them. The cat's tail slowly moved back and forth as she began pushing the mouse one way and then the other with her front paws. She allowed the little creature to move to the far side of the table leg several inches in front of her. Extending both paws, she reached forward and pulled the mouse back against the foot of the table leg.

Next, the mouse was batted one way, then the other, and pulled back against the table leg. The cat drew both paws back, giving the mouse a bit of hope that maybe it could get across the room to the safety of the cabinet. The cat allowed it to have its moment of hope. The mouse almost made it when the cat dashed that bit of hope. Timing it just right, the playful cat arrested the flight of its victim by almost casually rising, taking several steps, and pinning the mouse to the floor with a paw. Picking it up with her mouth, she brought it back to the original spot and dropped it. About this time, another cat came into the room and began watching the proceedings with a high degree of interest.

This newcomer cat wanted to play too, and that desire was telegraphed by its demeanor and every muscle twitch. Sitting on its haunches and sweeping the floor from side to side with its tail, she could barely contain the excitement she felt. She reminded me of a wound-up clock spring straining to be released. The activity of the cat and mouse game continued as before with an occasional "almost escape" to the cabinet on the far side of the room. At such times, the newly arrived cat could not help but move forward toward the mouse, only to be warned away by its owner.

Possession is law in the cat world, and both cats knew that. This other cat was law-abiding. Though her disappointment showed in the difficulty she was having in restraining herself, she sat back down and watched. The game of batting the mouse around, letting it go, and retrieving it lasted for quite some time. The little creature began to slow down as if it were losing its energy. The fur looked a bit bedraggled, and the escape attempts began to show a noticeable lack of enthusiasm. The mouse was discouraged and seemed to be giving in to the inevitable. Its condition finally deteriorated to the point it seemed to have no more will to continue. The cat, accurately discerning that there was no more fun to be had, just got up and walked away.

According to cat law, the mouse was now fair game. The cat that had been hoping for a turn at the mouse now had her chance. She quickly moved into position and began pushing the mouse about with her paws. There was little activity though. She lay there, studying the mouse, as if trying to decide what to do. Several further attempts at resurrecting the thing to a more animated state proved fruitless. It was completely done in. Cat number one had gotten all the good out of it, and there simply was no more to be had. This was a disgusting turn of events for the cat that had waited so long for her turn at play. Presently, she rose, somewhat disappointed, and just walked away.

It would have been a good time for the mouse to get up and head for the cabinet, but it had nothing left. A million miles or six feet might as well have been the same distance at this point. It was not getting up and going anywhere. I curiously watched the mouse for a while to see if it would regain enough energy to get up and leave. He was alive and breathing rapidly, I could tell. He was indeed all used up and not going anywhere.

Picking the mouse up by the tail, I took him to the back door and tossed him out. Several chickens rushed up as they always did, expecting scraps, whenever the back door opened. There was only the one mouse, and there were several chickens. The nearest chicken grabbed the mouse while the others tried to take him away. Chickens are not honorable like cats and don't respect the law of possession. The possessor of the mouse, however, was able to maintain control long enough for it to disappear down its throat. Chickens never play with their food. And, as I said before, they will eat anything.

Perhaps Dad did not stop and play sometimes, but his cats did. I found it interesting to note that while I had often entertained myself with his cats, they too amused themselves in their own ways. It seemed that was just the way it was at the time. I have tried to record the way it was honestly.

37

A MAMA CAT AND HER FUZZY KITTEN

MY OLDER brother Buddy enjoyed reading a good western novel by his favorite author, Louis L'Amour, when he couldn't do anything else. It happened to be such a day. It was bitterly cold, and he was inside trying to stay warm. The gas heater in the kitchen was turned up to the highest setting and seemed to be the color of the surface of the sun. Just about as hot too, I might add. Buddy sat in the chair at the kitchen table, sipping coffee and enjoying his book and the warmth of the gas heater. He had two companions with him, also enjoying the warmth. One was the large, very fuzzy, cat that sported a tail as fluffy as any owned by a fox. Nearby, and close to Buddy, was her kitten, which was a tiny version of herself. It closely resembled a little powder puff with a tail.

Entering the room and taking a seat across the table from my brother, I struck up a conversation with him. The mama cat was strolling back and forth in front of the heater. Never seeming to vary in her cadence and rhythm, she strolled one way, turned slowly, and strolled back the other way. Almost as if she were doing it in an absentminded way or maybe a designed way since her movements seemed to be so precise. She showed the precision of a sentry at Buckingham or one from an old movie, walking his post. During pauses in our conversation, we found ourselves watching the cat as if we were mesmerized by something in its movements. The cat's very fluffy tail inclined itself, slowly, far to the right and then equally far to the left. The movements seemed to be in very slow motion.

Suddenly, there was a puff of smoke as the tail erupted in flame. It had been inclined close enough to the gas heater for it to ignite. The kitchen was immediately filled with the odor of burnt fur. It was almost overpowering!

The cat's movements accelerated considerably for a minute or so before she slowed down to assess the damage. Buddy and I were both laughing pretty hard at what we had just witnessed while he opened the back door to vent some of the odor. The cat decided to leave at that point. I don't know if she just wanted to cool off or leave because of her injured dignity. The hair seemed to be completely gone on one side of the tail, and on the other side, it appeared to have had a rough time of it. We laughed and reworked the scene a couple of times in our minds before I left the kitchen for my room where I had been reading a book earlier. It was only a short while before I heard loud cursing erupting in the kitchen. I hurried back to see what was going on. This time, it was the little kitten that caused the excitement.

Buddy was not laughing now.

Between my brother's gagging sounds, his "Good God," and lots of cussing, I shifted my gaze from Buddy to the kitten on the far side of the room and back again. I had to be patient for Buddy to begin explaining what was going on. On that far side of the kitchen, a bewildered and somewhat shaken fuzzy kitten cowered. More cussing, another "Good God" or two and more gagging sounds erupted from Buddy.

"That's the stinkingest thing I've smelled in my life!" Buddy exclaimed. He looked like he was going to be sick. I knew the cowering kitten figured into this matter somehow, but how?

"What happened?" I asked. I knew I would have an answer soon and that it would probably be interesting. It was!

"That damned kitten just farted in my face!" he shouted. This was almost too interesting to be true!

"How in God's name did that happen?" I inquired with a grin. By then, I was already seeing this event as more promising than I could ever have imagined.

As Buddy began to regain a bit of his composure and stop the "Good Gods" that sprang from his lips now and then, he sat back down and filled in the details of what had occurred.

"I was sitting here reading," he said. "The kitten climbed up my pant leg to my lap. Then it decided to climb up my shirt to my shoulder. He laid on my shoulder and snuggled up against my neck. It felt warm and cuddly and kind of good, so I let him stay. He had his tail under my chin, and he went to sleep. Then the little ------- farted in my face! I snatched him off and threw him. I think he hit that wall over there. God, that's the nastiest thing I've smelled in my life!"

Luckily, the kitten was not injured, just shaken up a bit. It was unlikely the kitten was even aware of what had occurred before ending up by the wall. He was probably wondering how he had gotten from Buddy's shoulder to his new location across the room.

Well, there was no harm done, but we had grist for the humor mill that lasted for years. Whenever Buddy, maybe Danny B, and I happened to be together and conversation lagged or things got too quiet, I might inquire, "So, Buddy, you ever smell a cat fart?"

He might grin and perhaps embark on a retelling of just how

bad it had been. It was a question guaranteed to pull us out of the doldrums and get some conversation started again. With time and retelling of the story, I think the smell got worse and the kitten's flight across the room more spectacular.

I'm glad you had the cats around, Dad. They sure were fun— at times!

38

FISHING, HUNTING, AND TRAPPING WITH DAD

AS I had stated previously, Dad was not one to waste time. However, he did, on occasion, make a little time to go fishing or hunting, but this was not time wasted because going fishing meant we would have at least one meal with fish. Hunting meant squirrel hunting, and that meant squirrel with gravy at supper.

In my growing up years, Dad only went pond fishing two or three times that I remember. As a young adult, he had dug a pond for himself and Grandma. Its primary purpose was so the cows and mule could have a dependable, permanent water source in dry weather. It was probably only half an acre or so, but it was a pond. The cows drank from it and often stood in the water during hot summer afternoons to cool a bit. As children, we sometimes joined the cows there to play and cool off a bit ourselves. In the wintertime, we often slid around on the ice on the shallow side of it if we thought it was thick enough to support us. We stayed off the ice over the deeper water in case we might break through. The pond froze over a number of times each winter in most years. Usually, it was just a skim of ice, but sometimes up to an inch or so. The thickest was in 1961 when it froze to a depth of four inches. The temperature hovered at zero or just above for three days. Ponds rarely freeze over now because of the warmer winter temperatures.

When Dad dug the pond, it took him a while, he said. Whenever he had some spare time, he worked on it until it was completed. He plowed the area first with his mule and turn plow. Afterward, he hooked the mule's trace chains to the slip scrape and dragged the dirt away. This "slip," as he called it, was like a large deep shovel. Instead of a shovel handle, it had two handles attached to the back that resembled those on a plow or a wheelbarrow. With these handles, he could control the pitch of the slip as he skimmed up the loose dirt. With the mule pulling and Dad controlling the slip from behind, the dirt was pulled away to construct the dam of the pond. When the loose dirt was removed, the ground was plowed again, and more dirt was dragged away. It was slow, tedious work, but he eventually completed it and stocked it with fish after it filled with water. The livestock now had their permanent water supply. The remains of the stump of a large oak around which the pond was dug remained visible well into my adult years. It was one of the prominent features until it finally rotted away. The fish liked congregating near it, and it was a favorite place for the bream to bed. Therefore, it was naturally our favorite spot in the pond too.

One day, Dad surprised me when he asked if I wanted to go fishing with him. He had fixed up a couple of long cane poles and wanted to catch some bream for supper. This was the first time I had gone pond fishing with him since it seemed to be something he never did. We dug our worms by the pigpen and walked the two hundred yards down to the pond. The bream were bedding, and the water around the old stump was full of them.

It did not take long to catch all the fish we needed, and I remember the feeling that we were spending some special time together. The black-and-white spotted dog that had recently taken up with our family was with us. He darted back and forth chasing dragonflies and wound up teaching me a lesson I have passed on to my children and grandchildren. Be careful of hooks, especially if animals or other people are around. It's so easy to get snagged by a hook and very painful too. This dog ran into my fishing line while I was baiting my hook and pulled the hook deep into my finger. One of those words I knew but kept in storage just popped out.

Dad, sympathetically, ignored the word, but he responded to my howls. While I grabbed the line with my other hand to relieve the tension on it from the dog that was tangled in it, Dad removed the dog. He eventually got the hook out of my finger. He did not mention my use of the word that only adults were allowed to use, and I was thankful for that. Maybe he thought that under the circumstance, it was permissible to let something slip. Anyway, he let it slide.

We went creek fishing quite often together and were always accompanied by one or two others, usually Larry and Buddy. Creek fishing did not take Dad away from his necessary work since this fishing was always done at night. This is what we termed "setting hooks." It was, in fact, an overnight camping trip, but we did not call it that. We just called it setting hooks. It was a fun thing to do. We stayed in the woods, on the creek bank, all night next to a fire, making a "round" about once an hour to all the poles we had set along the creek for hundreds of yards in each direction. On each round, we removed the catfish and eels and baited the lines.

Preparing for the first outing on the creek each spring was exciting, but it involved a good bit of preparation. New poles were cut each year since the old ones might have become too brittle and break when a fish or eel was caught. Twenty-five or thirty new bamboo poles about twelve feet long were cut and trimmed. The lead and hooks were removed from the older poles for reuse on the new ones. The line was cotton and later, nylon. About an ounce of lead was used on each line because of the current in the water of the creek. Once the poles were finished, the lines were wrapped securely around each pole. Even so, the lines were often tangled when we got the bundle of poles to our proposed fishing spot. After all, the bundle may have been carried for a couple of miles through brush and woods and across several fences to our spot. A few tangled lines were a small price to pay for a night of excitement.

Our bait supply was crawfish. We seined them from various holes of water or ditches on the afternoon of our outing or the afternoon before. We broke the pincers from them as we took them from the seine and dropped them into the bucket. This was to keep the crawfish from killing each other in the bucket. Along with the poles and bait, we often carried bologna and bread to eat. Coffee grounds and a bucket or pot for boiling coffee were included, as were cups. Each of us carried a blanket since the air was damp and cool late at night.

As I got older, Dad did not normally remain with us through the night. He returned home and slept in his bed. Later, I understood that as something very understandable. Nights spent on the creek tended to be cold, damp, smoky, and generally sleepless. These things, in combination, led to a condition I would term a "creek-fishing hangover." I'm sure my dad had suffered his share of these in his lifetime and preferred not to risk having any more than absolutely necessary. I guess these "hangovers" tended to be forgotten by us younger folks because we were always anxious to go back and do it again in a few days. When summer advanced, our trips to the creek at night stopped. The heat, even late at night, was often oppressive in the woods along the creek, and the mosquitoes showed no mercy. This was something Dad had mentioned, but I still had to find it out for myself. There was always next year to look forward to and the exciting time for preparing everything for the first trip setting hooks.

Hunting, for us, was confined to squirrels. Others may have hunted quail or rabbits, and some were even involved in organized dove shoots. Dad went squirrel hunting early on Saturday morning before the sun came up and came back about an hour after sunup with several squirrels. This would not interfere with the daily work activities around the place. This only changed when Uncle Frank came down from Birmingham once each winter for a couple of days to visit Grandma and the rest of us. He always wanted to go hunting at least once. Dad would go with him, and I liked to go along too. Uncle Frank was such an interesting person to be around and someone we saw so rarely.

We went to the woods just before daylight as Dad always did when going alone. Picking out groves of trees that looked promising, we waited for the squirrels to come out of their nests in the trees and head outward to the surrounding trees or down to the ground to forage. Dad liked to wait until two or three squirrels were close by before shooting. His twelve-gauge shotgun was a single shot, and he had to reload quickly if he was to get two of them while they were near enough. Oftentimes, he would shoot and leave the squirrel where he fell and not move from his position. Presently, another squirrel might appear. Squirrels were not as plentiful then as they are now because so many people hunted and ate them.

Uncle Frank had less patience than Dad and was generally

not as successful hunting this way. He preferred the "vine-shaking" method that we employed after the sun was well up and the squirrel activity had abated. Many of the trees had large vines that grew from the ground around them and extended to the very treetops. They resembled the ones Tarzan might have favored as he traveled through the jungle.

Larry and I were usually the ones to shake the vines. We did this by tugging and snatching on them with all our might to create as big a disturbance in the tree as possible. Any squirrel hiding on a limb or in a clump of spanish moss, which hung just about everywhere, might be tempted to move out of his hiding place. When that happened, the cry would go out, "Ho, Ho, there he is!" A shot would quickly follow, and the squirrel would come down.

Now and then, a squirrel would land in a fork of the tree or get hung up by something else that prevented it from falling to the ground. Uncle Frank would not be willing to walk away and leave him. If it took six or seven shells to blast it free, he would blast away. When the squirrel was picked up from the ground, it would be a pitiful mess and not worth bringing home. It would then be tossed aside. Uncle Frank would not be made a failure by a hung-up squirrel.

Dad would not have wasted shots in a situation like this; he would have cut his losses and walked away. "You sho showed him, didn't ya, Frank?" he might have said, with a grin and a headshake.

When I went hunting with Dad and Uncle Frank, I was allowed to carry the single-shot .22 rifle Dad had purchased. I usually had only three or four cartridges in my possession and don't remember actually shooting a squirrel on one of these outings. It was fun just being there and a part of the activity though.

Dad may not have hunted all that much or fished very much either. He really made up for it in trapping though. From the times of my earliest memories, I do not remember my father not trapping in the wintertime. He trapped for three months out of the year, from the twentieth of November to the twentieth of February. He continued this until his health began to fail him a couple of years before his death. Even then, he tried to walk to the woods behind my house to catch a coon or two there, but he had to stop that in the winter prior to his death. His breathing difficulties and body pain had gotten too severe. Trapping was something he had always enjoyed with a passion. He had started doing it as a young man and eventually came to the point where it became his winter occupation. He enjoyed doing it, and he realized that by concentrating on trapping, he had an increased income during the winter months.

There really were not a lot of fur-bearing animals whose fur was worth going after. Bobcats had disappeared decades before and were all but worthless when they reappeared when I was a teenager. That changed dramatically by the time I came home from the service in 1979. Foxes, too, had no value, but that also changed about the time bobcat prices surged. Otters were rare and protected as were beavers. Tags had to be bought from the conservation department in order to trap and sell their furs. The value of beaver fur was very low. Otters were worth twenty dollars each, but they were scarce, and Dad had to walk many miles to catch one. The value of otters also went up along with foxes and bobcats. There were not many coons around when I was young, probably for the same reason that squirrels were not so plentiful. People had hunted them for food. Coons had almost no value as far as fur was concerned when I was growing up. This also changed in a dramatic way years later. There were muskrats about, and they were worth one or two dollars, which actually made them more valuable than coons or foxes. Dad trapped the muskrats whenever he located any along the creeks or in ponds.

Dad depended on the mink. These were the valuable fur-bearing animals when I was very young. They were not abundant, but they were valuable. A fully grown "bo" mink was generally called extra large. They were valued at twenty-eight dollars and fifty cents apiece by the F. C. Taylor fur company of Saint Louis, Missouri. This price stayed constant for many years. If Dad could bring home several of these each week, his income increased sharply. He did not catch one every day. Sometimes, he might go several days without any success. Again, he might bring home two in a day and repeat this for two or three days. Even as a child, I was always happy whenever Dad came home with two minks. Occasionally, he brought home a female mink, and it always disappointed him. He never liked trapping the females, and he released them whenever he caught one. However, sometimes one might have pulled the trap into the water and drowned because of the weight of the trap. The females were worth eight dollars because of their small size. Even though that represented almost a full day's pay as a carpenter, Dad did not want to catch one. It was better that they remain unharmed to reproduce and keep the mink population steady. Dad knew the creeks around our home for many miles about, as well as every branch and ditch. He never used any kind of lure or bait in his trapping in those days. He just understood how the minks traveled along the ditches and watercourses and where they would put their feet. He was skilled at getting them to put their feet where the traps were.

It was well after dark when Dad came in from checking his traps one day. Supper was long over, and most of the family had retired to their rooms. When Dad came in, I came into the kitchen to see what he had caught. He had left his croker sack on the floor and had sat down to eat his supper. He always used a sack to carry his traps and catches while working his trapline. I noticed slight movements coming from the bag and relayed the fact to Dad and asked him what he had in it. He informed me he had two bo minks—and that one must still be alive.

"Take them out and find out which one it is," he told me. I did and found that while the mink was not conscious, he was still alive.

"Get a boiler of water and hold his head in it," he instructed me.

I filled up the boiler from the water bucket, sat down on the floor, and picked up the mink. Holding it tightly by its neck and hind legs, I did as I was told. The mink began to convulse as it pulled the water in, and after five or six minutes, was no longer moving. This was all done in a matter-of-fact way and without emotion. Cruelty was not an issue, and there certainly was no pleasure in it. It was something that just had to be done, and it was done. Like hog killing or chicken killing, it was simply a fact of life. A fact I had learned and accepted—even at that age.

I stayed up late that night. Dad had two minks to skin, and he needed me to help hold the mink in the right position in his lap as he removed the fur. At night, he always skinned in the kitchen where there was enough light and warmth. He covered his lap with a feed sack, and I sat in front of him, facing him while helping to hold the mink steady. Dad was very patient and careful, no matter how tired he was. He had never cut a hole in a mink hide and always was conscious that any slip of the very sharp knife would devalue the fur. When he was finished, the fur looked like an inside-out sock. He slid it onto a board he had made a form out of for drying the mink hides. He scraped away the fat and muscle tissue with his pocketknife. He fastened the hide to this properly sized board with several tacks and a string and hung it in a corner of an unused room. He had a wire stretched across the corner of that room for a distance of three or four feet.

As days went by, the wire gradually had more and more furs hanging from it. When each fur dried sufficiently, it was removed from the form and hung back on the wire. I often stopped at this spot and admired the furs my father had hanging there, and I was so happy for him. I knew each fur there represented many miles of walking in freezing and sometimes wet weather. I also knew he had many disappointing days as well. I was happy for him if the wire got crowded.

There came a day every two or three weeks when there were enough furs to send to the Taylor Fur Company. Selecting his best-looking feed or "crocus" sack, Dad cut the seam on the side and bottom and laid the sack open on the kitchen table. He carefully made a bundle by laying the furs one atop another until they were neatly stacked. A larger fur, such as beaver or otter, was folded to the size he wanted the parcel to be. The stack of furs was wrapped neatly in the burlap sacking and tied with string. Any loose areas were sewed together with thread and a large needle. When he finished, Dad always had a neat and secure bundle. It had to be because it was valuable and would be sent through the mail. Dad's final act was to attach the "Taylor" tag to the bundle and send it off by the next day's mail.

Making sure the parcel got into the hands of the mailman often fell to me. This was an honor, but a frightening one as well. Dad gave me instructions to tell the mailman to "insure for two hundred and fifty dollars" or some such amount. I did not have a clue what "insure" meant and always wondered if I had said it correctly. I had repeated the line over and over to myself while waiting on the high bank at the side of the road for the mailman's car to appear. Blurting out the instruction in the way I had memorized it, I handed him the two or three dollars Dad had given me. I must have always gotten it right because the transaction never failed.

Dad trusted the fur company he did business with. He had to. When he sent his furs to them, he was at their mercy when it came to fair payment. He had to accept what they paid him. He had tried others but had been disappointed with them. About ten days to two weeks after sending his furs away by mail, an envelope arrived in our mailbox from the F. C. Taylor Fur Company of Saint Louis, Missouri.

Dad sat down at the table, took out the check, and went over the sheet where the furs had been graded and valued. Occasionally, he might express mild disappointment in the grading of a particular fur. In the next breath, he would utter an exclamation over the generous grading of another. When he folded up the paper and put it away, it was always with the feeling that he had been honorably dealt with and was satisfied with the amount they had remitted to him. There is no wonder he remained loyal to them through all the years he sent furs to them. Seeing the name "Taylor Fur Company" before me at this moment gives me a warm feeling. It would be very difficult for me to describe how important their honesty was to my father and to the whole family.

Fur price listing for 1931 with a shipping tag for
fur parcels sent to the F. C. Taylor Fur Co.

My first experience of going trapping with my father occurred when I was only seven or eight years old. It was a nighttime experience. It was late in the evening when Dad told Mama he had to check some traps along Ball Branch. I had never been with him and was anxious to go. He refused at first, but he gave in when Mama told him she saw no harm in my going along.

"He's liable to get sick in the cold night air," Dad warned.

I assured him I would not, and he finally gave in and said I could go.

"I'll be walking fast, and you'll have to keep up," he said, stating his one instruction to me.

I was happy and surprised Mama had spoken up for me on that frosty evening. It was totally unexpected, but Mama had moments of looking at life in a very romantic way. She had missed out on a lot, being an orphan and having been raised in foster homes. Perhaps she saw this as a special moment for a child and his father, and it appealed to her poetry-writing heart. I can picture her now, beside the warm wood burning heater, imagining our journey along the trapline. As Dad and I were experiencing that time together, she was recording her own version of it in a notebook on her lap. Years later, I read the poem she had written about that night. As it turned out, my going with Dad was as important an event to her as it was to me.

We angled across the pasture to the northeast of the house to Hatfield's store, which lay in a curve of Pettus Road. This was a graveled road I described earlier as intersecting the highway to our north and then running east toward Aunt Louise's house. We had to pass through the woods for some distance after crossing the pasture. Mr. Hatfield had a very small country store on the side of the road at a place where the road bent sharply to the right. It was also situated very close to Ball Branch, which ran under the wooden bridge a few dozen yards away. Dad needed new batteries for his flashlight. After purchasing the batteries, he visited with Mr. and Mrs. Hatfield for a few minutes. I had never been to this old store before and had not met these neighbors—even though they lived only a half mile or less from us across the pasture and woods—but I had heard their names many times in conversation. Mr. Hatfield was confined to a wheelchair, but I never knew the reason.

It was fully dark when we left Hatfield's store and headed for Ball Branch, which was now nearby. Dad was right; he walked fast. I followed along at his heels, and he occasionally shined his light at obstacles or places that might trip me up. Otherwise, I watched his movements carefully so I could follow him without tripping up. He checked one trap and then another, resetting them as necessary. Coming to one spot where there was a hole under the roots of a tree, we could see the wire of the trap pulled down into the hole. Pulling on the wire, Dad pulled an unhappy coon out of the hole.

"I knew something was using that hole, but I didn't know what," he informed me. Removing the coon and trap, he put them in his bag and continued.

At another place, along the water of the branch, he removed a bo mink that had been caught and drowned. He popped the water out of the mink's fur by swinging the mink sharply with popping motions. He was very satisfied to have caught the mink and carefully reset the trap in hopes of catching another there in the next few days.

We continued along the branch until all the traps were checked and then began retracing our steps on the return journey home. We did not leave the branch after reaching the place where it passed Hatfield's store, and we continued along it until the branch turned through the woods behind Grandma's house. Dad said he had to pick up something he had left in those woods earlier in the day. Coming to a fairly large and rotten stump, he began clearing the leaves and spanish moss that were on top of it. The stump was rotten in the middle and had a hole in the center in which my father had deposited a couple of rabbits during the day. After retrieving the rabbits and dropping them into his bag, we continued our journey home.

It was pretty late when we got home, and the warm bed with all its quilts felt very good. So good, in fact, I didn't want to leave those warm quilts the next morning and go to school. I remembered the warning Dad had given Mama the evening before that I might get sick in the cold night air. I felt I might be able to use those words to my advantage. I began to encourage such a condition in hopes that I would be allowed to stay in the warm bed. Perhaps I could convince Mama that the cold night air really had done its work after all. Coughing might help my case, I thought. Presently, I was able to generate a reasonably convincing cough and then another. Soon I was on a roll, and the coughs were coming! A few moans wouldn't hurt either. They did the trick!

Mama came in to check on me, and I told her I didn't feel good. "Maybe you shouldn't go to school today," she said. "You don't seem to have a fever, but I think it's better if you stay home in bed."

I successfully masked my happiness with what I hoped was a disappointed look.

A year or two later, I was to learn that I had a kindred spirit in the person of Tom Sawyer. It was truly amazing to me when I found out that we thought so much alike. This discovery helped dispel any guilt I might otherwise have felt in such situations like pretending to be sick. Obviously, what I had done was just human nature. If it was completely natural, then it would be expected that I, like Tom and other kids, would act according to nature's dictates. It was a thought that was both comforting and encouraging to me and one I embraced with all my heart. I was glad when I came to know Tom Sawyer. He made me realize I was normal. By the way, I began to feel much improved after the school bus had left our house that morning, and the coughs and moans suddenly stopped. I wonder if Mama noticed.

Dad told me there were muskrats in the pond. The pond was very low after the dry fall we had that year. The holes the muskrats had dug into the dam of the pond were clearly exposed along with the "runs" going from the holes to the water.

"You can set a couple of my old traps there if you want to," he told me.

Getting a couple of his older and weaker traps he wasn't

using, I took off for the pond. I had no problem setting the weak traps since I had practiced so much on the new ones he prepared each year. Following his instructions on placing the traps in the runs, I completed my trap setting fairly quickly.

When I went to bed that night, I could hardly contain the excitement I felt. Eventually, I did go to sleep, and when I woke up, I raced to the pond to see if I had caught anything. I had! There was one large muskrat in the first trap. It was to be the only one I caught from the pond.

Dad skinned the muskrat and stretched the hide for me on one of the wooden forms he had made for muskrats and mink. My muskrat hide was included in the next shipment to the Taylor Fur Company.

A few days later, Dad handed me a dollar and thirty-five cents, the price of my first fur. Not only was I a dollar and thirty-five cents richer, I was hooked on trapping! It was an occupation I pursued in the years following my military service. Just as it had been for my father, it became my source of income during the winter months for quite a number of years.

Christmas may have been the most exciting time of the year for me, but the arrival of the packet from the Taylor Fur Company had to be a very close second. The packet contained the projected fur prices for the season and several pages of traps and other items for sale. The lynx topped the list for valuable furs, but we didn't have any about as far as we knew and were unsure what they were anyway. I concentrated on those I knew something about and pretty soon knew the prices by heart. Next, my attention was drawn to the sales pages and all the interesting things offered for sale. I wanted everything, but I didn't have any money at my young age to buy anything. Dad usually wound up ordering one or two dozen number two, Blake and Lamb traps for mink and coons. Sometimes he would get several number threes or fours for beaver and otters.

A few days after my father ordered his new traps, he would receive them by mail. The new traps were to replace those that had become lost or stolen in the previous season or become too weak to trust. As I became old enough to begin practicing along the branch in the woods behind the house, Dad allowed me to use those older traps. The newer ones were too important to him for me to be using.

Dad always checked and made adjustments to his traps before the season started. Old, weak tie wire was removed and replaced with sound and reliable wire. This was to fasten the trap chain to roots or stakes driven into the ground to secure the trap against being dragged away by any animal caught in it. Dad "regulated," or adjusted, his new traps to suit him. This was done with a few taps with a hammer and several strokes of a file on the trigger. He wanted the trap to trip smoothly and quickly. Next, he fastened a doubled eighteen-inch tie wire to the ring of the chain. The chain and wire were then wrapped around the trap, and it was put aside for use.

There were a couple of occasions when friends stopped by to visit with Dad while he was getting his traps ready. People have a fascination for traps, especially if they haven't actually seen or held one before.

"How does it work?" or "How do you set one?" These questions were invariably asked, and Dad would demonstrate how the traps worked. Always, the person asking the question wanted to try his hand at setting one. That was a fun thing to watch. It usually involved a lot of grimacing and straining, and sometimes the person actually set it. Mostly, they failed. Dad often demonstrated the procedure again and talked the person through it a time or two. Once they understood the technique involved, they were generally successful. I liked to pick up one of the traps and set it to show I could do it quickly and easily, even at my young age. Dad might say something to the effect of "Put that thing down before you catch yourself" or "Be careful not to catch yourself." He never said anything before I actually set the trap. He knew I was showing off and allowed me to have my moment.

Anyway, the point would have been made that even a child could do it if he understood how and was not afraid to try. The trick to setting the trap was not in brute strength or in the grip but in knowing how to apply pressure.

Looking back over the years, I realize a lot of the excitement with trapping started right there in our kitchen. It was so exciting to look over the fur price list and imagine catching all those animals listed there and getting rich. Then, I could buy all those interesting things advertised on the included pages. I enjoyed watching my father adjust his traps and get them ready for use. I did not mind helping Dad hold the mink in the right position on his lap while he skinned late into the night. It was our special time together. The memories of these special times have come with me across the years that have gone by so quickly.

39

RELIGION AND IDENTITY

A FAMILY'S identity within a community begins with its name and its relationship to others within the community. What that family does to make a living or support itself financially may well be considered. Historically, in Western society, surnames were often given based on a person's occupation or something else others identified with that person. Even now, a part of our identity is based on what we do or how we contribute. Several families within our community had dairy farms. Some raised cattle, and others had subsistence farms and, possibly, part-time work off the farm for an income. Everyone knew them as farmers. Others had full-time jobs in town. Many mothers were homemakers and did not work outside the home or farm, though some did. We invariably know these things about those who live within our neighborhood or community. Just about everything concerning a person or family, whether good or otherwise, is considered in the matter of character or identity.

Looking back to the days of my childhood, I can attest that religious affiliation went as far in establishing a family's identity as just about anything else we could come up with. It was a rarity among families in our community, and in rural

Alabama in general, not to belong to a church. Churches were Protestant. Only in urban environments would there likely be a Catholic church or a synagogue. Church of Christ, Baptist, and Methodist were predominant in rural areas with many AME and a few Presbyterian congregations thrown in. Of course, there were others as well.

No matter how well people may have interacted socially or how friendly they might have been to each other, people were still conscious of each other's religious affiliation. After all, it is almost a given that members of a particular denomination will think their doctrine and manner of worship is the proper way. We all want people to worship the proper way. The opinions and mind-sets about what the proper way is create the divisions that lead to the formation of denominations to start with. The natural, likely conclusion of that thought is that others are erroneous in doctrine and worship. That can influence or maybe produce an impediment in our relationships even if it is a very subtle one. It is hard to dispel from our minds certain thoughts when we are not fully conscious they are there to start with. One thing is for sure though, in the days of my childhood, everyone knew the religious affiliation of just about everyone else in our community. That fact alone had some influence on the formation and the depth of many relationships. Therefore, church becomes not only important in our spirituality but is an issue in our relationships as well. It becomes a part of who we are.

Six youngest Brady children dressed for Easter, left to right:
Sandra, Dianne, Betty, Sharron, Larry, and Allen, about 1960.

Older sisters ready for church, left to right:
Verba Lee, Pat, June, and Daisy Anne.

James Lewis Brady (Buddy), second oldest of eleven children.

Thelma Brady (Mama) on a Sunday morning.

Thelma and Lewis Brady (Mama and Dad)
on Easter Sunday, about 1960.

My family was Church of Christ. That is about as conservative as a person could get, especially during the days of my youth. Members, in general, within the Church of Christ did not consider it a denomination, but, rather, the "true church" formed in Jerusalem in the first century. Only the members of this body were considered true "believers." Those who were not, well, they are in big trouble when Judgment Day comes! Baptism by total immersion "for the remission of sins" is a must. The Lord's Supper (Communion) must also be observed every Sunday for all believers along with faithful attendance at services. Instrumental music in worship is strictly forbidden as is choir singing. Women are forbidden to take a leadership role in services, including public prayer.

There has been a gradual change in the mind-set of many of those within the Church of Christ over the past three or four decades, and it seems to have developed some momentum of late. There is evidence of a softening of hard-line attitudes. That may cause consternation in the minds of some but delight in the hearts of others.

The church of my youth was awe-inspiring, yet frightening. After all, we are supposed to fear God. Judgment and punishment were emphasized far more than grace or mercy. When I sang of having "joy, joy, joy, down in my heart," I wasn't being truthful. It was fear. My fear did not give way to joy until I was a mature adult. I came to understand what the apostle John meant when he said in Christ we have the "truth" of God or see the "reality" of God. A real understanding of Jesus's purpose provides the joy, the comfort, and the hope we often sing about. When we are at that point, I guess we can truly sing with "the spirit and the understanding." I think I am at that point now and find my religion much more joyful and far less frightening, but let's go back to those childhood days when my religious training did not result in a lot of understanding.

We walked to church on Sunday mornings. We lived a little less than half a mile down the road from the church building. On Sunday evenings, we did the same as we often did on Wednesday evenings for Bible study. Our family did not own a motor vehicle, and Dad and Mama never learned to drive. Walking was a normal thing for us, so we didn't really think anything about it.

I mentioned earlier in this narrative that my first remembrance of walking to the Liberty Church of Christ building was from the old Mosley house on the Pintlala Old Road, which was to the north or several hundred yards on the opposite side of the church. We were staying there after our house had burned and while my father was building us another house across the road from our burned house. The journey along the scenic dirt road lined with trees draped with spanish moss was an adventure of sights for me at four years of age. The memories of all the other trips to church were from the site of our new house to the south. Those trips involved staying off the road—so we didn't get run over by passing vehicles—but we still made the trips exciting by playing along the way. Play stopped as we entered the church building. We were in a very special place. It belonged to God there, and we spoke in hushed tones. Playing or misbehaving was out of the question. If we could sneak outside, though, that was different!

Communion service at our church during that time was a most solemn occasion and was carried out with the utmost reverence. Only baptized members were allowed to participate, and it was done as a part of worship every Sunday. The Communion table was directly in front of the pulpit, and the emblems (bread and wine) were covered with a brilliant white cloth without wrinkles. The cloth appeared to be starched and ironed.

At the beginning of the Communion service, the covering cloth was carefully removed, folded, and laid to the side by those attending the table. After a prayer, the unleavened bread was broken, placed into four serving trays, and served to the congregation by those serving on the table. Each member broke a small piece off for himself as a tray was passed along each pew. I often wondered about the significance of the cloth covering the Communion trays and later came to the conclusion it was symbolic. Also, why was the bread broken and then distributed into the serving trays rather than having been distributed into the trays earlier? I suppose it is because the scriptures say, "He took bread and broke it." The Church of Christ has been known to be very particular about following the very letter of scripture. After the bread, the "cup" or wine is served, but in individual cups for obvious reasons. Here, it seems, we may have opted for the spirit of the scripture rather than the letter. If so, I'm happy and have no quarrel with that!

The sermons from the pulpit during my developing years tended to frighten me and convinced me beyond doubt that I was lost, without hope, and destined for hell. I really could not imagine myself ever being good enough to escape what awaited me. I wished I could be as good as those around me so I would have some hope, but I knew I wasn't. The dark-haired, square-jawed, and tanned preacher's baritone voice was powerful as if it were the voice of God himself. Looking back, I have no problem imagining a dark thundercloud around the pulpit or the smoke and thundering like on Mount Sinai. The preacher was a powerful and frightful presence! His messages were about the severity and the judgment of Almighty God, and he spoke on God's authority. I could easily imagine it was voice of God I heard thundering from the pulpit each Sunday.

Sundays were actually exciting for me in my very early years and as my childhood and awareness advanced. We didn't have a television and really did not know what one was anyway. Until I started school at six years of age, I had nobody to play with except for my sisters and brother Larry and an occasional visitor. Church was a place to see other children I knew, as well as a lot of other interesting people. I was not burdened with a consciousness of sin either, so that freed me up to enjoy myself more. I just had to remember to behave myself. God didn't have to get me—Mama was somewhere close by!

Sunday school was fun, and I liked it, at least until I got old enough to have a quarterly book where I was supposed to have my lesson completed when I got to class on Sunday. I managed to fill in most of the blanks before the class started. I liked the Old Testament stories. The Bible stories were all so familiar to me and didn't seem like they had happened so long ago. They were like recent history to me and were personal—not like they happened to a different people in a place far away and long ago. They were comforting. Even those about lions' dens, fiery furnaces, and giants named Goliath. God loved and took care of the people in those stories! He didn't let them get burned by fire or eaten by lions. These stories didn't have anything to do with sin and death or punishment.

One of my Sunday school teachers said he had once wanted to be a missionary and go off to "darkest Africa" and convert the heathens. I thought it would be nice and adventurous too, and I found myself wanting to go. Then he said he had changed his mind when he pictured himself in a big iron pot surrounded by hungry cannibals. I changed my mind too. There seems to be something especially bad about being eaten like a chicken!

A couple of the very old men would pray during worship service on their knees—or at least on one knee. They would pray for a very long time. I did not know how they could think of so much stuff to pray about, but they did. They prayed for everything and everybody and laid themselves bare before God. When they were through, there was nothing else to pray about. Even then, I knew they were good and sincere men and that God heard them. If I were God, I know I would have listened to them. Some of the younger men would read their prayers to God as if they were afraid to talk to him. When I started praying in church, I did that too. I was very afraid.

Most of the women in church wore hats. Even the young girls did at Easter. They always noticed each other's hats and commented on them. New hats always attracted attention even if the wearer denied it was new. I have mentioned earlier about the often-heard comment: "This old thing? Just something I had in the back of the closet." That might just as well have referred to a dress too. Even as a child, I could not understand why a woman would not admit to having something on that was brand-new. While they were pleased others noticed, I think they were careful about appearing extravagant. They might have been implying "I have so many hats and clothes in my closet that it's hard to get around to wearing all of them."

A couple of ladies were not as concerned about appearing extravagant and sometimes came to church wearing furs. One had two fox furs attached together and wrapped around her neck and shoulders and later came with four minks joined together and draped around her neck. Only their carcasses were missing. Another lady wore a mink stole. Mama made life very miserable for Dad for a long time after that. He was a trapper. If anyone should be wearing minks around her neck, it should be her! She tried for a couple of years to get him to set aside several minks for her to have a fur made to show off at church. At twenty-eight dollars and fifty cents apiece, Dad would not agree to contribute the minks. Each mink would have represented three days' wages on a carpentry or painting job. My father had eleven children and was still raising most of them. He had to be "practical minded," as he pointed out. Mama had to watch other people wear the minks and continue to fuss about Dad skinning them in the kitchen on winter nights.

I finally learned how to sneak out of church during worship service without Mama and Dad being aware of it. I would pretend to move back toward the rear as if I were sitting with Phillip Murrell and my brother Larry. Just before the service began, we would ease out the door and go and play. Playing usually meant we slipped into Phillip's Daddy's old car and played police chase till church service was over. When the service was over, we managed to blend in with the crowd that emerged as if we had been there all along. At other times, we sneaked away and went home and played or swam in the pond till everyone came home. Somehow, we convinced Mama we had just beaten them there. I'm sure that by slipping out, we managed to miss some pretty rough sermons that predicted what was in store for us when God got his hands on us. No doubt, we were in for a pretty warm time in the future!

Nothing was ever looked forward to at church more than the annual Dinner on the Ground. This coincided with our annual Gospel meeting, which lasted for a week. The Dinner on the Ground occurred on the Sunday, which began the week of our meeting. We ate a big picnic-style dinner right after the morning worship service. A long line of tables was set up under the trees, and everybody brought food. There was more potato salad and fried chicken than you could imagine. It was a time when someone like me could eat a lot of things he didn't normally get at home—or at least not very often. I tried to eat everything I could but still could only get just a sample of what was there. In the middle of the night, I often lay in bed wishing I had eaten some of this or that and a whole lot more fried chicken. I wished we could have had a Gospel meeting every week just so I could have enjoyed the Dinner on the Ground every Sunday. All those church services from Sunday through Friday would still have been a good tradeoff for some extra fried chicken.

I made it into adulthood and into those "middle years" and saw my religion and church attendance as comforting and not so scary. I have learned I can't be perfect, but the key is to do the very best I can. If I truly do that, then Christ supplies the perfection. I think about building a "spiritual house" as a carpenter builds a structure. He builds it as soundly as he can. A painter might come along and caulk, spackle, and provide a beautiful finish coat of paint. I can easily visualize Jesus as being the one who provides the finishing touches and makes the structure complete.

Who would have thought it? My brother Larry became a Church of Christ preacher and a missionary to Panama. He has done a lot of work over the past thirty years or so in that country as well as establishing a medical clinic in the interior. He has been the minister of a number of congregations in Alabama and is still preaching in a local congregation at the present time.

My sister Sharron Cates is married to Jack Cates who has been our minister at the Davenport Church of Christ for fifty years now. One of my older sisters, Verba Lee Ray, was married to Clyde Ray who preached for more than fifty years as a Church of Christ minister. He passed away several years ago. Mama was proud to have ministers in the family, but she was wrong in the prediction that I would be her preacher son. Well, even if I proved a disappointment in that regard, she still wound up with three preachers in the family! Mama was so happy about that. Three preachers would probably always outweigh a mink stole in bragging rights and trump any hat at church!

40

EXASPERATED TEACHERS AND A HOPELESS STUDENT

MY OLDEST sister is Daisy Anne. James Lewis (Buddy), my oldest brother, was born after her. Then came June Clara, Dannie Patricia (Pat), Verba Lee, Sarah Elizabeth (Betty), Lawrence David (Larry), Sharron and Sandra (twins), me (Allen Anderson), and finally Carol Dianne. There were eleven of us and about fifteen years separating the oldest from the youngest. By age and interaction, there seemed to be two groups of us with the dividing line being between Verba Lee and Betty. Therefore, the younger group of us were Betty, Larry, Sharron, Sandra, me, and Dianne. We were in school together, first at Pintlala, and then at Sidney Lanier High School in Montgomery. Pintlala was a country school in the community of Pintlala where we were raised and where we have all returned and continue to reside at present. Buddy and Betty are both deceased and rest in the family cemetery just outside my front yard.

Pintlala School consisted of grades one through nine and probably had only around 120 students. All the teachers lived in the community, and most had been raised in the community. People didn't seem to move around much in those days. Most of the children we started school with in the first grade were the same ones we graduated with in the ninth grade. There were few exceptions. Some of those at school were also with us in Sunday school at church. Our friendships began early in our lives and continue to the present. There were a few who came and attended school for a year or so and then moved on, but there were not many of those.

School was a frightening experience for the first three years or so. I was very quiet and shy, and the teachers were no-nonsense and strict. Betty was to watch over me when I first got to school, but that was little comfort to me since she was in another classroom as she was several grades ahead of me. Still, she got me into the custody of the first-grade teacher.

The classrooms had steam radiator heat that sometimes hissed and vented steam and dripped water. The steam radiators were strange and scary to me, just like everything else. Somebody said they could explode, but the janitor came in once in a while and adjusted them. I had never seen anything but heaters that used wood and coal as fuel.

The bathrooms had flush toilets, and I had never seen such a thing before. They were frightening when flushed—and noisy too! The water swirled and went down really fast with a sucking sound. I didn't know where it went, but I thought it might pull me down with it if I didn't stand back when I pushed the lever. Somebody said the water went deep into the ground. In our outhouse at home, I knew where everything went, and it didn't go very far. I had to watch out for chickens and wasps before I sat down. They were of less concern to me than the swirling water of the school toilet, which might suck me in and push me deep underground!

Every school day started with a devotional. The teacher read from the Bible and gave us a short lesson from the scripture she had read from. After that, she said a prayer and sent us to our desks to start her instruction. In the second or third grade, I was asked to read the scripture about Jesus coming into Jerusalem riding on an ass, but I would not say "ass." My older brother Buddy said that a lot at home and got in trouble for it, so I would not say it. I said "as." The teacher tried to get me to say "ass" for a long time, but I was embarrassed to say it in front of everybody and refused. Some Bibles used the word "donkey," but the teacher's Bible did not. I would have said that. I knew that "ass" meant "donkey" in this context, but I wouldn't say it. She finally gave up. I may have been quiet and painfully shy, but I have always been known as the most stubborn child most folks had ever seen. I never overcame that trait.

Punishment in class was always embarrassing. It often involved a trip to the cloakroom, which was on one end of the classroom. There, I sometimes had to bend over a chair and get a paddling from the teacher. The paddling really didn't hurt. It was the knowledge that the other children could hear the paddling taking place that really hurt. Sometimes, the teacher put an offending student outside the classroom in a chair beside the door. The principal came around about once an hour, and any student sitting in the chair had to explain the reason why. I never gave a satisfactory excuse when it was me in the chair and was taken to the office for a paddling and then sent back with a strong warning to straighten up.

On one occasion in the third or fourth grade, one of the girls took the teacher's paddle and began playing with it. Somehow, she managed to break the paddle. She was terrified about what would happen to her when the teacher came back to the room, and she began crying for no one to tell on her. We didn't, even though the teacher threatened everyone. Nobody told. In those days, nobody liked tattletales, even teachers. They might threaten, but they respected loyalty.

A friend named Larry was in my class during the second grade. He brought a big green-colored apple to school one day as a snack. At the beginning of class, he tripped and hit his face on the rim of a metal trash can. His lip was busted, and a front tooth was knocked out. He cried a little, but nothing could really be done as far as medical intervention. That was just the way things were at the time. He got over it and stayed in class. Later, he tried to eat the apple, but with the busted lip and lost front tooth, all he could do was nick the skin of the apple a bit. He tried it two or three times, but he realized he couldn't eat the apple. He offered it to me. It was a very lucky day for me because it was a big and pretty apple! I took it and ate it. I really felt sorry for Larry because I knew he really wanted to eat it but couldn't. I knew he was in a lot of pain too, but he did not carry on about it. His misfortune and friendship became my good fortune.

The older kids in school looked almost like grown-ups to us younger children. Even though they were eighth and ninth graders, we looked at them and respected them as we did adults. Sometimes, the older boys did things to the younger ones to establish dominance and put a little fear into them. Once done, though, they left them alone. In this way, it seemed the kids established an order in which each person knew his place. In that order, we could play together outside without any major problems or any tattling. If a problem arose, it was usually settled between those involved, and everyone was friends again. Rarely did the principal and his paddle have to get involved.

One day, while I was walking along the covered corridor to the boy's room, an eighth or ninth grader asked me the question, "Are you a member of the PTA?" I didn't know what to say, so I shook my head that I wasn't. He reached out with both hands and grabbed me in the region of both nipples and picked me up and shook me.

After dropping me, he walked away laughing and said, "We'll see tomorrow!"

I was with two or three others, but they ran away toward the bathroom. It hurt really bad, but I had gotten control of myself before I got back to the classroom. I didn't dare tell either.

The following day, the same boy stopped me and told me to pull up my shirt. I did, and my nipple areas were yellow and purple. He was satisfied and informed me I was now a member of the PTA. I was never bothered in that way—or in any other way—again. My friends who had run away? They showed me they had been made members of the Purple Titty Association too. When they pulled up their shirts to show me, their nipple areas were yellow, black, and purple. Swollen too! Suddenly, I felt I had gotten off easy. Both of them looked far worse than I did!

James, a student in the second grade, and I were sitting with our backs to a wall of the corridor leading to the lunchroom one day. It was winter, and we were enjoying the sun shining against that wall. I was listening to him as he was reading from a book. I was a third grader and a good reader. James was sick with a very bad cold. He had two long lines of green snot running from his nose. A shadow fell across us, and we looked up to see a ninth grader named Ricky looking down at us. He had the look all of us younger kids wanted to have when we got to be big like him. He was dressed in blue jeans with the cuffs folded back three or four inches. His socks were white, and he wore black penny loafers with dimes inserted into the slots. His black hair was slicked back with hair oil. It was hard not to admire the look even though I wasn't sure why he stopped and gave us his attention.

He reached into his back pocket, pulled out a folded, white

handkerchief, and said, "Here, take this and blow your nose, James." James blew his nose until the handkerchief turned green.

When Ricky was satisfied, he told James, "You keep that and blow your nose sometime. People don't want to see you with snot hanging out of your nose." With that, he walked away. He didn't make fun of James but got him cleaned up instead. He had also given up his white handkerchief. I found myself admiring him even more and wanting to be like him. I wished my hair could be black too, and I would like to slick it back like Ricky did. That could never happen though. My hair was red and curly. I don't think I ever managed to achieve the "cool look" on any day of my life. Redheads with freckles just can't seem to pull it off!

We did not have school "custodians" in those days. A person in that position was known as a janitor. The janitor did everything from cleaning the rooms, changing light bulbs, keeping the grounds clean, and doing anything else the teachers or principal needed to have done.

The janitor who took over when I was in the fourth or fifth grade was named Tom. He was black and was the only black person at our school. At that time, we used the polite and acceptable term "colored." We all liked him. We referred to him by his first name as that was the custom in our section of the country at that time in our history. There seemed to be far less for Tom to do on the grounds during the wintertime as he didn't have to mow all that grass. His main function then was to keep the radiators adjusted and the coal-fired boiler going to keep the chill out of the rooms. He spent the biggest part of the day in the basement area at the rear of the school where the boiler room was. The boiler room seemed half full of crushed coal in a huge mound that Tom shoveled into the furnace at frequent intervals. The room was very dimly lit and had the heavy, pleasing odor of burning coal. It was very warm even on the coldest of days. Tom had an old folding army cot covered with cardboard next to the wall far enough away from the furnace where it was warm, but not too hot. Beside it, he had his radio. I thought he had the best job in the whole world in the wintertime.

Our period of outside activity was called "play period" and not PE as it became known in later years. This period was largely unsupervised as we were used to being on our own and got along well most of the time. We played softball or basketball or engaged in other activities during that time. Occasionally, I slipped into the boiler room at the rear of the school, which was adjacent to the open area behind the school where we played ball. A couple of friends and I would spend some time with Tom and envy the fact that he had a warm cot and radio and a private place away from schoolwork and teachers. We kept a close eye out in case the principal came around checking on us during play period. Tom seemed to enjoy the occasional company and would sometimes tell us an interesting story. I always hated to leave the boiler room and go back into the cold air outside. I often imagined I was the one listening to the radio on the cot or maybe reading adventurous books. I liked reading. Books took me to interesting places on all kinds of adventures. I could read a lot of books in that warm, dim boiler room. Tom was the luckiest person in the whole world as far as I was concerned! I hoped someday I could have Tom's job.

A marble craze took hold at our school for a couple of years—until the principal put a sudden end to it. There was a period in which we spent a lot of time on our knees in the dirt shooting marbles. Everybody seemed to have a bag of marbles, and some of them were real beauties! A couple of boys had some steel ones, and one even had some very big ones that were very heavy. He really had a big advantage, and his marble sack kept getting bigger. We played for keeps. Playing for keeps was a big problem and was considered gambling. Gambling is sinful. We were warned to stop playing keepers, but we continued and just tried to keep it secret. Finally, the principal came around one day accompanied by Tom, the janitor, with a wheelbarrow. All the marbles were collected. It was said they were taken into the boiler room and shoveled into the furnace. Guess they didn't want us to burn in hell, so they sent our marbles there instead.

We lost our marbles, but we still had our knives. It was almost an assumption that a boy had a knife in his pocket. It was a country school, and most of us were farm boys—or at least country boys. Putting a knife in your pocket was almost a part of getting dressed. They were never considered weapons. They were tools and were sometimes used for entertainment.

It was not unusual for a teacher to say, "Allen, let me borrow your knife."

I learned the game mumblety-peg at school, but it wasn't all that popular. "Stretch" was more popular. It involved two people alternately flipping their knives into the ground and having the opponent stretch a foot to that spot. Another game was one of nerves where two people would alternately flip a knife into the ground near their opponent's foot. The first who lost his nerve was the loser. I only saw one person get stuck a little, but he had shoes on, and it was just a nick. Marbles could send us to hell and were taken away for our own good, but nobody ever suggested we surrender our knives or leave them at home.

At intervals during the school year, we were all assembled in the auditorium for different activities. One such frequent activity was a school singing session. In it, we were taught and sang some of the old songs together. It was a lot of fun and got everyone out of the classrooms for an hour. We were taught songs such as "Michael, Row the Boat Ashore" or "The Little Brown Church in the Vale." There were also "Way Down

Upon the Suwanee River," "Old Black Joe," and "Swing Low, Sweet Chariot." I suppose it was a way of keeping alive tunes from the past as well as breaking the monotony of the school environment. Sessions like that certainly made school more interesting.

About once or twice a year, we went into the auditorium, and all the students watched films together for a couple of hours. They were always interesting, though I wasn't really sure about the purpose of us watching some of them. Still, it was great, and I liked those times. It was nice to walk into the auditorium and see a big stack of film canisters beside the movie projector. That meant we would be there for a while.

Each year, we all participated in the rhythm band. At least up until a certain grade. It was to teach us to work together to make musical sounds, if you could call it that. I don't know how we were assigned the various instruments, but I don't believe ability was a factor. Probably favoritism prevailed. Some got lucky and got to play the triangle. That meant striking the triangle to make a high musical tone now and then. A lot of unlucky ones, myself included, clacked two sticks together. With a number of us doing that, and as the tempo increased, it sounded like a bunch of dried-up skeletons running. The really lucky ones, usually girls, got to play the bird whistles. Blowing on the dry whistle produced only a high-pitched continuous sound, but when partially filled with water, it made a trilling, warbling sound. Each person with a bird whistle had a gallon can of water so they could dip the whistle in for more water when needed. They had the best part of all. When the performance was over, there was always lots of water on the floor around them and some on their fellow students! I wanted to have a chance at the bird whistle or the triangle, but I never got to do anything but beat a pair of sticks together instead. I don't know who got lucky enough to beat the bass drum.

We practiced a number of times for our rhythm band recital. It was nice because we were not in the classroom; we were on a stage in the auditorium. When recital day came, we were all dressed in red and white capes with matching caps and paraded to the stage through the auditorium. Our parents had probably worn the same ones when they gave their recitals. It was a proud day to be dressed up so. I took my seat with the others and clacked away with my sticks like the others. I don't know if there was any rhythm there. I clacked when everybody else clacked and stopped when they stopped. The addition of the bird whistles, triangles, and bass drum made it sound as if the skeletons were shrieking and falling over furniture in a panic! That was the complete extent of my musical training.

We had programs on stage once or twice a year, and most students had some part, whether reciting or the girls showing off the dresses they had made. I remember my sisters all having made dresses and showing them in the "fashion show." We had occasional basketball games in this same small auditorium with our rival from the Pike Road School. We also played against them in softball. This happened a couple of times each year, and the site of the game alternated between the two schools. They were played during school hours, and everyone was let out to watch when the games were at our school.

Total education seemed to be the focus at school during my childhood. There was memory work, which included learning poetry, famous addresses or documents, and states and their capitols. Book reports were both written and oral and given every six weeks in front of the class. Multiplication tables were learned through twelve times twelve and recited. Certain home economics skills were taught—but only to the girls. We had our daily devotional activities at the beginning of the day. Boys were expected to participate in sports at whatever level they could. All in all, it was a very balanced approach to education. We all learned our book subjects, developed social skills, and improved in our outdoor activities at the same time.

Every year, the principal dissected a bullfrog as part of science instruction. The frog was alive, but it was stretched out and immobilized on a board. An ice cube was attached to his head by some means and rendered him unconscious. He was dissected, and each of us was allowed to view his beating heart and other organs. We looked at the webbing between his toes through a microscope and watched the blood cells flow through the capillaries in the webbing. After everyone had a chance to view the blood flow, the class came to an end. The frog was sent to the kitchen, and the legs were cooked. They were eaten by the principal as part of his meal. He maintained he dearly loved frog legs!

Pintlala School was built to resemble a Spanish mission. However, its design was called "Mediterranean." Five schools had been commissioned to be built by that design in the early twentieth century. Its first year of operation was 1922, and my daddy attended school there. I started there in 1956. When the bus was still a long way from school, I could see the black coal smoke billowing from the chimney above the school and could smell it too. I loved the smell of coal smoke. We often burned coal at home for heat.

The front of the school reminded me of the Alamo. The school was stucco and laid out in a large H design with the cross of the H being the Alamo part fronting the principal's office and auditorium. Two covered wings of classrooms fronted by columned corridors extended out to the side and then around the auditorium. A small sunken courtyard lay between each of these corridors on either side of the auditorium. The roofs were of gray slate. Grades one through four and the boy's restroom were along the right-side corridor, while the fifth through the ninth and the girl's restroom were along the left-side corridor. The classrooms were fairly large with very high ceilings and tall windows. The tops of the windows were designed to be pulled forward with a long rod to allow more air circulation and the lower sashes of the windows could be raised as well. The heat, as I mentioned earlier, was from steam radiators. The floors were of oiled wood to keep down the dust. A cloakroom extended the full length of the classroom on one end for coats and stored items. Punishment was sometimes administered there.

In the fifth grade, I moved to the corridor to the left of the "Alamo" entrance. It was a sign that we were growing up and moving up to where the big kids were. We started getting a sense of history beyond the Pilgrims and an introduction into science and such. We began developing a feeling that we were not little children anymore and soon afterward realized girls were more interesting than they once were, though we were not sure exactly why. We found ourselves wanting to impress them and get their attention, and we never wanted to look foolish to them. I carved a girl's initials on a tree in the edge of Murrell's Swamp—far enough into the edge of the forest though that nobody else might find it. Something was very different about life when we got to the left-side corridor from the auditorium!

We found ourselves a bit more aggressive on the left side. We did things to challenge each other and to act out and to assert ourselves. I guess that's called testing, spreading the wings, pushing the boundaries, or maybe growing up. At best, it was a confusing time. We eventually found girls were really different and interesting too. With that realization, life took on another dimension. Playing ball and romping with the other boys continued as it always had—but no longer with the idea of just impressing each other. We were becoming conscious that the girls were watching!

Two new classrooms were added beside the left wing of the old building. This new addition was not attached to the original structure except by a covered walkway. It had a modern look and had electric heat. The addition of these two rooms allowed the upper grades to spread out a bit. I still liked the older rooms the best because of the high ceilings, cloakrooms, and tall windows. Those were the rooms our parents had occupied before our turn came. There was something comforting about that.

We tried our best to make our time at school more interesting. While the teachers were instructing us with books and such, we made it our business to teach each other things that weren't in the books. I learned to make all kinds of useful gadgets and spent as much time as I could get away with in making them.

Noisemakers were great for making a girl squeal. They were made of a bobby pin shaped into a large letter "c." A rubber band was threaded through a button and then stretched between the two ends of the reshaped bobby pin. The button was twisted on the rubber band until it was wound like a spring. It was inserted into an envelope of folded paper and presented to someone. When the paper was loosened and the button freed, it made a whirring, fluttering sound in the paper. It was a fun thing to do, but it only worked once per victim.

Stink bombs were fun and easy to make. They could be set off at any time—even in class while the teacher's back was turned. The filler of a ballpoint pen was removed, and a bobby pin was inserted through the length of the spring and put back into the barrel of the pen with the end of the bobby pin protruding through the hole at the end of the barrel of the pen. A match was inserted between the rounded end of the bobby pin at the end of the spring with the head of the match touching the bobby pin. The two sections of pen were screwed back together, and if there was too much slack at the end of the matchstick, paper filler would take care of that problem. Pulling the end of the bobby pin outward and then letting go worked like a firing pin in a gun. The bobby pin hit the match head inside and set it off. When it ignited inside the pen, a jet of sulfur smoke came out of the end of the pen. It had a strong rotten egg smell!

Shooting spitballs doesn't require a lot of explanation. They can be thrown, spit, or shot with a rubber band or with a peashooter made of a piece of rolled-up notebook paper. There were usually a lot of them stuck to the clock or the wall around it. Everyone was a victim of spitballs now and then with no real harm done. Shooting someone with a spitball launched from a rubber band got the biggest response. They stung a bit when they hit the back of the neck. Paper clips shot like that really hurt, but they were reserved for the boys only. A girl would probably have screamed out loud, and that would not be good for the shooter.

Getting a thumbtack under a person was a real art in itself and sometimes involved using strategy and planning. I got a friend of mine so many times he got a little paranoid about ever sitting down. After several successive failures, I began doing a little experimenting. One day, he made a trip to the pencil sharpener, and I put a piece of notebook paper in his seat. When he came back, he glanced down at it, but then he sat down without removing it. He made frequent trips to the pencil sharpener because he always pressed hard with his pencil when he wrote and broke the lead far more often than anyone else. I filed away this bit of information about his ignoring the sheet of paper and used it to my advantage that afternoon.

During lunch break, I helped myself to a few dozen

thumbtacks from the teacher's desk. Later, when Thomas made a trip to the pencil sharpener, I put all the tacks in his seat and covered them with the piece of paper he had never removed before lunch. He sat down hard and sprang back up with the paper and a dozen or more of the thumbtacks stuck to his backside. He didn't holler out loud enough for the teacher to hear, but he made whimpering and moaning noises as he pulled the tacks out. He never sat down again without checking to make sure it was clear to do so.

I didn't think I would ever be able to get him again, but I did. The idea of partnering up with my friend Flynn was inspired. Flynn sat directly opposite Thomas on the next row. With me on one side and Flynn on the other, poor Thomas didn't have a chance. On cue, Flynn popped Thomas on his arm, and Thomas automatically leaned over to retaliate. I slid the tack under him and popped him on the arm on my side. In trying to get me back, he came down hard on the tack. There was whimpering and moaning again, and his hand shook as he removed the tack. I never did it again. He had suffered enough. After all, he was my closest friend in school. Until her death, many years later, his mother reminded me I had always been his closest friend. It was a good thing we were so close and liked each other—or our friendship would not have survived the tacks.

Girls wore dresses to school in those days, and boys wore long pants, usually blue jeans. Girls were spared from most pranks, but not always. When we learned about magnifying glasses and what they could do when coupled with a ray from the sun, we used that to our advantage. We might burn a leaf with the directed light from the sun through the glass or incinerate an ant or two. Now and then, we made a girl squirm in class. Choosing a victim at least two or three seats forward was the first thing. Directing a beam of light through the magnifying glass onto the back of her calf was second. After a few seconds or so, she would move her leg or reach down and rub it. Just getting a reaction was the objective—not to hurt her. That's the reason for choosing someone at least a couple of seats away.

Except for the crawfish down the blouse of a girl in the eighth grade, the girls were mostly exempt from pranks. This girl was more physically developed than most of the others, which made her the target of the prank. One boy had brought creatures to school on occasion to show them off and to get a reaction from the girls. On this occasion, it was a large red crawfish that looked like a small lobster. He had big claws. It wound up in the girl's blouse. It could have done some damage if it had pinched her, but she got lucky. In the hysteria that followed, several of the girls surrounded her, buttoned her up, and straightened her blouse. They finally got her calmed down. There wasn't much fuss made over the matter, and the owner of the crawfish reclaimed his property and took it back home with him that afternoon. I never really understood why the teacher didn't get involved since she was obviously aware of what was going on in the back of the classroom. Maybe she was thinking "boys will be boys." Perhaps she thought the girl deserved what she got for being so fully developed and having attracted attention to herself by that fact.

I believe it was the "crawfish boy" who came up with the idea of victimizing one of our fellow male students. This particular student was not shy about asking fellow students about the snack they may have brought to school. Snacks were actually rare things to see, but occasionally, someone brought a snack from home.

At times, he might see a snack in another student's desk and ask, "You going to eat that?" Obviously, he was hoping it might be offered to him, and he certainly would have accepted. This knowledge was used against him.

Conspirators got their heads together and worked out a plan. One would bring a Hershey bar the next day, and another would supply the Ex-Lax. On the following day, they met in the boys' room with several more of us as spectators for the operation they had planned. The candy bar and Ex-Lax bar were unwrapped, and the blending of the two bars commenced. The Ex-Lax and a pocketknife were warmed on the radiator, and the melted laxative was spread over the back of the chocolate bar. It was allowed to cool in the cold air coming in through the window. Afterward, it was rewrapped in its foil and slipped back into the "Hershey" sleeve. Lunch break being at an end, we returned to class where the candy bar was left on its owner's desk as a lure. The intended victim was in the next desk to the left and spied the candy rather quickly.

Before the hour was over, he had asked, "You going to eat that?"

The owner offered it to the victim and stated he wasn't feeling all that well and probably wouldn't eat it anyway. It was gladly accepted and disappeared rather quickly.

At the end of the school day, we boarded our buses for the trip home. The victim rode the same bus as I did, and his home was the second stop on the route for our bus. Before we got to his house, he was already standing by the driver and holding to the vertical metal rod directly beside the driver. He seemed to be in considerable distress. He didn't hesitate when the bus stopped, and as the driver opened the door, he ran a bit awkwardly across the road and into the stand of young pine trees beside his long driveway that ran through the pines. He was unfastening his belt buckle as he ran. I don't know if he made it in time or not.

We watched and grinned to each other, but we never asked

him about it later. That would have been admitting guilt about his condition. It was a prank that had worked perfectly, and we all admired those who had pulled it off so well. The knowledge of it was kept to a select few. I'm not sure if the victim ever knew what had caused the sudden onset of his condition!

Well, naughty or nice, we each got a Christmas present at school every year on the last day of school before our Christmas break, which began about one week before Christmas and continued 'til after the New Year. We got a gift because we drew names and exchanged gifts each year. All the gifts were put under a large Christmas tree in the middle of the auditorium, which had been decorated by a number of the older students.

We had the regular Christmas program each year in the auditorium with everyone in attendance. There was always the reenactment of the story of Jesus's birth complete with wise men and angels. We sang a lot of traditional songs together along with "Here Comes Santa Claus." The principal was then handed the gifts from under the tree and called out the student's name on each gift as it was handed to him. It took a long time to hand out about 120 gifts. It was the most exciting time of the year at school. For a number of days, all we could think about was Christmas, decorating, and practicing for the Christmas program. In the upper three grades, one of our teachers read Charles Dicken's *A Christmas Carol* to us over a period of several days. It was especially enjoyable hearing it read aloud in that manner.

Our bus driver stood by the door of the bus that was about to take us home in the middle of the school day. He greeted each of us, wished us a "Merry Christmas," and handed us a gift as we boarded. It was always the same and very special: a pack of chewing gum and a candy bar for everyone who rode his bus. He was a very kindly and thoughtful man. The parting salute to each person from the others as each exited the bus at their home was, "See you next year!"

Christmas celebration and the beginning of the break that followed was one of the most exciting times of the year at school. The most exciting was probably the last day of school when we also had a party. Two or three local businesses participated in the hosting of the festivities of that day—not the least of which was the local Coca-Cola Bottling Company. While others supplied cups of ice cream, cartons of orange drink, and snacks, the Coca-Cola Company gave us gifts we all remember after so many years. They gave us pencils, notepads, and rulers with their logo imprinted. We were always excited to receive them even though school was out for the summer. I think it was their way of saying, "Keep working!" The ruler was imprinted with the words: "Do unto others as you would have them do unto you." Even as children, we were impressed with what the Coca-Cola Company was doing and the interest they were taking in us. If memory serves me correctly, it was the only Coca-Cola bottling company that was privately owned.

Toward the end of summer vacation, Mama bought each of us some new clothes for school. I got two or three new pairs of blue jeans and shirts. Each of us got new notebooks and pencils along with lots of paper. I was always excited about the new items and promised myself I would be very organized at school this year and would be completely focused. This would be my best year ever, and nothing was going to distract me from being a good student. Like New Year's resolutions, these promises never lasted more than a few weeks. After that, I was the same distracted student I had been in previous years. I loved the outdoors too much for the teachers to have my full attention. I was practically hopeless as a student. The teachers had their hands full with me. They told me, often, that I had a good mind and were exasperated that I wouldn't use it. Actually, I did use it—but on more adventurous things outside the classroom. Theirs was not an easy job when it came to educating me. I have often wished I could go back through those years in a more focused manner and see what the result would have been for me *and* for them.

We finally made it through to graduation in the ninth grade. Most of us, that is. Bill, one grade ahead of me, drowned in a pond while swimming. He suffered cramps, went under, and didn't come back up. That was difficult for all of us. Eugene died of a bad heart. He was in the grade behind me and only attended for a few months. We all knew he was sick and felt very bad for him. He was a good student and very skinny because of his illness. One day, he didn't come back to school, and we found out he had died. It didn't seem fair to me, somehow, that he never had a chance at life in the way the rest of us did.

At graduation, our "prophet" stood before the audience, looked forward into our futures, and gave the predictions of where each of us would be in a few years. A few of the predictions were probably based on the accepted fact that the apple doesn't fall far from the tree, and if so, that is a valid assumption. Some did indeed follow in a parent's footsteps. Other predictions were on the mark too, but there were two or three misses.

We still had a while before testing our prophet's skill though because high school was still before us. I went on to attend Sydney Lanier High School in Montgomery with most of the others. It was a huge high school by any reckoning and considered one of the top schools in the nation. Coming from a little country school, we felt a bit intimidated and ill prepared, but we found out we were very well prepared after all.

Many eventually went on to distinguish themselves in various fields. I feel as if I should brag on some of them whose contributions were astounding, but I will refrain from doing so. Achievements can be measured in various ways, and I would not want to overlook or fail to note someone's accomplishment. I can only take my hat off to them, acknowledge their achievements, and be thankful I knew them. A student two grades behind me at Pintlala went on to become an astronaut and helped repair the vision-impaired Hubble Telescope on one of her space walks. It was diagnosed that the telescope needed some contact lenses! My younger sister, Dianne, also in that class, attested that this classmate of hers was the smartest person she ever knew! Dianne was a straight-A student, so that says a lot! I didn't come anywhere close to that level of perfection and really didn't care to. After all, being a trapper was just about as good as life could offer!

My teachers at Lanier had as tough a time trying to educate me as teachers had in the past. I never focused or committed myself to education until my senior year of high school. As a matter of fact, I dropped out from lack of interest but returned and completed my education. Upon returning, I applied myself as I never had in the past. I am happy I did that—both for my sake and for the pleasure it gave my father whose heart was broken when he found out that I had quit school. He wanted something better for me than he had experienced. He was a happy man when I returned to school, and the decision to do so was one of the best decisions I have made in my life.

I went on to serve in the Army Security Agency and gave a good account of myself. That was attested to by the document on the wall before me as I now write. That document references congratulatory communications received from the National Security Agency concerning my work and contributions. It would have made Dad proud to have read it. Perhaps it would have been nice for my teachers to have seen it as well. Maybe their frustration would have been lessened with the knowledge that their efforts were not completely wasted after all!

When I graduated high school in May 1969, I was already working with a paper supply company in Montgomery. Beyond my immediate situation, I had no ideas for the future. That was soon to change!

Part 2

VIETNAM

41

THE DUSTY CORNER

EARLY IN this narrative, I alluded to my military experience, which spanned nine years and nine months. Some of this experience involved a time of my life that I was uncomfortable talking about. The decision to leave much of my early military experience behind me was a deliberate and conscious decision, partly because of the sometimes-painful moments. Not that there was any great occurrences or traumatic events that caused me to feel this way. Rather, it was an accumulation of things in a time of great upheaval and change, not only in the country, but in my own life as well. I was comfortable in simply leaving it alone and thinking about it as little as possible.

I preferred the happier part of my military experience, which began with my marriage to Yoko Chinen in Okinawa on January 30, 1974. It was then that the face and character of my family changed dramatically and in a happy way. Events and circumstances that have come about in my life over the past six or eight months have caused me to pause and rethink my having pushed aside those things that made me uncomfortable. Perhaps it's time to reflect on some of those things. After all, they played their parts in influencing my past decisions and, ultimately, the course of my life. It is because of the impact my early military experience continues to have on me and because of the sound advice from a close friend that I am revisiting that time.

For several years, my children have been pushing me to retire and enjoy life a bit while I still have the health to do so.

"I can't do that," I always replied. "What will I do about health insurance? I'll have to wait until I'm old enough for Medicare."

My daughter, Mechi, began to investigate the possibility of picking up coverage through the Veteran's Administration. I was against this and was reluctant to pursue it. After a couple of years, she finally overcame my objections and began the process. It was then I fully realized my inability to remember details dealing with much of the experience I had "boxed up and stored away" in my mind. I found I could not recall unit designations, dates, and other information involving my military experience in Vietnam, as well as a lot of other things.

I also found myself in a highly emotional state when I awakened on the morning of the day on which I was to go to the VA to start the medical process. I had been racking my brain the day before trying to remember or retrieve information that seemed to be practically blotted out. This caused a fitful and difficult night with little sleep. It also caused me to have two extremely vivid but troubling dreams. Lying fully awake after having had them, I considered what my brain was trying to move from the subconscious to the conscious state. Feeling emotional and agitated, I knew it was important for me to figure out what was going on. It might as well have been someone shouting to me out loud: "Hey, listen to me! I want to tell you something!"

It did not take me long to decide what the message was that the dream center of my brain had sent me. This message, transmitted from one part of my brain to another, took the simple form of these two dreams that seemed perfectly designed to get my full attention. I had long ago learned to decipher what was going on in my mind, which sometimes resulted in troubling dreams, some of which reoccurred. However, if I took the time to think a bit and came to a satisfactory explanation for a particular dream, even the recurring ones, they never repeated. My dreams, however bizarre, always seemed to speak to an issue I was currently struggling with. Because of that, I learned long ago to pay attention to them.

The first of the two dreams on this particular night was about the cows I once owned. In that dream, it seemed my cows had strayed away from the pasture through untended fences many years before. I had never made an attempt to retrieve them, mend the fences, or keep up the pasture. The pasture had become overgrown with brush and had very few areas where spots of grass even existed. I could often hear the sounds of the cows far off in the distance. They were in some other place on the far side of the woods to the east of my house. In my dream, I found myself wondering about them and what their condition might be after all those years. Though I had no desire to get them back, occasionally, they came back on their own, and I could hear them close by and catch glimpses of them in the brush and in the occasional small clear areas. I debated whether I should fence them in while they were present so they could not disappear again, but I did nothing. The dream ended with the cows going back to that place on the far side of the woods, and I could once again hear them in that distant place. Later, as I lay in bed considering this dream, I was very aware I had experienced it before but had made no attempt to understand it. Now, here it was again and being replayed in exactly the same way as I remember it from years earlier!

The second of the two dreams on that night concerned the old barn on the place. This barn has fallen into a sad state of disrepair after not having been used for so many years. It is practically falling down, and only junk is stored there. Going into the middle area of the barn is like entering a dark and damp room. Now, even the dirt floor is muddy most of the time. This was the area of the barn that had once been dry and where we had stored hay for the cows and mule. The abandoned mule stall is to the right and adjoins this section.

My dream began with my opening the door to this middle area of the barn and stepping inside. I was struck by the sensation of a peculiar warmth in the air and the feeling that it was produced by body heat. I detected a presence and immediately knew it was my father. There was the smell of peppermint and other odors I have always associated with him. *How can he be here though? He's been gone for so many years!*

As my eyes adjusted to the dimness, I began to see things. Items hanging from nails turned out to be clothing. Blankets hung like tapestries along the outer wall, and I could not see any light filtering in. Instinctively, I concluded the blankets were hung to prevent someone on the outside from peeking in through the cracks between the boards. They also helped keep out cold drafts and made the place more secure. There was a chair to the left of a pallet on the floor, a pallet still warm from the sleeping person who had occupied it.

It was my father—I knew with a certainty! A father dead for so many years was actually right there with me! He had never gone anywhere. Though he was there, I could not see or touch him. I could only sense he was there. I knew, when I awakened from the dream, that my father represented memories I have had with me for so long. Memories that were in a dim place. I had put them there among the other junk where they would not be a bother to me, but I could not deny them. They were a part of me, and they were as meaningful as the relationship Dad and I had before death took him away from me. The cows, which I was apparently satisfied to leave on the far side of the woods in the earlier dream, represented the same. Perhaps the woods helped ensure the separation. The overgrown pasture gave the cows no place to return to. Though they tried on occasion to return, there was nothing for them to feed on in the overgrown pasture, and they drifted back to the far side of the woods.

Having awakened, following the two dreams and considering them, I had no difficulty in accepting that they were related and conveying the same message. Memories and thoughts that I had pushed aside or insulated myself against were still there. They were waiting for me to accept them back! A process that had been set in motion the day before when I began trying to resurrect certain things deep in my mind. It was proving to be a bit painful for me to do so as I had been satisfied to leave things as they were. For me, consciously trying to recall these things I had deliberately stored away for so long was like letting a genie out of his bottle. I wasn't sure I wanted to. In the past, when certain thoughts came into my mind, I was usually able to just push them away by putting my mind on other things. That decision to put my mind on other things had become a habit a long time ago. Soon, however, I had to make a decision as to whether I wanted to break that habit or continue in it. A good friend gave me advice that encouraged me to stop pushing things aside.

I called that friend, George Baird, on the morning after the dreams. He was the only person I felt I could talk to about what I was experiencing. George and his wife, Marianne, live in Plymouth, Massachusetts. George and I are good friends and served together in Vietnam. He is more than just a brother in spirit. I have always looked at his family as an extension of my own. Therefore, George seemed to be the one person I could turn to in my present state. I would soon be going to the VA and could not remember many things about our time together in Vietnam and was in a panic. The dreams were strong indicators of the distress I was feeling and seemed to have increased it.

When I called, Marianne answered the phone. She knew something was wrong as I had difficulty expressing myself because of my emotions. "Let me wake up George," she said.

When George came on the line, I was finally able to get the words out that I couldn't remember the important information concerning our joint assignment there in Vietnam. As a matter of fact, I couldn't remember much of anything! I had spent so many years not thinking about it that things just faded away and had all but disappeared. Until that moment, I had not realized the extent to which I had pushed those thoughts away.

When I left Vietnam, I was told not to talk about the part I played because of secrecy concerns. The best way to ensure this was to not think about it at all. Eventually, it became a habit, but it also shielded me from any unpleasant memories. I now found myself in a deep emotional distress because of the nearly blank slate my mind had become. From his bed in Plymouth, Massachusetts, George began helping me reconstruct information that I could no longer recall. That information was helpful and served me in the same way that reference points do for someone who has become lost. I felt much better after George and I had talked awhile.

In preparing my petition to the VA, my daughter, Mechi, had done a lot of research and legwork for me. She had visited the office of the Veterans of Foreign Wars on my behalf. It was located on the campus of the Veteran's Administration hospital in Montgomery. They gave her all the necessary forms and paperwork with the instructions needed to fill them out properly. They were carefully highlighted with colored marker and sticky notes. She was to request and obtain copies of all medical records from my doctors. This, she was told, would greatly speed the process when the VA reviewed my petition. She had done her work well! The documentation and paperwork with accompanying records were flawless, and the submission of them went without a hitch. It then became a matter of waiting to hear from the VA after they received and reviewed the documents. I did not have to wait long. I received notification that I was to report to the Veteran's Hospital in Montgomery for an initial medical screening. Now, the time had come that I had dreaded for so long and had only come about because of the insistence of my children.

A few hours after having experienced that fitful and dream-filled night and having awakened George and Marianne in Massachusetts, I headed for the VA complex in Montgomery. Carrying my bag with the thick binders of medical records, filled-out forms, and other documents, I took a few deep breaths and headed across the parking lot away from my car. Only the thought of the time and energy my daughter had invested kept me from turning around and going back home.

It's not going to do any good, I thought to myself. I had convinced myself of that even before we began the process. I passed a man coming in my direction from across the parking lot. We made eye contact, and he smiled and nodded a greeting as he passed. I returned the greeting, but remember thinking, *I'm glad I don't look like that.* He looked older than he probably was and not particularly neat in his dress. He reminded me of someone who might be on the back side of life. Soon, I saw a couple of other men who looked similar to the first and then still another sitting in the designated smoking area. These three men appeared to be close in age and appearance, perhaps my age. They reminded me so much of the first man I had passed. The biggest difference in all four seemed to be the varied grayness of their hair and the length of their whiskers, from bristles to full beard. I found myself once again wanting to turn and head back to my car.

I'm not like that, I thought again. *I'm not one of them.* I continued to walk, however, and noticed that each one had nodded, smiled, and spoke to me as I passed as if they were acknowledging something or someone they were familiar with. I returned their nods, smiles, and greetings and began to think. Later, I realized these four people had given me a lot to think about!

I survived the day at the VA after all. I went through a benefit processing as well as an initial physical screening. During the physical examination, I was asked several probing questions designed to look beyond the physical. I was not prepared for that. I denied having any special problems along those lines. It was a reflex answer. I kept wondering how I might change my response and tell her of the distress I had begun to experience. At the conclusion of the physical examination, I was asked again if I were sure there was nothing else I wanted to add. She must have known. I told her I had not been completely open with her and that I had something to say. It took me a moment to compose myself and tell her about the emotional distress I had recently begun to experience.

"I really didn't want to come here and do this," I said. "My children are concerned and have been urging me to come here for some time, and it's begun to cause me problems. I've always been happy and comfortable in leaving everything behind. I have never had the least bit of a problem by doing that. Now, it's trying to come back, and it's a bit unsettling for me!"

She said there was someone she would like me to talk to. "I'll set it up if you wish," she added.

I indicated I was interested, but as it turned out, it was a couple of months before I got a notification. By then, things had begun to settle back down, and I did not wish to pursue it.

The VA Hospital was a very depressing place for me. Not by the way I was treated, but what it represented to me. It represented those things I had disassociated myself from. I could not have been treated more kindly by those who worked there. The staff was very helpful and courteous.

Many times, I heard staff members say, "Thank you for your service!"

I soon found myself responding, "Thank you for yours and for your kindness!" The veterans I met on that first day and subsequent visits were friendly and quick to acknowledge others and strike up conversations. They were always willing to be of assistance in helping me in my confusion about locations in the hospital or of procedure. Most did not look like the guys I had seen outside on my initial visit, but some of them did. I do not remember any of them being unfriendly or unhelpful. This gave me even more to think about concerning my long, self-imposed isolation from anything dealing with the military.

I must have been thinking a lot about all the veterans I had seen on that first day—even more than I could have realized—because I dreamed again sometime during one of the following nights. It was to be one of the most revealing dreams I had ever had, and the message was completely clear. It spoke of the self-imposed isolation from my fellow veterans that had existed for so long with the only exception being my friend George. This dream turned out to be the beginning of the end of my isolation, which seems to have begun around the end of July 1971.

In this latest dream, I found myself in a small, almost bare room. There was one table in the room. One table surrounded by four chairs with no other furnishings. Across the table from my position, the wall was actually a curtain partition from one corner of the room to the other. It reminded me of the biblical description of the veil of the temple dividing the Holy Place from the Most Holy Place. It represented a barrier for me. I was seated facing this curtain with three others with me around the table. Pablo Caudillo was to my left, and George Baird was across from me with his back to the curtain. To my right was an unknown person whose face I could not see. It was blotted out. We were dressed in sky-blue uniforms, an odd shade of blue. Later, I came to realize it was the background color of the patch that represented our organization, the US Army Security Agency, an intelligence-gathering agency. We were not talking. We were just there, looking at each other as if there was no need to say anything at all.

A young woman parted the curtain, stepped inside, and gave us a smile and a questioning look. "Why are you sitting here by yourselves?" she asked.

"This is where we are supposed to be," I answered.

"No," she said. "You are supposed to be in there with everybody else." She pulled the curtain aside and revealed a large banquet hall with a thousand or more faces looking back at us.

"No," I said again. "We are supposed to stay here. Anyway, they can't see us."

With that, those in the banquet hall began to gesture for us to come and join them. Some stood up and smiled as they beckoned for us to come, and others clapped. There were all kinds of uniforms in that hall: army, marine, air force, and navy. There were no sky-blue ones though besides the four at our table.

The young woman, who was obviously a waitress, turned and faced me again, smiling. The smile changed to a look of concern, and she asked me, "Why are there tears in your eyes?"

"Because I'm not invisible anymore," I said. "All these years I've been invisible, and I'm not invisible anymore."

"Then go," she said.

The four of us stood up from the table and started toward the parted curtain and those beckoning to us. First, the faceless one. Then, George, Pablo, and myself. My dream ended at that point, and I woke up. Even before I was fully awake, I knew the significance of this dream. There was to be little need for analysis. While the meaning of the dream was immediately clear to me, the "faceless one" was a bit of a mystery.

A few days later, I told George about my visit to the VA and of the dream that had occurred subsequent to that visit.

His reply was straight to the point and indicated the depth of understanding about the issues I was dealing with. "Allen," he said, "your problem is you internalized and suppressed everything and did not talk about your experiences. You were told to keep quiet about your service, and you did. You did it to the point of repressing those things. You need to start dealing with them. It's time you started thinking about that time and talking about it too. We were all told to keep quiet about our service and were bound to do so. We were all debriefed to that effect, but we're not bound by that any longer. People are writing books about it and have been for several years. I've got something I'm going to send to you for Christmas that you will find quite interesting. It will get you to thinking about things and will really be of help to you."

I was happy I had shared the dream with George. He had come to the same conclusion I had concerning its meaning. It was time to end my self-imposed isolation. The time was right.

George was true to his word. In a couple of weeks, I received a package from him. In the package was a nicely made black baseball cap. Embroidered on the front was "Army Security Agency." Under that, the words "Always Vigilant." Over the years, I have received a couple of nicely made caps proclaiming "Vietnam Veteran," but I never wore them. They went straight into my closet and are still there on the shelf where I put them. I felt no inclination to put them on. When I received the hat from George, things were different. I sat and looked at the hat for some time as it lay on my desk before picking it up again and putting it on my head. Walking out of my study, I went to the closest mirror to see how it looked on me.

I liked what I saw and found myself smiling and thinking, *Wow, this is great!* I suppose I never expected to see the ASA shoulder patch again or the words "Army Security Agency." Here were the words and the shoulder patch being reflected back at me in the mirror from the front of the cap. Suddenly, I found myself thinking, *Here is a cap I will wear. It will never be in the closet like the other caps!*

I returned to my study, took the second item out of the package, and laid it on the desk. Sitting there, I looked at it for a while—not believing what I was seeing. It was a book, published in 2013 by iUniverse, LLC, and authored by Lonnie M. Long and Gary B. Blackburn entitled *Unlikely Warriors: The Army Security Agency's Secret War in Vietnam 1961–1973*.

They really were writing books about us, just like George said! I looked at the front cover for a long time, digesting the words and image printed on it. Finally, I flipped it over and read the introduction on the back, which described the clandestine arrival of the first American military personnel in Vietnam, ninety-two members of a secret organization: the Army Security Agency.

I knew I was going to read this book! In the forty-five years since I had left Vietnam, I adhered to my policy of never reading anything about that conflict or making it a habit of watching movies, documentaries, or TV shows where that was the subject matter. I just didn't care to be reminded of it. *Just leave it alone*, I thought.

The book lay on my desk for a couple of weeks, and I occasionally picked it up and read the front and back of it and put it back down. Finally, I opened it and began to read. I'm so glad I did! It was factually accurate, well written, and interesting. By the time I was two-thirds of the way through the book, I realized I had come to an understanding of the significance of the fourth man in my dream with the sky-blue uniform and the blotted-out face. I still cannot see his face in my mind, but I know who he represented and have resurrected his name. This book has caused me to think about certain things, and it has given me the desire to write down a few of them as well. My thanks to Lonnie Long and Gary Blackburn for that!

As I began to consciously think back on that time, I found myself remembering more and more. First the bigger things and then the smaller details, even trivial things started coming back to me. I have begun jotting two- and three-word notes down so I don't forget the little things that are popping up. Incredibly, I find that most are not troublesome, but are amusing! Some are amusing but shouldn't be, and that's a bit troublesome. I guess that says something about the desensitizing effects that can occur in the environment so many of us found ourselves in. It may also speak of a certain coarseness that tends to set in when putting men in an environment away from the softening influence of their families or sweethearts. I remember the desperate lonely times that set in, especially on holidays when the thoughts of family could not be pushed aside, but there were also those other times that were difficult experiences. Some were physical occurrences while others happened "between the ears" and left their indelible marks. I have debated with myself which likely left the biggest mark on me. I am inclined to believe it was the latter. Not specific events or occurrences, but the changes that took place in my mind and thinking. Someone very close to me remarked when I came home, "You are different now." I knew that I was too.

42

RESPONDING TO THE CALL

THERE IS no better place to begin than at the beginning. At nineteen years of age, I was out of high school and working for a paper supplier in Montgomery. School had been a boring experience for me, and I finally dropped out before graduating. I had never fully applied myself to my studies in any grade that I am aware of. The teachers may have had my body, but they never had my full attention. Fish, squirrels, birds, trees, and anything connected with the great outdoors had that. I was a hopeless case for any teacher. There were occasions when exasperated teachers reminded me that I was very bright. However, that doesn't do anyone any good at all if such a one is just not interested. Apparently, I was not bright enough to grasp the implications carried in such statements, and they failed to motivate me. The only subject that ever really interested me in high school was ROTC. I might have skipped two or more days of school in a given week, but I never missed a Friday.

That was the day of the "in-ranks" inspection. I stayed up most of Thursday night preparing my uniform, brass, and shoes so I could get my usual perfect inspection score the following day. I had been completely fascinated by the army since I was eleven or twelve years old. Finally, however, I made the decision to quit attending school. I don't know who broke the news to my dad, but he came into my room that night with a sad expression on his face.

"I heard that you quit school," he said.

I told him that I had.

"Son, I'm afraid you will find that it's the worst decision you have ever made." With that, he turned away with a sorrowful expression and walked out the door. He never got angry, shouted, or berated me. He just turned and went out the door. I was stunned by the look on Dad's face. It might as well have been that someone had told him I had died. Throughout the whole weekend, I was haunted by that.

On Monday morning, I went back to school, and for the very first time, I began to apply myself completely to my studies. I had to go an extra year to make up the lacking credits, but I did it with all A's. My dad was a very proud man for that!

I read a lot while growing up, including newspapers and news magazines. I watched every evening news broadcast I could and kept up with what was going on in the world. The biggest event of my time during high school and afterward was the Vietnam War. It seemed to occupy most of the time devoted to news broadcasts. I was highly patriotic and accepted any broadcasts or news releases by the media or government as I had accepted biblical truth. Communists? Bad! Vicious people, evil liars, and a threat to all decent people. Americans and democracy? The decent people! The virtuous of the world and the defenders of goodness! Three and a half months after finishing high school, I suddenly decided to be one of these "defenders of goodness." Leaving work on my lunch hour, I walked the few blocks to the courthouse and stated my intention to enlist. Two days later,

I found myself being processed at the Gunter AFB Induction Center—but in a way I had never imagined.

"Sorry, son. The army will not take you. You've got a weak eye," he said.

I stared at the staff sergeant in disbelief.

He leaned back slightly in his chair and looked across his desk at me through dark glasses that concealed his eyes. I had never considered the possibility of rejection and was completely stunned.

"What about the marines?" I asked.

"No," he said.

"Air force or navy?"

"Same," he added.

My disappointment showed. There was no way I could hide it. I wanted more than anything to serve my country, and this obvious rejection only made that desire stronger.

"It's a pity," he said. "I've been looking over your test scores, and they are impressive. You certainly rank at the top. Perhaps there is something I can offer you if you're interested. Ever heard of the ASA?"

I indicated I had not and asked what it was.

"It's the Army Security Agency. I can't tell you much about it though." He glanced to his left and to his right and then appeared to be looking past me to see if anyone was listening. Perhaps someone with big ears was close by, and they did not need to hear our conversation. "It's rather secret and hush-hush. Has to do with intelligence. I can tell you this—it is incredibly interesting work and will put you in equally interesting places. You'll not be able to talk about what you do. Don't get me wrong, you won't be wearing a cloak and stabbing people in dark alleys, but you'll be serving your country in a very special way. Interested?"

I was!

"One more thing. You'll have to agree to a four-year enlistment. Are you willing?"

I was! I would have agreed to twenty at that moment!

A few minutes later, I was the newest member of a shadowy organization called the Army Security Agency. There probably is not a professional angler anywhere in the world who could have reeled in a catch any neater than this man with the dark glasses. Almost three months later, after basic training, I arrived for training at Fort Devens, Massachusetts. I found that a friend and classmate of mine had been recruited by this same man about a week before me. This friend was David Marshall, who later would have a career with the Montgomery Police Department. Afterward, he was elected as the sheriff of Montgomery County several times and was, without question, the most effective and popular man to hold that post. Death has recently claimed this good and competent man. I was fortunate to have grown up with him and played ball and gone hunting with him on a couple of occasions as teenagers. It was quite a coincidence that we were to go through training together at Fort Devens. Afterward, our paths diverged and took us to different parts of the world.

Fort Jackson, South Carolina, was to be the place where I would receive my basic training. I arrived in a blistering heat wave in September 1969 and left in brutally cold conditions in late November.

"We will tear you down physically and mentally," we were told. "Then we will rebuild you the way we want you to be."

The breaking down started from day one. We quickly found out there would never be enough rest or food for the next two months. On many nights, we were rousted from our bunks by our drill instructor and into formation in our shorts. The next hour or two would be spent in low crawling up "Drag-Ass Hill" repeatedly. Sometimes the low crawling was under our own ancient wooden barracks. Diving under one side and crawling rapidly out the other side was a most unpleasant experience in the dark, dusty confines of a very tight crawl space. It was an agonizing time of being kicked in the face by other trainees and crawling headfirst into brick pillars that could not be seen.

Afterward, we had to clean ourselves up and try to get a few more minutes of sleep before five o'clock rolled around. Going to chow at the mess hall was an even worse treatment than the nighttime low crawling for some. All of us had to do our bit on the horizontal bars and the low crawl stretch before getting into the chow line.

Chubby guys had to endure the added torment of the telephone pole. They lay on the ground side by side with a telephone pole across their upper torsos and did sit-ups together until everyone else had made it through the chow line. Then they could eat, if they could! These guys were the most transformed of all, physically, by the time our training was complete.

None of us were allowed enough time to eat and were often ordered to dump our food and get out of the mess hall. Each platoon had to make room for the next in line, and we often were not allowed to sit, but rather followed the wall from the end of the serving line to the garbage cans near the exit. Whatever was not consumed at that point had to go into the cans. Sometimes food went into my field jacket pocket before I dumped my tray. On three or four occasions, someone managed to steal a loaf of bread from the mess hall. Once, a whole cooking sheet of apple pie was stolen. I was one of the fortunate ones who got some of the pie. I also lucked out with the bread a time or two. On these lucky occasions, the feeding frenzy took place in the boiler room atop the coal. We ate the pie as fast as we could, using our bare hands. We were taking no chances of losing out to someone else.

The instructor held the M-16 high over his head for all of us to see, and then the class began. It was very early in our training cycle. We were inside on this day and would become familiar with this weapon. He stated the nomenclature and characteristics of the M-16. He then stated, emphatically, its deadly capabilities. "If Jesus H. Christ walked in that door there, with this killing machine, with this lethal weapon, I could blow a hole ... etc., etc.!"

I fully expected Jesus to show up with lightning bolts about that time, but the instructor was spared in that blasphemous moment. I had never heard anyone breathe out threats toward Jesus before and decorated with such profanity too! I wondered about the wisdom of doing so. He was letting us know that with such a weapon, he feared no one—not even Jesus. It was almost a "come on, if you dare" challenge, and Jesus did not show up. The Vietnamese fared far worse. The reshaping of us mentally had really kicked in.

For the next few weeks, notions that the Vietnamese were people who deserved to continue living were gradually driven from our minds. As a matter of fact, they were less than people. They were never referred to as such. They were ninety-eight-pound monkeys in black pajamas. They were gooks and zips (zipper mouths because of the abundance of gold or silver teeth.) They were "Charlie," the ones we were being trained to get rid of. To do that, we were being taught to despise them and not see them as people. Although hatred for the Vietnamese, in general, was not voiced, it might as well have been. The effect was the same. Our mentality was in fact being restructured, just as promised at the beginning of training. Learn to hate your enemy, and it will be easier to kill him. You certainly can't kill your enemy by loving him to death! It just doesn't work.

We learned that immediate response to orders or instructions is a must in a military setting. That is one of the biggest and most important things to get across to an individual being trained. It is also one of the most difficult things for many people to accept. So, much of training is devoted to getting a person to respond appropriately and without hesitation. A lot of what we might have been put through in training seemed pointless and without meaning, but we did it anyway. We might have grumbled privately, but did not openly question and ask, "Why?"

Falling in hastily at midnight in underwear and low crawling over and over, up the hill or under the barracks, had this goal in mind. Respond! By the time our basic training was over, we were in the best physical shape of our lives. We had been torn down and rebuilt as promised. We had learned to respond immediately and without question. We were now ready for the next phase. This was the advanced training in which each soldier would be made proficient in the tasks he would be expected to carry out. I was about to enter a world I had not dreamed existed, and I was to find myself in a training environment for a long time. By the time I arrived in Vietnam, I was among the most highly trained people to serve there. Still, I was naïve, and when I arrived, I had just celebrated my twentieth birthday.

43

FORT DEVENS, MASSACHUSETTS

MY TRAINING for ASA took place at Fort Devens. It would be my first winter in a snowy climate. I had experienced snow a few times in my life, but not many. We had plenty of ice in the wintertime in Alabama, but few occurrences of snow. In 1961, an ice storm hit that paralyzed us for several days and kept the temperature down to near zero for about three days or so. The ice was four inches thick on the pond, and holes had to be chopped in the ice for the cows to get water. It was a once-in-a-lifetime experience for us. Generally, the average daily temperature was colder when I was younger with much more ice than we ever experience now. That's true for just about everyone though. Massachusetts was still far different from Alabama, being such a long way to the north. There seemed to be snow on the ground during most of the winter while I was there, and the average temperature was colder. Somehow, the winter there did not affect me as much as the winters had in Alabama. I don't know the reason for that, but maybe it was because the temperature didn't seem to fluctuate as much in

Massachusetts. Maybe it's because, as some might say, "It's a different type of cold."

At Fort Devens, I met George Baird. A friendship was established that has endured and grown to this very day. Knowing I was a long way from my Alabama home and lonesome, he invited me to go home with him for the weekend. His family home was in Brockton, Massachusetts. We would ride with a couple of other guys who also lived in the state and were going to visit family for a couple of days.

Before departing for George's house, he turned and said, "There is something I want you to know before we get to my house, so it won't be a surprise to you. My mother is Japanese, and I'm half-Japanese."

I told George I knew something was different about him, but I had refrained from asking. I had never met an Asian before and was intrigued. I had finally met my first and had not even been aware of it. I couldn't wait to meet his mother and the rest of his family. I was a painfully shy person and found it very difficult to engage people I did not know well in conversation. Many times since then, I've wished it were not so because I would have loved to have conversed with them a lot more, especially the sister named Barbara!

I found out that George had a brother, Richard. There were also three small sisters: Dianne, Shirley, and Patricia. Then there was the sixteen-year-old sister: Barbara! I was completely taken in by her stunning Amerasian good looks. She was the most beautiful sixteen-year-old who had ever breathed air! Drop-dead gorgeous? That term had to have been coined just for her. I couldn't talk to her. I wanted to look at her, but I was afraid to do that too. She might say something, and I would have to respond. Just being around Barbara was like being in heaven and in torment at the same time!

George's family was Baptist. I sat in the back seat of the family car as we were about to depart for church. George would drive with Barbara sitting in the front passenger seat. George remembered he had neglected to bring his Bible and got back out of the car to go fetch it.

Barbara turned and faced me. I was already panicking before she said anything. Barbara asked me something, and I tried to answer. I really did! My mouth was dry with my tongue stuck to its roof, and I was incapable of forming words. It was an hour-long minute before George came back, and it took a long time for my heart to settle down and my tongue to come unglued. I told him later to not ever do that to me again!

About a year later, Barbara and I wrote each other a couple of letters while I was in Vietnam, but I never got over the paralyzing fear of talking to her—even on paper.

I met George's girlfriend, Marianne Pelaggi. I don't think there are any introverts in the Pelaggi family. They all seem to be musically inclined, happy, and outgoing people. Perhaps, that's the Portuguese coming out—or maybe the Portuguese side is competing with the Italian side. On the weekend of my visit, we were going to attend a stage production of *The King and I*. It was performed in a community theater, and many of Marianne's family had roles in it. I had never seen such a thing before and was completely impressed! Marianne's six-year-old sister seemed to know all the songs as well as everyone's lines. Marilou put on her own show for us at the Pelaggi house. She could have held her own with Shirley Temple and with my favorite, Margaret O'Brien. It turned out to be one of the best couple of days of my entire life, and I was fortunate to have another weekend visit with them later. It was very hard to go back to Fort Devens both times.

We had a Christmas break from training, and I was able

to go home to Alabama to have Christmas with my family. I really needed that since Christmastime had always been such an important time for my family. My actual training period began after the Christmas shutdown. I think I had been on permanent KP duty while in "hold," waiting for my training to begin after Christmas.

Once training began, it began in earnest. We learned the Morse alphabet and responded in code as an instructor shouted out the character. It was done carefully and in stages. As we learned the alphabet, we also were introduced to it in perfect Morse code or "canned code." Then, our proficiency training began by copying tapes of perfect code. First, at 2.5 groups per minute, and building in speed at each student's own pace. A group is five letters, just like in typing class. Soon, I was accelerating in speed proficiency beyond most of the class, along with two or three others. We began to have special privileges because of that and were granted afternoons off from training. I was several speed levels ahead of most until I hit fifteen groups per minute. Fifteen groups per minute seemed particularly difficult for me, and I stalled at that speed for a couple of days. I found myself losing ground and others closing the gap on me. I didn't like that. I was proud of the lead I had opened up and the special privilege of afternoons off. In desperation, I cranked my speed to eighteen GPM and began to copy.

After a couple of hours, I dialed back to fifteen and passed it with perfect copy. It seemed to be the rhythm of fifteen GPM that had been giving me problems. However, the experiment of dialing up the higher speed taught me something. I continued to dial up higher speeds and then dropping back to pass lower ones and regained my lead. I learned a valuable lesson in the process: push yourself to the limit, and anything less is easy. I don't know the speed I had achieved by the end of training, but it was probably around twenty-four GPM.

Perfect code or "canned code" is one thing. Hearing the real thing from a sloppy operator amid background interference is quite another. I was soon to be introduced to that. The question that came into my mind immediately upon hearing such code was "What the hell was that?" The introduction to real, over-the-air code (recorded, of course) was awaiting me at Two Rock Ranch, California. I heard and copied my first Vietnamese operators there.

"What the hell was that?"

Allen Brady, Fort Devens, Massachusetts, ready for training in the Army Security Agency, 1970.

Allen still healing from a face-first
encounter with Massachusetts ice.

George Baird and Barbara Baird (brother and sister)
at home in Brockton, Massachusetts, about 1970.

George Baird in the barracks at Fort Devens, 1970.

Marianne Pelaggi, George's future wife, 1970.

44

TWO ROCK RANCH

MY EXPERIENCE at Two Rock Ranch lasted for about thirty days. It allowed us to hear Morse transmitted in a real environment by real operators, the ones of a sort that we would soon be listening to, daily, in our first assignment. We learned of the difference between heaven and hell. Two Rock Ranch was heaven. Many of us thought of that place and longed for it so many times after we left it. It was the perfect assignment. The climate? Great! The locals? Accepting and extremely friendly. The people at Two Rock? Family. It was the type of place that once left, was dreamed about as one of those perfect places on earth! Tucked away in the rolling hills near Petaluma, it was the most ideal setting imaginable.

We walked the three hundred or so yards down to the training facility each morning. Herds of deer were everywhere as were the gigantic stacks of hay bales from the hay that had been cut from the vast antenna field that spread out over the meadowland of Two Rock Ranch. Oftentimes, fog partially obscured the low hills all around until the middle of the morning. Evening temperatures were in the soft warmth range, while the July mornings required a blanket. Norman Rockwell could not have painted a better scene, and the climate could not have been more agreeable!

The scenery and physical environment matched the camaraderie between trainers and those being trained. To say the people at this intelligence-training facility were close-knit would be the grossest of understatements. Look up Two Rock Ranch on the internet if you do not believe me. You will be amazed! We left heaven though—some say for hell. By contrast, that may well have been true. In a sense, we surely contribute a lot in the making of our own personal hell. In the torments that were to afflict me later, I may have found mine. If so, I had found it in ways I would not have anticipated. I was that loyal, patriotic guy who had accepted all things as gospel truth. That was soon to be tested by the question even Pontius Pilate once asked: "What is truth?"

Truth is in fact, reality. Truth is also subjective. (Now here is a statement that will surely get me in trouble!) How a given thing might affect one person as opposed to another is interpreted as reality by either. I had never considered that concept before. That idea eventually challenged—and, in fact, changed—my whole belief system. It was to become something that was to test me and my thinking to this very day, but that was still in the future. Now, I was being trained to listen to the enemy, locate, and identify him, and may God or the powers that be have mercy on him.

I found I was very good at my job. So were others just like me. Years later, I lay in my bed at night and heard the young Vietnamese operators transmitting, arguing back and forth as to who was the worst operator and wondered what had become of them. I wondered how many, along with their comrades around them, had fallen victim to people like my friend, George Baird, who were so deadly proficient at "fixing" their position in a matter of several minutes. George had won a Bronze Star for that very thing, but that is a story in itself.

Before leaving Two Rock Ranch, we had a big party. Along with soft drinks, there were kegs of beer, plenty of hot dogs and hamburgers, and a live band playing the favorites of the time. The hippie movement was in full swing and maybe at its peak. Woodstock was an event that was still fairly fresh in the minds of most of us. Some of the music on that day had been played at Woodstock. The words "Next stop is Vietnam" and "Whoopee, we're all gonna die" blasted from the speakers. Just about everyone at Two Rock was in attendance for our final bash before we began packing up and processing for our trip overseas. We had this final "family" event to remember fondly from time to time in the coming year when, in our minds, we wanted to escape for a few minutes. But, for now, we were preparing to make our departure for that which we had been trained over the course of most of the past year.

Our intelligence brass was removed from our collars and replaced with a second "US" emblem. All references to ASA were forbidden from that moment on. We were now "XYZ." I don't know if that was official or suggested as a joke. Anyway, we all referred to ourselves as XYZ after the brass was switched. We had all known from the beginning that Vietnam would be our destination. We also had been told, from the beginning, with winks and smiles, that ASA does not go to Vietnam. Sometime between the removal of the brass, joking about the XYZ cover, and processing in Vietnam, we became "Radio Research." We were soon to become aware of "Davis Station" at Tan Son Nhut AFB in Vietnam, named for the one who many have pointed to as the first American combat casualty in

Vietnam. He was a Morse interceptor just as we were. I guess, just like us, he was not there either—not as ASA, anyway. What is truth? Since then, I've struggled with that question more than a few times.

45

OFF TO VIETNAM!

THE FLIGHT over had been long with some small talk between us and feeble attempts at making jokes. Most of the guys were wrapped up in their own thoughts and probably wondering the same thing as me: *What's really awaiting us when we land in the country we've heard so much about?*

I sat near the rear of the plane and studied the water stains on the inside of the long tubular fuselage during most of the trip. *It must be pretty old and leaky,* I thought. *I hope it makes at least one more trip without coming apart.* It seemed to warp and wiggle as if it were a fish swimming or a snake slithering. "God, I hope we make it," I prayed.

The couple of stewardesses looked tired and seemed to have not quite made the cut for more glamorous destinations. I wondered how often they had been assigned to flights such as this one. Perhaps this type of flight was all they could get. Maybe they had volunteered to make flights such as this. If so, that would put things in a whole different perspective.

I wondered about all kinds of things on the trip over. There was plenty of time for me to ask myself plenty of questions. A few weeks later, as it turned out, I found I had begun thinking of these two girls occasionally and realized they had begun moving up the scale from near plain to beautiful. Yes, I'm sure they were tired on that long flight. Maybe that's what put the "plain" idea in my head. There were a lot of us for them to take care of. They had lavished so much attention on a group of pretty nervous guys and had made our trip as pleasant as they could. They were the last American women I saw for a long time. Looking back to that time from the present, I must say that I appreciate them so much more now.

After landing in country at Tan Son Nhut Air Base, we were put aboard a military bus and transported some distance away for in processing. The bus had metal mesh screening across the windows. Someone said that was to prevent some guy from riding by on a motorcycle and tossing a grenade into our laps. That made a lot of sense, but it made us a bit apprehensive. It also gave us a firm appreciation of the mesh across the windows.

We made it to our destination and began the somewhat-confusing process of in processing. I don't remember much of that after all these years. I do remember looking at one of the metal buildings and seeing holes in the metal that I took to be shrapnel holes. They might well have been, but they might also have been there for years. I wondered if they had occurred during the Tet offensive in 1968. *I'll probably see a lot more stuff like that*, I thought. *For now, I'd be better off paying attention to getting processed.*

As with any in processing, there is a lot of "do this, go there, follow me, hang tight, etc." When you're following blindly and not thinking for yourself, what is there to remember? We were assigned a place to bunk down and clean up and were finally released for the day. Tomorrow, they would begin sorting out who was who and in which direction each of us would be going. Now we could hit the showers, clean up, and relax for the evening.

It had been more than twenty-four hours since our last shower in the States, and the climate here was hot and humid. We all tried to be the first to get to the showers, so we all got there about the same time. The area along the long, common sinks and mirrors was all occupied as guys shaved and brushed their teeth. The place was as crowded as any dance floor, and the rest of us, towel wrapped, waited for an opening. There was scarcely any personal space between us, so modesty had to be left behind—or so it might be thought!

Suddenly, someone shouted, "There's a woman in here!"

The alarm was picked up, amplified, and repeated two or three times by others, and the result was amazing. The packed floor thinned considerably and immediately. Someone could have shouted, "Grenade, grenade!" and not have any better results in reducing the number of guys in the room. I don't know where they went, but they went somewhere, fast!

Being somewhere in the middle of the room, I suddenly found myself with all the personal space I could have wanted. I was looking straight into the face of a grinning woman only five or six feet away. She didn't just grin—she laughed too. Her sudden appearance had effectively scattered the newly arrived Americans as completely as any tossed grenade could have done. She seemed to have enjoyed the reaction, and I suspect she had done this kind of thing before. This little woman had put to flight a bunch of highly trained American soldiers, and she had done it only with her sudden appearance among us!

Highly trained does not equate to experience or worldliness. We had no worldly experience at this point, and many of us had recently been in Sunday school. Several weeks later, we were used to such occurrences, and we didn't go to Sunday school anymore. As time passed, it became a common thing for us to see one or two women in a shower area picking up discarded razor blades and soap. Americans are known to be wasteful, and there was a lot of use to be gotten from a nearly depleted soap bar or a cast-aside razor blade. Without actually admitting it, I think we might, at times, have left soap that we could have used a bit more or razor blades that did not quite need changing. Though some of our attitudes may have begun hardening, we were still soft in others. I am reminded of the Old Testament story in the book of Ruth. In it, Boaz directed his servants to leave a little extra grain for gleaning in his fields for the women who came. Maybe we didn't go to Sunday school anymore, but the lessons we had learned there were never totally forgotten.

46
WELCOME TO NHA TRANG

WHERE EACH of us would be going had been established and the orders cut. I and a number of the guys I had been trained with for so long would be going to the 330th Radio Research in Nha Trang. I didn't know where Nha Trang was, but someone said it was a few miles north along the coast from Cam Rahn Bay. Well, that didn't help a lot either. It really didn't matter since it was someone else's responsibility to get us there. That would be the air force, and we would be transported on one of their C-130s. We were to get our gear together and get ready for transport. It was another of those "Do this, follow me, hang tight, and finally get aboard" moments.

"Getting aboard" meant entering the aircraft with our duffel bags, securing them, and finding an empty seat. Cargo was lashed down along the sides and in other parts of the plane. Along the middle were two rows of cargo-netting seats facing each other. Most were occupied by Vietnamese. They appeared to be families on the move since they had a lot of personal possessions with them, including several chickens and a pig. I'm not kidding! There were four chickens tied by the feet in a bundle and one small pig with all four feet tied. The animals seemed to belong to one family.

As I looked in disbelief, Mom and Pop looked back at me and grinned. I had seen scenes like this before in movies, seemingly, more than once. Those scenes usually involved a dilapidated aircraft in some banana republic or perhaps involved a raggedy bus or truck. This was for real though, and this was a US military aircraft! Several of us guys found places to sit among the local color. I didn't have another GI next to me with whom I could talk, so all I could do was look around and feel out of place.

I must have been an interesting person to look at with my red hair because everyone seemed to be watching me. Grinning too. They were always grinning at me! They knew I was brand-new. My green combat fatigues were right off the shelf and hadn't seen a washing yet, and the jungle boots still had that "just-issued" look. I had always been somewhat shy, not very talkative, and easy to blush when embarrassed. Likely, I was red-faced then, sitting there among these grinning and curious fellow travelers. I couldn't help being curious too. Now and then, I took another look in Mom and Pop's direction and studied them—and their pig and chickens. *I can't believe this,* I thought. *The United States government has just spent $50,000 training me, and I'm sitting here among the cargo sharing a ride with chickens and a pig!* I've wondered since if the chickens and pig even noticed me. If they did, they were probably grinning at me too!

We eventually made it to Nha Trang with our flight path roughly following the coastline. Someone from the crew said that was the safest route as we were more protected from any hostile fire that might be directed at us. There was none. We were safely on the ground at Nha Trang Air Base, and I began looking around for evidence of any recent hostile actions such as shrapnel holes and craters. I saw none. That made me breathe a little easier, though I was still apprehensive about what I would find waiting for me when I reached my destination. At this point, I was probably only two or three kilometers from it.

I do not remember how we made the trip from the air base to the 330th Radio Research Company located on Camp McDermott. Likely, we were transported in a deuce and a half (a two and a half-ton truck.) We rolled in through the large opened wire gates past barbed wire "aprons," coils of concertina wire, and lots of sandbags. Somebody had worked for a long time stretching that much wire and filling all those sandbags. The guards were both Vietnamese and American. A couple of hundred yards past this point was our new home. We were processed in at the orderly room, went to supply, and issued our field gear (flak vests, helmets, protective masks, web gear, etc.). Though we had been trained on M-16s, we were issued the older M-14s. They were noticeably larger and heavier. We also received our bedding with instructions to follow an NCO to one of the "hootches" where each of us would be bunking for the next year, God willing.

A hootch is simply a tropical barracks. It is a wooden, open bay-type of building with a tin roof. The sides were screened from the ground to the roof with board sides up to about four feet in a louvered design. The screen was obviously for mosquitoes and bugs while the louvered style of the board walls kept the rain from spattering in and allowed for as much fresh air as possible. The roofs had a wide overhang to protect against the rain hitting the screened-only portions of the walls. The hootch had a screen door on each end and a blast wall encircling it about three feet from the building. The blast wall was a hollow boxlike affair constructed of wood and was two feet thick and about three-and-a-half feet high. It was filled with sand and sandbags. The blast walls were to protect us from any shrapnel from blasts occurring on the outside. Of course, one occurring inside was an obviously different story. They also gave us something to take cover behind if the need ever arose. Between the various hootches were bunkers constructed of large metallic half pipes covered with thick layers of sandbags. They were to be used as shelters during rocket or mortar attacks but were pretty useless to us. I'll explain why later.

Having followed the NCO into our new quarters, we were instructed to grab an empty bunk. As luck would have it, mine was the closest to the door. I didn't realize why nobody had chosen it until later. Anyway, it was to be mine since it was the only one left. I didn't really mind until I realized the mosquitoes got to that one first and were likely too full of my blood to make it to the second. We secured the rest of our gear, brought it in, and stowed it for the evening. We were told exactly where to put the flak jacket and the helmet (steel pot). The jacket was to be slipped under the bunk about where our heads would be if we had to suddenly roll off the bunk and take cover. The steel pot was placed on the floor so we could look directly down on it if we rolled over and looked down. In the military way, I didn't ask questions—I just did it.

The old-timers, the guys with the jungle fatigues that had faded some, told us it was important to our survival that we learned to listen to them. We were going to get hit in the morning, and it would probably occur around five-thirty or afterward. At least they were betting on it as the signs indicated we would be. It can be a bit more than a hunch when it is your business to listen to enemy communications. That was the business of everyone in the 330th Radio Research. Times had been selected by everyone (except us, the new ones) and betted on, as to the time of the first rocket strike. That procedure was carried out, on paper, in the same manner of an office football pool. Just after daybreak, or at least in the morning hours, was generally the favorite time for the VC to fire three or four 122-millimeter rockets onto our compound. It was something they enjoyed doing to let us know they were thinking of us. Apparently, they got bored at night and used the cover of darkness to set the rockets up in the hills that overlooked the camp on two sides. Some say the rockets were set off by timers so the VC could slip away before they fired off. I don't know about that, and I don't know that it really mattered. When they fired the rockets, they came to us. That's what really mattered!

I turned in for the night and hoped to get a little sleep. I lay atop the bedding in my shorts and T-shirt, sweating in the tropical heat. One of the old-timers, who had probably been in country for several months, gave me a bit of advice. He was sitting at a small table writing a letter by lamplight.

"Nug (new guy), don't go to sleep like that. Cover up. The mosquitoes will eat you alive!"

I indicated I had heard and promptly fell asleep. Later, I woke up, and the guy was still sitting there writing his letter. I was itching badly on my arms and legs and looked down to see they were covered with mosquitoes. It was almost as if I had grown brown fur! Springing up from the bunk, I was busy swatting and rubbing mosquitoes away.

"Told you, didn't I?" he said with a grin.

I found my bottle of army-issued repellent, which resembled lightweight oil, and rubbed it on my legs, arms, neck, and face. Nobody liked the stuff since it made you oily and hotter, but it also worked. I lay back down and pulled the sheet up to my chin, which was what the advisor was hinting at from the beginning. I was able to go back to sleep with the sound of mosquitoes buzzing about my head looking for an unprotected spot.

The next sound I heard was one I have never forgotten

and was to hear many times in the next year. It was as if the atmosphere was separated by a piercing "Kaaa-raaaak," followed by a boom that fairly bounced me from my mattress! I must have instinctively turned in the air and rolled to my right toward the floor. My head hit my steel pot, and I groaned out loud and said something that I shouldn't write here. I pushed the pot aside and tried to slide under the bunk, but my flak vest was in the way. I was conscious of at least one other person farther down also cursing about having bashed his face or head against his steel pot. I also heard laughing—probably from someone with faded fatigues who had pulled this stunt before. The rocket blast was not a stunt, though, but it was factored into the "Welcome to Vietnam joke."

"Hit the bunker, hit the bunker," was the next thing I heard. I was partially under my bunk and scrambled out, grabbing my flak vest and steel pot in the process. I was hastily donning them as I headed for the bunker outside the hootch. I didn't take time for pants, boots, or anything else! Too late. The bunker was full. I don't know how many of the guys got into it, but the faces looking back at me were Vietnamese, both men and women. It was already daylight, and they had just arrived for their camp duties. They were looking back at me and grinning very nervous grins. Obviously, there was no room here, and I was standing in the open, so I reversed course and went back to the blast wall that surrounded the hootch and crouched behind it. I was not alone either.

From that moment on to the end of my time in Vietnam, I never ran for that bunker. I simply went and stood behind the blast wall. Within three or four months, I found myself standing there from time to time admiring the show, fully exposed to the rockets except below the waist just like everyone else. We had all developed a fatalistic attitude in the short time we had been there. I started making it a habit to bring something to drink. Might as well make the most of the situation! It was as if we had turned these situations into social events. As terrifying as a nearby rocket blast might be, it was also exciting to experience! It took a little time to come down off the adrenaline high after the "all clear" was sounded.

47

A THORN IN THE FLESH

MY PERSONAL sign was to be "AA." This personal sign was a local personal identifier. It was to be attached to all of my intercepts so everyone from the local level to NSA could determine who was responsible for an intercept if need be. I was the VCOB interceptor. VCOB stands for Vietnamese Communist Manual Morse (Political). My job was to copy certain known targets and to search for unknowns, copy, and identify them. Also, to fix their position, geographically, with the aid of direction finding. This is where George Baird, his network, or others like him came into play. I took my job seriously. The Army Security Agency, or Radio Research, was incredibly good at what they did. It was almost impossible to hide from them. Whenever I was not occupied with a VCOB intercept, I rolled the frequencies and searched for military targets and identified them, if possible, and fixed their locations. We were a "thorn in the flesh" to VC communicators and were referred to as such. I know because I copied those very words myself. More about this later.

We had been exposed to the communications of the Communist Vietnamese at Two Rock Ranch for about thirty days and had gotten over the initial shock of hearing real communications. We had even gotten to the point where we could copy those communications, but not as well as we needed to. We found ourselves sitting "sidesaddle" for a while in Vietnam. This meant we were plugged into a radio receiver with an experienced interceptor until our copy was about 90 percent of his copy. We were then considered suitably qualified to be on our own. This "sidesaddle" may have been for just a day or two for one guy or a week for another, depending on the person's ability. I progressed quickly and was assigned to political intercepts as my primary mission with unidentified military intercepts as the secondary. I learned very quickly the unique sound of the transmitters and operator characteristics of the VCOB operators. Learning these operator characteristics was like detecting accents in other people's voices that might indicate their national origin or from which region of our own country a person was from. Upon hearing an unidentified VCOB operator, I almost instinctively knew he was political, one of mine. It was as if they all had the same teacher and shared the same transmitter. The transmitter sounds were incredibly similar. On the other hand, the military operators tended to share sloppy characteristics as if hastily trained and deployed to their jungle hideouts. They argued a lot. These are the ones I later imagined as young kids arguing about who was the worst and who should surrender the key to a more competent (less sloppy) operator, kind of like kids arguing in a family setting.

I liked rolling the frequencies when I wasn't copying a VCOB. Picking up unidentified transmissions, fixing the location of their transmitters, and identifying them gave me a sense of accomplishment. A request for a geographical "fix" on a target transmitter or unidentified intercept might go as follows:

"George, I have a UI (unidentified) on frequency 8405kc."

"What's he doing, OB?"

"He's chattering, George."

"Qsa imi? (What is my signal strength?) Msg imi? (Do you have a message for me?)"

"RGA." (Roger, go ahead.)

"Got him, OB."

OB is me. I am referred to as OB because I am the political Morse interceptor.

After George said, "I got him," we ceased communication with each other while he communicated with his "net" to get a fix on the geographical location of the unidentified transmitter. I would continue to copy the unidentified transmitter and also "roll" the frequencies, searching for the one he was communicating with. Quite often, I located the other end (transmitter) and began copying both ends at once: the first contact in receiver A and the other end in receiver B. "A" would be coming into my right ear and "B" would be coming into my left ear. Each bit of copy from either end was labeled "/A" or "/B" to keep track of who was saying what. I would then attempt to get George's people to get me a fix on "B," the other end.

In several minutes, George would contact me and say, "I got a fix. You ready for it?"

"Go ahead, George," I might respond.

"He is at PK273504, accurate to one hundred meters," or some such response.

That would be the coordinates of the transmitter and the suspected accuracy of the location of the transmitter. That is an uncanny fix in its accuracy and should be very scary to the guy who is transmitting. A hundred meters is as good as being fully exposed to whatever someone might decide to send your way. That's scary! Scarier still would be those rare times when I was told the fix was accurate to ten meters. That could be equal to a death warrant. It was doubly fulfilling to get a fix on both ends of an intercept—even more so if we were to identify them. Even if we did not identify the intercepts, valuable information was still gained concerning the location of the radio transmitters and the fact that enemy units were at those locations. We could follow up on these UIs as others saw fit.

It is almost impossible to overstate how good the Army Security Agency was when it came to locating and helping identify enemy units. Not only that, but there was a wealth of information from the daily intercept and decoding of the messages those units sent to one another. We really were a thorn in their flesh!

Allen and George, Nha Trang, Vietnam, 1971.

George Baird, Nha Trang, Vietnam, 1971.

Pablo Caudillo, Nha Trang, Vietnam, 1971.

48

PRACTICAL JOKES
AND SANITY

IT SEEMS that most guys acquire a nickname. As I stated, mine was OB, and OB stood for "political Morse." I also was very shy and blushed easily when embarrassed. So much so that I was called "Scarlett." Therefore, I was known to some as "the Scarlett OB," just "OB," or perhaps as "Scarlett." Because I was also from Alabama, a few referred to me as "Reb." I did not take offense to whatever I was called as it was in good-natured fun. We all got along very well together, and few if any problems or disagreements arose. We played lots of pranks on each other, especially while we were actually intercepting. That was to break the tension and served almost as a relief valve for us.

"OB, do you need any fallopian tubes?" the nug with the clipboard asked. I was busy rolling the frequency spectrum looking for unidentified transmitters and was surprised and confused by the unexpected question.

"What's that?" I asked. Someone standing behind the new guy was grinning and gesturing to play along so I knew the joke was on.

"Do you need any fallopian tubes for your receivers?"

I pretended to check by adjusting several knobs and replied "Yes, I do. Receiver A needs one."

"Male or female?" he asked.

"Female," I answered.

"Nothing for B?"

I pretended to check B receiver and said, "Yeah, better take care of B too."

"One or two, male or female," he asked.

"Two, male," I responded.

He wrote the info down on the clipboard and stepped over to the VCIB operator (Viet Communist Intelligence Net interceptor).

I looked back at the grinning guy who seemed to be behind the joke, and he signaled that I would get the lowdown later. For now, "keep a straight face" was the order of the day.

After the newbie (new baby) had finished taking orders for fallopian tubes from all of us, he turned the list in and was congratulated on the fine and complete job he had done. To be sure, no one had ever done better!

I was as dumb as the guy with the clipboard and asked the architect of the joke, "What the hell is a fallopian tube?" He explained, in a brief way, the difference between male and female and the part the fallopian tubes played in a woman's reproduction.

Okay, I told you I was not yet a very worldly person. As it turned out, I had plenty of company who answered the nug's questions without having a clue about what he was asking of them. I don't know who the joke was really on. Was it the nug—or us?

"Scarlett, what is your average frequency for today?" Another nug with a clipboard was standing there with his pen poised to copy my response.

I was not allowed to voice it aloud. I had been warned he would be coming around and to be ready to play along. I had "averaged" the frequencies of all my intercepts and had it written down for him to copy. I uncovered it and allowed him to write it on his clipboard. I had it classified "top secret/w code word" affixed. He went to the other interceptors and copied their "average frequencies" down as well.

Afterward, as instructed, he averaged these frequencies and had the result verified by the chief. This alleged supersensitive bit of information was put into a folder marked "Eyes Only."

The unsuspecting nug was told to take it into the intel shop to a certain major. He was to ask for the major's identification card and compare it to the ID badge he was wearing. Then, and only then, could he show the major the highly sensitive "average frequency" of the day. He was informed he was allowed only to open the folder briefly so the major could memorize the frequency written on the page. Under no circumstance was the major allowed to touch the folder or view it for more than five seconds.

I—and everyone else—would have loved to have been one of the flies on the wall of the intel shop when said nug showed up with that "Eyes Only" document containing the fictional bit of extremely sensitive material known as the "average frequency." I don't know if the major congratulated him for doing the job properly—or threw him bodily out of the intel shop!

The best time to really "get" a new guy was while he was sitting "sidesaddle." The first day was always the best choice. It bordered somewhat on outright dangerous at times, but boys will be boys. The best of all the sidesaddle pranks involved a large loose bundle of carbon paper. Making sure the new guy was out of his chair and away for a minute was all the time needed to get everything set up. The bundle of carbon paper was taped very loosely under the chair with duct tape. Someone made sure the victim was distracted when he came back to sit down so he would not notice the bundle of carbon paper that had been made ready for him.

Waiting till he had started copying code again, the person designated for the privilege lit the carbon paper with a cigarette lighter. The result was frightening and immediate. The chair and operator seemed to partially disappear in the flames! Carbon paper ignites and burns at an almost explosive rate. Before pulling this prank, we had to be sure there was a charged CO_2 fire extinguisher at hand. Since the carbon paper engulfed the chair so quickly in flames, the person holding the extinguisher had to discharge it quickly to keep the victim from being burned or inhaling the flames. The result was as if a fiery explosion had occurred. It was a fun thing to see—but not a fun thing to experience! I know because I have been on both ends of that prank. It was all in fun though, and it broke the tension for a few minutes. I don't recall there being any really hard feelings. That was not really a consideration anyway since the victims were just nugs being broken in. They had to take it and respect the guys with the lighter-colored fatigues.

Other jokes were lighter in their nature and not dangerous. Rubbing carbon paper on the "cans" of the headsets caused large black rings on a person's cheekbones when they took the headsets off. Sometimes, grease pencil was used if someone could steal one temporarily. That caused a few chuckles, but no harm. It might be followed by a comment such as "Whatcha been doin', big ears, eavesdropping?"

Paper flags might be fashioned and slid onto the rods that the can portion of the headsets slid up and down on. This gave the interceptor a head-bobbing, flag-waving, cartoonish appearance as he copied an intercept. Occasionally, someone would take his Zippo lighter and set the flags on fire. That was fun and relatively harmless too, but it got a big reaction from the operator. It also broke the tension for a while.

Sending a bogus message to a nug was always fun. By setting the frequency control knob to a particular spot between signals and plugging in a Morse key to the back of the receiver, a message could be sent to the guy operating from that receiver. Transmissions could be sent that were tailor-made for that operator. It might reference something personal about him and breathe out threats to him in particular. It could be pretty unsettling for a new operator that someone knew who he was, where he was, and that he was listening! We, the O5Hs were not trained in transmitting, and our skill level was not particularly high in that area. Any transmission we made tended to be a little rough, but that probably made them sound a little more genuine! It is possible we might have sometimes enlisted the support of an O5D (like George Baird) in that prank. They were well trained in transmitting. I'm not sure about that though.

There were smaller pranks played, such as lugging a heavy wooden box of ST1s to different locations. I saw the box finally with the stenciling on it: STONES. Also, there was sometimes the demand for a QRM eliminator, and a nug was dispatched for one to signal maintenance. QRM is "man-made interference" in international Morse jargon. If there was too much man-made interference around a signal being copied, a nug was advised of the immediate need of a QRM eliminator. The "eliminator" consisted of a large steel block with a couple of knobs attached and a gigantic roll of copper wire that had to be rolled rather than carried. Of course, the nug was always cursed soundly for dragging his heels and of his slowness in bringing the apparatus.

He had to take the apparatus back as it was always too late to be of use.

The list of pranks like this ended only with the imagination, but they served a purpose. They released tension and kept us reasonably sane.

49

THE RAMP

THE PLACE where all these pranks occurred was in a structure and collection of intercept vans under a large tin roof. The vans were backed up to openings in this wooden structure under that roof. The structure itself consisted of a twelve-foot-wide hallway extending about forty feet with the vans on either side projecting outward like rooms. There were three vans on one side of this hallway and two on the other, which we knew as "the ramp." As a matter of fact, the whole affair was referred to collectively as "the ramp." In those rooms (vans), we did our work.

There were six intercept positions in each of the three vans where the O5Hs (interceptors) copied their assigned targets and searched for new ones. Each operator had two radio receivers in order to copy both ends of a communication. We used typewriters with a continuous feed of six-ply fan-folded paper. The typewriters were unique in that they typed in uppercase letters only. They were known as "mills," and we were jokingly referred to as "mill monkeys."

One van had equipment of a very sensitive nature that I probably should not discuss—even now. Another was where the O5Ds worked. They worked with others like themselves and were scattered in various locations around the countryside. They also had capabilities of communicating with aerial (airborne) direction finders. Using direction-finding techniques, they got a "fix" on the locations of the transmitters we were listening to. They also had other capabilities that aided in the identification of a transmitter that might disappear but be suspected of transmitting somewhere else later. The value of that capability is obvious. That was radio fingerprinting, and fingerprints don't lie. A picture of a transmitter's wave signature was printed out on graph paper. If that transmitter disappeared but was suspected of resurfacing later, it could be identified by this "fingerprint." It was another tool to use in tracking a unit attempting to conceal its movements or identity. At one end of the ramp was another area from which analysts and linguists would sometimes emerge. A small shop where maintenance on the intercept equipment was performed also lay in that direction, as did the intel shop and hideouts of seldom-seen people and various spooks.

We kept our steel pots and flak jackets close to us while working. Should we experience incoming fire, we slipped on our flak jackets and balanced the steel pots on our heads as best as the headsets would allow. It is very possible we might intercept something valuable at such a time, so we did not stop our listening and copying during the times of incoming fire. There was only one instance where all stopped, but that was because of a direct hit on the ramp by a 122-millimeter (some say 107-millimeter) rocket. More about that later.

The ramp was within an enclosed area of about an acre or a bit more. It was surrounded by barbed wire and only had one entry point, which was controlled by a guard shack. There were two or three other wooden structures in the enclosure as well as five or six bunkers. On one corner of the small compound was a guard tower looking out over a village of shanties on the other side of the perimeter wire. This tower had a guard in it at night and watched in the direction of the village.

I spent a night in that tower from time to time. The guard shack was about forty meters or so from the tower. The nights I spent in that tower were long since the duty was from dusk till dawn. That is a long time to stay awake and keep the mind occupied! I studied the shanties across the wire and all the family activities going on around them. They were as close to me on that side as the guard shack was behind me. I thought it was a pitiful way for people to have to live. The structures serving as houses appeared to be put together with a variety of scavenged or salvaged materials. Some appeared to be not much more than lean-to affairs, often with an open side. Some families cooked on a small fire outside, while others cooked inside. A few of the dwellings were much better than others, but collectively, it was a shantytown. Watching the activity going on there was the biggest thing I did during a long night in the tower.

The first time I entered the guard tower, I made myself comfortable on the seat and stowed my snacks, canteen, and web gear. I had a couple of warm cans of soda and two packs of cigarettes, as well. It was hot as usual, and I was covered with mosquito repellent, which made me sweat even more. Hot or not, I kept my steel pot on, as well as my flak jacket. After all, that was a pretty exposed position about sixteen feet up for everyone to see. The protecting wall of the tower came up almost to my shoulders when I was seated. The walls were a foot or more thick, but hollow. They had been filled with sandbags at one time, but many were missing. There was little protection for me from about my navel up. The missing sandbags were lying around the base of the tower, and I wondered about that. That mystery was solved during the night when a dog showed up and started sniffing around the base of the tower among the sandbags that used to be up higher protecting people like me.

Obviously, people like me had entertained themselves on long nights by bombing snooping dogs with them. I was tempted to do it myself but decided I would rather have the remaining sandbags between me and an incoming round. Anyway, the dog eventually went away. He was one of the several camp dogs that hung about and lived by the generosity of the Americans. Had he been on the other side of the wire, his life expectancy would be very short. He was a large/medium breed and would have fed a number of people. The camp dogs got a lot of scraps from around the mess hall and certainly would not be considered poor choices for the cooking pot. They would not have stood a chance on the other side of the wire.

It was difficult to remain completely alert all the time during the long night. The fact that I was all alone was a great motivator. The fear that came from being almost completely exposed also kept me from dozing off after a few hours in the tower. I sat there with my M-16 across my lap (we had finally had our M-14s replaced with M-16s). Sometime during the middle of the night, my head was knocked forward by something that made a loud *clang* against the back of my steel pot!

Sniper! I thought. I wheeled around with my weapon at the ready and faced the direction of the MP at the guard shack. I fully expected to take a hit. There was no sniper. It was the MP. He was standing out from the shack, facing me, and looking surprised. He raised both hands to the sides, palms up, and made a gesture as if to say, "Sorry, didn't know I could throw the rock that far!" Not only had he thrown it that far—he was dead on target! Well, boys will be boys. At least he knew I was awake, and believe me, I was!

When the MP on duty was not throwing rocks at someone

like me, he was guarding the access into the ramp compound. His job was to check the badge of everyone who entered against the person's face. Things that went on inside that wire were considered top secret, and access was strictly controlled. The fact was, everybody knew just about everybody else, and that included the guards. Each person coming past the guard had his photo badge hanging from a chain around his neck. The guard glanced toward the badge, but I never saw one stopping and doing a comparison unless it was some new guy entering the compound.

One day, the VCIB operator laughingly asked me to check out his badge. I looked at it, but it was not his photo on it; instead, was a photo of Chairman Mao Tse Tung. He had cut it out of the *Stars and Stripes* newspaper and placed it over his own picture. "Man, I've been wearing this for a whole month," he said.

Another guy decided to try the same thing and did it with a picture of Mickey Mouse. It worked for him too, but Mickey Mouse stands out a lot more with those big, black ears, so he didn't press his luck. Once was enough to satisfy him and provide him with a funny story to share in the future. Therefore, Mickey Mouse only worked with us for one day. I don't know just how long Chairman Mao continued to work in our compound!

One night, while busy copying an intercept, I looked up to see a strange face looking at me. Strange in the sense that I had not seen this person before, and he looked bewildered. He had several days of whiskers on his face, and his fatigues were covered in dust or mud. He made me think of a grunt just in off patrol. I continued with what I was doing and noticed him moving down the ramp and looking around slowly. He didn't seem to know where he was and appeared to be completely drunk.

After a couple of hours, everybody was laughing about the incident. The guy really had been drunk and totally lost too! He had been rounded up, grilled by intelligence officers, threatened repeatedly, and ended up just about signing his life away. I was told that when he was let go, it was with the warning he better not ever open his mouth about what he had seen or discuss the incident in any way. I was also informed he was cold sober and awfully frightened when he was released. As it turned out, he was only looking for the place where the movie was to be shown. He was a bit off target, it seemed. A movie was usually shown in the area near our hootches on a four-by-eight-foot plywood screen each evening. I have a feeling that when he got out of our compound, a movie was the last thing on his mind! Afterward, he had to start from scratch to regain his former drunken high, and it probably took a whole lot more alcohol to get the job done.

As it turned out, the MP on duty had to make an emergency latrine visit and grabbed an incoming O5H to watch the gate for a minute. Well, if a trained guard can let in Chairman Mao and Mickey Mouse, what can you expect from an O5H who has no interest at all in guarding a gate? I felt bad for the MP and wondered what had been done to him. I also wondered if he was the one who had beaned me with the rock. If he was the same one, I had no hard feelings toward him and hoped he got off easy.

50

PURPLE JESUS

WHEN WE were not performing our duties as interceptors, we were free to do pretty much as we pleased. We drank. We drank to kill time, to help us to forget, to help us sleep, and for just about any reason we could come up with to have another one. This was contrary to the way we had conducted ourselves just a few months before. Then, it was mostly sodas we consumed, but not a lot of alcohol. Things were far different now. Now, it was alcohol and a few sodas. The more popular brands of beer were difficult to find, and once found, were not in very abundant supplies. There seemed to be a much larger supply of less popular or unpopular brands, and that was very suspicious. The suspicions turned out to be well-founded. Certain people in high positions were found to have been in collusion with beer suppliers and had been profiting. That was taken care of, and the situation eventually began to improve a bit. Sometimes, beer cans had a bit of rust on them from having been in the pipeline for a while. Some say they had seen pallets of beer stored in the open and exposed to the tropical weather. Still, once it got to us, we drank it! We drank it cold if we could get it, but warm if we could not. We drank the harder stuff too, but far less often.

One of the instances of drinking the hard stuff stands out in my mind far above any of the others. It was the "purple Jesus" party. We had been in country for several months when it was decided we were going to have a party. Someone with a bit of authority had some steaks brought in from Cam Rahn Bay. A charcoal grill was acquired. It appeared we were about to enjoy our first and only steak while in Vietnam. I may have gotten one and may have enjoyed it, but I'm not really sure. We had been introduced to purple Jesus a short time before the coals were ready to receive the steaks.

"What is purple Jesus?" I had asked earlier.

"Just bring any hard liquor you have," I was told by the one who was spreading the word. "We'll start making it at eleven hundred."

I was to find that purple Jesus was a very special concoction, not unlike the Kickapoo joy juice in the *Li'l Abner* comic strip of my youth. There's a bit of everything that isn't good for you in it. Everyone showed up at the designated time with whatever he had or could acquire that fell into the category of strong drink. Into the big cauldron, contributed by the mess hall, it went. After the liquor was all in, a gallon can of Concord grape juice concentrate, also donated by the mess hall, was added and mixed. Dip the cups in!

The big problem with PJ was the fact that it was basically straight liquor that went down too easily because of the smoothing, buffering effect of the sweet Concord grape juice concentrate. It was deeply purple, but that didn't explain the "Jesus" in the name. That was explained later. After a few trips to the cauldron, a person began to forget who and where he was. The steaks were being dropped onto the grill at that point. One of the guys grabbed a steak from the grill before it even had a chance to warm up good. He ate it raw! He held the steak in his hand and tore away pieces of it with his teeth. It was washed down with more PJ. One of the Vietnamese camp workers screamed in terror when he came too close to her and ran away, still screaming.

I decided to wait for my steak until it cooked, but I don't remember the point when it did so. I am assuming that I ate the steak and enjoyed it. I was glad later that I was very moderate in the amount of PJ I had consumed. After a while, the laughter began to die down a bit for some, and the purple Jesus began reemerging in projectile form from some of the ones who had really poured it down! Occasionally someone could be seen holding on to a blast wall or leaning forward with his hands on his knees retching convulsively, all the while moaning, "Oh, Jesus. Oh, Jesus!" This was not the wedding feast at Cana, and Jesus had no part in it. We were responsible and had to suffer the consequences. Jesus was not going to help any of us recover; only time, a bunk, and lots of puking could do that.

I suffered, but not like many of the guys, because I had consumed far less. Still, it took me until the following day to fully recover. For days, the evidence of the party remained everywhere in the form of deep purple areas on the clay ground. We never had a "purple Jesus" party again during the remainder of my tour in Vietnam. Nobody even suggested we do so. Once in a lifetime is sufficient! It is good most of us confined our drinking to beer because we did a lot of it.

51

COMMUNICATING WITH THOSE BACK HOME

DRINKING WAS the activity that seemed to be mixed in with the other activities that occupied us. Guess that was our idea of multitasking. We were letter writers. It seems most of us wrote several letters a day. We were creative in our letter writing and often competed for new and original ideas to make the letters more unique and more interesting. I once wrote a forty-foot long letter on toilet paper, which included sections written by George and Pablo.

We had begun passing letters to each other so we could share in writing a letter to someone we were close to. People back home came to know who our friends were and included their names in their correspondence. It was as if everyone's family size was increasing because of the letters. Like our practical jokes while intercepting, letter writing was our outlet when not listening to the enemy. It was a desperate attempt to stay connected to something in a sane world that we longed for so badly. Every day of letter writing was one more day we could mark off our calendar. I wrote to Mom and Dad and to the girl to whom I had become engaged just before leaving for Vietnam.

Those letters were written daily. I wrote to several friends back home on a frequent basis and received letters from them. I wrote to a couple of girls I had met while in Massachusetts during training and to several girls with whom I had become pen pals since. These were people I was introduced to through friends. Most of these girls I never met. Only about two or three of them had I ever laid eyes on before. They just enjoyed communicating with guys and brightening their lives up a bit. However, I got marriage proposals from two of them!

We made tapes too. We got very good at recording voice tapes on cassette and learned the art of fading from voice to music and back. We even learned to dub voice over music. We could fade out the music and have only voice or fade out the voice and have only music. Or, we could have voice with the background of music appropriate to our mood when making the tape. Letter writing had become almost an art form for us, but we did even better with the tapes. It became one of the biggest ways for us to escape and to find some sort of emotional release. We were always looking for ways to improve our productions and for new things to include. We each sent tapes to our sweethearts and to each other's sweethearts as well. We included all our pen pals back in "the world." There were always tapes flying back and forth across the Pacific between us and those who were special to us. Several of us would gather to listen to a new tape someone had received or to make one together. We drank as we listened, sometimes laughed, and sometimes got very quiet as we thought about home or the one whose voice we were hearing at that moment. Even if we had never met that person, or others on the tape, they were special, and sometimes it was hard not to get emotional.

Occasionally, the recipient of the tape might stop the tape and say, "Sorry, guys, this part is a bit private." That might require a headset for a moment or two of privacy and a bit of fast-forwarding. The headset would be unplugged, and then we were included again. As I think back to those times, I feel as if I have once again experienced what I felt at those moments, so many years ago. Even now, I find I am a bit emotional in this moment of thinking back. I'm waiting, too, for the headsets to come off, and for someone to hit the play button again, so we can continue listening to the voice of someone who had become so special to all of us.

52

AT WAR WITH MOSQUITOES AND RATS

MOSQUITOES WERE a real nuisance. Every evening, as the sun was going down, a truck outfitted with fogging equipment drove throughout the camp fogging for mosquitoes. I would swear it did absolutely no good, but who knows how bad it would have been if there were not some attempt to control the pests. When the sun went down, the mosquito repellent came out. OFF mosquito repellent was included in every care package we received from families and friends back home. The variety of packaging and applications methods available were surprising. There was the liquid in a squeeze bottle that could be squeezed onto the body and rubbed in. That was less popular in the tropical heat and humidity, but not as bad as the military variety. There was a can that dispensed foam that was rubbed on, which didn't seem to make a person feel too awfully uncomfortable. It seemed to disappear into the skin with no residue, so it was preferred, but not commonly received in our care packages. The spray was popular, and we had a very abundant supply of that. It was so much easier to use and could be sprayed over clothing and body.

We did not care so much for the army-issued brand of repellent. It came in a flattened, plastic squeeze bottle. Oftentimes, a bottle of this is evident in pictures taken of soldiers in Vietnam. It was commonly seen tucked behind the band that secured the camouflage covering on the steel pot. It was good when there was nothing else to use. It worked extremely well, but because it felt oily, it was less popular than the OFF from home.

Right Guard deodorant was popular in mosquito control even though the manufacturer would have frowned on our using it for that purpose. This was done more for entertainment purposes and revenge than large-scale pest control. When the mosquitoes got particularly bothersome as we sat on a bunk and talked—or if conversation began to lag—the Right Guard and Zippo lighters came out. Spraying Right Guard through the flame of a Zippo lighter created a mini flamethrower. We had competitions on who could turn the most mosquitoes into little diving sparks. When we added in the right sound effects, we had a mighty good time shooting down a few "zeroes." Each shoot down called for another drink or two. It made us feel like we were administering a little payback.

Sometimes, we actually used the Right Guard for its intended purpose of making us smell a little better. A good instant shower could be had in a pinch if a regular shower was not possible. Simply spray a little deodorant straight up above the head and let the mist settle over the body. It didn't make a person feel any cooler or cleaner, but he might smell a little better!

Pablo had the only mosquito net I was aware of. I don't know how he was lucky enough to possess it. He had a ritual of untucking it from his mattress and pulling one corner of it clear enough for him to check for mosquitoes. After he was satisfied it had been purged by spray and swats with a folded copy of the

Stars and Stripes, he climbed into his bunk and secured the net around him. How Pablo could go to sleep with two or three of us sitting around and carrying on is beyond me, but he did. I guess it was the sleep of the innocent because he was certainly a decent guy with a bit of class. He was really too good of a guy to have to been in association with people like us, but that was his lot in life.

When Pablo was sleeping a bit too well or if we were feeling particularly devilish, we might decide to have a little fun at his expense. One of us, usually George, would carefully pull the mosquito netting from under the mattress corner and fold it back. With so many mosquitoes, it did not take long to encourage a few to join Pablo under the netting. Shortly, he would be wide-awake and smacking mosquitoes. He would then have to go back through the routine of purging the net. He might get upset with us, but that was as far as he took it. After all, he was a nice guy. Also, our fatigues were faded a bit more than his, and he had to respect that symbol of our "time in country."

There was an ongoing campaign to keep the rat population down in our camp. I saw a number of bait stations that had been placed between the blast walls and the hootches, as well as in the bunkers and around the mess hall. Even so, I had several encounters with rats that I have never forgotten. Rats don't exactly terrify me as I grew up on a farm with lots of rats, but I do hate them. As a matter of fact, I despise them. My first encounter with a rat in our camp involved several other guys and one terrified guy with a loaded .45-caliber pistol.

Five or six of us were sitting around on a couple of bunks shooting the breeze during the day when a rat shook us up pretty good. It wasn't really the rat, but the guy chasing the rat with the loaded forty-five! The rat was darting around between us as this guy, whose thinking was somewhat questionable, was trying to get a bead on him. The floor was concrete, and we didn't know where the bullet was going to go when he pulled the trigger.

We scattered in every direction hollering, "Don't shoot, dammit, don't shoot!" He also turned in every direction trying to get a fix on the rat while we continued to change our courses and stay out of the line of fire or ricocheting bullet. Mercifully, the rat finally disappeared in the confusion without the forty-five being fired. We all made a note that this fellow was deathly afraid of rats and always had that loaded pistol at the ready in case he encountered one. We all knew he was an unstable person too, which was another reason to keep an eye on him!

My second encounter with a rat occurred while I was sleeping. I was unaware of what had happened until I woke up. Many of us understood and appreciated the value of alcohol as a sleep aid. I learned that value very early on in my experience at Nha Trang. It was not just because of the heat or mosquitoes but because of the fear in letting my guard down while sleeping. Therefore, I had to make myself sleep. On this particular night, I slept pretty soundly, thanks to a little extra sleep aid. I woke up in the morning, and it was daylight. I realized there was a throbbing pain coming up my arm from my right hand. That hand and arm were hanging off my bunk nearly to the floor. When I lifted the arm to look at the throbbing hand, I saw a bloody index finger on that hand. The skin was chewed pretty badly up to just above the first finger joint.

I knew I had gotten chewed by a rat while sleeping and could not believe I had slept through it. I had a bottle of rubbing alcohol and set about cleaning the finger as best I could. It hurt like blue blazes when I poured the alcohol over the finger, and I could feel my heart beating in the throbbing of that finger. It didn't make a lot of sense to me that the rat didn't go ahead and eat the finger after going to all the trouble of peeling it! Perhaps, in my sleep, I had kept snatching it out of his mouth. Maybe he finally got frustrated and left.

Encounter number three occurred several months later. My bunk had been moved to the opposite side of the hootch and was now the second in line. Pablo was first. I began waking up during the night or in the morning with the peculiar feeling that something had been sleeping with me. Sometimes, I felt as if I sensed something crawling across me or jumping to the floor from my bunk. I began to notice that on these occasions, there was a peculiar and suspicious warm area between my legs just above or below the knees.

One night, I woke up with this feeling of unease and reached out, turned on the small light, and directed it toward my legs. My legs felt warm, and on the sheet at that spot was a nest-like depression with several rat droppings in it. I got the creeps! He must have felt me stirring and got out of the bed before I was fully awake. I didn't sleep much more that night, but he did not come back. On several subsequent nights, he did, and I awoke each day to find the depression in about the same area with rat droppings in it. I thought about that rat a lot. I knew he had begun sleeping with me every night. I wondered why he picked me and why he should feel comfortable enough with me to share my bunk on what had become a continuing basis. This occurred for several more nights before I decided the relationship would have to end. I wasn't sure about what approach I should use to try to get rid of this nightly visitor. *Guess I'll try a straightforward approach*, I decided. *I'll lie in wait and try to smash him with something when he shows up.* That decided, I made sure I would stay as clearheaded that evening as the situation required.

Pulling the sheet up to my chin, I placed a jungle boot on

my chest and gripped the canvas upper part in my right hand. I turned off the light and waited. *It will be a long, sleepless night,* I thought, *but maybe I can smack him good.* I guess my friend was wanting to turn in a bit early or was missing me because I only had to wait a minute or two before I felt the sheet move. He was climbing up the sheet from the left side of my bunk! I had to force myself to lay there and breathe normally. The ambush was well laid, and I did not want to spring it too early. Friend rat must have gotten very comfortable in his sleeping arrangements, because he went directly to his spot and settled in and lay still. I felt my legs beginning to warm up as he lay there, but still I waited. I knew I would have a better chance if he were sound asleep.

Something told me the time was right. I mentally judged the distance several times and pictured myself doing a quick sit-up and bringing the boot down just so. When I thought I had the movement worked out, I drew a breath and acted. I sat up and in the same motion brought the boot down hard on the spot just below my knees. It was a direct hit! I felt the boot heel strike something soft and heard the squeal of the surprised rat. I suppose I hurt him too. I knew I got a solid hit on him! I heard him hit the floor and then a sound as if he had bumped into something while running. I dropped the boot to the floor, reached out for a cigarette, and lit it. I lay there smoking and congratulating myself for springing the trap so well and neatly. I had not had time to finish the cigarette when loud cursing erupted farther down toward the other end of the hootch. More cursing came from others wanting to know what the hell was going on.

"A g—d— rat just got into my bed," was the response, shouted out loudly enough to wake everyone.

I lay there, grinning, and finished my cigarette. *Buddy,*

I wonder where your rat came from? I asked mentally, still chuckling to myself. It was a rhetorical question. The real question was why this particular rat liked sleeping with people. I guess he was trapped in the hootch and hung around out of sight during the day as best he could and found a comfortable bed off the concrete at night. To sleep with people at night indicated he had little fear of them. If he had slept in my bed for a couple of weeks, that might have indicated he liked me best.

I'm starting to feel bad about the whole thing now. I may have been his best friend, and I've treated him so badly! Maybe he was the one who chewed me up a few months ago and has been feeling remorseful about that. Lately, he might have been trying to make it up to me! Now, I've obviously hurt him, and he has run to another bunk to find comfort, only to be rejected. I'm starting to think I'm a terrible guy. Or, maybe, just maybe, I'm thinking this way because I've been copying code too long!

53

BABY, EVERYBODY'S SWEETHEART

"BABY" WAS our dog. She belonged to everybody, and each guy made it his business to look after her and spoil her. Her real name was not Baby, but I've had to change it here for sake of sensibility and not needlessly offending anyone. Some say she came down from Pleiku when a detachment of our guys moved down to join us. I really don't know where Baby came from if that is not true. It's possible she was born and raised right there, in our camp at Nha Trang, but I'm inclined to believe that the story of her coming from Pleiku is accurate. She was a medium short-haired breed with red fur. She was very fat and seemed to have gotten even fatter by the time I last saw her and headed back to the States.

Baby was said to be the only female dog in camp, but there were several larger male dogs I saw from time to time. The other dogs were usually together around the mess hall or some other place getting a few scraps. Baby didn't get out much as the guys were pretty protective of her. They fed her and gave her plenty to drink. She didn't have any reason to get out much unless it was to pee or take care of business. Her diet was not exactly a healthy one. She got snacks with lots of canned shoestring potato chips and plenty of beer to wash everything down with. She preferred the beer over everything else and was not particular if it was a popular brand or not. When I was introduced to Baby, I was told it would be nice if I could put a beer out for her before I went to sleep.

"What should I pour it in?" I asked.

"You don't have to put it in anything, just open it and set it on the floor. She'll take care of it," I was told. The floor was concrete, so I did as I was instructed and left a can of beer beside my bunk for Baby when I turned in for the night.

During the night, I came awake with a start. I knew I must have heard a noise, and I lay there, stiffly, listening intently. *Maybe this is the night when someone will manage to slip in and cut my throat right here in my bunk.* It was a thought that was on my mind every night. I stared into the darkness while protecting my throat with my arm, but I couldn't see anybody hovering around me.

Another noise—a metallic thunk—as if something had hit the floor. Then, a strange lapping sound. It sounded like a dog lapping, and it was. I reached out and flipped on the small lamp.

Baby had turned the can of beer over and was lapping it from the floor. This is how she drank her beer during the night. During the day, it was poured into a large glass ashtray, kept for that purpose, or a bowl. Sometimes during the daytime, Baby consumed a couple of beers in a short period of time and then went to sleep. Presently, she would get up and go to the screen door and indicate she needed someone to open it for her. Someone was always willing to get up and let her out. She must have had a big and full bladder because she went out and peed for a long time. I mean, she peed a lot! Afterward, she came back in and lay down again. After several naps and trips to the door to empty her bladder, she let us know that she would like to have a beer or two. After a couple of beers, the process would repeat itself. Somewhere in her drinking sessions, someone decided she needed a little solid food as well and opened a can of shoestring potato chips or gave her some other snack.

Baby had puppies while I was at Nha Trang, which proved we could not watch her all the time. I suppose that, even intoxicated, her natural cycles came into play, and the several male dogs in camp were very happy to make her acquaintance. I don't know what happened to the puppies she had, but they were all spoken for. The puppies were fat butterballs—just like her! I wondered how many of them eventually made it into someone's cooking pot. It is possible some eventually did because of the culture and dietary habits of the populace. I hope Baby never did. She sure was fat, and with the beer diet, probably would have been very tasty!

One day, during the monsoons, when it was rainy and damp all the time, I saw a strange sight. I was sitting down writing one of my numerous letters when Baby walked by dragging a shirt. Actually, she was dressed in the fatigue shirt, and it was buttoned in a way to protect her body from the damp while allowing her legs to move freely. The tail of the shirt trailed behind her like a royal mantle, and she seemed perfectly content to be attired so. I wonder how much time some guy had spent in dressing her up and making her comfortable at the same time. I knew it was one of my fellow O5Hs. Nobody else would be that crazy or sentimental toward this dog we were all so fond of. I smiled, shook my head, and went back to my letter writing. Baby, you're really something, you know that?

Allen Brady with Ski, one of Baby's puppies at Nha Trang.

54

CRAZY—OR A NEW NORMAL?

SOMETIMES, PEOPLE did things that might indicate the pressure of our situation was wearing on them a bit. At times like this, they might do something or act out in a way that would arouse such a suspicion. These incidents might seem to play out as some prank or joke, but they indicated a person wasn't exactly acting or thinking normally—even if I give wide latitude for what was acceptable under what we had adopted as our new normal. So, there were occasions when people exceeded normal or new normal behavior.

After an afternoon and evening of intercepting code, several of us decided to take the basketball and shoot a few hoops since we weren't sleepy and there was no movie being shown on our outdoor plywood screen. It was too late at night for movies. We hadn't gotten so far along in our relaxation habit of drinking that it would prevent us from at least a few minutes on the small concrete pad that served as a basketball court. It was well after midnight, and the spot where we were had a couple of dim lights. They were for security and also to light the way to the outdoor latrine and the outdoor urinal. The urinal was a metal trough about four or five feet long with a pipe on the underside that carried the urine into an underground sump. There was no flushing capability, so it could be smelled even where we were a few feet away and far beyond. The latrine was just beyond the urinal. It was nice as far as latrines go as it had concrete floor, and there were six or seven holes to choose from. They even had toilet seats on them and paper too.

The waste was collected in cut-down barrels that were pulled out from behind each day and taken away to be emptied. It didn't matter to us at the time that the barrels were said to have originally contained Agent Orange. Whether this was true or not, I don't know. It certainly was not an issue at the time. Getting some relief when we needed it was the issue. The latrine, like just about everything else, had a tropical-style architecture with a screen door, screen and wooden walls, and a tin roof. Opposite the latrine and urinal, on the other side of the little ball court were several hootches that were our homes. Mine was about twenty or thirty meters away. The closest was about ten to fifteen meters from where we were. The first sergeant and the other NCOs were housed there.

Suddenly, fire from an automatic weapon erupted and sent us nose-diving for the concrete. None of us had weapons with us, and all we could do was look for a crack to crawl into. Naturally, we assumed the fire was directed at us. We were the only ones outside, so, obviously, we would be the targets. Just as the firing stopped, I forced myself to pick my face up from the ground and look for the shooter. He was directly in front of me about a dozen meters away with his back to me. He had just emptied a twenty-round clip through the doorway of the NCO hootch. The screen door had been propped open with his foot as he fired. Now, his clip empty, he pulled his foot back, and the door banged shut. He turned and walked in the direction of my hootch, but he entered the doorway of the one beside it instead. It lay between mine and the NCO quarters. When he went inside, the screen door banged shut behind him. He had been in no particular hurry and had taken no pains to conceal himself.

By then, we all had managed to pick ourselves up off the ground and stared in the direction of the disappeared shooter at a complete loss as to how to react. Before we even had a chance to discuss the event or say, "What the hell?" the door of the NCO hootch opened and the first sergeant staggered out and walked unsteadily toward us.

He must have taken a hit, I thought.

He continued staggering in our direction until he had stumbled past us and stopped at the urinal. We all gathered around him, trying to talk at once, but he simply looked at us as if completely confused by our presence around him. He went ahead with his business of urinating, glancing at one then another of us as if he were trying to make sense of what we were going on about.

When he was finished, he turned as if he wanted to get away from us and the mosquitoes, but he paused long enough to ask the question, "What are y'all talking about?" His total body language indicated a very drunk first sergeant who wanted to get back to his bunk. We explained how someone had emptied a twenty-round clip into the doorway he had just come out of.

He looked as we pointed in that direction and asked, "Anybody get hit?"

With all of us saying "We don't know—we better check," he turned and waved us away with a "forget it" gesture and left us standing there. Nobody had been hit, as it turned out, and very little was said about the incident. It was as if nobody knew it had occurred except the several of us who had looked for cracks to dive into. Well, the guy with the empty clip too, but he kept quiet. I can only conclude that almost everyone else that night was in a similar condition as the first sergeant. That is not an unreasonable assumption, considering how we constantly tried to relieve pressure on some overly taut nerves.

One day we received instructions for everyone to turn in their protective masks, or gas masks. I don't know what the reasoning was behind the order. It did not make sense, but everyone turned in their masks. Everyone, that is, but me. I don't know why I did not comply, whether I had not heard about the order or was just slow in reacting to it. Anyway, my mask stayed right where it had been for quite a while—in the bottom of my duffel bag.

A day or so later, while writing a letter, I smelled the distinct odor of tear gas just as I heard the alarm being shouted, "Gas, gas!" Then the clanging of the metal gas alarm. I jumped up quickly, emptied my duffel bag, and donned my protective mask. There was nothing to do but sit back down and wait for the all clear. We weren't under any sort of assault, and no other alarm sounded that might give cause for concern.

After several minutes of observing people running here and there, cussing a bit, and occasionally hearing someone coughing, I began to hear various ones passing the word that it was "all clear." I noticed that everyone who happened to see me sitting there with my mask on seemed to give me a questioning—and maybe accusing—look. The word must have gotten out about my mask because when things began to settle down, guys were stopping and eyeballing me. Some of them smiled knowingly and said nothing, while others looked at me with suspicion and asked why I conveniently had a mask at my disposal on such an occasion. I suppose everyone kept mum about their suspicions because no one of any consequence showed up and asked me about why, when the tear gas canister had been set off, I was the only one with a gas mask!

In a short while, the story was out about what had occurred. The hut that contained the orderly room and CO's office had been cleared out with a CS canister. This hut had an AC unit a few feet from it with the air traveling through a flex duct from the unit to the orderly room. Someone had placed the canister where the gas would be carried inside through the duct. I swear it was not me! I had not gotten that crazy yet. Circumstances could easily have convicted me though. I did have the only protective mask. I did not realize at the time that some had already begun to eye me with suspicion, but for a completely different reason. It seems some had the opinion I might be more than just an O5H. I was the most surprised person around when I heard of that! I'll explain.

Just about anywhere we find ourselves in a military setting, it is likely that there is an individual who is not happy being there. He would be firmly convinced that the military is not for him and that he needs to be a civilian again. The sooner, the better. Well, we had ours. We shall call him "Brightman" and will not use his true identity. Brightman was very capable, but his desire to get out of the Army Security Agency and the army itself became a near obsession with him. Energy that should have been spent to further our work and make him a valuable addition was diluted and perhaps, neutralized by his intense desire to get out. His only real value, from my perspective, was in the bit of entertainment he occasionally supplied in his quest for freedom.

"I've got a drug problem, sir," Brightman informed the commanding officer. He had once again requested to see the CO and had once again been granted his request. The CO was perfectly aware of the strict penalty for someone in intelligence work being associated with drugs in any way. It was something that had been pounded into our heads continually while we were in training. So much so, that any one of us would have avoided an area where marijuana was smoked lest a trace get onto our clothing—or that we might be judged guilty by association. That was before we got to Vietnam, where the environment had changed everything, and the pressure was on.

People suddenly began looking for ways to cope and to forget. Even in ASA, some people began using drugs at a mind-numbing rate. Squeaky-clean people who would never have even allowed themselves to be around the stuff just a few months before were often using something now. That something was mostly marijuana. This was the new reality the commanding officer faced. If he acted against every operator who was suspected of drugs, mainly grass, he would have few interceptors, analysts, or linguists. The CO recognized it was a tricky business in dealing with these matters and took the approach he thought best in dealing with Brightman.

"Put them here, Brightman," the CO ordered, indicating his desktop.

Brightman complied and dropped the dope on the desk.

They had been through this once before.

The CO picked up his trash container and swept the dope into it. "Get the hell out of my office, Brightman, and don't come back again, got it? Get the hell out!"

A taste for drugs was not the issue; the CO knew that. A strong distaste for the army was. The commander was smart enough to understand that this was the case with Brightman. He had seen people before who wanted out, including Brightman, and he wasn't going anywhere!

Brightman came up with another plan he was confident enough in that he thought it deserved a try. One of the guys told me Brightman made him a proposition one day of a sexual nature.

"Come on, Brightman. I know what you're up to! You're not queer," he responded. When telling me of the encounter, this fellow operator laughed and said, "He's just trying to get someone to turn him in." He went on to tell me Brightman had recently made the same suggestions to a couple of others and received the same response both times.

"Get away from me, Brightman. I know what this is all about, and it won't work," they had responded. All he needed was for just one guy to report him with an accusation. That's all it would take! He would gladly admit to it and be on his way out. Unfortunately for him, he couldn't convince the CO he had a drug problem, and he couldn't convince others he was homosexual. People just didn't take him seriously! He would have to come up with something else. He needed to get arrested for something, he decided. So, he came to me.

On the day Brightman showed up in my hootch, I was straightening up a few personal things and cleaning out my footlocker. He and I were acquaintances but not friends. Most of us knew each other because of the work, but our circle of friends tended to be far smaller and layered. Ours was only a distant working knowledge of each other. When Brightman showed up, hung around, and started making small talk, I began wondering what might have occasioned this unexpected visit from someone with whom I had never had a real conversation. Turning my back on him and straightening the little five-inch mirror hanging on a nail in a two-by-four, I could still see him behind me. He bent down and placed something in my footlocker. He had no sooner straightened up when I was already there and looking down to see what he was up to. There were two joints of weed in my footlocker, side by side! I didn't touch them.

I simply turned to him and said, "Brightman, I don't know what you're up to, but get your stuff out of my locker and get out of here!" Of course, this was said more colorfully than I've written here.

He looked at me and asked, "You mean, you're not going to arrest me?" It had not been accidental that I had seen him put the stuff in the footlocker. He knew I was watching.

"What do you mean, arrest you?" I asked.

"You're not CID?" he asked.

"No, I'm not CID," I responded with alarm. CID is Criminal Investigation Division. "I'm an O5H, and that's all," I answered.

So, they were suspicious of me after all. I had thought so because in the evenings, when I came upon them in groups smoking, the talk died down. I could smell the grass burning long before I got to them. While I was close by, they were enjoying their Marlboros, but each had his other hand behind his back. There was a red glow back there too. Somehow, I had gotten the reputation of being a bit too straight, and that had aroused suspicions. OB might be CID, undercover! I wasn't! I'm sure that disappointed Brightman, but I was what I was: an O5H who didn't smoke dope. I just drank a lot. Brightman picked up his two joints and left.

My parting words were, "Brightman, tell them they are wrong." I didn't want to worry about the VC and at the same time worry that the other guys thought I was spying on them. I remembered being in discussions a couple of times about undercover CID agents who were found out or suspected. Things got rough for them. While I generally accepted such things as nothing but tall tales and in the category of urban legend, I really didn't want to find out on the personal level. Brightman was the only one who ever "offered" me dope, and in doing so, he learned the truth about me. When I left Nha Trang,

Brightman was still there. I'm not sure if he gave up trying to get out or not. Nobody ever smoked dope around me, which proved I was never totally in the clear with them.

I had mentioned before that sometimes people did things that just did not make sense. The grenade on the cooling unit of the cold storage locker of the mess hall was an example of this. I don't know who found it, but it was good they did. I did not have firsthand knowledge of this. I got it secondhand or thirdhand. Sometimes, the grapevine is very accurate in the information it passes on, and sometimes, it is not. It seems that on a particular day someone found a grenade on the cooling unit of the cold storage locker at the mess hall. The pin of the grenade had been pulled, and a rubber band held the spoon down. It was the obvious intention of someone to allow the sun's intense heat to help in the delayed detonation of the grenade. Hopefully, the sun's heat on the metal would be enough to warm the rubber band enough to stretch and loosen the rubber sufficiently to allow the grenade to explode. It was said that someone discovered it, and it was safely removed. It sounded like a true story, and even if it weren't, it added to our sense of unease and kept us from totally relaxing our guard.

If it were true, it might serve as another example of how a person's thinking becomes mixed up in a constant pressure environment. For it is as unlikely someone acting on behalf of the VC did this as it was that he put the CS canister in the AC duct serving the orderly room. Likely, it was one of us. There were more people around the mess hall area than in any other area on camp, far exceeding the number in the ramp compound or in any of the hootches. If any one of them wanted to do some damage, that would be the place to do it. Of course, someone may have wanted to make a statement about the chow! I've thought this over a bit, and I have the suspicion it was a prank gone to extremes. After all, ours was a place where a guy might take a notion to clear out the orderly room with a CS canister or empty a twenty-round clip into a sleeping quarters at one o'clock in the morning and walk away!

55

ATTITUDES HARDEN A BIT

ONE EVENING, I was busy with an intercept when there came a sound of a detonation of some sort. It did not sound too awfully close, so I was not particularly alarmed by it, but it was plenty close enough. I heard it quite distinctly over the sounds coming from my headsets and felt it telegraph clearly through the floor of the intercept van at the ramp. It did not sound like a rocket strike, and I thought it might have been a mortar round or something of that nature. It was a dull *ka-whump* sound.

I kept copying my intercept, but I reached out for my flak vest on the floor and put it on. Next, I balanced my steel pot on my head, on top of the headsets. I kept listening for a repeat of the sound, expecting the next detonation to be closer. There were no repeats, which did not follow the usual pattern of incoming rounds. The camp alert siren did not sound, which it normally did in such a circumstance. I was a bit mystified, but I continued to copy. *Guess I'll find out what has happened once the grapevine gets fully activated,* I thought.

It seemed only several minutes had passed when a fellow O5H popped into the room from the ramp with news about what had occurred.

"Man, you won't believe what just happened," he announced excitedly as he came in.

I turned to him to hear what he had to say because I knew it had to do with the "ka-whump" of several minutes earlier.

"It was down at the gate," he said. The gate was the camp gate, about 250 meters away. "Some drunk ARVN just caught a grenade! He wanted to play VC down at the gate, so he went into the barbed wire apron beside the gate. The ARVN guard must have thought to himself, *Oh, you want to play? Let's play!* He tossed him a live grenade. He won't be playing VC anymore!"

ARVN is South Vietnamese military.

The O5H rushed off, laughing a bit to spread the news to everyone who hadn't heard. I took off my steel pot and flak vest and laid them on the floor by my chair. I did not need them, after all. I resumed copying my intercept target, but I found myself smiling a lot in the process. I kept seeing the surprised expression of that crazy, drunken fool in the wire as the grenade came toward him.

The sounds of the Morse code did not drown out the sounds of the other guys laughing and joking about the idiot who wanted to play VC. Once again, boys will be boys—whether they are American boys or Vietnamese boys. We saw the humorous side of the situation, but we felt no sympathy at all for the one on the receiving end of the grenade toss. It may be a disturbing thing to admit, but this lack of feeling was indicative of how our general attitude had continued to harden for some of us during the course of a few months. In all honesty, the attitudes of many of us toward those who we were supposed to be helping may have never been entirely sympathetic. Our individual reasons for serving may well have been different. Perhaps, in some cases, it was less a desire to assist the Vietnamese than to serve our own national interests as patriotic people often do. Some might have had romantic notions of warfare and didn't want to miss out on the adventure. People generally got over such notions. Others, likely, didn't really have a choice and would have been drafted had they not volunteered for the longer hitch with ASA. Whatever the reasons, sympathy for the Vietnamese was probably not the supreme motivating factor.

"Free Lieutenant Calley," began to appear on the hard copy of our intercepts. We called these our "skeds" or scheduled intercepts. That also applied to the hard copy of any intercepts—even the random or unidentified ones. These intercept copies were collected periodically during the course of the day and taken away for analysis. The intercept operators began showing their support for Lieutenant William Calley, who had been accused of mass murder at the village of My Lai. He had recently been convicted. We demonstrated our show of support by typing in the words "Free Lieutenant Calley" at the beginning and end of each copy that was submitted to the analysts. It was something we agreed to do and was not limited to Nha Trang operators. The fact that we supported Lieutenant Calley is a good example of what the general attitude was for many of us and showed a clear lack of sympathy toward those we were supposed to be assisting, even, defending.

The massacre at My Lai actually occurred fairly early in 1968, but it did not become a full-blown issue until the end of 1969. If memory serves me correctly, of the fourteen officers eventually charged, only William Calley was convicted in early 1971. By then, I had been "in country" for quite a while, and I might have been considered an "old-timer," though I was still twenty years old. Frustration levels were high for many throughout the armed forces serving in Vietnam. The war had dragged on for far too long, and there was little hope for an outright victory. It seemed an almost impossible task to defeat an enemy that was spread through the general population and countryside. When it is difficult to distinguish friend from foe and frustrations mount, it is almost a given that something like the incident at My Lai will occur. However, we might expect such a thing to occur on a smaller scale than it did. Likely, on much smaller scales, such incidents may have occurred more often than we might have been aware of or care to admit.

Within the ASA, we, too, were not immune to suffering frustration. These periods of frustration might lead us to ask a "why" question. Perhaps, it might be after one of the frequent episodes of rockets coming in on us. It would really be a reflex question. "We know where they are. Why not just do what is necessary and blow them away?" Information, that's why! We got a wealth of information in knowing where they were and what they were up to. It's better to listen to them every day and keep track of what they are up to and keep a fix on their location than to lose that capability by acting inappropriately. Kind of like prostate treatment that sometimes requires "watchful waiting." When the situation becomes severe enough, the doctor will act. Until then, you may have to live with the discomfort, take pills, and pee frequently!

We actually understood and accepted the wisdom of controlling the desire to respond. The decision concerning how the situation was handled was not ours to make anyway. Our job was to get as much information as we could on the enemy that would help others do their jobs—even if the situation was often uncomfortable and frustrating for us. I sometimes stopped, from time to time, by the corkboard that served as a bulletin board on the ramp and read through some of the recent intercept copies posted there. These were the English versions of decrypted messages we were allowed to read. They often contained something humorous or of particular interest because of some peculiar bit of included information. An after-action report of a VC sweep through an area indicated they had "captured" two bicycles and a buffalo and cart. That may sound funny, but they had a use for the bicycles and the cart. Another message reported that troop strength in a unit was at 70 percent with 30 percent of those having dysentery and low morale. Again, seemingly trivial but very useful information. Some intercepts were too sensitive to release and would violate the "Need to Know" principle had they been posted.

Stopping and reading some of the intercept transcripts helped remind me why we did what we did every day. In a smaller sense, it helped calm some of my personal frustration, but it could not address the deeper and larger issues I had begun to deal with. Those issues often arose out of the question that I alluded to early on: "What is truth? That question pops up again with the incident at My Lai concerning the events and attitudes that resulted in the massacre there of innocent people. Those killed included children, young women, and the elderly, obviously not enemy combatants. Those involved in carrying out the massacre had been through a protracted period of trying to deal with a situation they could not seem to bring under their control. They were also still reeling from the effects and injuries sustained in the general Communist offensive we knew as the Tet Offensive. The question of who was friendly and who was enemy was, sometimes, very difficult to answer. It became frustrating to the point that truth didn't matter so much anymore. They acted—and in a very gruesome way. The facts of what had happened had become pretty common knowledge by the time we began showing our full support for Lieutenant William Calley. We had the facts, most of them, but they mattered less than what we wanted to believe or accept. By disregarding those facts, we could not hold ourselves as innocent in our attitudes after typing in "Free Lieutenant Calley" on our skeds. In so doing, because of frustration and our unwillingness to accept the facts, we were also saying that truth really does not matter. We gave tacit approval to what happened at My Lai, and that disturbs me still.

56

THOSE UNEASY FEELINGS

I NEVER felt completely at ease at any time while serving in Vietnam. There were no real front lines. Wherever a person found himself was the front line. The general offensive of Tet proved this. There were areas that were much safer than others, to be sure. We knew the enemy was around us, and that was borne out by the fairly frequent rocket strikes directed toward us. There were enemy positions we were aware of nearby and were firmly fixed by our direction finding and daily intercepts. We simply monitored them.

One, in particular, we named Nha Trang Charlie because his position was only several kilometers from us. We listened to everything he communicated. We did not see him as a really big threat as long as he stayed put, and we knew what he was up to. One of his functions was to provide R and R (rest and relaxation) for Viet Cong. We knew from our intercepts that the VC soldiers were given a small amount of money on special occasions and allowed to go into Nha Trang to relax a bit—the same place that some of us went. Other units had different functions, and that was to make it as difficult for us as they could. They let us know they were thinking about us. There were times when we had to take extra precautions against the possibility of VC sappers slipping in during the night and blowing up a few things—or us. I had to stand guard at my quarters because of that. Thankfully, the sapper attacks did not occur. The fact that we had good information of their likelihood allowed us to prepare. That, in itself, may have kept these incidents from occurring. I stood guard and drank with the senior NCO who was in charge of the guard detail during one of these incidents. That did not mean I was not vigilant, but it passed the time and helped both of us stay more relaxed.

Perimeter guard was no fun and could play on the nerves a bit. I stayed there all night, alone. There were, however, Chinese guards (Taiwanese) about a hundred meters to my left and to my right. About once an hour or two, they clanged on a piece of metal as their sergeant or officer of the guard drove by in a jeep to check on them. No one checked on me throughout the whole night the way the Chinese checked on their guards. I was left completely alone, but I did have a field phone. I spent my time swatting mosquitoes, smoking cigarettes, and plotting various fallback positions or escape routes if the VC hit my position. The time crawled by ever so slowly!

A woman hung around on the dirt track outside the wire for quite a while earlier in the evening. Occasionally, she would look at me across the twenty meters of barbed wire apron and fence and smile. She never got a customer. As the evening dragged on, she obviously lost hope and eventually walked away. It was a bit lonelier after she left because she was at least a presence. Later, I was told that this prostitute was also a deaf mute. I found myself feeling sorry for her. Life must have been very tough for someone like her in such an environment.

Daytime was not so bad. I could see all around me during the day, and there was plenty of activity. This was not so at night.

Nighttime was different. Even going to the latrine could play on the nerves a bit. It was dark in there, and my imagination kicked into overdrive. Somebody could have been lying in wait for me to come in and sit down. When I sat, I experienced the almost overpowering feeling of another person's presence in the darkness. I kept my hunting knife in my lap. I felt as if someone was lurking about and waiting for an opportunity, maybe even coming up out of the hole next to me, as if he were emerging from a tunnel. I protected my throat. I never went to the latrine at night if I could help it.

Going to sleep meant a person had to let his guard down completely. This was very hard to do. We had all heard stories of people getting their throats cut while they were asleep. Of course, these were tales and legends, like ghost stories around a campfire, but that did not matter. I drank a lot to help me go to sleep. Even so, sounds had a tendency to wake me. I learned to ignore the nightly barrage of outgoing artillery fire that was directed at the hills nearby. As loud as it was, it became only background noise and was ignored. Sometimes there seemed to be a "short round," and my mind acknowledged it as a departure from the normal sounds. The sounds that woke me up tended to be the ones out of the ordinary or unexpected. It was a defense mechanism. It might be Baby turning over a can of beer and drinking it or an unexplained sound that would have me laying there, listening and waiting. I began to sleep on my side with my forearm across my throat and my hand locked behind my head. If someone wanted to cut my throat, they would have to pry my arm up first! It took me thirty-five years to break this habit. I did it then only because my shoulders had gotten so bad that I could no longer put an arm in that position. I then started sleeping on my back with my arms crossed on my chest.

It frightened my Japanese wife, and she said, "Don't do that.

You look like a dead man!" She had never noticed I had slept with my throat covered for so many years, yet when I departed from it, she noticed it, and it frightened her. Because she had never noticed, she never knew I had slept with my arm across my throat for all those years because of those hundreds of uneasy nights so many years before.

On a certain day, I showed up thinking I would be doing my normal work of intercepting code. I was wrong. On this day, I would be on burn detail. I had never been on burn detail before and did not know what it entailed until I received my instructions. We generated a huge amount of classified paper trash in the performance of our duties. Most of this trash was top secret and had to be disposed of properly. The trash had been stored in brown paper bags as it was generated, stapled shut, and labeled "Classified Trash." They were collected and placed inside of a secure wire "pen," which also contained an incinerator. These bags of classified trash had to be disposed of by burning on a particular schedule. This pen with the incinerator and classified trash was within the ramp compound next to one of our sandbagged bunkers.

The procedure for destroying the trash included burning it to ashes and then mixing the ashes with water into a slurry in a fifty-five-gallon drum of water. There would be nothing remaining of any top-secret material except a black mud. Pretty simple, actually.

There were a lot of bags to be burned. It looked like there must have been two or three hundred bags piled in the pen next to the incinerator. I started the fire and began feeding it with the bags. They burned well with the tremendous amount of carbon paper the bags also contained, but there were so many of them! Occasionally, I opened the door of the incinerator and stirred the material with a long iron rod. It wasn't a difficult job, and it was a departure from my normal duty of intercepting communications. I didn't mind. At least, I was doing something different. I might even go so far as to say I was enjoying myself. That is, until the rockets started coming!

They were not particularly close, but they were close enough. The camp-alert siren sounded. I plastered my body against the sandbagged bunker next to me after the first rocket hit the camp. I saw people running for bunkers. Soon, all activity ceased except the first sergeant running past me for a nearby bunker. I was completely ignored. I knew I could not leave the mound of classified trash, but I was caught in the open.

"Top, what should I do?" I called out to him as he passed with his forty-five-holster slapping his leg as he ran.

"Keep burning!" he shouted over his shoulder as he disappeared toward a nearby bunker. Soon, there were no more people running around. There was nothing. No movement of any sort and almost no sound. It was as if the whole world had ground to a stop. There was only me and the incinerator. Also, a huge pile of top-secret material. I pondered what I should do. Remembering the words of the first sergeant that I should keep burning, I rushed to the incinerator and threw several bags into it. Next, I ran back to the inclined, sandbagged wall of the bunker about five meters away and inclined my body against the sandbags. This left me in a position to peek over the top of the bunker. I looked up in the direction of the hills on that side to see if I could see anything. There was nothing to see except the hills themselves. Somehow, I felt, somebody up there could see me. Surely, they had to! The only living and moving thing in camp was me. I felt very vulnerable. Since I was the only thing moving, I must be providing a perfect target for the next rocket or sniper!

Suddenly, I felt as if I were in the very center of a bull's-eye target, but I kept burning. I tore myself away from the relative cover and safety of my position and ran to the incinerator and pitched in a few more bags. I wondered how far a sniper could shoot, and I was hoping I would be out of his range. Even as I was moving back and forth between the incinerator and the sandbags, I could not shake the feeling that I was the only target around for rocket or sniper—and that somebody had a bead on me! I do not remember a time when I felt more vulnerable. There was not a single human being stirring, bird singing, or dog barking. Only the loud cracks and booms of the rockets. I felt absolutely alone!

In those few minutes, that relatively exposed position was to become the loneliest place on the face of the Earth, as far as I was concerned. It was one of the most uncomfortable feelings I remember experiencing. I felt much better as people eventually emerged from the bunkers after the all clear had sounded. None of the rockets had fallen within the small ramp compound where I was. The amount of comfort one can feel in the presence of another human being is amazing. The remainder of my burn detail went much better when everyone was out of the bunkers. If anyone up in those hills was looking for a target, they had a lot more than just me to choose from! There is a lot to be said for the safety of the herd and of the comfort of being lost in it.

57

VERSUS SPY: A GLIMPSE OF THE MORE SERIOUS SIDE

HAVING MENTIONED earlier about our ability to intercept enemy communications and locate their positions, a couple of examples might be helpful in understanding the importance of this capability. The Communist Vietnamese were aware that we had the ability to both listen to them and locate and identify them. This made life very difficult for them, at times, but there was not a lot they could do about it. Much of their communication was conducted in Morse code at all levels and required a longer transmission time. It is difficult to secure such communication except by manual encryption of message texts. Some of this encryption was breakable on our level, and some required NSA decryption. We got frequent and accurate fixes on their positions, as well as a wealth of information through message content. This was done by the intercept operators (O5Hs) and the direction finders (O5Ds). The analysts and linguists were invaluable in their expertise. The direction finders operated from several locations spread out over the countryside. Some of these were ground based while others were in fixed-wing aircraft. These were known as ARDF, or airborne direction finding. This was very helpful for Americans and their allies in planning and carrying out military operations.

The knowledge of our activities was officially confined to a select few because of secrecy requirements. Even within our organization, we operated on a very strict "need-to-know" basis. Information gathered was passed up the line to the NSA for their analysis and to a few others who depended on the intelligence information we helped supply. Otherwise, people were ignorant of our existence. We kept our mouths shut, listened, and established the locations of the enemy.

George Baird had been sent to Pleiku for a period of time. As I stated earlier, he was an O5D, or direction finder. One of his "fixes" was on the transmitter of a unit a few kilometers from one of the firebases in the region. Fixes on the transmitter showed the position of the transmitter was shifting, indicating the unit was on the move. It appeared the unit was positioning itself close to the firebase. A final and very accurate fix confirmed the fact that they were very close, and that could only lead to one conclusion. They were about to do mischief against those on the firebase. That conclusion was also confirmed by their communication content. The information was passed on that the enemy unit was now in very close proximity and preparing an assault. Acting on this intelligence, countermeasures were implemented, and then all hell broke loose! The unit was caught totally by surprise and was effectively destroyed.

For days, this unit had been carefully creeping forward toward its target, kilometer by kilometer, perhaps a bit each night. Though they used the cover of darkness in their advance, the Viet Cong's radio transmitter was signaling their position. As far as they were concerned, their movements were concealed by the darkness, and in the daytime, they probably laid low. ASA was listening and plotting their position changes. They might as well have been traveling right along with them. This is an example of how effective the operators of ASA were and the result of the proper use of the information they supplied. George Baird received the Bronze Star medal for this action and others similar to it in the twelve months he served in Vietnam.

Lieutenant Lee was a Republic of Korea or ROK officer. He was also an intelligence officer, but I did not know that when I first met and talked with him. We talked about everything but that. That's just the way it was. Certain things were kept quiet about and left out of the conversation. He knew George, and he also knew George and I worked together. Lieutenant Lee did not get where he was by being stupid. I'm sure he knew we were in a related field and refrained from asking too many questions. George took karate instruction from Lieutenant Lee and knew him much better than I did. I had never actually had a conversation with him. George admired and often described this man's ability and mastery of martial arts. He tried convincing me to join in for some instruction, but I chose not to do so.

One afternoon, I reported for duty and was informed I would have the evening off. That was a very rare event as we were expected to listen to enemy code every day. However, there was almost always one extra operator, which allowed each person to have a day off about every month or so. We usually would not know that our name had finally gotten to the top of the list until the trick chief informed us once we showed up for duty. My name came up, and I went back to my quarters to relax for a while and decide how to celebrate my good fortune of a day off. Problem was, my closest buddies were working, and that kind of put a damper on things.

As the afternoon wore on toward evening, I decided to go to the small Korean club only about fifty meters from where I bunked. Their small club was in a tropical-style hut, and

Americans like me enjoyed going in for a large bowl of noodle soup, some cucumber kimchi, beer, or something harder. There was very little activity in the Korean club on this late afternoon, so I had nobody to sit and pass the time with—until Lieutenant Lee came in. I had never seen him there before and was surprised when he came in and asked to sit down. We sat facing each other across the table for a while and had a couple of drinks together. It began getting dark outside, and I noticed that he occasionally checked his watch. Finally, he stood up and indicated he had to go. Before leaving, he asked me if I was going to stick around for a while.

"I won't be gone all that long, and if you're still here when I come back, we can have a couple more drinks and talk some more. There's something I have to do."

I told him I had nothing to do and that I would probably be there for some time.

He nodded and left.

The Korean lieutenant did not come back for a long while. It seemed to be two or three hours later that he came back in and sat down. I bought him a drink, and he began to sip on it. He didn't say anything right away. I think he may have been giving himself a chance to collect his thoughts and decide what he was comfortable with sharing with me. I was taken totally by surprise by what he said when he started talking.

"I just lost a jeep," he said. "That's my second one!"

Having no context, the words didn't mean anything to me. I waited for him to continue.

He sipped his drink a bit, looked at me, and continued talking. "I went to meet one of my contacts," he said. "I parked the jeep and walked to the place where I was to meet him. When we had finished our business, I headed back to the jeep. Before

I got to it, it blew up! Someone may have slid a grenade into the gas tank."

I was not knowledgeable about many such things, but I did know that the filler neck of the gas tank could easily accommodate a grenade, but the detonation would have to be slightly delayed. It's possible that it involved the rubber band trick—or perhaps the jeep was destroyed by some other means. However, it was sometime later that I actually reflected on those things. While sitting across from Lieutenant Lee, I could only marvel as I listened to the amazing story of his narrow escape. People other than his contact were obviously waiting in the dark for this Korean officer. They were in the know and had laid a pretty good trap for him. It was just plain good luck and the timing having being off a bit that delivered him from what would have been a pretty horrific ending!

I was pretty shocked by his close call and the fact that he had shared the information with me. It was only then I realized he was an intelligence officer. That he confided in me indicated he knew more about me than I had realized. As earlier stated, he knew that George and I were friends and that we worked together. Though I had not discussed my work with him, I later got the feeling that he already knew about it. We shared a couple of more drinks before he stood to go, saying he had a bit more to do concerning the affair. I stood and shook his hand and wished him well. I still do not know why Lieutenant Lee sat, talked, and shared drinks with me that day or why he confided in me in that little tropical Korean club. I thought a lot about that later. Mingling with unknown people while meeting informants and undercover people was likely a pretty hairy business. The pressure must have been enormous! Maybe he couldn't release the pressure the way we could and desperately needed someone to talk to. I kept this business to myself for more than forty-five years until I shared it with George several days ago.

Pure chance—or luck as we might choose to describe it—may very well happen more than we realize. As with the ROK lieutenant, chance played a big part in my most memorable intercept during the year I was in Vietnam. I had a few minutes before the scheduled time when my next intercept target would be making contact with his "out stations." I was free to search the frequencies for targets. Soon, I could hear the sounds of a transmitter being tuned and stopped out of curiosity to see who it might be. He began broadcasting call signs I did not recognize. Though he was also on a frequency different from any of my assigned targets, he was in the frequency range of my usual targets. He seemed very familiar in the sound of his transmitter and the rhythm of his hand on the key. It sounded exactly like a VCOB, one of mine. I settled in and copied him as an unidentified, but possible VCOB.

The operator of the unidentified intercept indicated he was about to broadcast a lengthy message and went directly into it. His signal was loud and clear. He was an excellent operator with a good hand on the key. What took me by total surprise was that the message was not encrypted; it was being broadcast in plain Vietnamese. I had copied plaintext transmissions before, but more out of curiosity and boredom. I had never seriously copied a plaintext message in Vietnamese before, but I had no problem with this one because of the clarity of the transmission. I found myself enjoying what I was doing and proud that I seemed to be getting perfect copy. I had copied for quite a while before I began to feel pressure to drop this intercept and get ready for my regularly scheduled target who would soon be tuning his transmitter. I closed out the unidentified intercept and placed the copy where the analyst could pick it up. He came almost immediately and took the copy away as I was rolling to the frequency of my target intercept. The VCOB target came up as scheduled and had no message for his outstation, and that station had nothing for him. They ended their transmission after a brief exchange.

As I was closing out the copy on this intercept, a very excited linguist rushed in wanting to know if I had just copied the unidentified. I told him I had, and he quickly informed me I should go back to that frequency to see if he was still up. He was.

"Copy him!" he almost shouted. He turned to two other operators and commanded, "Roll to his frequency!" I called out the frequency, and they rolled to it and began copying as well. I had never witnessed such a sense of urgency in anyone's voice concerning an intercept. The fact that three people were now copying the same transmission made it seem that something of extreme importance was occurring.

The linguist stood behind me and read the copy over my shoulder as I typed it out. Once he looked over the shoulders of the other operators but came back to me. My copy was about as perfect as it could be.

After a period of time the linguist said, "Okay, OB, you can drop him."

I closed out the intercept and handed him the copy. Looking up at him, I asked, "Do you mind telling me what that was all about?"

"That message was directed to us!" he said.

"What do you mean, directed to us?" I asked.

He responded, "The message started by saying, 'This is a warning to you big-eared chair soldiers at Nha Trang. I know you are listening." He went on to say we had caused them problems and that we had been a thorn in the flesh long enough. We were warned, according to the message, to be sure we understood that they were about to do something about it."

At first, I found it almost impossible to believe what the linguist was telling me. I had almost, by chance, intercepted a message that practically had my name and address on it. No wonder it was such a tidy and clear transmission with probably the best operator on the key. It reminded me of one of the jokes we had played on some nug a couple of times. They wanted to make sure we had no trouble picking up this transmission. We didn't even have to go through the problem of decrypting it. It was perfectly clear for the linguist to read!

Once the "I can't believe this" moment had passed, I shared the threat with the other guys, and we all got a good laugh out of it. We knew we were very effective in our work and that we were a real problem for the enemy through their communications. Here they were, actually admitting it and describing us as a "thorn in the flesh." It felt kind of nice being noticed and even complimented by the enemy! It didn't matter that the compliment came in the form of a threat. We got a few more laughs out of it. The time came when it wasn't funny anymore. A few days later, several rockets came in, and the ramp took a direct hit. One intercept van was destroyed, one operator was killed, and several others were wounded. The enemy operator had made sure that we knew revenge was coming. They had made good on their threat!

I was not on duty at the time of the strike and was in my quarters. A friend of mine was in the latrine with his pants around his ankles when the rockets came in. He thought the latrine had been hit because of the deafening kaaraaack-booom and the sound of gravel and shrapnel hitting the walls and tin roof. He found himself in the floor, facedown, with his britches covering his boots. His one thought, he told me, was that he didn't want to die like that. He would at least want his britches to be in order and not around his ankles!

In a moment, someone shouted the news that the ramp had taken a direct hit. Word came we were to stay away. There was already enough confusion there. The attack had occurred during the morning hours and had effectively shut down operations on the ramp. This had been the second attack of the day. The first had been at daybreak. The hours between this second attack and the time I came on duty early in the afternoon had been spent, by those on duty, in cleanup of the ramp and moving another van into the place of the destroyed one that had been pulled out. The replacement intercept van was operational by the time I came on duty. It was then manned by the guys I came on duty with.

The ramp area was still a mess even though the debris and other evidence of the blast was partially cleaned up. There was still blood, however, and sand. Each of us pitched in as we could and cleaned the place a bit more. The sand had come from sandbags that had been opened, poured over areas of blood, and then scooped up. There had not been time to clean it completely. Some of the plywood panels that made up the walls of the ramp had been blasted loose but put back into position. Two of them were perforated over their entire areas with shrapnel holes. Someone was throwing a shirt into the trash. The fatigue shirt belonged to one of the guys who had been taken away wounded. I identified it by his name tag stitched to it. It looked as if a colony of rats had chewed it up! It had been hanging on a nail or hook during the rocket strike. I rescued it and gave it back to the owner when he returned to duty a couple of weeks later. He was our youngest operator and was a Cajun from Louisiana. He was proud of this souvenir and of his very perforated hide! He often walked around naked to display those "million-dollar wounds."

I have wondered about the stories he had for his friends when he got back to Louisiana. I'm just glad he got back to Louisiana.

The seat cushion of the metal swivel chair at my radio position had a hole in it that had not been there before. This position was in the van beside the one that had been destroyed and replaced. I probed the hole in the cushion with my finger and discovered that a piece of shrapnel was embedded there. I was able to retrieve it and was happy I had not been in the chair during the rocket strike. It was about an inch and a quarter long and resembled a piece of chewed gum. The place where it was embedded seemed to suggest an emasculation for anyone who might have occupied the chair. Luckily, no one had been in it at the time of the rocket strike. It was a somber time for all of us, but we made it through the evening and accomplished our normal intercepts. It took me a long time to link the very unusual and threatening intercept of a few days earlier to the deadly accurate rocket attack. It seems our enemy had made good on the threat that I had laughed about—a threat sent to us in a message I had intercepted almost by pure chance!

Operations continued normally over the days and weeks that followed. The direct hit on the ramp was a sobering reminder of what could happen at any time, night or day, to any one of us. Some of the evidence of what had occurred on that particular day remained in place and was visible until I left the country. I had wondered, on occasion, why it had not been removed. Perhaps someone had determined that it needed to remain as a visual reminder to all of us, a reminder that this was serious business despite our pranks and the jokes played on each other.

As I had done so many times in the past, I stopped now and then by the cork bulletin board and read some of the decrypted messages that were posted there for our entertainment. Also, they educated us as to the types of things we sometimes intercepted. These tended to be the more amusing intercepts or something with a peculiarly interesting content. Drier, technical intercepts were not generally included as were the ones too sensitive for everyone to see. One intercept, transmitted in four-digit code and broken by our people, was fascinating to read. I read the English translation of it so many times that I remember, generally, how it went, even after forty-five years.

This intercept was made by our VCIB interceptor. This operator intercepted messages between intelligence stations and agents in the field. The message had been transmitted from an intelligence station to an agent in place in one of the cities, possibly Saigon or even Nha Trang. Such messages were sent "in the blind." This means they were transmitted without receiving a response. A one-way communication. They were transmitted at very specific times so the field agent would know when to be listening. Because we routinely intercepted these transmissions and were able to decrypt them, we knew what the field agent knew. This particular message contained the instructions that an agent was to follow in making contact with another to exchange information. It went something like this. (I have substituted A and B for the street names because I have forgotten them.)

"Tomorrow, at 2:00 p.m., you will be on the corner of the intersection of A Street and B Street. Stand beside the lamp pole on the east side of A. Wear a white shirt with red bow tie and have a folded newspaper under your left arm. Someone will ask you, 'Will there be any relief from this heat?' Your reply will be, 'When the monsoons come.' If no contact is made, next transmission will be at 4:00 p.m. tomorrow."

A few weeks after the rocket hit the ramp, I was standing at the board and reading this and other intercepts again. I had taken notice that a lot of the papers on the board, including the intercepts, had spots all over them. They were grease spots. In the middle of many of them was a brown speck from a bit of matter that had dried. I realized I had flecked a few of them off with my fingernail in an absentminded sort of way. It dawned on me I was flecking away the dried flesh of some of my friends. They were small pieces, even tiny, but still, they had come from them, bits that had sprayed outward from the blast. No one had cleaned them off or changed the papers mounted there. They were allowed to remain on the papers on the corkboard and the plywood wall to which it was mounted.

Once I realized the significance of these dozens of small oily spots scattered over the bulletin board and the plywood wall, I found myself reflecting on them from time to time when I stopped there to read an intercept. Occasionally, I flecked away one or two more of the tiny bits of dried matter on or around the board while I was standing there reading or just looking. This area of the ramp where the corkboard was displayed served as a constant and real reminder to me about the situation we were in. *We play our pranks on each other to escape the seriousness of what we are doing,* I may have thought. *We cannot, however, escape the fact that this is a very serious business. Another accurate strike on the ramp could well occur at any time—whether we are engaged in a prank or an intercept. That tin roof above us offers no protection except from the elements. Just as the intercept had implied, they know we are here, and they could very well get lucky again.*

The VC creeping up on that firebase, and then being destroyed, had the cover of darkness. The darkness provided them a measure of the comfort of concealment as they moved. If they thought it also provided them with safety, they were wrong. Those of us listening knew of their presence and had fixed their positions through their transmitters. It was as if we could see them through their transmitters. It proved costly and even fatal for them.

The ROK lieutenant went to meet his contact at night. Others knew about it and were right there and waiting. Only a few seconds and luck had preserved him. That was strike two for him. I didn't know what eventually became of him and have wondered if he might have finally been called "out" by a third strike. George informed me recently that Lieutenant Lee had indeed survived.

There was the ramp from which we gave the enemy such fits. We knew where they were and a lot of what they were up to. They knew that we knew and also knew where we were. They determined to exact their pound of flesh, which they did with their very accurate rocket fire on the ramp.

The agent on the ground in the city unknown to me did not know we were receiving his instructions at the same time as he was getting them. *Did he know—or did his contact know—that there were others near the lamppost on the east side of A Street?* Whenever I stood and read that intercept, I had a mental picture of a bunch of us looking down and observing what was unfolding on that street corner as if we were watching a movie. However, I don't know how it may have ended and have wondered since about whatever happened to those two agents.

You can play all the pranks you wish, make light of the situation, and attempt to divert your attention from your surroundings for a few minutes, but you cannot escape the serious nature of the work that is going on. Even purple Jesus cannot do that. It only numbs you to it for a while. When you get through puking, you find yourself back in a real world again. We knew what we did was deadly serious stuff. We did it, stayed quiet about it, and dealt with it in our own peculiar ways.

58

PUTTING IT IN PERSPECTIVE

PERSPECTIVE IS important. I remember leaving Two Rock Ranch in California. I was off to serve my country. That was the uppermost thought in my mind. We were under the threat of Communist encroachment, and it was important I do my part in stopping it. I had no doubt about the fact that I was doing the right thing. Whether I was ASA, XYZ, or Radio Research did not matter. I just wanted to do my part. I was told the government had spent $50,000 in the year training me to do my part. Okay, so I was to go to my assignment accompanied by a pig, four chickens, and their gold-toothed owners. That did not really matter either. I was still very special, I thought. I was serving my country and doing it as a part of the intelligence community—something few people had the opportunity to do. That was a special feeling!

The commanding general of the Army Security Agency, Pacific, came to Nha Trang one day. He and his entourage ate the noon meal in our mess hall during that visit. That evening, two of the cooks and I got together to visit and chat awhile, as we often did. They were friends of mine. This evening was completely different, however. When we got together, these two cooks seemed to be on top of the world. Their faces were literally glowing in their happiness, and they could scarcely contain their excitement. They relayed to me what had happened following the noon meal. After the meal, they said General Wolfe had asked to see the cooks who had prepared the meal he had just eaten. When they were presented to him, he began to compliment them profusely.

"I have never had a finer meal in all of my military experience," he said. "Who cooked the pastries?"

"I did, sir," responded Tommy Bulger, one of the cooks.

"Son, I have never enjoyed pastries more than the ones you prepared for us today! You fellows have done so well with the limited resources you have. I want you to know no one could have done better. I want you to also know that I appreciate so much the effort and pride you have obviously taken in the preparation of this meal. It is encouraging to know we have people like you feeding these men here."

As Tommy and Gary, these two friends of mine, excitedly relayed to me what had transpired in the mess hall that day, I found myself looking from one to the other, almost in disbelief. It was as if God himself had complimented them, and they seemed to be, as I stated, on top of the world. It was at that moment I learned one of my most valuable lessons, not only of Vietnam, but of life itself. I had thought of myself as important. I was, after all, a member of a group of highly trained people. What I did was very important, and people may have lived or died according to how well I did my job. My commanding general had not complimented me or any of those I worked with. I didn't even see him. He complimented the cooks, the ones who supported us and tried their best to please us. Their job was a thankless one, and all they likely heard was complaints. I had done my share of complaining, so I know.

When these two friends of mine and I got together, we never

talked about certain things. We all knew it was forbidden to do so. We talked about other things: home, families, and such. I was aware they were cooks. Though they were friends, I felt my job was much more important than theirs. Certainly, it was more prestigious. The excited looks I observed on the faces of these two friends seem to be always before me. I finally came to realize they were really proud of how they did their job. They were as proud of their work as I was of mine. As I began to reflect on this, I came to the realization that their job was much more difficult than mine. Sure, I had trained for a long time, put everything into my job, and was quite good at what I did. The cooks did too. The difference was that we really didn't appreciate the effort they put into their jobs. They had to satisfy countless people who could not seem to be satisfied. I had only to do my job, and everyone was satisfied. These two friends of mine certainly had the more difficult task!

I have stated previously that I made a conscious decision not to think about Vietnam over the past forty-five or so years. I was just fine with the idea, and it became a habit, but the lesson I learned from these two friends has stayed with me far more than any other lesson I can immediately recall. The general who I spoke of never spoke to me, as I said, at least not directly. He had spoken very clearly through the words that uplifted these two friends of mine when he took the time to thank and compliment them. His message came to me through them just as clearly. I haven't forgotten it. Everybody has a part to play, and every part is important. I know what I did made a contribution to our efforts in Vietnam, but I am no more important than any other person who contributed. Many contributed far, far more!

Allen in a social moment with two friends (Tommy
and Gary) from whom he learned a valuable
lesson. Tommy Bulger, left. Gary R., right.

Earlier, in this writing, I mentioned the dream that seemed
to signal the beginning of the end of my self-imposed isolation,
a dream of a table in a room with four men at it, separated by
a curtain from the general military population in an adjoining
hall. In that dream, we were told it was okay to pass through that
curtain and join in with everyone else. This dream was about
the Army Security Agency and of its separation by secrecy. The
blue of the uniforms in the dream represented the blue on the
ASA shoulder patch. As we passed through the curtain, we were
led by the one whose face was blotted out in my dream. He was
followed by George, Pablo, and then me. I now can put a name
to the man with the blotted-out face. I know who he was, and
his name is inscribed on the wall of the Vietnam memorial.
I shall withhold his name though. It has occurred to me the
faceless man could also represent any of the scores of men from

the Army Security Agency who gave their lives in Vietnam. Somehow, it is fitting they were allowed to pass through the curtain first in the form of this one man. Certainly, they are deserving of the first and highest honors!

59

FROM VIETNAM
TO OKINAWA

WHEN I left Vietnam in July 1971, I was sent to Okinawa, Japan, but my orders did not say Okinawa, Japan. They read that I would be going to USASAFS Sobe, Ryukyu Islands. That would be Torii Station, an intelligence station at Sobe, Okinawa. I didn't have the faintest idea of where the Ryukyu Islands were and was not familiar with Okinawa. Since it was an inter-theater transfer, I knew it would be in the same theater of operation, and therefore in the same military operational area I was already in: the Pacific. Everybody else was about as dumb as I was about this place I was going to.

Somebody finally said, "I think it's the place they call the Rock." He was right. I arrived on the Rock about thirty days later, after I first went Stateside for a month.

It was nice being home, but oddly, I felt out of place at times. My mind was often back in Vietnam with George and Pablo. Every day, I found myself wondering what they were doing at that moment. A couple of people observed I was now "different." I was twenty-one years old and only one year older than when they had last seen me. I felt different somehow, but I really could not explain it. Like I was many years older—not just one. I found myself wanting to reach out to those I had missed so badly and, at the same time, wanting to be alone in my thoughts. I felt happy about being home and guilty at the same time that I had left George and Pablo behind.

I bought a car within a day or so of getting home. After all, I did need transportation while I was at home. Mom and Dad never drove or owned a vehicle. The car was purchased from the Joe Scott Motor Company in Montgomery. It was a clean and shiny used car, but I thought it needed washing and waxing anyway, which I decided to do at home under a mimosa tree in the front yard. I was on my knees, shining the bumper and wondering what George and Pablo might be doing, when there was a tremendous karaaack-boooom! It sounded like a rocket had detonated above me! I found myself partially under the car, not realizing how I had gotten there. When I found out where I was and had extricated myself, my first thought was that I hoped no one had seen what happened.

A thunderstorm had come up, and thunder had crashed overhead, taking me by surprise in my thoughts. I looked around. Dad was on the front porch looking up and around at the sky. He looked everywhere except in my direction, which told me he had seen and was trying to disguise the fact. He had been on the porch to be near me and to enjoy the fact I was home. He had been in torment while I was gone and had prayed for me every day. I found he had kept a picture of me in his Bible so I could be at church with him every Sunday. The picture was still there, between the pages of his Bible, when he died a number of years later. In the picture, I was wearing jungle fatigues. I had sent it to him from Vietnam.

I married while I was home on leave. Given the circumstances, it was a mistake. While I knew things were different with me, I went ahead with the plans I had made a year earlier. I didn't want to feel I was going back on a promise, though I had reservations. It turned out to be a mistake that hurt a lot of people. I was, in fact, different, as others had noted. I should have acknowledged it and put things on hold, but I did not. After my marriage, I headed off to Torii Station in Okinawa.

At Torii Station, I resumed the same type of duties I had been doing in Vietnam with the exception that people were not trying to kill me while I carried out those duties. Well, I guess that was a plus! I found myself listening to the Chinese military communications. They were not difficult at all, and I found myself really enjoying intercepting their communications. They were so easy that it seemed almost like child's play. Somebody thought I would be a good choice for North Korean diplomatic communications, and I agreed to give it a try. They were slightly difficult at first, but I soon got the hang of their communications. I got to the point that I could anticipate their actions. It was almost as if I knew what they were going to do before they knew it. I was obsessed with copying them. On most days, I got 480 minutes of copy on an eight-hour shift, which is 100 percent copy. It was not work for me; it was a challenge and fun.

One day, I observed the Korean operators acting in a peculiar fashion and took note of it. I alerted the other two operators to the fact and told them to make notes and to pass them along to me. Together, we were able to establish they were making changes in their communication strategy, and it worked out precisely according to my predictions. In sharing the information, following up, and cooperating, we were able to pass along to NSA what we had discovered. We were each commended in a communication from NSA for the valuable observations we had made. It was a feather in the cap for everyone at Torii Station, and we were recognized and honored for it. That acknowledgement, in the form of a letter of commendation, is the only award from the military I have kept as being truly meaningful. It is posted on the wall in front of me. When I ask myself if I ever really made a difference, I can look up, read it, and answer, "Yes!"

My marriage went sour almost from the beginning. I'm not really sure if either of us was completely to blame. Basically, I think we were both good people, but the circumstances were too much to overcome. Sometime around September 1973, we divorced. We had actually only spent a couple of weeks together after our wedding before I left for Okinawa. That isn't much of a married life, but it was enough to give happy moments that led to a lot of pain. Sometimes I wish it had never happened, but at other times, I'm glad it did. Either way, I cannot change it and am thankful for the memories and for my daughter, Theresa, born of that union.

I married Yoko Chinen on January 30, 1974. I have stated earlier in this narrative that this is the date of my second birth. The first seems to have been when I was four years old, and I felt I had come alive when our house burned in 1954. When I was married to Yoko, I was twenty-four years old. On that day, I laughed, and I cried. I was that happy! My life had started all over again.

Okasan (Mama) wanted to see the marriage certificate. She looked at the Japanese certificate and then at the American one from the American Consular Office. She studied both of them carefully before smiling and laying them aside. She worried for her daughter and wanted to be sure everything was on the up-and-up. When she was satisfied, she told her youngest daughter, Misae, to go around the corner to the local store and buy a bottle of beer. When it arrived, she poured a glass and gave it to me. She now welcomed me as her son. She smiled a lot. I had never seen her look as happy as she did at that moment. I think, until she saw the marriage certificate, she was always a bit suspicious I might change my mind or abandon her daughter. When my own mother passed away, I reminded myself I still had a mother in Okinawa. I made a promise I would never neglect her, and I kept that promise completely. We became even closer than before, and I did everything I could to help support her and take care of her needs.

On Christmas, the New Year, and on her birthday, she received special gifts from me. She knew they would be coming and announced that fact to those at the day care center she went to on most days. She was never disappointed. She passed away recently at the age of ninety-three, and it left a huge emptiness in my heart. Her picture is on the wall in front of me, and I look at it almost every day.

When I met Yoko, I knew from the beginning I wanted to marry her. I spent as much time as I could with her and visited her home and family every time I had a day off or on those days when my working schedule allowed it. Yoko's mother was a widow and was raising her last five children alone. Her oldest daughter, Masako, was born in World War II to her first husband who was a civilian casualty of the war. Masako was married with children when I met Yoko. I tried to help Okasan and her family in little ways because I knew they were struggling. Yoko was working since she was the oldest of those living at home. She had dropped out of high school to help out. She made almost no money by our standards of the time, and what little she made was given to her mother.

Yoko's family had an acre or two of sugarcane that needed harvesting, and I volunteered to help. Yoko was skeptical about that offer and admitted she had never seen an American actually doing any manual labor. I insisted I had grown up on a farm and knew how to work, including harvesting sugarcane.

I had a couple of days off and showed up on the day of the harvest. Several people had already been working and had cut down a good bit of cane. One person was assigned the task of tying it in bundles so it could be carried to the roadside for pickup. My offer to cut was turned down, as they didn't trust me to cut cane and not myself. It was decided I would be the carrier instead. However, they were not sure if I could do that either. After all, I was an American. I carried all the cut cane from the field and actually caught up with the cutters. I practically ran the whole time—with one bundle on my shoulder and another under my arm. At times, I had to wait on the cutters and the one tying the bundles. At the end of the day, I was completely done in, but they were impressed.

On the following morning, I came to the cane field ready to get the job finished. I believe they were surprised to see me, but they seemed happy I had come back. I secretly showed Yoko the bruised area from the base of my neck, across my shoulder, and partly down my arm. It was from the cane bundles bouncing there as I trotted to the roadside with them. I made her promise not to tell. We finished the field that day, and I had carried out every bundle except for the first two, which had been used to demonstrate to me how to do it and where to stack them beside the road. It took about two weeks for the bruising to disappear and for me to be pain-free again. It was worth it though because Okasan had been impressed to see an American actually doing work. I felt good about it too because it was the sort of thing I had grown up doing on our little one-mule farm in central Alabama. In a way, it was like recapturing a bit of what I had left behind and sorely missed from time to time.

A little over a month after we married on January 30, we

left for the States and our new life together. I was the happiest person on the face of the Earth! We arrived in the States on March 4, 1974, and our forty-five years together have been happy ones. I left military service in May 1979 for my family home in Alabama. I brought Yoko from 391 Misatosan, Okinawa, to 391 Hope Hull, Alabama. We have raised our children and are enjoying our grandchildren whenever we can see them. At present, we are enjoying each other's company as retirees. As stated before, we did not share our childhood years together, but having entered our second childhood, we intend to make the most of these years.

Both of us had started from humble beginnings and in difficult times, but those times were long ago, and any pain we may have felt because of those difficulties has actually become cherished memories. I don't think either of us would want to change a thing since the events of our childhood are what ultimately brought us together. I am thankful for the ashes of 391—both here and in Okinawa.

Yoko Chinen (Brady), Torii Station,
Okinawa, January 30, 1974.

Yoko on that happy day, January 30, 1974. Married to Allen!

Allen at Torii Station's chapel, reflecting
on the future, January 30, 1974.

A very happy Toshi Chinen, my new "mother."

Yoko at 391 Hope Hull, Alabama with
stepdaughter Theresa, 1974.

Yoko with daughter, Melissa (Mechi), 1977.

Yoko with son, Charlie, 1977.

Part 3

LIFE MOVES ON

60

CONCLUSIONS ABOUT LIFE AND FAMILY

THE YEARS between my early childhood and the time I went into the military service at the age of nineteen were full of memories of my home life and of other people. I have described some of the interactions between myself and my siblings but not really all that much. I barely mentioned most of my ten sisters and brothers, and I omitted the vast majority of those things I could have written about. Space alone prohibited the inclusion of so much I might otherwise have recorded.

We had a lot of interaction during that "premilitary" time and resumed our close associations after that nearly ten-year period had passed. We've had well over thirty-five years of close contact in which to create new memories since then. We live nearby to each other, and most of us attend the same church. Yes, it's still the Church of Christ. Our family gatherings are frequent, and we all eat a lot. It's a wonder we are not all heavier than we are. Occasionally, one or another has to shed an extra pound or two. That's to be expected, though, in a family where each had learned in childhood something about the basics of cooking and have always enjoyed our food. We each were expected to do our part and still do. We come together frequently and enjoy meals and good times together.

A get-together moment for the eleven Brady kids:
(left to right) Buddy, Dianne, Verba Lee, June, Betty,
Sharron, Larry, Sandra, Pat, Daisy Anne, and Allen.

We have a lot of good cooks in my family. As with good cooks anywhere, each one in my family tends to have certain dishes they are known to prepare well. When we have any type of gathering, each person is invited to bring the special items they do well and have been established as family favorites. Yoko might be asked to bring collards and fried corn bread. Sharron may show up with her pot roast and Sandra with her baked beans. Dianne contributes her brand of mashed potatoes. Daisy can be counted on for one of her cakes she is noted for. Everybody brings something tasty to the gathering, and several tables are usually required to display all the food that has been prepared. We take a moment to thank God for the food and for those who have prepared it. We then set about in an earnest attempt to demonstrate our appreciation for it by consuming far more than we should. Always, we spend the better part of a day enjoying the meal and each other's company. It is rather sad, toward the end of the day, to observe various family members in the process of packing up their dishes and leaving for their respective homes. There is some comfort, however, in knowing our gatherings are frequent and that it will only be a short while before the next.

I have considered that the uniqueness of the special dishes contributed by various family members are a testament to our individuality. We all appreciate the specially prepared food each family member brings and the commitment of each to contribute to the enjoyment of us all, but there are some foods everyone seems to have a good recipe for. It is kind of like something we have in common, like our genetic pool. Our genetic pool is immense, and the likelihood of good recipes for building individuals is virtually endless. In our family, we have redheads, blondes, brunettes, and those with black hair as well. Many have blue eyes, but there are brown eyes galore. I haven't made it my business to investigate the eye color of all my relatives, but I know I can find lots of green, gray, and hazel mixed in with the blues and browns. Most of us are of a fair complexion. Some are tan or have olive complexions, and a few are red-brown to dark brown. There are tall ones, short ones, slender ones and those who may be a bit on the fluffy side. Everyone presents a different version of Brady, but we have Brady in common.

It is like that dish we have in common: mashed potatoes. Have you ever considered how many ways there are to make mashed potatoes? The possibilities are endless. Everybody draws upon this endless storehouse of possibilities as freely as they have drawn from their genetic storehouse. How often have we whipped up a blend of ingredients into our unique version of mashed potatoes? Everyone starts with their favorite potato. There are several popular varieties from which to choose. One person may decide to use a potato masher and do it the old-fashioned way and maybe even leave a few lumps for texture. I grew up eating these "true" mashed potatoes, and they were good. Most people prefer using an electric mixer now. By varying the mixing times and speeds, a product is produced that may turn out creamy or as light and fluffy as a cloud. Most everyone uses milk in varying amounts as they do with butter. One of my sisters has puddles of melted butter on top of hers. Another sister often adds the interesting taste mayonnaise supplies. Salt is a must, while black pepper is a possibility. However mashed potatoes are prepared, they are always an enjoyable addition to a meal. Should a dozen people prepare their brand of mashed potatoes, no two would be exactly alike, and each would be as individual as the preparer's fingerprints.

Whether we are serving up for others some product of our kitchen or a bit of ourselves, we are offering something that is uniquely us. We often question ourselves as to whether what we are serving is good enough or if it might have been made a little better. Perhaps I should have left this out or added a little bit of that. In the writing of this book, I have often questioned myself along those lines and have also considered how even small things might have influenced the direction of my life. What would I have added or taken out if I had the ability to do so? How would that have affected the outcome of my life? Would it have made my life better and more enjoyable or less so? I have thought a lot about that, especially after a recent conversation with my brother Larry. Well, maybe not all that recent. It was actually quite some time ago. He and I were having a conversation about times past, our experiences and memories, mainly from our childhood years. Larry, almost sadly, announced that he wished that he could go back and undo or change certain things he was not proud of. If he had it in his power to do it over, certain things would be different. I nodded in agreement as I listened to him, for he was expressing my thoughts as well. It is likely most people have entertained such thoughts. As he had expressed what each of us was thinking, I chose to answer for both of us.

"Larry," I responded, "we are the results of not only our environment, but of our thoughts, decisions, actions, and everything we have involved ourselves in, whether good or bad. Change one of those things, and you may change what you have become today. We are familiar with the scripture that reminds us that 'all things work together for good for those that love the Lord.' All things, whether good or bad. If we eliminate the bad, we have eliminated some of the building material that has been used to make us what we are. It's not a matter of you or I changing anything, but whether we use that to some good end like influencing us to do better and to make better decisions in the future. Sometimes, the bad things we do or the feelings of regret we experience actually inspire us to better things. I'm sure we all adjust and even compensate. Change one thing, Larry, and you may have never had a career in the air force or become a minister. You might never have started Panama Missions and helped all those people. You may never have written your books. You and I are the result of all the things in our lives, both good and bad. All things, together, have brought us to where we are."

In the time since we had that conversation, I have become even more convinced of the value of mistakes, failures, and hardships in our lives. Perhaps failures can be even more valuable than successes at times, especially when they inspire us to better things we might not otherwise even have imagined possible.

Today, I am what I am, and I cannot change that. I'm not

sure I want to. When I look back over my life, I come to the conclusion that I am satisfied, and I am happy. The memories of my childhood are with me yet and will forever be. That is good, for there are so many pleasant ones. My military career? Experiences and lessons that I will never forget, along with the special bonds that were formed and continue to exist. My first marriage when I returned from Vietnam ended a short time later in bitterness that hurt a lot of people. This hurt is a deep regret of mine from which I wish everyone could have been spared. All I can do now is to acknowledge it and use it to make me a better person; I cannot change it. I thank God for the daughter, Theresa, born in that short marriage and for the person she has become in spite of my mistakes. She is a person I admire so deeply.

The author's oldest daughter, Theresa.

My second marriage occurred in 1974 in Okinawa, Japan. There, I married Yoko Chinen of 391 Misatosan, Okinawa. Me? From 391, Hope Hull, Alabama. A coincidence of addresses that still amazes me. It is as if it were a mark of fate, and our marriage marked the beginning of my adult life even though I was almost twenty-four years old and had been in the army for four and a half years. Along with Yoko, I was blessed with a lot of Japanese relatives who have become so dear to me. I cannot imagine life without them, especially my second mother, Toshi Chinen. Yoko further blessed me with two additional children: Melissa (Mechi), and Charlie.

All my children are married and have kids of their own, some of whom are married too. With one great-grandchild and a second on the way, I'm very conscious that I'm getting older much faster than I would like!

Allen, Theresa (daughter), Melissa (daughter),
Yoko, Charlie (son), about 2000.

Charlie, Melissa, Yoko, and Allen.

My parents and grandparents have been gone from this life for some time now. My mother was the last, having died about six years ago. All my aunts and uncles have been dead for quite a while. Even though all these family members are dead, they are, strangely enough, still alive to me. I can see them in my mind as clearly as I ever saw them in life. The only difference seems to be that I appreciate each of them even more today.

Some of my cousins are now buried in various cemeteries. Several of my nieces and nephews occupy the cemetery just outside my front yard. My older brother Buddy rests there alongside his wife who died with their unborn daughter still in her womb. The family I knew as a child has gotten smaller with the passage of time. It contracted a bit each time one person breathed their last, but the family grew again as another took their first breath of life. Even though death has claimed so many family members, the family has continued to grow and expand. That is the natural way of things. However, I see my family as unique; it has grown through births and marriages and through its attitude of inclusion. Because of that attitude, many have been included as a matter of the heart, and as such, become part of us.

On a Friday night several years ago, I witnessed a sad event on NHK, the Japanese channel on my satellite television. News footage showed the arrival in Japan of the bodies of a number of Japanese citizens who had been killed in a north African country. They had lost their lives, along with others, in a terrorist takeover of a petroleum refinery. It was a glaring example of the willingness of certain groups in our world today to sacrifice innocent people in the furtherance of their own agendas. The fact that the event I was witnessing at the time involved a nation and a people I had come to love made the scene all the more painful to watch. Only a couple of years before, on this same NHK channel, I had watched scenes of the rushing water and the devastation left behind by the massive tsunami. I felt a deep sorrow and anguish for those who tried so desperately to stay ahead of the oncoming water, only to be overtaken by it. It still affects me when I think of that event.

On the Saturday morning following the return of the Japanese victims of the terrorist takeover, I came into my private chamber and reflected on what had occurred. I remember it as having been a cold and overcast January day. It somehow suited my mental state as I replayed the scenes of the newscast in my mind. Looking about me, I studied the faces of Otosan and Okasan. I looked at the other items that were displayed about me that remind me of how much my world has changed. Those things, along with the American and Japanese flags, testify that my world is broader than it once was.

The smaller world of my childhood exists only in memories. The few acres of once-farmed fields are overgrown now. The mule has been long dead, and the wagon decayed to dust with only three of its wheels remaining. These wheels, along with a few other remaining artifacts, are reminders of the much smaller and less complicated world of that childhood. The small farm and community have given way to an environment that includes far-flung places in this country and in the world. My family is no longer defined in terms of only those with whom I shared that little farm as a child. It has come to include more than those few aunts, uncles, and cousins I saw occasionally. In fact, the very face of my family has changed and is evidenced by the older photographs of it versus the more recent ones.

Wagon wheels and cast-iron wash pots
from the long-gone one-mule farm.

Snapshots taken at any of the more recent family reunions quickly reveal the ever-changing face and makeup of my extended family. Gone are the days when a picture of my family reveals only light-skinned or Caucasian faces. Such a photograph now will reveal a family that includes Asian faces as well as black and Hispanic ones. Some of the family members have varying percentages of Creek Indian blood and are proud of that fact. One of these, Billy McCain, shows very pronounced Indian features. It was Billy who first began referring to my family as "the Brady Bunch," even before there was a television show by that name. Our family has continued to grow and has changed as it has done so, both in makeup and in attitudes. Just as the Brady family outgrew the confines of its small farm existence and identity, so also has our society gone through tremendous changes during that same time. Change is good if we make it so and make those changes while remembering those things that are important. It is good to hold on to our treasured memories and move forward with positive attitudes and, hopefully, changing those that have not served us well.

Allen Brady: "Not sure we're liking the empty nest."

Yoko Brady.

I count it a tremendous blessing my family now includes so many people of diverse backgrounds. If I were to look at a photograph of a family reunion, it would be difficult for me to identify any face I would be willing to blot out of the picture. I love and accept them all. When misfortune or tragedy strikes any of them, I feel it deeply. When I consider things that have affected those in my community and state, I am saddened or made happy according to the circumstance. They are a part of me, and what affects them, affects me. My family has grown, and so has my love for it. It has grown beyond those within the fences of the small farm of my youth, it and has transcended the borders of my state and country. Strange as it may seem, I see it as a blessing to be so deeply touched by events in foreign countries unfolding on my television screen. Tears came to my eyes as I viewed the scene of terrorists' victims being brought home to Japan on that Friday night. The heartbreak and grief felt on that side of the world was felt here as well. It was as if it were happening to my own family, and it was. My family is a large family. I love my family!

Thelma Brady (Mama) in her golden years.

The Brady Cemetery entrance.

Inside the Brady Cemetery, "the most peaceful place around."

Mama's stone and inscription. Mama often
escaped into a world of poetry.

Plaque mounted at the entrance to the cemetery
admonishing all to "Remember only my best"
(from poem written by Mrs. Lyman Hancock).

Epilogue
WE LOOK FORWARD

"Honey!" my wife called out. "Honey, come quick and look at this!" Abandoning the coffee maker where I was pouring my morning coffee, I hurried toward the sound of her excited voice to see what was requiring such immediate attention.

"Hurry up and look over there!" she commanded with excitement. "Is that a fox?"

Peering over her shoulder through the screen door, I scanned the area she appeared to be looking at and emphasizing with her finger against the screen. She had judged correctly. Less than a hundred yards away was a beautiful red fox. With nothing to obstruct our view, we could see it clearly. Barely slowing in its forward movement, it ducked slightly as it passed under the lower strand of the barbed wire fence separating our place from that of our nearest neighbor, Jimmy Todd. The fox's choice of a crossing place between Jimmy's property and mine seemed logical as the barbed wire fence joined the woven wire fence of my garden at this point. It was likely well known to the fox and a frequent crossing point. Its movements were graceful as it almost seemed to float across the upper part of the yard and then the pasture with the cloud-like tail matching the grace of the body.

"You don't think it has rabies, do you?" Yoko asked with some concern.

I continued to watch the fox as it disappeared into the fringe of brush and weeds that surrounded a huge pile of tree trunks and stumps that had been pushed together several years before. "No," I said. "It is probably living in that big pile and is just going home." As I turned away from the door and headed back to the kitchen for my morning coffee, I made a mental note to be careful in following through on my plans to burn that pile this summer. It was nearly a hundred feet across and probably harbored a lot of wildlife, baby foxes included. *I'll be careful and do it in stages*, I thought to myself. *That will give any animals a chance to get away.*

As I enjoyed my morning coffee, I reflected on the changes I had seen come over my wife since she had retired several months earlier. The fox was only one of many things she had pointed out to me lately. She seemed to be looking out the door at the world a lot now—when she wasn't actually in the yard or garden working and making the place more attractive. There are daily comments and observations about the creatures around the house she never appeared to notice before. She has finally realized the squirrels actually own the place and that chipmunks are under every building and shed around. She reports an occasional snake sighting and reminds me she doesn't care to have them around. My assurances they are not poisonous do not comfort her. Good snakes are dead snakes, and the bad ones should be confined to the other side of the Earth. She has placed bird feeders around the yard for songbirds and for hummingbirds. The feeders seem to be multiplying while I'm at work.

Yoko is constantly pointing out interesting birds that show up to eat, and she asks me what kinds they are. I'm ashamed to say I can't identify many of them. Yesterday, she pointed out two matching birds and said, "Those must be husband and wife."

"Probably so," I answered, smiling and wondering about the little bird wedding. It doesn't matter that we never got an invitation. *The birdseed in the feeders can be our wedding gift,* I thought. The flower beds around the house have never been so neat, and the rose bushes have never been as full of blooms as they are now. Her garden plot on the right side of our broad front yard continues to increase in size as more ground is tilled and planted. She has learned to use the garden tiller, and it appears family and friends will be well supplied with fresh vegetables this year. Her new interest in gardening promises to make things a bit easier for me.

Yes, she has definitely gone through a change, I thought, *with all the new things she is noticing and doing. Those things she is continually pointing out to me in the present are reminding me so much of that which is past.*

My mind drifts back to Mandy Norman, the very special old black woman who still occupies a warm place in my heart. She seemed to notice everything and had such a descriptive way of relating what she saw. Though she has been dead for many years, my memories of her are still strong and pleasant. I remember my frequent visits to her house, her well-swept yard, and her interest in the goings-on around her place. She had so many interesting stories about foxes and such. The thoughts and memories that come to me are comforting, and I find myself wishing I could go back to her place one more time. Mandy had plenty of chickens too—just like we used to have. The sight, sound, and smell of those chickens were a big part of my childhood and early adult years, but those days are gone. *Say! We can get chickens! If we get chickens, it will be like going back and bringing something forward! I'll give that idea some thought.* In reality, that thought has been resting on the back burner of my mind for quite a while.

The telephone rang, and it was my sister Sharron calling. "Jack said you mentioned you might want to get some chickens again for the grandchildren someday."

"Yes, I thought about it a few times and thought I might enjoy having some again," I answered, wondering what she was leading into.

"Angie bought six baby chicks for the boys, and we need to get rid of them," she continued. "If you want them, we could bring them to you tomorrow."

Though I had been considering the issue of chickens as far back as a couple of years, I had never carried that thought to a serious level. Suddenly, the issue was being forced, and my brain kicked into gear. *Baby chicks would be nice, and I'll have twenty-four hours to prepare to receive them,* I thought quickly.

"Sure, I'll take them," I replied.

She seemed relieved, somehow, when I repeated my assurance that I would be pleased to have them. Having finished the conversation, I continued my interrupted toothbrushing and shaving. Several minutes later, I heard the sound of my brother-in-law's voice in the kitchen. The twenty-four hours had shrunk to about five minutes!

Entering the kitchen, I found a relieved and excited Jack Cates talking to my wife. On the sunporch adjoining my kitchen was a cardboard box containing six bewildered baby chicks that had found themselves suddenly disowned. Accompanying them and in a pile were all their worldly possessions. There was a ten-pound bag of chick starter feed and its accompanying feeder. Also, a watering apparatus, a heat lamp (with extra bulbs),

486

and a roll of cardboard with which to construct a temporary enclosure for the little ones. Apparently, everything was part of a kit offered for sale by a local supply house to any unsuspecting parent with small children. It was also apparent my relatives were not going to give me any time to reconsider. It may have been guilt that caused Jack to leave so abruptly after depositing the chicks and their belongings at our house. Whatever the reason, Yoko and I were left studying our new charges and wondering if I had made a rash decision. It seemed we were now stuck with the results of that decision—and the fact that our family size had increased by six.

The chicks remained on my porch for the next week while the odor of their presence increased day by day in the house. One adventurous chick proved to be an escape artist and had to be recaptured twice after searches that involved moving furniture. Evidence it had spent some time outside the box lay everywhere. It seems I had forgotten something that gets people into trouble. Biddies come into this world cute and fuzzy and attractive to little children and idiots like me. God designed them that way. That is what hooks us into adopting the little eating-and-pooping machines. I had forgotten how much care they needed and how messy they were. I knew I had to get a coop built and soon. Later was not an option. Some materials were already on hand, but I needed some lumber and screws along with a few other items to complete the project. A trip to Montgomery and sixty dollars later, I had what I needed.

Building the chicken coop took a whole Saturday, but it was a work to be proud of! It was impenetrable to snakes and to any predators that might attempt to tear through the wire. The coop was partitioned in the middle with a wooden divider that could be slid out to give chicks more room as they grew larger. I was also careful to build it on supporting legs that kept the chicks several feet off the ground. After a coat of forest-green paint, the project was finished. It now stands under the edge of a shed in the yard, complete with a heat lamp and drop-down curtains to protect the youngsters from the cool night air. They seem quite content in their new home and have gotten along well with the business of young chickens, eating and pooping.

"Are you going to name them?" someone asked.

Don't be silly, I thought. As I began to compute the cost of building a chicken house and then a pen with a covering to protect them from hawks, my thinking began to change. *This could end up costing me $1,000—or maybe even $1,500. Those are expensive chickens! I will have to name them, and their names will have to be memorable too. Perhaps, later, when the pen is built, I'll buy a few dozen more chicks and spread the cost per chicken out a bit. We could have a good supply of chicken and eggs.*

"No," my wife said, apparently indicating that we are not cannibals. "We'll buy our chicken and eggs at the store."

That is something I had not counted on, but I won't worry about that right now. There is too much else to do. I'll have a while to figure out which friends and associates will be eating the eggs, but I won't bother myself with that detail just yet.

Suddenly, the first name came in a burst of inspiration. As I looked down at the chicken that had begun to grow feathers, I announced out loud, "Her name is Sundae!" Her body is mainly white or cream colored with the head and shoulders being reddish brown, kind of like vanilla ice cream with syrup poured over it. *She reminds me of an ice cream sundae,* I thought. I found myself very pleased with the name and my ingenuity. The remaining five were more similar in appearance with reddish feathers and some white- or cream-colored ones mixed in. *They will be a bit more difficult to distinguish from one another by appearance.*

In a second moment of inspiration, I named another Excuse Me. I had noticed while the others pecked at the freckles on my hand inquisitively while I was feeding them and changing the water, she pecked me as if she had an attitude. If she could talk, she might have been saying, "Excuse me! Did I invite your hand into my personal space?" I thought her name was another clever idea until it occurred to me her attitude might change and I couldn't identify her anymore. *Like the anticipated eggs, that's something I'll worry about when it happens.*

By then, I was fully inspired. There seemed to be more inspiration floating about than had existed since the New Testament was written. I realized I was on a roll! Little Red would be the name of the dainty-looking almost solid red one. Houdini would be the name of the sunporch escape artist even though I could no longer identify which chicken it was. Somehow, it seemed appropriate to allow that name to float between the final three chickens. That would keep things from getting complicated. So now they have names: Sundae, Excuse Me, Little Red, and three named Houdini.

I have become attached to our additions and have discovered I look forward to the few minutes of tending to them each morning and evening. Along with the pleasure of taking care of our young chickens, I have developed a renewed interest in the simple things occurring around me. It is good to watch the birds again and to observe a fox close by. Only today, we saw two Canada geese near the pond with three young ones between them. We had suspected the geese were nesting nearby. Later, they marched across our front yard toward Jimmy Todd's place, almost matching the course the fox had followed earlier, but in reverse. Three more geese were in attendance and were bringing up the rear. I got the feeling they were prepared for a rearguard action should any predator show up.

Experiencing these things seems to have taken us back to an earlier time in our lives when day-to-day living seemed less hectic and more joyful. Now, with the chickens, it seems I have reclaimed another bit of what once was; in a sense, I am coming full circle. In this reawakening, the joys we experience each day are almost childlike. I cannot push aside the feeling I have entered my second childhood. Childhood can be a blessing with its simple joys, wonderment, and pleasurable moments. I hope for a full measure of these this second time around. Somehow, it seems as if I have been away and am now home again.

The old story of the prodigal son suddenly comes to mind. He desperately longed for his family and yearned to return home. He did and was happy. I am happy too, and Yoko shares that happiness with me. The heartache of the ashes in both of our childhoods have long ago given way to the happy thoughts and fond memories of growing up in similar fashion but in distant places. Having missed spending our first childhood time together, we are determined to make the most of the second. We now have that opportunity, thanks largely to events set in motion long ago and outside our control. I think we are ready too. I don't know what else we could add except for a pig or two. There are plenty of childhood memories there! After all, we do have a good place for a pigpen to the southeast of the house. The spot is in a generally downwind direction. Maybe we could tolerate the smell—or maybe not. I might have to think long and hard about that one! Hmmm, perhaps we should just scrap the pig idea after all. The prodigal son and I would likely agree that we should leave well enough alone! There are certain things best left behind!

Okay, we'll have no pigs this time! Goodbye and farewell from Hope Hull, Alabama.

Allen and Yoko at home in "Mama Down Yonder's" old house which has changed a lot in the past 150 years. Farewell! Best wishes to all our family—wherever you may be!

A Note to My Wife

Honey,

> When I Think about
> This road we have travelled
> I give thanks
> That we have reached our present destination,
> And when I think about
> Where this road might lead us,
> I give thanks
> That we have the time to travel another day.

From the poem "I Give Thanks" by Pablo Soto Caudillo, my friend and one of those in my dream with the blue uniform. Used with permission from his book *Pieces of Thoughts and Feelings*.